MURDER AT LA CAPPELLA

By Camilla Trinchieri

Murder in Chianti
Murder at Vigna D'Oro
Murder at La Cappella
Murder at Villa Salviati
Murder in Pitigliano

MURDER AT LA CAPPELLA

Camilla Trinchieri

Allison & Busby Limited
11 Wardour Mews
London W1F 8AN
allisonandbusby.com

First published by Soho Press as *Murder on the Vine* in 2022.
This paperback edition published by Allison & Busby in 2026.

A CIP catalogue record for this book is available from the British Library.

10 9 8 7 6 5 4 3 2 1

ISBN 978-0-7490-3368-2

By choosing this product, you help take care of the world's forests.
Learn more: www.fsc.org.

FSC www.fsc.org MIX Paper | Supporting responsible forestry FSC® C018072

Printed and bound in Great Britain by Clays Ltd. Elcograf S.p.A

EU GPSR Authorised Representative
LOGOS EUROPE, 9 rue Nicolas Poussin, 17000, LA ROCHELLE, France
E-mail: Contact@logoseurope.eu

A NOTE

Many people live in my Tuscan series. Some, like Nico, Perillo and Daniele, are the backbone of the mysteries. Some, like Tilde, Nelli and Stella, are vital to those three, but they also exist on their own. They are part of the world I have stepped into. They live in Gravigna, Greve or other villages. They belong. So do the people who step in and out of the stories. Some appear unbidden, wanting their moment. I let them in so that I can be part of this world that is slowly coming alive in my head. I want that world to come alive for you too. I know, so many foreign names to keep track of. You can get lost. I want you to stay with me and so, for this third Tuscan mystery I have added a list of characters at the back of the book to help. I hope you enjoy the trip.

Thank you,

Camilla Trinchieri

GRAVIGNA,
A SMALL TOWN IN THE CHIANTI HILLS OF TUSCANY

CHAPTER ONE

A Sunday in mid-October, 10.35 a.m.

Nico Doyle sat on the balcony of his small, rented farmhouse dressed in his running shorts, a faded Yankees T-shirt, his feet bare, eating the last of his toast. The overbearing summer heat had finally retreated, leaving warm days and cool nights. The three swallows that slept between the wooden beams on the balcony ceiling had already flown off on their long migration to South Africa, leaving their empty nests waiting to be refilled in the spring.

He had a free day ahead of him. Tilde didn't expect him at Sotto Il Fico until dinnertime. Looking out at a view that still surprised him made whatever sadness he had from the past disappear. The colours of an Italian autumn were mostly muted – varying shades of yellows, browns, greys, faded greens. Italian maple trees did not offer eye-stopping splashes of New England red. The only strong colour came from the deep dark green of the cypress trees in the distance.

Nearby the leaves of his landlord's olive trees glinted silver in the bright sun. Beyond the grove were neat rows of Ferriello vines, their leaves yellowed, their grapes already picked by hand. The harvesting of the olives would begin at the end of the month. Last year Nico had joined his landlord and the day workers for the harvest. Perched on an ancient wooden ladder, he'd shaken branches, hand-picked clingers, showering the green fruit onto the black nets below. He looked forward to helping out this year too. Payback was two bottles of the best olive oil he'd ever tasted.

A series of shots rang out from the woods behind the farmhouse. The hunting season was open and the quiet of weekends was now pockmarked with rifle shots. The sound made Nico look over at the small table where Perillo, maresciallo dei carabinieri of the Greve-in-Chianti station, was downing his third espresso. They had met just over a year ago thanks to the sound of a single shot followed by a dog's yelping that had sent Nico running into the woods. He'd adopted the dog. OneWag was now asleep at his feet. The maresciallo had become a friend.

'I never asked you,' Nico said. 'Do you hunt?'

Perillo shook his head. 'I don't see the fun in it.' He'd popped in on Nico without calling first. Nico had been surprised to find him at his doorstep early on a Sunday morning but had welcomed him in with a smile and immediately offered him breakfast. Nico's dog had greeted him with a swish of his tail and a good sniff at his shoes.

Perillo pushed his empty plate aside and reached for his pack of cigarettes. 'You're a good man for taking me in and feeding me. It's not the bacon and eggs breakfast you once promised' – Perillo tapped the unfiltered cigarette on the table – 'but I'll concede toast slathered with ricotta and acacia honey is very good.'

Nico reached down to pick up a bowl filled with new potatoes sitting next to OneWag. 'I didn't know you were coming.' For a moment, the maresciallo's serious expression had led Nico to think something bad had happened, but Perillo had eaten breakfast and said nothing. Nico knew that whatever was on his friend's mind would eventually come out.

'What are you going to do with all those potatoes?' Perillo asked. Nico was always trying to come up with new recipes for the restaurant run by Tilde, his dead wife's cousin. It was an odd hobby for an ex-homicide detective, Perillo thought, but then being an unpaid waiter at the restaurant was even odder.

'I'm going to peel them,' Nico said, 'and I know not to ask for your help.'

'That is an unfair assessment of our friendship.' Perillo reached into the back pocket of his jeans and pulled out his rolled-up newspaper. 'For you, I will spread this yet unread paper at your feet to catch the peelings.'

'Very generous of you, Maresciallo.'

Perillo sat back in his chair, fingering his cigarette. He wasn't in the best of moods, hadn't been for weeks now. It was Ivana's idea to talk to Nico. As an American and some years older, Nico would have a different perspective.

From under the table, OneWag eyed the spread-out newspaper. He raised his snout and sniffed. The paper must have given off a warm smell because the small dog took a few steps and curled himself into a ball on top of it.

'Ehi, Rocco, get off.' Perillo shook one edge of the paper

to get the dog to move. He'd given OneWag a name he could pronounce. The dog, being smart, answered to both names. He now gave the maresciallo his *Do I know you*? stare. He didn't budge. Paper was much warmer than tile.

'It's okay,' Nico said. 'He'll get covered with potato skins. That'll teach him.'

'O Sole Mio' rang out from the suede jacket hanging on the back of Perillo's chair. He reached for it, checked who was calling and swept his finger over the screen. 'Vince, didn't I tell you I was taking the morning off?' Perillo put the phone on speaker.

'You did, Maresciallo, but a Signorina Benati insisted I call you.'

'For what reason?'

'Her bartender has been missing for three days.'

'Take down the details, tell her we'll look into it, then send her home.'

'She won't go until she talks to you. She says you met her last September. She's the manager of the Hotel Bella Vista.'

'Of course, I remember her. Offer her a coffee from the bar. I'll be there in half an hour.' He slipped the phone back into his jacket pocket.

'Nothing serious, I hope,' Nico said.

'The last time we went looking for someone, the missing woman had decided to solve a fight with her husband by taking off to Paris for a week. Keep your fingers crossed that it's not more serious than that.' Perillo eyed the cigarette he was still holding for a few seconds, then slipped it back in the pack.

Nico noticed but didn't say anything. He'd never seen Perillo, a heavy smoker, put a cigarette away before.

'I'm thinking it would be good for me to stop smoking,' Perillo announced, as if reading Nico's thoughts.

Nico dropped the peeled potato back in the colander and picked up another one. 'Excellent thinking.'

Perillo kept staring at the cigarette pack. 'It takes courage.'

Both quitting and voicing his worries, Nico thought. 'Far less courage than hunting down a murderer.'

Perillo leant forward, dropping his elbows on his knees. 'I did a terrible job with the last one.'

'You found the guilty party.'

Perillo shook his head. 'I've become a man I don't like.'

A strong statement from a man who came across as very sure of himself, sometimes even pompous. Nico dropped his peeler in the colander and turned to look directly at Perillo. 'What man is that?'

'A man who eats and smokes too much, who worries about getting old.' Perillo looked down at his feet. 'I don't trust my own capacity to move forward. I'm full of doubts. I don't recognise myself.'

'Where I'm from, we call that a midlife crisis.'

'You had this crisis?' Perillo didn't wait for an answer. 'Did it make you feel like a lesser person?'

'Not lesser, just different. I did go through a period of obsessing about the changes in my body and my brain, then Rita got sick. I quickly realised how lucky I was to just be alive.'

The idea of something happening to Ivana made Perillo shiver. She had become his axis. 'I feel like a weakling.'

'Whenever my thinning hair or a new ache gets me down,' Nico said, 'I remind myself that having most of my wits still with me is pretty damn fantastic.'

Perillo looked out on the olive grove, the fields beyond, thinking of Ivana soon coming home from Mass, starting to cook the Sunday meal, waiting for him. Thinking of Signorina Benati waiting for him at the station. Nico was right. What he had was good: a wonderful woman who still put up with him, a job he enjoyed, a good friend in Nico. He would need to remind himself when the doubts crept back in, as he was sure they would. 'Thank you, Nico. You've lifted my spirits.' Perillo stood up. 'Tell me the truth – I wasn't really so ineffective with the last murder, was I?'

Nico picked up his peeler and a potato. 'Not at all. You led a team effort with great tenacity and intelligence.' He was exaggerating a bit. Daniele, Perillo's right-hand man, had been the tenacious one. 'The Three Musketeers, isn't that what Ivana called us?'

Relief spread across Perillo's face. 'One for all. All for one. Thanks again for breakfast and the boost. I have to get back to Greve.'

'You're welcome. I may not have any bacon in the refrigerator, but I've always got ears on me.'

'I'm counting on that. I'll see myself out. Ciao, Rocco.'

OneWag conceded a tail swish.

As the sun continued to rise and spread light over the olive grove, Nico turned his mind to a happier subject – a surprise for his adopted family at Sotto Il Fico – thinly sliced potatoes layered with crumbled sausages, sliced onions, Parmigiano, a sprinkling of rosemary and a sweep of olive oil.

* * *

Laura Benati stood up from the bench outside of the maresciallo's office as Perillo rushed into the station. He was a short, stocky man, with a handsome face, a strong nose, lots of black hair and appealing dark eyes. The first and last time she had seen him, he had shown up at the hotel in uniform, asking questions after a man had been murdered in Gravigna. Afraid his presence would upset the guests, she had tried to get rid of him as quickly as possible, had even fed him a lie. Now she was the one who needed his help. She hoped he would be kinder than she had been.

Laura extended her hand as Perillo came near. 'Thank you so much for coming.'

Perillo took the woman's hand and studied her for a moment. She was somewhere in her late twenties, with a lovely pale face and rounded cheeks. Last year she had worn her wavy blond hair loose and something very pretty. Why did he remember those details and not her first name? Today she wore a severe dark blue dress, and her hair was pulled back into a tight bun. Perillo came back to the present and shook her hand finally. 'Ah, yes, Signorina Benati, I remember you well.'

'I'm sorry I've interrupted your Sunday, but I've learnt that when you have a problem it's always best to deal with the top.'

'Absolutely,' Perillo said with a smile, enjoying the small ego boost. He opened the door to his office and indicated for her to enter first.

Laura looked around the large room. There were only three chairs – a straight metal chair in the back next to a computer, a wooden armchair behind a large ink-stained wooden desk in the centre of the room, and directly in front of the desk, the straight one she now sat in.

Perillo had followed her in. 'You want to make a missing person report,' he said as he lowered himself into the armchair. 'Is that right?'

'Yes. Cesare has been gone three days now. He didn't—'

Perillo raised his hand to stop her from going on while he took out a notepad from his desk drawer. 'Please be patient with me, Signorina Benati. My computer scribe, Brigadiere Donato, is filling his eyes with art in Florence this Sunday. It is up to me to write down your details.' He didn't trust gum-chewing Vince to get it all down correctly and Dino was painfully slow.

'A tape recorder is faster,' Laura said with an authoritative tone.

Perillo bristled. Daniele had been trying to convince him to tape interviews, but tapes could be cut, erased, the machine could break down. Besides, he couldn't stand to listen to his voice. He poised his pen on his notebook. 'The name of the missing person?'

Patience, Laura thought. Her very sensible suggestion had met deaf ears. 'Cesare Rinaldi. You must remember him. You interviewed him last year. He's the bartender at the hotel. He didn't show up for work on Friday. He's never missed a day since I started working at the hotel eight years ago.'

Perillo remembered the old man with his crafty eyes, a thin, sculpted face and long white hair pulled back in a ponytail. He'd come away from talking to Cesare convinced the bartender knew more than he'd told. 'He is obviously a man devoted to his work. If I remember correctly, he's been at the hotel since he was a kid.'

Laura shifted in her chair. 'I'm sorry, that's not true.'

'Isn't that what you told me?'

'Your presence at the hotel made me nervous, and, without thinking, I repeated what Cesare always tells his guests. He likes to impress them with his devotion to the job. It gets him good tips.'

'Lying to a maresciallo is never a good idea, especially during a murder investigation.'

'I know. I apologise.'

Perillo gave her a hard stare. Her lie did not say good things about her. She lowered her eyes. He put pen to paper.

'Please give me a detailed description – age, colour of eyes, hair, his height, build, et cetera.'

'I have it right here.' Laura handed Perillo the envelope she'd been clutching. 'I've written it all down to save time. I've included a photo of Cesare.' She tightened her jaw, angry at herself and filled with guilt. Not for the lie. For waiting too long to come here. What if he'd had a heart attack, or fallen, hurt his head and was now lying in a ditch, unable to move?

Perillo extracted the folded sheet of paper from the envelope. The photograph landed face down on the desk. He turned it over. Cesare looked back at him with a smile, his arm around an equally happy Signorina Benati. They were both holding flutes filled with prosecco or champagne. A flowered garden in the background. 'You were celebrating something?'

A wistful look slid across Laura's face. 'His eightieth birthday, last year. We gave him a party in the back garden of the hotel.'

Perillo flipped the photograph and placed it on his

desk. The missing man's obvious happiness made him uncomfortable. Perillo knew he wouldn't be happy turning eighty. He unfolded the sheet of paper and had to narrow his eyes to read. Getting old was humiliating and scary. 'Thank you, Signorina Benati. You've been very thorough.' All of Cesare's physical details were there. Even what he had worn the last time she had seen him. No wife, girlfriend or boyfriend. A nephew, Pietro Rinaldi, was the only relative. His phone number was written next to his name. *Cesare is a loner*, she had written at the end.

Laura sat on the edge of her chair, leaning as close to Perillo as his desk allowed. 'Can you please send out your men to find him? I'm afraid something bad has happened to him.'

Perillo saw the care and worry on her face. *Was Signorina Benati just a compassionate soul, or did she love this old man?* he wondered. Cesare may have left some clues she misunderstood. In the Paris case, the husband had not understood why his wife's best clothes were gone. 'First, tell me what you have done to find him, so we don't lose time.'

'Cesare is supposed to check in for work at four in the afternoon. On Friday, when five o'clock came around and he still hadn't shown up, I called him. He didn't answer and I left a message. I took over at the bar and called every half hour. I got annoyed, then angry. His not showing up had never happened before and I didn't have a substitute ready. By the time I closed the bar at midnight I was tired and thought he may have taken the day off to calm down.'

'Calm down?'

'There was an incident at the bar on Thursday night. Cesare spilled a tray of drinks on a hotel guest. The guest then complained to me that Cesare had done it on purpose and did not apologise. I apologised on Cesare's behalf and the hotel's, didn't charge him for the hefty bar bill, and that was the end of it.'

'Did you get Cesare's version of the event?'

'I didn't try. I wanted to give him time. That guest is one of those entitled men who snap their fingers at the help. I had to stop myself from snapping at him several times.'

'The name of this guest?'

She hesitated. She shouldn't have spoken ill of him.

Perillo kept his eyes on her. 'I doubt I will need to disturb him, but just in case.'

Laura nodded. 'Dottor Eugenio Vittori. He's a very successful businessman and has been coming to the hotel for years.'

'Thank you,' Perillo said. *Incident with Dottor Vittori*, Perillo wrote in his notebook, wondering if the man's title was legitimate. Too many men enjoyed putting an honorific in front of their name to give them status. He looked up. 'Please go on.'

'When he still hadn't shown up yesterday afternoon, I went to his house.'

Perillo squinted at the list of details Signorina Benati had written down. 'That would be Via Vigneto 18?'

'Yes. It's just a few kilometres down the road from the hotel. His motorcycle was gone. I had already checked at the hotel. Sometimes he leaves it there overnight, preferring to walk home.'

'Do you know the make of the motorcycle?'

'The make is on the sheet of paper I gave you. A 1972 Ducati 750GT.' How he loved that motorcycle. She'd often find him at the car park of the hotel before reporting for work, polishing every nook and cranny of that old relic. Pietro had told her the model while they were going through Cesare's house. *'It's worth a lot of money. I hope he didn't wreck it,'* he'd added.

Perillo looked from his notebook. 'And the license plate number?'

'I'm sorry, I don't know it. Pietro doesn't either.'

'We can find it easily enough.' A job for Daniele. 'You went inside the house?'

'Not alone. I didn't have the keys. I banged on the door, shouted at the windows, rattled the glass. Silence. I called his nephew, Pietro, who came as soon as he could, maybe an hour later. He lives in Castellina. His address and phone number are included in the note I gave you.'

Perillo quickly checked. He found the nephew's address and phone number on the other side of the sheet of paper, along with her name and information. *Of course, Laura.* He repeated the name in his head to plant it there for good. 'Did the house give off any clues? Suitcases gone. Clothes missing from the closet.'

'It's a small house, two rooms, a bathroom and a kitchen. It didn't take long to look. The closet didn't have any empty hangers. Most of his clothes were on the floor or tossed on chairs.' She'd stared at the pile of unwashed dishes, the unmade bed, the dirty socks left on the bedroom floor. The disorder had surprised her, made her uncomfortable, reminded her of the mess her life had been. Cesare always kept the bar meticulously clean. She felt she had entered the home of a man she didn't know. 'The house was very disordered, but it didn't look ransacked.' If Pietro hadn't been with her, she would have put order to Cesare's home. She liked order now, wanted it for Cesare.

'Did the nephew have any idea of where his uncle could have gone?'

Laura shook her head. 'No. Pietro said he hadn't spoken to his uncle lately. We went knocking on the doors of the houses nearby. There are only three. No one knew anything. We went to Panzano, where he does his food shopping. The vegetable and fruit vendor sold him two apples Friday morning. That's the only thing Cesare bought in Panzano.'

Perillo made a note about the fruit vendor. Only two apples bought, which probably meant Cesare wasn't planning on going on a long trip. 'Did you spread the news of his disappearance to neighbouring towns? Here in Greve or Gravigna?'

'Pietro was supposed to do that by going to the bars and cafés. I couldn't. Managing the hotel is more than a full-time job.' She raised her hands. 'Cesare's always stayed close to home.'

'You wrote that Signor Rinaldi is a loner. You also wrote he's been a bartender at the hotel for thirty-eight years. I wouldn't think that is a job a loner would choose?' It was important for Perillo to get a sense of the man.

Laura had sometimes thought something had gone wrong in Cesare's life early on, something that bore a heavy weight. 'He loves his job very much, but maybe it made him a loner. Think of all those hours listening to guests unloading their problems or just talking to hear their own voices.' She preferred to think that was the real reason. 'I liked to watch him sometimes. He was very attentive. He laughed with his guests, teased them, commiserated with them, sometimes offered suggestions. The guests loved him. They left generous tips. But when he wasn't working, he wanted to be alone.' Laura glanced at the photograph lying facedown on Perillo's desk. At that birthday party he claimed she was the only friend he ever needed. She had found it sad, but it had also warmed her heart. Now Cesare was missing. He needed help. She felt it in her heart. He wouldn't just walk out on a job he still loved after thirty-eight years. He wouldn't walk out on her. They were friends.

'Any hobbies that might have taken him somewhere?'

'He has a small vineyard on his land. He likes to joke that he's the only Tuscan who mastered winemaking on a small island.'

'What island?'

'He wouldn't say.' Laura leant forward, her expression intense. 'I've told you more than you need to know. Now can you send your men out to find him?'

Perillo bristled again at her authoritarian tone.

Laura understood. Eight years of dealing with demanding guests and overworked staff had taught her to grasp a person's reaction quickly. 'I'm sorry, Maresciallo, but I'm beside myself. Cesare is a good friend.' She had started out at the hotel as the owner's assistant when she was only twenty. Two years later the owner had gone back to Florence and left her in charge. Cesare had patiently guided her into her job, taught her 'patience with a smile,' which she had now lost. 'I have told you everything I know.'

Perillo acknowledged her words with a nod and picked up the office phone.

* * *

Daniele felt the vibration as he stared at Michelangelo's sculpture of a naked man, a slave, the sign said. The man's face was unfinished, but his strong body was pushing forward, trying to free himself from the rough block of marble encasing him.

'Don't you feel his anguish?' Stella asked.

What Daniele felt was embarrassment, something he had not felt in front of the naked *David*. This sculpture was sensual. The slave seemed to be writhing and it made Daniele think of sex. The phone continued to vibrate. Daniele continued to stare. He was blushing.

'I much prefer it to the *David*,' Stella said. This was their second Sunday together. The first time she had taken Daniele to the Uffizi to open his eyes to her world of art. Today the Accademia. Stella slipped her arm around his. Brigadiere Daniele Donato was a sweet, gentle man. She felt safe with her new friend.

Daniele enjoyed the warmth of Stella's arm and put his hand over the pocket of his slacks to stop the phone's vibration.

'I think you better answer,' Stella said. 'It could be your mother.' She knew they were very close.

Daniele took out the phone and looked at the screen. 'It's the maresciallo.'

'Answer. I don't want you to get into trouble.'

'I'm allowed a day off!'

She unhooked her arm. 'I'm sure it's important.'

Daniele sighed and placed the phone next to his ear. 'Yes, Maresciallo?'

* * *

Perillo hated bringing Daniele in, but his notes needed to be deciphered and faxed along with the information Laura Benati had brought. The young Venetian had become his right-hand man, naïve and astute at the same time. 'I'm sorry. I need you here at the station. We have a missing person to find.'

Next Perillo rang Vince's extension. No answer. He glanced at his watch. Almost lunchtime. Vince was probably off somewhere filling his ever-expanding stomach. Laura fidgeted in her chair as Perillo tried Dino's extension.

'Yes?' Dino said. He was a man of few words.

'Call the Florence Prefecture and tell them we're reporting a missing person and we'll fax them a photograph and personal information. They're here on my desk. Let them know we'll send more information later.' Perillo put the phone down and answered Laura's questioning look. 'I assure you we will do all we can on our end, but it's the Florence Prefecture that activates the search for a missing person. The fire department will get involved. In a few hours trained search dogs will come down from Florence and start sniffing.'

Laura gave him a half-smile. Something was being done . . . finally. 'They'll need his clothes.'

'Yes, the more body odour they have the better. Bring a suitcase full. I don't know how many dogs they'll be sending down.'

Laura stood up. 'I'll get them. Pietro left me the keys.'

Perillo raised his hand to stop her. 'Just one more question.'

One that had taken up a small space in his brain. 'How is Cesare's state of health, as far as you know?'

'You'd have to ask his doctor. I think he goes to the one in Panzano. He never complained about anything except creaky joints.'

'You haven't noticed any memory loss? Him not remembering how to make a cocktail, for instance? Sometimes people go missing because they forget how to get home.'

Laura sat back down on the edge of the chair. Was it possible Cesare had just wandered off, kept walking, his mind in a fog? A heartbreaking thought. 'He has slowed down. He sits on a stool now behind the bar. Before he always stood. And he's less patient, but I haven't noticed any loss of memory. He doesn't repeat himself or ask the same question over and over again, if that's what you mean.' But they didn't talk to each other as they used to. The hotel had become very successful. They were both too busy, and when the day was done, too tired. 'Even if he can't remember how to get home, someone would have found him by now.'

'That would depend on where he wandered off to.' Perillo looked at Laura's stricken face. 'We'll find him, Signorina Benati. We'll find him.'

'Please do.' Laura stood up again and quickly left the room.

Nico slowly opened the door to Sotto Il Fico, afraid to drop the dish he was balancing in one hand. OneWag sat and waited to see if the dish lost its balance and crashed. The dish did not move and the door to the restaurant closed. The dog gave one last sniff to capture the disappearing smell of crisped sausage meat and took himself off down the hill to check what was new in town.

'Buonasera, Nico,' Elvira said from her usual command post at the far end of the narrow room. She was wearing one of her white Sunday dresses. Each day of the week had a different coloured dress. 'I see you've brought us another one of your ideas.' Her voice lacked enthusiasm.

'An idea yesterday. Today a reality. Buonasera to you too.' Nico was used to Elvira's grouchy ways. They had become friends, although she would probably never admit it. He understood that she was trying hard to assert herself as the owner of the restaurant. The place was really in the hands of her resented daughter-in-law, Tilde, with some help from Enzo, Elvira's adored son. Old age, loneliness, diminishing joys, jealousy – Nico thought that was more than enough to make anyone grouchy. He walked between the tables towards her, holding up his dish like a waiter in a fancy restaurant might usher in a renowned specialty. 'I will eat my hat if you don't like it.'

Elvira harrumphed. 'You don't wear a hat.'

'I'll buy one.'

'You should at your age. Your hair's thinning. What is it?'

'A sort of lasagna made with sliced potatoes instead of pasta.'

She waved the dish away. 'Give it to Tilde. She's the cook. What is your age?'

He was going to be fifty-nine soon. 'I'll tell you if you tell me yours.'

Elvira picked up her *Settimana Enigmistica* and started a new crossword puzzle. Nico understood he was dismissed. He planted a quick kiss on Elvira's crow-black dyed hair and took himself and his dish to the kitchen.

Tilde was wiping the cap of a huge porcino mushroom

with a damp cloth when he walked in. As always, she wore a perfectly ironed apron over a dress. Her long chestnut-brown hair was gathered under a green kerchief. She looked up and smiled at him. 'You're early.'

Nico smiled back as he slid his dish onto the scarred wooden counter. 'Ciao, Tilde.' Seeing Tilde always gave him joy. He loved her for being Rita's adored cousin, for welcoming him with open arms when he came to Gravigna almost a year and a half ago to attempt a new life in Rita's hometown. He watched Tilde pick up another large porcino. 'Where are these beauties going to end up? In risotto or fresh tagliatelle?' Fall was the peak season for porcini mushrooms.

'These are too beautiful. They'll go in the oven with a dozen more. A splash of olive oil, garlic, a generous sprinkling of parsley at the end and you have a dish fit for the gods.' Tilde eyed Nico's foil-covered pan sitting on the counter. 'What did you bring?'

'Something humbler. Since you're not closing down the restaurant like everyone else—'

'The townspeople like to eat out too,' Tilde interrupted. 'We'll stay open only for dinner this winter. Alba and I need the mornings. We're going into the cantuccini production business.' Nico picked up his pan. 'What I was trying to tell you is that I came up with a winter dish you might like. That's the reason I'm early. Is there a free oven?'

'All three for now.'

As Nico turned one oven on, Tilde said, 'I heard Cesare, the bartender at the Hotel Bella Vista, is missing. What can you tell me about it?'

Nico shrugged. 'Nothing.' Only five hours had passed

since Perillo had received the call. Once again news had travelled fast. The Gravignesi were proud of their stellar grapevine.

'Salvatore hasn't involved you?' Tilde asked. A lot of people in Gravigna called Perillo by his first name. He was a regular at the town's only café, Bar All'Angolo, and in his cycling days would sometimes come to Sotto Il Fico with his fellow cyclists. Even though Perillo was a friend, Nico couldn't bring himself to call a maresciallo of the carabinieri by his first name. Besides, the men in the detective squad back in New York mostly used last names.

'Why would he involve me?' Nico asked. 'He needs search dogs, not me. You called the missing man Cesare. Do you know him?'

'I met him when Babbo died. He showed up at the funeral and told me they'd played football together in high school. They lost touch when Cesare went to Germany to get work. He said he was sorry he never contacted Babbo when he came back. He seemed like a nice man, a sad one. That was my impression. I hope he's all right and they find him quickly.'

Nico checked the oven temperature – 205. He slipped his dish on the top shelf, happy he'd finally got the hang of converting Fahrenheit to Celsius in his head. 'If he's still in Tuscany, the dogs will find him.'

CHAPTER TWO

On Monday, after his early morning run and a quick shower, Nico drove into town with OneWag for his usual breakfast at Bar All'Angolo in the main piazza. It was a routine he had established within a few weeks of settling in Gravigna in May last year. The noise and activity of the café, with tourists and locals enjoying their espressos and cornetti, had made him feel less lonely. He had found a friend here, the Dante-quoting Gogol. They had breakfast together every day of the week except Sundays, when Gogol went to Mass.

'Ciao, Nico,' Sandro said, picking up empty espresso cups from the counter, dropping them into an already full wire basket that would go into the dishwasher. He didn't look happy. Sandro Ventini, owner of the café with his husband, Jimmy Lando, usually stood behind the cash register, making change with a smile, or serving customers.

Jimmy did the hard work of manning the blistering-hot coffee machine and baking the cornetti. Nico thought it was an unfair distribution of labour but knew it was none of his business.

'Is Jimmy still in Florence?' Nico asked once the last two local patrons had left.

Sandro started Nico's americano. 'I wouldn't be doing this if he wasn't.'

Nico was selfishly disappointed. Jimmy's continued absence meant breakfast would again be without wholewheat cornetti hot from the oven. He always had two. 'How did his mother's operation go?'

'She survived.' Sandro's regret was clear. 'Now he's the one who's sick with a bad cold. He'll be home this afternoon.'

There were no good feelings between Jimmy's mother and Sandro, according to the Bench Boys, four old pensioners who spent their days exchanging opinions on a bench in the piazza. Jimmy's mother would not accept a gay marriage.

'Wish him well,' Nico said.

'What shall I give you to eat?' Sandro asked. 'Do you want a ciambella or a bomba?'

OneWag perked up his ear. Both were fried dough stuffed with either custard or jam. Most of the sugar coating ended up on the floor.

'Just the coffee, thanks.' OneWag gave his boss a disappointed look and hurried out to the piazza. Nico went back to reading *La Nazione*, the Florentine daily newspaper the café provided.

Gogol, standing at the door, watched the dog scoot between his legs. '"Haste deprives dignity to every act,"' he warned.

'Buongiorno, amico,' Nico called out, glad to see him and relieved his friend had given up asking him to identify the Dante quotes Gogol liked to spout.

'"Another sun came to the world,"' Gogol quoted as he and his cologne-sprayed overcoat made their slow way to Nico's table. It was the overcoat he wore all year that had given him his nickname after the short story, *The Overcoat*, written by the Russian writer Gogol. 'It is our good fortune we're still in it, my friend,' the old man added. 'At least for today.' He stopped; his eyes aimed at the perfectly empty table. '"If you want that with you I sit, I will."'

Nico heard the implied *but* and fought back a smile. 'I'm sorry, but the butcher hasn't made your crostini yet. Last night his wife decided the tourist season was almost over and he should offer food and wine only at lunchtime.' Nico pulled the chair next to him away from the table. 'I do want you to sit down. Can I get you something else?'

Gogol squinted at the glass-enclosed offerings at the end of the L-shaped counter. After a long moment, he said, '"Here it is best to abandon every hesitation." Two ciambelle with custard, please.' Gogol lifted the ends of his coat and sat down. 'To survive one must adapt, which reminds me that the missing man must be adapting to the forces of nature. Last night the weather was not amicable. I sense he has not been found yet.'

'I guess not. I saw a search dog on my run earlier.' The rising sun had picked up the gold in the retriever's coat and he had stopped for a moment to watch. The dog's head stayed low, moving like a periscope trying to centre the target. His handler, long leash in hand, followed murmuring encouragements.

Sandro looked up from the plate he was filling with Gogol's order and saw the maresciallo at the café door. 'Ciao, Salvatore. Any news of Cesare?'

'Nothing yet.' Perillo held his right arm away from the entrance, his hand holding a lit cigarette between his middle and index finger. He was wearing his preferred outfit – jeans and a white shirt, topped by his much-loved brown suede jacket.

Nico looked at Perillo and wished he too had worn something warmer and neater than a rumpled cotton shirt. The temperature had dropped a few degrees since yesterday. 'Ciao, come in,' Nico said. He'd noticed the cigarette and tried to keep his expression neutral.

'Sandro, a double, please,' Perillo called out, raising his thumb, which meant he wanted it corrected with grappa. 'It's only my third cigarette,' he said to Nico. 'I've been up all night.' Perillo dropped the half-smoked cigarette on the pavement, stomped on it and walked in and over to the counter. Sandro was putting Gogol's two ciambelle and Nico's americano on a tray. The big steel coffee machine was already dripping the maresciallo's coffee into a white cup. On the counter the grappa bottle was open.

'I'll take the tray with my espresso,' Perillo said. 'You know Cesare Rinaldi?'

Sandro nodded. 'He used to come in here once in a while when we first bought the place ten years ago. He'd sit in a corner and watch us work for an hour or so. He said it brought back his young days. Supposedly he had worked for the previous owner for a couple of years. Cesare wasn't a nice man, but I guess every lost human being deserves to be found.'

'How was he not nice?'

'I don't know. That must happen to you. A person walks in and some kind of guard goes up. Here you are.' Sandro put the full espresso cup on the tray.

'Yes, that's happened,' Perillo said. 'Some instinct left over from our animal days. Thanks for the coffee.'

As Perillo walked towards their table, careful not to spill the double coffee, Nico pushed the newspaper off the table to make room. Gogol observed the maresciallo lower the tray and toss down his coffee the instant he sat down. There was no contentment in this man, Gogol decided. He pushed the plate with the two ciambelle towards Nico's friend. '"Your low spirit comfort and feed with good hope."'

'You are kind, Gogol.' The old man's generosity surprised Perillo. Not sure whether Gogol was crazy or just following his own drumbeat, Perillo never felt at ease in his presence. 'Thank you. I will accept half of one.' Perillo split the ciambella in half with Gogol's fork and pushed the plate back to the old man.

'Any news?' Nico asked.

'None so far, but a man can't just disappear.'

'Agatha Christie disappeared,' Sandro said as he wiped down the counter. 'Eleven days, I think. Jimmy's read all of her books. The man's probably enjoying a vacation. I know that's what I need.'

Perillo pushed his chair closer and lowered his voice. 'Men armed with his photograph are checking train and bus stations, airlines, airports in Florence and Pisa. We've just started. So far no sighting in the Florence hospitals. We're not done with the walk-in clinics and doctors. We do know that the man was in very good health for his age, which I hope means he's not lying in some ditch from a heart attack or a stroke.'

'What else do you know about him?' Nico asked softly.

'I called his nephew, Pietro. I didn't get the feeling he was worried about his uncle's disappearance. Laura Benati seems very attached to Cesare, either because he's a very good bartender or he's a nice man, at least to her. She's lovely. I'm meeting Cesare' – Perillo glanced at his watch – 'in ten minutes. He's delivering some bottles of his olive oil to Enrico.' He bit into his half ciambella, careful to catch the oozing custard.

'Cesare has lost his way?' Gogol licked custard off his finger. 'There is goodness in his heart. Cesare was the shield I hid behind when school turned dark.'

Nico knew that Gogol had been constantly bullied. Perillo swallowed quickly. 'You know him?'

Gogol shook his head slowly. 'I fear his eyes are "not struck by sweet light."'

Underneath the table, Perillo touched his balls, a gesture meant to ward off the evil eye. 'If you're predicting the man is dead, I hope you're mistaken. For his sake and for Signorina Benati's.'

Gogol looked at Perillo with sad eyes. '"Oh, sweet brother, what would you wish me to say?"'

To avoid a rude answer, Perillo bit into the last piece of ciambella. Gogol's remark had put him in a bad mood.

'Have you checked with the police?' Nico asked. 'Cesare could have been arrested.'

'There is no love lost between the carabinieri and the police. The people at the Prefecture are in contact with them.' Perillo leant back in his chair to pull out the handkerchief

Ivana always slipped into the right front pocket of his jeans. 'Nothing's come up so far.' He wiped his mouth and stood up. 'Thanks for the ciambella, Gogol. Ciao, Nico. I'll pay you later, Sandro.' From the other side of the bar, Sandro raised his thumb and continued to fill the glass shelf under the counter with squares of schiacciata and tramezzini. OneWag had wandered back in and now sat in front of the counter, looking up at Sandro with a soulful look. The bar phone, a squat, black one from sometime in the fifties, started jangling. OneWag perked up his ears and turned towards the sound, food momentarily forgotten.

'That weird noise always intrigues him,' Nico said.

Sandro continued to fill the shelf with paninis waiting to be heated, which parents would buy before picking up their children from school. No one dared show up at the school doors without a snack.

'Want me to answer?' Nico asked Sandro. 'Yes, thanks. I only have two hands.'

Nico walked quickly to the phone. 'Bar All'Angolo.'

'Where's Sandro?' an annoyed voice asked.

'He can't come to the phone right now. Can I take a message?'

'Ah, Nico. Ciao. It's Jimmy.'

'Oh, ciao. I didn't recognise your voice,' Nico said, annoyed his American accent always gave him away.

'My nose is stuffed up and I've run out of gas. Sandro has to come and get me. Tell him I'm a few kilometres before the turnoff for Montagliari.'

'Wait a minute.' Nico looked across the room. Sandro was putting the last panino in place. 'Jimmy needs you.'

'Only when he feels like it and, lately . . . well, never

mind.' Sandro strode towards the phone with a thunderous look on his face. He grabbed the receiver. 'Dearest, what is it this time?' He listened with eyes closed.

Gogol looked up with a grin. He had cleaned his plate. A curl of custard on his clean-shaven chin was the only sign there had been food at the table.

Sandro turned his back to Nico and Gogol and lowered his voice. No one else was in the café. 'Filling the tank is not my responsibility. It's your car. I have my own car to worry about. Whenever you go to your mother's you stop thinking. You turn into a six-year-old.'

Nico nudged Gogol and walked his fingers across the table. Gogol understood and slowly rose out of his chair. Nico slipped enough money to pay for everyone's breakfast under his coffee cup and stood up. OneWag barked and scampered out the door, ready for whatever came next.

Sandro turned back to look at Nico and lifted his hand. 'Nico, please wait.'

Nico stopped. Gogol muttered his usual goodbye. 'Tomorrow, if I live,' and shuffled off with his scent.

'You'll live,' was Nico's answer.

'Jimmy, I will not close down the café. I'll find some good Samaritan to bring you some gas. Ciao.' Sandro slammed down the phone and looked at Nico. 'I do love him, but sometimes I could—'

'I understand I am the good Samaritan,' Nico interrupted, not wanting to hear the rest.

'Can you? Free breakfast for you and Gogol for a month.'

'No need for that. I'm glad to help. There's nothing I have to do right now.'

Sandro clapped his hands. 'You're a gift from the gods. I'll get an empty canister for you from my car.' He slipped away from behind the counter. 'If anyone comes in, I'll be back in two minutes.' Sandro rushed out.

Nico waited by the open door. The piazza was empty. Last week the large linden tree that hovered over the benches had been full of yellowed leaves. Now the leaves carpeted the ground. Luciana came out of her florist shop, two doors down from Bar All'Angolo. Seeing her, OneWag scooted over to say hello.

Luciana and OneWag were friends from his street days. She had always had a biscuit for him. He wagged his tail once, got his head scratched and followed her as she approached Nico. She was wearing one of her countless black tent dresses that did little to hide her vast body. Her most distinctive features were large hazel eyes and a small head tightly covered by thick henna-tinted curls.

'Buongiorno,' Nico said, crossing his arms over his chest. Luciana had the uncomfortable habit of always hugging him whenever he bought flowers for Rita's grave.

'Ciao.' Her wide face spread into a smile. 'I saw Sandro rushing off. Where's he going? It's time for my morning snack.'

'To his car. Give him two minutes.'

'I'll give him five. You should join me for a schiacciata stuffed with figs and prosciutto. The figs are perfect right now and the prosciutto, as you well know, is the best in the area.'

Schiacciata, which translated to 'flattened,' was the Tuscan way of saying what he knew as focaccia. Luciana's husband, Enrico, had the only salumeria in Gravigna. He also owned a bakery on the outskirts of town. His olive bread loaves always sold out. 'I'd be happy to join you,' Nico said, as his stomach could use some food, 'but I can't. I'm sorry. I have an errand to run now.' Maybe he'd indulge when he came back.

Luciana pushed her lips into a pout for two seconds, then smiled. 'Stop by the shop later. I have some beauties that will sell out quickly. Chrysanthemums the size of my head. Almost the same colour. I bet Rita never saw anything like them when she lived in New York. The asters you bought last week must be wilted by now.'

Nico thought there was reproach in her eyes. Lately he had slowed down his visits to Rita's grave. Last year he had gone daily. Once his friendship with Nelli had deepened, he found himself trying to stay afloat in a whirlpool of mixed emotions. Now he was avoiding both Rita and Nelli, which only left him feeling one emotion – guilt. 'Consider three of those beauties sold. I'll pick them up later.'

'Bravo.' Luciana hugged him, crossed arms and all. 'I'll pick the prettiest.'

Nico took a step back. 'Look, here he is.' Sandro was striding towards them, a large plastic canister in one hand.

'Who ran out of gas?' Luciana asked. She liked to know whatever happened in the town.

'Jimmy,' Nico said.

'Here you are, Nico.' Sandro handed over the canister and some money. 'You know where to go?'

Nico nodded.

'Thank you. You are the saint of travellers.'

'That's Saint Christopher,' Luciana said, suspecting Nico

wasn't Catholic. No, of course he was. Irish father, Italian American mother, she remembered. But Sandro, married to Jimmy, had surely forgotten his saints. 'Where are you going?' she asked Nico.

Nico pretended not to have heard her question. Let Sandro tell her if he wanted to. 'See you both later.'

Surely sensing the start of an adventure, OneWag barked once and ran towards Nico's car.

Jimmy was standing next to the open hood of an old, much-dented green Ford parked on the western shoulder of the road. As Nico's car approached, Jimmy started waving both arms. Jimmy was a short, muscled man in his early thirties with a round pale face and drooping jet-black eyes that matched the colour of his hair. Nico honked to acknowledge him and looked for a place to park. On his side, the shoulder was blocked off for a few kilometres for repairs. Luckily Jimmy had run out of gas in the middle of a long straight stretch of Route 222, a busy state road that joined Siena to Florence. Nico had perfect visibility and swung the car across the two lanes. As he parked a few metres behind Jimmy, OneWag leaped over Nico's lap and stuck his nose through the two-inch window opening.

'You stay here,' Nico said. OneWag started barking and wiggling. They could see Jimmy approaching. Nico guessed his dog was happy to see the café owner, who sometimes tossed him bits of leftover pastries that OneWag caught on the fly. 'Stop it, OneWag!' The dog's paws scratched at the window; his bark became more insistent. 'Calm down.'

'Ehi, ciao, Rocco,' Jimmy said with a grin on his face and a stuffed-nose voice. He swung open Nico's car door.

OneWag leaped out before Nico could stop him. Jimmy spread out his arms to Nico. 'American friends are the best. I won't hug you. Don't want you to get my cold.'

Cursing silently, Nico lifted the now heavy canister from below the passenger seat and squeezed himself out of the small space of the Fiat 500. He handed the canister to Jimmy, as he kept track of OneWag, who had ignored Jimmy and was now sniffing the back of the Ford.

'Thank you for doing this,' Jimmy said. 'I don't know why I always forget to look at the gas gauge.' He took out a tissue and blew his nose. 'Sandro has threatened divorce.'

'He doesn't mean it.' Nico was still looking at OneWag, who was now up on his hind legs, sniffing the bottom edge of the Ford's boot.

'Have you got food in your boot?'

Jimmy looked back at his car. 'A moth-eaten blanket even the thief who broke the lock wouldn't take.'

'Well, something is in there now and my dog wants it.'

'You look. Bang on it and it pops open. I'm filling my gas tank.' Jimmy walked to the Ford's open hood.

Nico stepped closer to the back of the car and caught a faint odour that stuck in his throat. He bent down and picked up OneWag. 'Jimmy, come back here a minute, please.'

Jimmy put the canister on the ground and walked back. 'What's wrong?'

'Maybe nothing.' He picked up the dog. 'Hold onto OneWag, please. I'm going to open your boot.'

Jimmy pressed a squirming OneWag against his chest. 'What do you think is in there?'

'We'll see.' Nico banged his fist on the lid of the boot.

It popped open a few inches. The smell was stronger now, but not gag-inducing. Nico lifted the lid higher and saw a plastic sheet loosely covering something bulky. He leant forward. A man's boot stuck out of one end of the sheet. He used his pen to lift the plastic on the opposite end and saw the back of a man's head and neck. At least he thought it was a man based on the size of the shoe. Nico stretched out his arm and pressed two fingers against the carotid artery in the neck that pumped blood to the brain.

Jimmy stepped closer and peered at the dark shape. 'What is that?' OneWag whined to get free.

Nico pushed the boot lid shut. 'I'm sorry, Jimmy. We'll have to wait here for the carabinieri.' He took OneWag from Jimmy's arms, whispered, 'Good boy,' and dropped the dog back in his car.

'What's in my boot?' Jimmy asked with a tremor in his voice.

'A dead man, I'm afraid.'

Jimmy's face blanched. 'Dead? Are you sure?'

'I'm sure.'

'No, you're kidding. Right?' Jimmy asked with a laugh. 'This is some bad joke.'

Nico took his phone out of his pocket and dialled Perillo's number. 'I'm afraid not.'

Jimmy's stomach heaved. 'Dead in my car? How? Why? Who is it?' He tugged at Nico's sleeve while Nico explained the situation to Perillo. 'Did you see the face? Is it someone I know? Oh, God, please don't let it be someone I know.'

'I didn't look,' Nico said in answer to Perillo's *Who is it?* question.

Jimmy threw his hands in the air. 'Shit! Fuck! I don't

believe this.' He looked up at the clear, just-another-beautiful-day sky. 'God, why me? Just because I never got around to fixing that stupid lock? I don't deserve this. Sandro will have my head.' He whipped out his phone.

Nico grabbed Jimmy's hand. 'Please ask him not to come. The minute Maresciallo Perillo gets here, I'll take you back in my car.'

Jimmy jerked his hand away from Nico's grip. 'I need Sandro here now!'

'I know you do, and I know that Sandro will want to come rushing down here, but Maresciallo Perillo doesn't want bystanders.'

'Sandro won't listen. He'll come. I need him. Salvatore Perillo is going to think I put that body there.'

'Did you?'

'Are you crazy?' Jimmy walked away a few steps and punched numbers on his phone.

To give Jimmy some privacy, Nico leant his face against the driver's window and muttered reassurances to his still-excited dog.

'He doesn't believe me,' Jimmy said as he walked back towards Nico, all colour drained from his face. 'He thinks I just want him to come down here. He said you'll make sure I get back.'

'Of course, I will.'

'God, I don't know what to do, what to think. You have to believe me, Nico. The last time I looked' – Jimmy stopped to swallow a few times, as if the memory had got stuck in his throat – 'the only things in that boot were the spare tire and the blanket.'

'When was the last time you looked?'

'Five days ago. Parking in Florence is impossible, so whenever I visit my mother, I leave the car at the Villa Costanza car park and take the tram in.' Jimmy clasped Nico's arm. 'Do you think it's a homeless person who was looking for a warm place to sleep? It gets cold at night now. Maybe he was drunk and he passed out? The lid came down. Or he overdosed?' Sandro had taught him to think up possibilities when things happened that scared him. For scary, a dead man in his boot won the championship. 'Maybe he just had a heart attack. You think that's what happened?'

'The maresciallo will figure it out,' Nico said. *Maybe a homeless man. The boot he'd seen was far from new.*

Jimmy buried his face in his hands. 'Oh, God, poor man, and it's my fault.'

Nico took hold of Jimmy's arm. 'Come on, why don't we wait in my car?'

As the two men and a dog waited in silence in the Fiat 500, many cars sped by on their way south or north, unaware a dead man was waiting to be recognised.

The carabinieri's Alfa Romeo screeched to a stop just on the other side of the road. Perillo got out slowly from the passenger side. A reluctant Daniele checked both sides of the road before getting out of the driver's seat. Dealing with a corpse had turned what had started off as a beautiful Monday into a terrible day. It was a selfish thought he was not proud of.

Perillo stopped in the middle of the road and turned to his brigadiere. 'Come on, Dani. Bring the photograph.'

Daniele reached in the back seat for the photo and his

Canon camera case, then, after making sure no cars were coming once again, stepped out of the Alfa.

Perillo joined Nico and Jimmy in front of the Ford. 'Sad business,' he said.

'A tragedy!' Jimmy buried his nose in a tissue.

Daniele ran across the two-lane road and acknowledged Nico with a smile of relief. Police business was always easier when Nico was around. It helped Perillo keep his temper under control.

OneWag stretched himself up as far as he could against the window to say hello, to smell the car again.

Perillo held out his arm in front of Jimmy. 'Step away, please.' Jimmy gave a vigorous nod. 'Yes, thank you. I leave it to you. I don't do well with death. I threw up at my aunt's funeral.

Terrible business. I'll sit with Rocco.'

'Please don't let him out.' Nico waited to see Jimmy settled in the driver's seat of his car, putting OneWag on his lap. The dog kept his body stretched out against the window.

'Show me,' Perillo said. Nico popped open the boot with his knuckles. He didn't want to smudge more possible fingerprints, just in case. Daniele stood next to Nico and closed his eyes.

Perillo sniffed. 'Not so bad. He hasn't been in here that long.'

'Jimmy says the car was parked at Villa Costanza for five days while he was in Florence.'

After slipping on a pair of latex gloves, Perillo leant into the boot and pulled the plastic away. The man was lying in a foetal position, his back to the opening.

'Is it the missing man?' Nico asked.

Perillo stepped out from under the boot. 'This man has grey hair cut short. In the picture I have Cesare's got a ponytail. It still could be him, but I can't see enough of his face without turning him around. I hesitate to move him in case he didn't die of natural causes.'

'I don't think he covered himself in plastic to die a natural death.'

'I can hope, can't I? Maybe he was cold.'

Nico pointed to the camera case hanging from Daniele's shoulder. 'Your brigadiere has come equipped.'

Perillo sighed. 'All right, Dani, snap away.'

Daniele removed the station's digital camera from the case. He took his time cleaning the lens before nearing the open boot, careful not to look too closely at the body. Viewing the dead through a lens made it somehow easier, less real. He snapped photos from various angles, repeated the shots with the flash attached. He was intent on doing a good job, proud that the maresciallo had found a school hobby of his useful.

'That's enough,' Perillo said finally, knowing Daniele would keep going until the battery ran down.

Daniele turned his back to the boot and lowered the camera. 'You'll need his photograph.'

'Let me turn him over first.' Perillo moved closer and carefully pulled the shoulder towards him. The head stayed facing the back of the boot. 'Shit!' Perillo leant further into the boot, slipped one arm under the man's bent legs and lifted them up and over. The rest of the body came with them, still partially covered by the plastic sheet. Now he could see the damage done to this man.

Perillo reached one hand back out of the boot and tried

to snap his gloved fingers. Daniele handed him Cesare Rinaldi's photograph.

A moment later Perillo appeared from under the boot's lid. 'It's our missing man.' He pulled the lid down. 'Looks like he's been stabbed more than once. Dani, call Barbara at the prosecutor's office and tell her we have another murder on our hands. Also, get forensics down here and the medical examiner. Tell them to hurry up. It's almost time for lunch.'

Daniele hesitated. 'Maresciallo, wouldn't it be faster if I drove the car to Florence, left Signor Rinaldi with the medical examiner and dropped the car at the forensics lab?' The thought of driving with a dead man in the boot made his knees buckle, but at least he'd be doing something, instead of just standing near a dead man and his smell, waiting for who knows how long.

Perillo said, 'A good and generous thought, Dani, but the inside of the car could be the crime scene. We don't touch it.'

Daniele nodded and walked away to make the phone calls.

'I wish we could grab his phone,' Nico said. He could see it sticking out of the back pocket of the dead man's jeans.

'We'll get it back. Dani's good at guessing passcodes.' Perillo glanced at Nico's car. Jimmy was staring at him with wide eyes. OneWag, his face still pressed against the window, barked.

'I better take Jimmy home,' Nico said.

'Please do. And not a word to anyone.'

'Too late, I think.'

Perillo turned towards the direction Nico was staring at. Across the street, a grey Renault was now behind his Alfa

Romeo. Laura jumped out. 'Have you found Cesare?'

'What are you doing here?' Perillo shouted. 'You can't come any closer.'

Laura started to cross the lane, but cars coming from both directions stopped her. 'I saw your Alfa race down the road. You found him. I know you did. Is he hurt?'

'Get back in the car and leave, please, Signorina Benati. Go home.'

Jimmy saw Laura, the woman who had given Bar All'Angolo a big boost by ordering a daily supply of his cornetti for the hotel. Why was she here? He waved at her and was about to lower the window to call to her when he remembered Sandro telling him Cesare Rinaldi had disappeared. Jimmy buried his face in OneWag's neck. *Sandro, please, don't let it be him.*

Laura stepped onto the road. 'You have Cesare's photograph.' A car honked and sped past on Perillo's side of the road. She did not move.

'His face is hidden,' Perillo said. 'I cannot touch him until the medical team comes.' Nico, standing next to him, shuffled one foot. Perillo clasped his hands together. 'Please go home or back to the hotel. I'll let you know as soon as the medical team arrives and we can move him. Please, Signorina.'

Nico watched as the woman squared her shoulders and seemed to grow taller.

'I understand. There's a time and place for bad news and this isn't it. I know Cesare is in that truck. I see it on your face, Maresciallo. I will wait for you at the hotel to give me the official news.' She got in the car, made a quick U-turn and drove back the way she'd come.

'An intelligent woman,' Perillo said as he watched Laura's car get smaller and smaller the further it got.

'Yes, she understood you.' Nico walked to his car, opened the door and grabbed OneWag from Jimmy's lap before he could run to the boot again. 'Come out, Jimmy, and get in on the passenger side. I'm taking you home.'

'Not home,' Perillo said. 'First take him to the station and have one of the men take his fingerprints and DNA. Forensics are going to need them as soon as possible.'

Jimmy moaned and got out slowly, as if his joints had stiffened with the wait. He stared at Perillo with wide eyes and a grey face. 'Laura's wrong, isn't she? It's not Cesare Rinaldi.'

'I don't know yet.' Perillo narrowed his eyes at Jimmy. 'Does it matter? Is Cesare a friend of yours?'

Jimmy shook his head. 'It's just that Sandro told me he'd disappeared, and then Laura—' He pointed a finger at where Laura had stood just a few minutes before.

Nico stepped between the two men. This wasn't the time to question a frightened man. 'The Ford is out of gas,' he told Perillo. 'There's a full canister by the hood. Let's go, Jimmy. Call Sandro and tell him you're going to the carabinieri station first.'

Jimmy took out a fresh tissue and blew his nose, his eyes still on Perillo. 'I'll get my car back?'

Perillo took Jimmy's arm and led him around to the passenger side of the car. 'As soon as possible.'

'How soon?'

'It depends on the forensic team.'

Nico got into the driver's seat. OneWag jumped out of his arms and into the back seat. He stretched out and dropped his head on his paws. Nothing exciting was going to happen now.

Jimmy opened the passenger-side door, muttering, 'What am I thinking of? I'll never get in that car.' He turned to look at Perillo again. 'Do what you want with the car, but please bring back the canister. It belongs to Sandro. He's very possessive of his things.'

As the Fiat 500 drove off, Daniele joined Perillo. 'Forensics said they'll get here as fast as they can. Barbara wished you good luck.'

Perillo frowned. 'Does that mean I'm getting Della Langhe again?'

'She didn't say.' Daniele looked down at his feet and hoped he wouldn't blush. He hated lies, but he'd only followed her advice. *'Looks like it,'* is what Barbara had actually said after he'd asked who the substitute prosecutor would be. *'Don't tell him now. Why ruin the day for both of you?'* There was no exchange of love or respect between Della Langhe and the maresciallo. Della Langhe, a snobby Tuscan aristocrat, treated the Neapolitan with condescension.

Perillo looked at his watch. 'I better call Ivana.' He punched in the home number. 'Ciao, bella. You guessed it. A dead man in a car boot . . . Yes, I know. You can heat them up for dinner.' He listened, nodding. 'Yes, I know. It's not the same. I'm sorry. Ciao.' Perillo swiped off and gave Daniele a dejected look. 'Lunch was fresh tagliatelle with porcini mushrooms followed by roast pork on a bed of onions, celery and carrots!' He sighed loudly. 'Our job is full of sacrifices.'

'Indeed, Maresciallo, but I called Vince to bring us sandwiches from the café.'

Perillo raised his eyebrows in surprise. 'And a thermos with espresso?'

'Yes, Maresciallo.'

Perillo's face broke into a wide smile as he gave Daniele a resounding pat on the back. 'Brigadiere Donato, you are going to go far in your career.'

Daniele blushed.

CHAPTER THREE

The lunch hour was over. Nico was in the kitchen cleaning out the plates Alba and Enzo brought in from the terrace.

'Your potato pie was a success,' Tilde said. 'Elvira and Enzo cleaned their plates.'

Nico laughed. The compliment was nice, but after the discovery of a murder, being back in the restaurant with people he considered family was much nicer. 'Your mother-in-law looked up from her crossword puzzle when I walked in and gave me a rare smile. I assumed it was for the pie.'

'What do you think of adding some hot sausage to add a little spice?'

'You're the chef. You can change it any way you want.'

A light knock on the kitchen doorjamb made Tilde turn to look.

'Ciao, Tilde, Nico.' Nelli tugged at the long grey braid

slung over one shoulder and looked at them with worried blue eyes.

Nico felt himself tense up. 'Ciao.'

Tilde smiled. 'Ehi, bella, what a nice surprise. I haven't seen you in a while.' She gave Nico a quick look of disapproval.

Always the man's fault, Nico thought. Well, maybe Tilde was right. No, only partly right. After an enjoyable winter and spring taking walks together on hiking trails, feeding each other, making love, they had both taken a step back.

'Are you here for lunch?' Tilde asked. 'Nico made a delicious potato pie, but it's all gone. I can heat something else up.'

Nelli shook her head at Tilde and then looked at Nico. 'How are you?'

'I'm fine.' Her eyes seemed to soften. 'Why do you ask?'

Because I care, she wanted to say, but didn't. 'I heard you found a dead man in Jimmy's car. Is it true?'

Tilde gaped at Nico. 'Did you?'

Nico nodded. 'The Gravigna grapevine is up to her usual lightning speed.'

Tilde tilted her head at Nico. 'Her? Men are just as gossipy as women.' She turned to the sink and started rigorously scrubbing a pot. 'Whoever the spreader is, the news certainly didn't reach here. Isn't that right, Nico?'

'I don't gossip,' Nico said in his defence.

'It's not gossip. It's news we need to know,' Tilde directed at Nico, a frown on her face.

'I didn't find out from the grapevine,' Nelli said, wishing she hadn't come. 'After breakfast, Gogol came to my studio. He was sitting quietly while I worked on his portrait when he suddenly said, "Nico has found another dead man," and then he quoted, "Hear ye not the pain of his cry?" I thought—'

Nelli was interrupted by Alba appearing at the door with a stack of dishes. 'That's the last of them.' She handed them to Nico and turned to Nelli, who had moved away from the door to give Alba room. 'Ciao, I'm glad you're here.' She kissed both of Nelli's cheeks. 'This place needed some brightening, isn't that so, Tilde?'

Nico got another disapproving sideways glance.

'Thanks, Alba,' was Tilde's answer. 'See you at five.'

Alba wiggled her fingers, said, 'Ciao to all,' and was gone.

Nelli reappeared at the kitchen door. 'Since it's obvious that the cry of pain referred to the dead man and not to you, I'll go back to my studio.'

Nico put the stack of dirty plates down on the counter. 'No, wait a minute, Nelli. There's no way Gogol could have known about the dead man unless Sandro told him.'

'He didn't leave my studio. He just knew. He feels things we don't, just as animals hear vibrations the human ear doesn't.'

'Jimmy believes Gogol has ESP,' Nico said. 'I didn't believe it when he told me, and I still don't.'

'You are too attached to the ground beneath your feet.' Nelli's tone was not complimentary.

'I find comfort in being grounded.'

'Too bad. Goodbye.' Nelli disappeared from the doorway.

Tilde reached out and poked Nico's arm. 'Go after her.'

'No.'

'What happened between the two of you?'

'If I knew I'd tell you.' He needed to figure it out, but it wasn't all his fault, was it?

'Maybe you should ask Nelli.'

'Maybe I will.'

Nico picked up a dirty dish, and with a knife, started scraping leftover food into the garbage can. 'If you find out anything useful, let me know.'

Tilde hit him with a dishcloth. 'God, men are impossible.'

During a break, Nico called Perillo. Asking about the murder was more comfortable than a self-examination. 'Ciao, where are you?'

'In the park across from the station, thinking.'

'That's good. No need to ask what about.'

'Not about the murder,' Perillo answered. 'My soul is waiting to be restored.'

Perillo's soul only reacted to food. 'I guess you didn't have lunch.'

'A sandwich standing on the side of the road while we waited for the medical examiner.'

'Did you get any useful information from him?'

'Gianconi thinks he's been dead four days, which means he was killed the day he disappeared. He was stabbed four times. Heart, chest and two in the stomach. We'll know more after the autopsy. Forensics is still working on the car. The plastic sheet was bloodied in parts, wiped clean in others. They didn't find any clear fingerprints. The phone had been wiped clean.'

Nico heard the inhale, the slow exhale. Perillo was smoking. So much for good intentions. 'Did anything come of your meeting with Cesare's neighbour this morning?'

'His name is Mattia Gennari, someone we need to look into. He claimed Cesare's disappearance was simply a manoeuvre to get Mattia to offer more money.'

'For what?'

'Cesare's land. It abuts Gennari's. Gennari's land is smaller. So is his house. If Rinaldi sold him the land, Gennari could build a bigger house.'

'You mean the land is designated for agricultural use?'

'Yes. The size of the house is determined by how much land you have. Cesare's home has two rooms on the ground floor and two rooms above.'

'A bigger house, I hope, is no reason to kill a man. Is the Investigative Unit going to be involved? Capitano Tarani worked out all right last time.'

'I don't know yet. I'll catch up with you later. I have an appointment to keep. Ciao.'

Nico went back to work. Thanks to Nelli's visit, he too needed his soul restored.

Perillo followed Laura Benati across the large entrance hall of the room at the back of the Hotel Bella Vista. As his was an official visit, Perillo was dressed in uniform. Laura was wearing the blue dress he'd seen earlier.

They walked past the cozy bar room where Perillo had chatted with Cesare last September about a hotel guest. Not so long ago, Perillo thought, careful not to look at the empty space behind the bar counter.

'Cesare's nephew is waiting for us,' Laura said as she turned a corner. 'I called him after I came back. It will save you an I-regret-to-tell-you trip to Castellina.' Her voice lacked warmth.

'Thank you. It's not an easy job.' A job that always gripped his stomach.

'I believe it's always best to get what's painful over with quickly. All I told him was that you had news for us.'

Perillo followed Laura across another room, this one crowded with comfortable armchairs and thick wooden coffee tables covered in picture books. Laura opened a door. Pietro Rinaldi turned away from the window. He was a big, bulky man, somewhere in his fifties with a receding hairline, a wide face, jowly cheeks and tired eyes. Splotches of white paint covered his sweatshirt, jeans and boots.

A *house painter*, Perillo thought as he stepped into the room. He introduced himself and held out a hand.

Pietro shook it quickly and stepped back as if the maresciallo gave off a bad smell. 'You found Cesare?'

'Why don't we all sit down?' Laura said in a soft voice and lowered herself into the closest armchair.

The two men followed her example. Pietro crossed his arms over his chest, as if to ward off what the maresciallo was about to say. 'Let's get it over with.'

Perillo took a deep breath. 'I'm sorry. Your uncle, Cesare Rinaldi, is dead.'

Laura leant back in the armchair and closed her eyes. She'd been sure he was dead. It was the only explanation for his disappearance. Yet the maresciallo's words struck her heart with surprising force.

Pietro tightened his arms across his chest. 'His heart gave out? He'd been complaining about chest pains.'

'He was stabbed in the heart, chest and the stomach.'

Laura sat up, her eyes wide with disbelief, her mouth gaping.

'Poor man,' Pietro said with no emotion behind his words.

'I am truly sorry,' Perillo said. Stupid words that were of no help, but what else could he say? He quickly explained how and where Cesare was found. 'We will need you' – he turned to Pietro – 'as next of kin, to identify him.'

'Sure. What about the Ducati? Did you find it?'

'No, we did not.'

'Cesare kept it in excellent condition. It could be worth more than fifteen thousand euros. Are you going to look for it?'

Perillo nodded, mentally putting nephew Pietro on top of his suspect list for now. He accepted a murdered uncle without a blink, but worried about his motorcycle. 'Even if we find it, forensics will need to hold onto it for some time.'

Pietro's response was a grimace.

Fighting tears, Laura walked over to the window. *How could anyone not love Cesare? Her gentle, kind Cesare? What monster did this?*

She watched a guest picking up chestnuts from under the big tree. Cesare had dubbed that chestnut tree 'Il Vecchio,' claiming it was the only living thing in the place older than he was. She squeezed her eyes closed to stop the tears, to shut down the memories she knew would start hissing at her, coiling themselves around her chest. She had to stay strong this time on her own. Cesare could no longer help.

Perillo's eyes stayed on Pietro. 'I need the keys to Cesare's house.'

'Laura has them.'

'No,' Laura said from the window. 'I gave them back to you before the maresciallo came.'

Pietro shrugged. 'I forgot. Anyway, you won't find anything. Laura and I already looked.'

Perillo stood up. 'You weren't looking for a murderer. The house will be sealed until forensics has finished. I also need both of you to come to the Greve station to have your fingerprints and DNA taken for elimination purposes. The sooner the better.'

'The sooner for you,' Pietro said in a surly voice. 'I happen to be on a job, and from where I live, Greve is not around the corner.'

Perillo straightened his back and squared his shoulders. It always helped him face unpleasant people. 'The sooner to find your uncle's killer.' He held out his hand.

Pietro dug into a pocket of his jeans and dropped a heavy iron key into Perillo's open hand.

'Thank you, Signor Rinaldi. I will also need to ask you some questions. I expect you tomorrow morning at nine o'clock.'

Pietro's left eye started to twitch. 'I didn't kill him.'

Perillo ignored the statement and turned to Laura, who was still looking out the window. 'Signorina Benati, you will also come in the morning?'

'Yes. I'll do anything to help find the bastard. Cesare was very dear to me. My grandparents lived across the road from him. We used to play together.'

'Tomorrow, then.' Perillo put on his hat and left the room. 'I'm sorry, Laura,' he heard Pietro say. He stood still to hear more.

'What did you do to get Cesare so upset?' Laura asked.

Silence followed.

Perillo found his way to the exit.

* * *

Vince kept turning back to look at the vastness of the Villa Costanza car park as he followed Daniele to the snack bar. 'There are more than four hundred spots here!'

'Five hundred and five,' Daniele said.

'He couldn't have been killed here. It's all out in the open. Nothing to hide behind.'

'There's shelter between two parked cars.'

'Come on, Dani. That's too risky. Cesare must have been killed elsewhere. You think Jimmy did it? Stabbed him, stuffed him in the boot to throw him down one of the many ravines we've got in Chianti. Could be, right?'

Daniele kept walking. 'The snack bar is just ahead, near the ticket dispensers.'

'Slow down, Dani. I'm out of breath.' Thanks to always feeding his hunger, Vince was on the heavy side.

'Stop talking.' Daniele had offered to exercise with Vince a few mornings a week. Vince had only laughed.

After a nervous tug at the bandoleer over his uniform jacket, Daniele stepped inside the snack bar with the optimistic name of TuttoBene. *All is well.* The space was large and impeccably clean, with a long U-shaped counter in the centre, which two servers making coffee stood behind, handing out sandwiches. A line of small tables ran along the windows that faced the tram tracks.

As Daniele walked further into the room with a panting Vince, a man sitting at the last table looked up from his laptop. Seeing two carabinieri uniforms, he stood up quickly and walked towards them.

The manager, Daniele thought. A man in his late thirties, with a receding hairline and tired face, neatly dressed in pressed blue slacks and a collared light blue jersey. Daniele met him halfway and introduced himself and Vince, who was hovering behind him.

'Buonasera. I'm the manager here, Giovanni Sant'Angelo.' He shook hands with Daniele and offered his hand to Vince, who didn't notice, as his eyes were assessing the display of sandwiches in the glass cases below the counter. The manager stuffed his hand in his pocket. 'What can I do for you?'

'A glass of water would be great,' Vince said.

Daniele turned to frown at Vince. 'Go ask at the counter.'

Vince nodded happily. The counter was exactly where he wanted to be. He'd already spotted an irresistible schiacciata stuffed with salame and mozzarella.

'Maybe it's best if we spoke outside,' Daniele said, noticing stares from a few of the customers.

'Yes, of course,' the manager said. Instead of taking the walkway where a few people were coming and going, the manager led Daniele to the car park.

'A man may have been stabbed to death here on Friday,' Daniele said.

The manager stopped to look at Daniele, taking a moment to digest the news before asking, 'What makes you think it was here?'

'The body was found in the boot of a car that was parked here for five days. The medical examiner says the man was killed on Friday, when the car was still parked here.'

They resumed walking. At five o'clock in the afternoon, the place was half-full of tourists' rental cars and those left by commuters. 'The lot is video monitored. Whatever happened that day will show up in the video. I don't see how I can help you.'

'We are waiting to receive the footage, but it's always good to ask if anyone noticed anything unusual.'

'The cleaning crew didn't mention any blood,' the manager said. 'Every morning they're at the door, waiting for us to open. They would have said something. Here.' He stopped and reached into his back pocket for his wallet. From a side pocket, he extracted a card. 'This is the company that takes care of keeping the car park pristine.'

'Thank you.' Daniele slipped the card into his trouser pocket. 'I also need a list with addresses and telephone numbers of the people who were working in the coffee bar on Friday.'

'I understand. I will have to check the schedule on my laptop. You can start with Miremba. She's behind the counter now. On Friday she worked a double shift to fill in for someone who got sick.'

'Miremba?' Daniele had never heard that name.

'She's Italian,' the manager said. 'Born at the end of the tram line of all places – Scandicci. Her parents are refugees, one of the lucky ones who made it across. They fled Uganda.'

'It's a beautiful name,' Daniele said. 'I'd like to talk to her now.'

'Certainly.' The manager started walking back quickly, head down. 'I always think it is best to get things done right away. The place is quiet now.'

Daniele kept pace as he watched the manager speak to his feet. Probably the man was just eager to have the carabinieri's visit over with. Vince was leaning over the bar counter, saying something to a young Black woman, when Daniele walked in. She was laughing, her shoulders shaking, long, graceful fingers covering her mouth.

Vince straightened up once he saw Daniele walking up to the counter with the manager. 'I didn't know where you'd gone,' he said.

Daniele said nothing, absorbed by the woman's chiselled face, her smooth, gleaming, dark skin, her large eyes filling with worry. 'Is something wrong?' she asked the manager. The manager looked at Daniele to do the talking. Luckily, they were alone on this side of the counter.

Daniele introduced himself first, then said, 'I just need to ask you a few questions. It won't take long.'

Miremba's eyes shifted to the manager's face.

'Go on,' he said. 'Outside.'

She gave Daniele a big smile. She'd obviously been given good news. 'Give me two minutes.'

Daniele walked out of the snack bar with Vince following and complaining. 'You sent me to get a glass of water and then you disappeared. I thought we were a team.'

'We are. How was the sandwich?' Daniele stopped at the end of the walkway, not sure where Miremba would be coming from.

'Good, but Miremba, did you see how beautiful she is?'

'I did.'

'She liked the police jokes about us. Do you know the one about a woman telling her friend, "Yesterday my car was stolen." The friend asks, "Did you go to the carabinieri?"'

Daniele chimed in, '"I did, but they said they didn't do it." Very funny, Vince. Now she's going to think we're imbeciles.'

'No, I don't,' Miremba said, walking up from behind. 'Thank you for waiting. I needed my cigarettes.' She towered over Daniele and Vince in her TuttoBene uniform: tan, long-sleeved jersey and matching slacks. The normally bland colour looked vibrant against her dark skin. She had taken off her apron. 'Can we take a walk? The manager doesn't want me to smoke where the customers can see me.' She started walking without waiting for a response.

Daniele caught up with her easily. Vince lagged behind.

'What did you want to ask me?'

Daniele repeated what he had said to the manager.

Miremba stopped and lit a cigarette. She inhaled deeply, turned her head away from Daniele to exhale slowly. 'The body was found in what kind of car?'

'An old green Ford. I don't know what kind.'

'With a lot of dents?'

Daniele felt a surge of excitement. 'Yes. Very dented.'

Vince stood between them now, sensing that something was being revealed. His head moved from his teammate to the beauty, as though watching a tennis match.

'A Ford like that was parked where I like to park my car. We get a free pass, so we can park where we want. I parked next to it. It was there at least four days. Right by my flower bed. It's not really mine, but it's my spot. When I get out of the car at six-thirty in the morning I like to be greeted by daisies, begonias, whatever gets planted. It cheers me up.'

'You worked a double shift that day.'

'Yes, I did. Whenever anyone can't make it, I volunteer. I need the money. I'm getting married in June.'

'Congratulations!' Vince said. 'Who's the lucky man?'

Daniele didn't give Miremba time to answer, 'When you went to your car after work on Friday, did you notice anything different about the Ford? For instance, did you see blood on the ground next to it?'

'The lot is well lit at night, but I didn't see blood, but something did happen.'

Vince leant in between them not to miss a word.

'My keys had disappeared in the mess I keep in my bag. I put my bag on the boot of the Ford and started rummaging. The boot popped open.'

'You looked inside?' Daniele asked.

Vince stared at Miremba. 'You saw the body.'

'I saw an empty space and an old dirty blanket. Maybe that wasn't your car. If it was, the murder happened after eight-thirty that evening. That's when I go home.' She extinguished what was left of her cigarette with her fingers and slipped it into her cigarette pack. 'I better get back to work. I see the manager is coming to get me.'

The manager lifted a hand holding a piece of paper. 'I have your list, Brigadiere.'

Daniele held up a hand to say he was coming. 'Did you close the boot?'

Miremba lifted her shoulders with an apologetic look on her beautiful face. 'I didn't think to. I should have, I guess. I was tired.'

'Thank you, Miremba, and congratulations on your marriage.' Daniele turned and went to meet the manager, who had stopped halfway. Now the list of Friday's employees was no longer important. If Cesare was murdered in the car park after eight-thirty, they would all have gone home.

Daniele took the envelope and pocketed it. 'Thank you.'

'I am happy to be of help. I hope Miremba was helpful.'

'She was.'

'I'm glad. She's my best employee.'

With Daniele too far away to interrupt, Vince followed Miremba as she started walking back. 'Tell me, bella, who is the lucky man you're marrying? I'm trembling with envy.'

Miremba lengthened her stride. 'A carabiniere. That's how I know most of you aren't imbeciles.'

Daniele had heard the exchange but said nothing as he and Vince got back in the Alfa. They rode back in silence. As they entered the carabinieri station, Vince tapped Daniele's arm.

Daniele stopped. 'What is it, Vince?'

Vince gave Daniele a woeful look. 'I am an imbecile, aren't I?'

'Somctimes.'

'Thank you, Dani.' Vince popped his gum. 'That's better than always.'

Nico walked over to the old olive tree under which he usually sat during a break in his day, grabbed the chair and took it to the vegetable garden. The unusual move made OneWag sit up and start to follow his boss. At the open gate, he sat back down and gave Nico a yearning look. The vegetable garden was forbidden territory.

Nico opened the chair and positioned it behind the long bed shared by broccoli and the newly planted black cabbage, a cousin of kale that was popular in Tuscany but had taken him a while to get used to. Tilde showed him how to make a hearty soup out of it, adding white beans, garlic-brushed toasted croutons and a double swirl of new olive oil.

Nico sat down, stretched out his legs between two

broccoli heads and closed his eyes. Peace. He wanted peace. To stop thinking of that body in Jimmy's boot. To stop hurting Nelli. To stop feeling guilt about Rita. The single olive tree, with its speckled shade, had been his refuge during the summer. Today he needed to be with what he'd grown. The plants had fed him, the flowers along the fence had coloured his view.

Tired of waiting, OneWag whimpered.

Nico opened one eye. He saw two begging and mystified eyes staring back. The same look he got when he was late feeding his mutt. 'Sorry, buddy. This morning was rough for you too. Just watch where you put your paws.' Nico closed the one eye and moved his head sideways to catch some sun.

OneWag gave a contented bark, jumped over the broccoli bed and settled underneath the chair.

Sometime later, OneWag woke up, one ear catching the sound of wheels turning. He reluctantly stood up and trotted out of the gate.

'Ehi, OneWag.' Aldo Ferri made his slow way out of his car. His barrel of a belly had not got any lighter.

OneWag swished his tail once. There was no need to send a warning. Aldo was Nico's landlord and friend.

'Where's Nico?'

OneWag walked to the back of the small stone house, checking every once in a while to see if Aldo followed.

Nico had heard Aldo and walked out of the gate to greet him.

'Ehi, Nico, you've trained OneWag to be an usher.' Aldo spoke an accented English to the hundreds of tourists who paid to be wined and dined by a successful Tuscan vintner.

He was proud of being able to pronounce OneWag almost correctly.

'Ciao, Aldo. He just wants to make sure he doesn't miss anything. If you see him sleeping, watch how one ear is higher than the other. He's catching every word.'

Aldo raised his eyebrows. 'Every word?'

Nico laughed. 'Maybe I give him too much credit, but he does know a lot of words. The ones he doesn't know, I guess he picks up by tone of voice. He's quite a mutt. I'm very lucky to have found him.'

Aldo gave Nico another sceptical look. 'I believe it was the other way around.'

'His luck then.'

OncWag sat down by the gate with a dignified look. He'd manoeuvred a sit-down with the vegetables once. Twice was risky and humiliating in front of a witness.

'I was going to come by the winery,' Nico said. 'When do you need me to pick the olives?'

'In two weeks, we'll be happy to have you.' Aldo noticed the folding chair sitting behind a row of broccoli heads. 'What happened to contemplating life under a two-hundred-year-old olive tree? My grandfather probably planted this one.'

'Sometimes you need a different perspective.'

'Yes, I heard. You and Salvatore have another mess on your hands.'

'Perillo and Daniele are bearing the load of this one. I only do backup.'

'I don't believe that. With you on the team, whoever did this doesn't have a chance.'

'I like your flattery and optimism.'

'Well deserved. Get me a chair. I'm too heavy to stand all day.'

Nico wondered why Aldo was here. The rent wasn't due yet and it was a busy time for the winery. 'Did you know Cesare?' Nico asked as he handed Aldo the chair and retrieved his own, making sure to close the gate.

OneWag let out a sigh and stretched out on his side.

'He served us drinks. He was a nice man, always willing to listen. We had quite a few drinks in that bar. Cinzia considers his daiquiri the best she's ever tasted. She was always asking for his recipe.'

'I didn't know you are bar hoppers.'

'Only when we eat out. She likes to close the evening with a bar stop. We've been to all the bars in the area, but the bar in the Hotel Bella Vista is her favourite.'

'That's where she found your previous manager.'

Aldo scrunched up his nose. 'That's right.' That manager had turned out to be a bad one.

'Do you know anything about Cesare that might help?'

'You should talk to Cinzia. She thinks something unpleasant happened to him. Every time we were in there, she wanted to sit on one of those hard stools with no backs so she could talk to him. After one daiquiri too many, she asked, "What makes you so sad?"'

'Did he answer?'

'It took him a while. After taking care of a few other guests he said, "Getting older." That put an end to any more questions. He zeroed in on Cinzia's weak spot. She's as beautiful as the day I met her, but she won't take my word for it.'

'You don't worry about getting older?' Nico was

thinking of the conversation he'd had with Perillo Sunday morning.

'Why worry if you can't do anything about it?' Aldo said. 'As long as I can do two or three push-ups and still get up from the floor every morning, I'm fine.'

'That's how I feel about running, although I admit, it's hard some mornings.'

'I'm sorry about Cesare, but that's not the reason I came over. You now have another murder on your hands, and we worry about you. Please come to dinner anytime you're free. You dictate the menu, Cinzia will cook it.'

'Thanks. I'll eat anything she cooks.' When Aldo's wife found out Nelli was out of the picture, she'd invited him over every week. He'd gone only a couple of times, using his commitment to the restaurant as an excuse. Cinzia and Aldo had become Nico's good friends, but their efforts to cheer him up had made him uncomfortable. He had felt on display. Worrying about him because of a murder was more welcome. 'I'll have to check with Tilde first. She shouldn't need me much anymore, with the tourist season almost over.'

'Don't I know. The tourist agencies have stopped booking dinners at the winery, which means no extra income until the spring.' Aldo used his push-up arms to lift himself out of the chair. 'Walk with me to the car.'

Sixteen long footsteps took Aldo and Nico to the other side of the stone house. OneWag met them in front of Aldo's car.

Aldo opened the back seat door. 'Help yourself to six bottles of my 2018 Chianti. A present from us and hold the waterfall of thank-yous. None are needed. Ferriello wine will get those murder-solving cells of yours working again.'

'I'll say just one. Thank you.' Nico reached in and lifted the bottle. 'I'll let Cinzia know about dinner.'

Dinner at Sotto Il Fico was long over when Nico said good night to Tilde and whistled for OneWag. The dog, who had been fast asleep on the church steps, jumped up and ran to his boss. Nico picked him up and caught the smell of turpentine. 'You've been in Nelli's studio again, huh?' Nelli and OneWag had taken to each other like bread and butter. Now that Nelli wasn't coming to the house anymore, the dog sought her out as often as he could.

OneWag barked.

'Of course, you have.' Nico put him down. OneWag barked again and started trotting down the hill. Nelli's studio was at the bottom.

Nico whistled. 'Wrong direction, kiddo.' The dog knew perfectly well the car was parked next to Sant'Agnese Church. An obstinate OneWag continued trotting down the hill just in case.

Nico's phone rang. 'Ciao, Perillo.' He started walking up to the car. 'How's it going?'

'The case or me?'

'You.'

'Not well. I thought I was done with murder.'

'Mine was a hope, but here we are.'

'You'll help?'

'Of course. One for all, all for one.'

'Thank you. I appreciate it. I sent Daniele to Villa Costanza this afternoon.' He told Nico what Miremba had said. 'I'm counting on the surveillance videos to show us something. I'm supposed to get them tomorrow or Wednesday.'

'Even if Cesare wasn't killed there, the tapes will at least show someone putting him in Jimmy's boot. Knowing the boot was sitting there open for anyone to use is a plus for Jimmy.'

'The videos will tell us more.'

Nico was finding it hard to think of Jimmy as a possible murderer. 'Who's the substitute prosecutor?' Substitute prosecutor was the Italian way of saying deputy prosecutor. 'I hope not Della Langhe.'

Perillo's laugh turned into a cough. 'None other. He texted he was putting all his trust in me to resolve the case quickly. No Capitano Tarani this time. He added he was grateful the victim was not a man of renown.'

'Renown to his family and friends, I hope.' Nico opened the car door and was happy to sit. He'd been on his feet since five o'clock. It was now just past midnight.

'To one friend certainly – Laura Benati. I don't know about the nephew, Cesare's only relative. He didn't seem in the least upset his uncle was dead.'

'Maybe he was looking at the positive side of things. I suppose he inherits.' OneWag jumped on Nico's lap and nudged the arm he was holding the phone with. It was his way of protesting not going to Nelli.

'Then he should be happy. Daniele and I spent the evening at Cesare's home with two men from forensics. The place was a mess but didn't look ransacked. It reminded me of my bachelor days. No computer, but we got Cesare's phone back. Daniele is trying to crack the passcode. We found a handwritten will, rolled up and stuffed inside a vase in his bedroom by his bed. It's dated nineteen years ago and duly signed and witnessed by two people. Pietro gets the house and the land. Two and a half hectares with a vineyard, but not the much-desired Ducati. Cesare wanted to be buried with it like the Vikings with their horses.'

'Is the land worth a lot of money?'

'You mean is it a possible motive for murder? We'll look into that, but land designated only for agriculture is worth less. Cesare added a codicil two years ago. He leaves his money, I'm quoting now, "to Laura Benati, who always deserved love."'

'He loved her,' Nico said. Nico had told Rita she was his joy every day after she got sick. Why had he waited so long to tell her? He was full of regrets about Rita. 'How much money?'

'To be discovered along with who killed him.'

'Listen, Perillo, you're in the park outside the station, smoking, and I'm in my car ready to go home. Put the cigarette out and go to bed. Tomorrow we'll deal with Cesare's death, okay?'

'Daniele found something very interesting hidden between the pages of a book.'

Nico turned on the engine. 'Whatever it was, tell me tomorrow. My day is done.'

'Now so is mine,' Perillo said. 'I'm glad you came to live in Chianti. 'Notte.'

'Thanks. I am too. 'Notte.' Nico put the stick shift in reverse and started backing out of the parking spot. OneWag put a paw on Nico's arm and whimpered.

'Not a chance, buddy. It's bedtime for both of us.'

CHAPTER FOUR

Sandro looked up from unloading the small dishwasher. 'The murder got you out of bed early, eh? I just opened five minutes ago.'

'You could say that.' Nico, with a sleepy OneWag in tow, walked up to the counter. 'Buongiorno.' He'd skipped his morning run to check up on Jimmy before the curious locals stormed the café. 'How's he doing?'

'He's in the back, starting to bake. I told him to stay home, that I could manage without him for another day.' Sandro lifted his head, his eyes wide awake. 'Did he listen? Of course not. Want your americano now?'

'If you've got time.' Nico walked to the back of the room and shouted to a closed door. 'Buongiorno, Jimmy. I'm glad you're here, and not just for your baking skills.'

The door opened to show Jimmy wrapped in a large apron. 'Ciao, Nico, I'm glad too.' He spoke with a stuffed-nose voice and an anxious face. 'Please explain to my husband that I need my life to return to normal. Normal is being here at six o'clock in the morning, turning on the oven, taking my cornetti out of the freezer, dipping them in sugar and baking them.' He looked down at OneWag, who was licking his shoes. 'Yes, I spilled some sugar. My hand is not so steady this morning, but don't worry, Nico, I won't burn your cornetti.' Jimmy retreated. The door closed.

Nico walked back to the counter. Sandro was filling a large cup with some hot water. OneWag stayed by the back door, checking the floor for more sugar. 'Perillo will want to talk to Jimmy about Cesare.'

'I know, that's why I wanted Jimmy to stay home, at least for today. He's really shaken. He needs time to gather his thoughts and find his strength again before Salvatore floods him with questions.' Sandro poured the shot of espresso into the cup with hot water, placed it on a saucer and put them on the counter in front of Nico. 'Careful, the cup's hot.'

'Thank you.' Nico breathed in the bracing smell of the espresso. He'd skipped making coffee at home. 'I'm sure Perillo will understand what a shock it's been for Jimmy.'

'I hope you're right. Finding a dead body in your boot is terrible. Finding the murdered body of someone you hate is horrifying.' Sandro grimaced as soon as the words were out. He quickly turned his back to Nico and busied himself wiping the already sparkling espresso machine.

Nico picked up his americano and walked over to a table to leave Sandro alone. OneWag, having licked up whatever sugar had spilled from Jimmy's shoes, padded over to sleep under Nico's table. Sandro had just dropped an interesting piece of information and questions started churning in Nico's mind. Why did Jimmy hate Cesare? Did Jimmy hate Cesare enough to kill him? Kill him and then leave the body in his boot? That made no sense.

Nico drank down the coffee one gulp after another, scalding his tongue. Good, he deserved that. Jimmy was one of the good guys. If only he could stop thinking like a damn detective.

'If only people would stop getting murdered.'

Nico turned to look at the speaker, a young, attractive woman dressed in a grey skirt and a beige blouse that peeked under her tweed jacket. 'How did you read my thoughts?'

'Because you spoke them out loud. I'm sorry. I couldn't help commenting given what has happened.'

Nico stood up. 'Buongiorno. Nico Doyle.' He shook her already extended hand.

'Laura Benati.'

'I'm sorry you lost your friend.'

'Thank you. Nelli tells me you're a good friend of the maresciallo's and have helped him solve cases in the past.'

'You know Nelli?'

'You sound surprised.'

'I am, but I don't know why.' The unexpected mention of her name had embarrassed him somehow.

'Some of her landscape paintings of the area hang in the guest rooms. I hope you'll offer to help the maresciallo this time too. I'm sure he will need all the help available. Cesare was a good friend of mine. And so is Jimmy.' Laura smiled. She was proud of herself. She'd beaten back the guilt snake.

Sandro walked out from behind the counter to greet

her. Laura hugged him, kissed both his cheeks. 'How is Jimmino?'

'Sniffing and baking.'

'Ehi, Jimmy,' someone called from the open door of the café.

Sandro's shoulders sagged. 'God, here they come.'

Both Nico and Laura turned to look. A group of villagers was pouring into the café, their faces filled with fear or anxiety or simple curiosity.

Sandro slipped back behind the counter and barricaded himself behind the cash machine. Laura nimbly avoided the onrush and sat herself next to Nico to watch. Nico recognised some of them. Luciana, the florist; Oreste, the barber; Gustavo leading the other three Bench Boys; Gino, who owned the trattoria in the main piazza. With them came a flurry of questions and comments.

'Where is Jimmy?' 'Is Jimmy all right?' 'Was there really another murder?' 'Who was it?' 'A bartender. I heard it on the local news last night.' 'Jimmy's not a suspect, is he?' 'I'll vouch for him.' 'What did the maresciallo say?' 'Is Jimmy going to get rid of the car? If the price is good, I'll buy it from him.' 'Is he going to be arrested?'

Sandro raised his hands. 'Signori. Signore. Buongiorno.' He gave them his usual welcoming smile. 'Service will be slow this morning as I'm alone here. Jimmy is in the back, baking for you. Now, how can I help you? One order at a time, please.'

Since forming a line of any kind was an impossibility for Italians, Nico knew those orders weren't going to line up. The group huddled together by the cash register, the orders came in a jumble, mixed with more questions and comments.

Nico stood and quietly walked out with OneWag in tow. Laura left with him. In the piazza, as each started to go in different directions, Nico said, 'I just want to reassure you, Signorina Benati, the maresciallo is very good at his job.'

'I hope you're right, Signor Doyle.'

'Nico.'

'Laura. I'm going to see him now. Buongiorno, Nico.'

'Arrivederci.' It meant, 'see you again,' which he intended to do to find out more about her friend and bartender, Cesare.

As Laura walked away to her car, Nico looked at his watch. He had time to kill before Gogol would show up. OneWag was looking up at him as if to ask, *What's next*?

A rigorous walk to replace the missed run would be good. Nico headed towards the newsstand. Just beyond it was the turnoff to an unpaved road that wound uphill through several vineyards. It would be a good hike. He'd almost reached the newsstand when he heard Luciana's voice.

'Wait, Nico, please.'

He turned around to see her black shift billow around her body as she hurried towards him, her face red with the effort.

He walked back towards her.

She stopped with her arms outstretched. 'You poor thing, Nico. You opened the boot and there was poor Cesare. Knifed to death. Terrible. Terrible. My heart will give out it's beating so wildly.'

As soon as Nico reached her, she hugged him with more fervour than usual. Nico forced himself not to stiffen this time. Luciana was having an emotional meltdown, something he suspected she thrived on.

'You have to talk to Enrico. Please.'

'I'm always happy to talk to your husband.' His olive loaves cut open and stuffed with prosciutto and caciotta brought Nico happiness. OneWag was a big fan too.

'He knows something about the murder,' Luciana said. 'Ever since we heard it on the local news last night, he's been odd, fidgety. Usually, he's so quiet I can't even tell he's in the room. After the news, he was picking up things, putting them down again, changing channels every minute. Going to the kitchen, coming back empty-handed. I kept asking him to talk to me. He yelled at me. Nico, he has never yelled at me. The man has always had the patience of a saint. Talk to him. He trusts you.'

'I will, but he could simply be upset that a man was murdered. Did he know Cesare?'

'He knows Cesare's neighbour, Mattia Gennari. They play in the Verdi Orchestra together.' She took a step back to spread her arms out. 'Mattia is a big man, as round as a beach ball. He should be playing the tuba instead of the flute. Oh, but his notes are lovely. You are coming to Greve for their last concert of the season on Saturday?'

'Of course, I am.' Last year he'd gone to many of them with Nelli.

'Good. Talk to Enrico. He knows something.'

'Then he should talk to Perillo.'

'That will never happen. Three years ago, Salvatore fined Enrico for opening the shop an hour too early. Enrico has a lot of love in his heart, but he never forgets.'

'Well. Thank you for telling me.' Nico started walking backward. 'I'll be at the salumeria later to pick up the restaurant order.'

'Thank you. I want my quiet husband back.'

* * *

'Thank you for coming so early, Signorina Benati,' Perillo said as she walked back into his office. He had waited for her to wash her hands after Daniele had finished taking her fingerprints. They both sat down, Perillo at his desk, Laura across from him. Daniele slipped back into the room and took up his post in front of the computer.

'I would have come in the middle of the night if it helped find Cesare's killer.'

'It would be very helpful if you told me everything you know about him.'

'Cesare was a kind, generous man, but very private. As I already told you, he was a loner. It was work and home for him. If he had any friends besides my grandmother, he never mentioned them. I first met Cesare at Nonna Celestina's house. I think I was six or seven.' Laura could see him now, sitting in Nonno's armchair holding up a skein of bright red wool in his two hands while Nonna wound the wool into a ball. The next time she made her weekly visit to Nonna Celestina, Cesare was in the garden kicking a football. Tall and skinny, with a smile splitting his long face.

'Play with me?' he asked.

'Football is for boys.'

'Dolls won't give you strength.'

Scrawny as she was, she had liked the idea of being strong very much. They stopped their weekly football games only when she went to the university in Pisa.

Laura looked up and met Perillo's unexpectedly kind gaze. She moved uneasily in her chair. 'I'm sorry. I got lost in the past.'

'The past is important. The seed of many crimes is buried

in the past. One memory can lead to another and, suddenly, a window or a door is opened.'

'I was only remembering how we used to play football. He was a good friend of my grandmother's. They'd gone to school together, and when she got married, she moved to a house down the road from his.'

'Does she still live there?' He was going to send Daniele with his unintimidating ways to canvass all of Cesare's neighbours. Laura's grandmother could be a good source of information.

'She passed away ten years ago, and Nonno moved in with us in Montagliari.'

'Can you give me your grandfather's name and the address?'

She didn't want to. 'He didn't like Cesare being around Nonna so much. He will only have bad things to say about him.' He would also say bad things about her.

'The bad things can sometimes also be helpful.'

No, they never are, she thought. She didn't want lies said about Cesare, who had picked her up off the floor and put her back on her feet.

Perillo dropped his arms on the desk and leant forward. 'Signorina Benati, I need every piece of information I can get, truth or lie.'

Laura felt her shoulders sag. How could lies help? They only hurt. 'If you think so, Maresciallo. Duccio Gualtieri.' She gave him the address.

He looked back at his brigadiere to make sure he'd typed the information on the computer. Now, with the new keyboard Daniele had insisted on, he no longer heard the keys being pressed.

Daniele nodded with a smile. He loved his new keyboard, especially how it unnerved the maresciallo. Having his Sunday with Stella cut short still had him in a disloyal mood.

Perillo turned back to face Laura. 'What about your parents? They must have known Cesare well to allow you to play with him?'

'They didn't. They worked too hard to pay attention to what I was doing.' What extra time they had went to Gabi, her perfect sister. 'My mother works at the Greve Coop as a cashier. My father passed away when I was seven.'

'I see. Let's get to the present. What can you tell me about Cesare's relationship with his nephew?'

'Not good,' Laura answered. 'Pietro showed up at the hotel about a month ago. Cesare asked me to take over the bar for ten minutes and they went off to talk outside. When he came back, Cesare was shaking with anger. I asked if I could help in any way. I was willing to take over the bar for the night, but Cesare refused.' She remembered the tremble in his voice when he'd said, *'I'm fine.'* It used to hurt her that he would never open up to her about his life. He knew so much about hers. After a while she learnt to accept his silence, attributing it to the big difference in their ages.

'Did he ever mention his neighbour, Mattia Gennari?'

'Only obliquely at the beginning of summer.' The bar was closed. Cesare had turned off the air-conditioning and was cleaning up. She remembered the sudden warmth as she'd entered to wish him good night.

He had looked up from behind the counter. *'Ehi, Lalla, what are you still doing here?'* He used her childhood nickname only when they were alone.

'I'm staying over. I have guests leaving at dawn to catch their home flight in Rome.'

Without asking, he'd made her an Aperol, her favourite drink. *'You work too hard.'*

'So do you.'

Cesare then crossed his arms on the counter and gave her a rare smile. *'I do it because I love it.'*

'I know you do. What else do you love?'

'I love the land, the house my father left me. It was as an act of love he hoped would help me. How can I give that up? I will never give it up.'

'An act of love always helps,' she'd said, remembering his kindness and wondering what help Cesare had needed.

'Do you remember what he said?' Perillo asked when Laura's answer didn't come right away.

'Oh, I'm sorry. Yes, I do remember. Cesare said that his neighbour would never understand the love he had for the land his father had given him.'

'Signor Gennari was trying to buy Cesare's land.'

'Was he?' That explained why Cesare did not want him coming to the hotel. Why hadn't Cesare told her the reason? 'I didn't know.' It made her feel foolish. Peripheral. She hated that.

'There was no mention of any animosity between them?'

'He never said anything of a personal nature to me. I was surprised he had even told me that much about Gennari.' She'd also been pleased. Laura crossed her legs and snuck a look at her phone lying on her lap. The leg movement had lit up the screen, showing the time. She needed to get out, breathe air free of death. 'Maresciallo, I need to get back to the hotel.'

'I understand but allow me one more question. Was there ever any animosity between Cesare and one of your guests, any reason one of them might want to harm him?'

'Dottor Vittori is the only one I know who disliked Cesare. He kept telling me to fire him and get a young bartender. He's a difficult, pretentious man, but I can't believe he would actually want to harm Cesare.'

'Do you know the reason for the dislike?'

'Maybe because Cesare didn't cater to him.'

Perillo got on his feet. 'Thank you, Signorina Benati. If you remember anything else that might shed light on your friend's death, please let me know.'

'Certainly. I am as eager as you are to find Cesare's killer.'

Perillo looked at her stricken face and wanted to believe her. 'Arrivederci, Maresciallo.' Laura looked across the room at Daniele, who had stood up the second she had. 'Arrivederci, Brigadiere Donato.'

'Arrivederla, Signorina.'

The café had quieted down when Nico came back from his hike to have his breakfast with Gogol. An exhausted and panting OneWag stayed outside, lapping up water from a bowl Sandro always left by the door. Nico walked to the counter to pick up his breakfast. The half-dozen locals having their espressos or cappuccinos kept an eye on Jimmy, who was back at his usual post in front of the enormous espresso machine, ignoring them.

Sandro picked two wholewheat cornetti from the glass case and placed them on a plate. 'He hates mosquitoes, but he doesn't kill them,' Sandro said, holding out the plate.

'Thank you.' Nico took the plate and nodded. The message was clear. Jimmy may have hated Cesare, but he didn't kill him. Believable, even though it came from a man in love, but unfortunately for Jimmy, Perillo wasn't going to take it as proof of innocence.

Nico joined Gogol, who was sitting at the far table by the open French door. OneWag, thirst abated, had dropped down onto the cool tile floor at the old man's feet to recuperate. With a wide, toothy grin, Gogol pointed to the lard and salame crostini he had managed to cajole out of Sergio, the butcher. '"In church with the saints, in the tavern with the gluttons."'

'That can only come from hell.'

Gogol closed his eyes in approval.

Nico bit into his perfectly baked cornetto and chewed slowly, savouring the taste. 'How did you ever guess I found a dead man yesterday?'

'"Now had arrived the hour when air blackens."'

'It was daylight.'

'Does death not darken the air for you? The death of love? You have darkened the air for someone who is an angel.'

'I don't wish to darken anyone's air,' Nico said. Gogol was upset that Nico and Nelli had stopped seeing each other.

'"Your soul has been assailed by cowardice."'

'Maybe you're right, Gogol. I need to do some work on myself, but now, tell me, how did you know I found a dead man?'

'He knows,' Jimmy called out from across the room. The man had the hearing of an owl. 'I told you. Gogol has ESP.'

'It was just a coincidence, wasn't it?' Nico asked.

Gogol lowered his chin behind the upturned collar of his coat, avoiding Nico's gaze.

'You knew Nelli would worry and come to the restaurant. You wanted me to see her, didn't you? See that she still cared. Yes, I did see, and it made me feel horrible, is that what you wanted?'

The old man wrapped his coat around his frail body and stood up. '"No more I tell you, no more I answer you." Tomorrow, if I live.'

'You'll live.' OneWag followed Gogol out. Nico went to the cash register to pay for breakfast.

Sandro pushed Nico's money back. 'I told you, breakfast is free. One favour to another.'

'Thanks, both of you, although favours are supposed to be free. See you tomorrow.' Nico walked out of the café just as the first half of the Bench Boys, Gustavo and Ettore, walked towards their bench from different directions.

Perfect timing, he thought. 'Buongiorno!'

'What's good about it?' Gustavo asked with a scowl as he reached the bench and lowered himself gingerly. He'd added a bright red scarf to his attire – the temperature had dropped. 'Another man murdered in these parts. We're back to Sodom and Gomorrah.'

'Buongiorno, Nico,' said the always more cheerful Ettore, tucking his hands into the pocket of his thick hand-knit sweater. 'Don't mind Gustavo. His ulcer is acting up again.'

Gustavo turned to stare at his friend. 'Can't you get anything straight? Simone has ulcers. I have acid reflux, makes me cough all night. My wife is ready to throw me out of the house. That's how good today is.' Gustavo looked up at Nico standing in front of him. 'If you're here to pump me for information to hand over to Salvatore, sit down. You're cricking my neck.'

'I have just one question.' Nico sat down next to him. 'Did you know Cesare?'

Gustavo raised one thick grey eyebrow. 'And why should I? He's not from Gravigna.'

'He was from Panzano,' Ettore chimed in. 'We went to lower school in our own town, the liceo in Greve. Cesare was at the liceo with us.'

'What are you blabbing about?' Gustavo snapped. 'Nico asked me, not you.'

Ettore gave Gustavo a look of infinite patience. 'Then answer him.'

Gustavo tucked his hands under his armpits and gave Nico his full attention. 'We were on the school football team together along with Tilde's father. I played goalie. Cesare was an attacking midfielder. He knew how to use those long legs of his. He gained respect because of how he played, but we stayed away from him when not on the field.'

'Why?' Nico asked.

Gustavo shrugged.

Ettore leant forward so that he could look at Nico sitting on the other side of Gustavo. 'He was different. Didn't talk much. Didn't mix. And there were rumours.'

Gustavo raised his hand in front of Ettore's face. 'Death wipes one's slate clean.'

Ettore sank back into the bench.

'He was murdered,' Nico said. 'That makes whatever you know about him important.'

'Rumours have no value,' Gustavo announced. 'They are like farts, diffusing stinking air.'

'You should tell him,' Ettore insisted. 'It could be important. He didn't graduate, you know.'

Gustavo tightened the scarf around his neck, as if a sudden wind had risen. 'All it took was a hug. There are many kinds of hugs. Hugs of gratitude or to say goodbye, to share happiness. Or an innocent hug of friendship.'

'Jimmy and Sandro are lucky to live in a more forgiving time,' Ettore said.

Gustavo closed his eyes with a frown. 'You say stupid things, my friend. There is nothing to forgive.'

'But it's true! Now they can get married!'

'And what is that to you?' Gustavo shot back.

Ettore stared at Gustavo with his mouth open. 'What do you think it means to me? Nothing at all. I was just remarking that times have changed. What do you say to that?'

Nico stood up before the disagreement between the two men escalated. 'Arrivederci, and thank you.' Maybe Cesare was gay. If he was, did it have anything to do with his murder? Thwarted love and jealousy were strong motives, but Cesare was an old man. Could passionate emotions still be that destructive so late in life? Nico thought of his own hesitations with Nelli. Was age stopping him?

He crossed the piazza, whistling for OneWag. It was time to pay a visit to the salumeria. It was still too early to pick up Enrico's bread for the restaurant, but Luciana's comments about Enrico's reaction to the murder needed following up. A few steps up Salita della Chiesa, the uphill road that ended at the foot of Sant'Agnese, Nico whistled again. Usually, one whistle was enough to have OneWag come running. As Nico was about to pass the first side street, he noticed that Nelli's studio door was open. Well, that solved the mystery of the missing dog. Nico hesitated. He should apologise to Nelli, but he wasn't ready for the long overdue heartfelt talk he owed her. She too must have things to get off her chest. *Don't be an asshole. Just go*!

Nico entered the side street and as he stopped in front of the open studio door, the familiar smell of oil paint and turpentine hit his nose. It brought back the sensation of hugging Nelli after her day at the studio. A smell that he had enjoyed until their unequal expectations had soured their friendship.

OneWag, half buried in a folded blanket on the stone floor, casually looked up at his boss and offered him a half wag of his tail. Nelli was hidden behind a large canvas propped on an easel, with only her paint-splattered jeans and equally colourful boots showing.

'Ciao, Nelli.'

'Ciao. You can't have Rocco. He's posing for me.'

Nico took a step inside. It was a small room with only one window bringing light from behind Nelli. 'I didn't come for the dog. I'm sorry I was curt with you yesterday. Finding a body in Jimmy's boot did rattle me.'

Nelli peeked from one side of the canvas. A white streak of paint curled over her cheek. 'I know. Being rude isn't like you. Not even now. I appreciate the apology.' She smiled at him.

Nico had the sudden desire to kiss that curl of paint on her cheek. 'Maybe we could have dinner soon?'

Nelli retreated behind the canvas. 'Yes. Why not?'

'I'll call you.'

'Hm-hm. Close the door, please. I don't want Rocco to

follow you just yet. In half an hour he's all yours.'

Maybe he deserved it, Nico thought, but he still didn't like being dismissed. 'OneWag knows where to find me. Ciao.'

'Ciao.'

Nico walked out. OneWag looked at him but didn't budge. *Ungrateful mutt. Maybe Nelli should keep him.* Nico stopped himself from slamming the door.

Enrico's multicoloured beaded curtains parted, and Alba came out of the store with a half-wrapped sandwich in her hand. 'Ciao, Nico bello.' She gave him a quick kiss and held up her sandwich. 'Mozzarella and crushed olives. It's the end of the world. Sorry, I don't share. See you Sotto Il Fico.' That was Alba's attempt at humour. See you underneath the fig tree – Sotto Il Fico – was the name of the restaurant where they both worked.

Alba bit into her sandwich as she climbed up Salita della Chiesa with her usual undulating hips. Nico parted the bead curtain and walked into the salumeria.

Enrico smiled. 'Good to see you again, amico.'

Nico, happy for the welcome, smiled right back. 'Me too, Enrico. All is well?'

'The bakery hasn't delivered your bread yet.'

'I just came to say hello. Luciana reminded me about the last concert of the season on Saturday. I look forward to hearing you play the violin again. Do you have another solo?'

'No, no, may Santa Cecilia be praised. I can relax this time. Excuse me.' Enrico used a hooked stick to take down a prosciutto hanging from a beam in the ceiling. He gave the haunch a pat. 'I have to fill some restaurant orders with this beauty, the Hotel Bella Vista included. The dead man, Cesare Rinaldi, bartended there.' Enrico shrugged. 'Sad story, but people still have to eat.'

Using a long, thin knife, Enrico started cutting off the thick pig skin with its fat. 'Mattia Gennari's flute has the spotlight on Saturday. Debussy's "Syrinx". Three minutes of soul-stirring music that demands great control. It's our last concert. We've worked hard to make it the best and, now, with Cesare's death, Mattia is not himself.' He shook his head. 'We had a rehearsal last night. He had no control. The notes fluttered. I'm worried. Our last concert has to be perfect.'

'I know Mattia and Cesare were neighbours. Were they also friends?'

Enrico ignored the question and lifted the prosciutto onto the slicing machine. Enough skin and fat had been removed to show the pink meat surrounded by a quarter of an inch of white fat. The first time Rita had offered prosciutto, Nico had removed the fat, an action that had been considered sacrilegious. '*What you've done is like separating a baby from her mother's nipple.*'

Enrico held out a slice. 'This one's for Rocco. Where is he? I don't hear him barking for his treat.'

'He's with Nelli.'

'Wise dog.' Enrico took that slice back and held out another one. 'For you. This one's best.'

'Thanks.' Nico popped it in his mouth, fat and all. 'Heavenly as always.'

'On the subject of friendship between Mattia and his now-murdered neighbour, if they had been friends, the

"Syrinx" notes would flow from Mattia's flute as a tribute to his memory. And now you have to excuse me. I need to concentrate on cutting perfect slices. Bring Rocco when you pick up the bread. I'll have some salame ends for him.'

'If I can tear him away. Ciao. I'll see you at eleven for the bread.'

Enrico nodded as his arm went back and forth on the slicing machine.

Nico left the store and headed towards a short side street halfway up the hill that led to a terrace with benches. The kids who usually used the terrace to kick a football around were in school. He hoped to find it empty. He had information for Perillo. The terrace was empty as he had expected. Nico chose the bench closest to the parapet and looked down at the park that divided the medieval part of Gravigna from the new. He loved the whole town, old and new. And the people. He just needed to do some thinking about what he wanted for himself and what Nelli wanted. She had been the first to pull back. He'd been relieved, afraid the relationship was becoming too strong. Too binding. It took less than a week to feel hurt, a feeling that he fought. As for an explanation, she didn't offer, and he didn't ask.

Nico's phone rang. He looked at the screen. Perillo. He was ashamed to realise he felt relief it wasn't Nelli. 'Hey, Perillo, how are you?'

'There's nothing like a murder to stop me from feeling sorry for myself. I'm in the car with Daniele driving to Castellina. Did you know the Etruscans founded it? Dani just told me. He's becoming a regular scholar, thanks to Stella. There's nothing wrong with blushing, Dani, as long as you keep your eye on the road.'

Nico sat back on the bench. He was happy Stella and Daniele were friends. She would put calcium in his bones. 'Why are you going there?'

'Cesare's nephew ignored my order to show up at the station. He didn't even bother to call. Now he won't answer his phone.'

'If that's the action of a guilty man, he's incredibly dumb.' A football came flying over the parapet and hit Nico's knee. He looked down and saw Beppe.

Beppe, the newsstand owner's son, called out, 'Ehi, Nico, throw it back.'

'Hold on a minute,' Nico said to Perillo and stood up. He picked up the ball and threw it to Beppe, who caught it on the fly.

'Good throw for an old man,' Beppe said. 'Listen, I have information that might solve the murder, but first the maresciallo has to give me the scoop. And you have to tell me what it was like opening that boot. It must have been revolting, the smell, blood smeared everywhere. My readers swallow that stuff up.' After the last murder he had started a gossip blog he considered honest reporting.

'I'll tell the maresciallo.'

'So, what was it like, Nico?'

Nico didn't answer, picked up the phone and sat back down. Below, in the park, Tino, the butcher's son, who should have been in school, kicked the ball. Beppe ran after it and kicked air.

'That was Beppe, right?' Perillo asked.

'Right.'

'From what Daniele told me about Beppe's blog, he considers the truth a matter of speculation. I'll chat with him, but now I've got more important people to talk to. Pietro for one. He has the only motive I can think of. With Cesare dead, he gets the land and can sell it to the neighbour Gennari. I know that gives the neighbour a motive too. They are both unpleasant men, which makes me feel better about them being suspects.'

'Getting the land is a good motive if they both knew what was in the will. I had a talk with Enrico. They play in the Verdi Orchestra. Enrico implied that Gennari had no love for Cesare, but according to Enrico, Gennari's now very upset. Enrico's worried Gennari will mess up his solo at Saturday's concert.'

'He's next on my list. So far Daniele has not found the passcode to Cesare's phone.'

Nico overheard Daniele protest. 'I need time.' And then Perillo reassuring his brigadiere. 'You'll get it, Dani, but slow down. These curves are killers. I want to stay alive.'

Nico chuckled. Perillo drove his own car, a Panda, as if he were competing in the Monaco Grand Prix. The road up to Castellina had sharp, relentless curves, but the views of the valleys below each side of the road were stunning – lush green trees and bushes leading to olive groves and a quilt of vineyards that were now yellowing. For a moment, Nico's mind travelled back to his first visit to Castellina with Rita. They'd walked along the narrow streets looking at all the stalls. It had been his first encounter with an Italian market day. He'd expected to find fruits, vegetables, salamis, cheeses. They were all on display and for sale, but then came the underwear stalls, the makeup, the sewing threads, the cookware, the colourful clothes hanging from the spikes of the umbrellas swaying with the wind. Rita had fallen in love with a cheap brown leather jacket he was sure would fall apart as soon as they got back to New York. But she wanted it and he bought it for her. It never did fall apart, and now it was with her back on home ground. A bittersweet thought.

'Ehi, Nico. Are you still there?'

'Yes, I'm here.' He really did need to figure out if he could love Nelli and still keep Rita in his heart. 'Don't you have an interesting something you wanted to tell me last night? Something Daniele found in Cesare's home besides the will.'

'Ah, now you want to know.'

'I had a good night's sleep.'

'I was going to get there because it's something you have to work on without me. At least to start. He's more likely to open up to you.'

'Who is?'

'Jimmy. Cesare kept his picture between the pages of a book. He must have been in love with him.'

'Or Jimmy was his long-lost son,' Nico said.

'Now I think you're in Beppe territory. Talk to Jimmy, please. Approach him when Sandro is not around. Maybe he and Cesare had a love affair.'

Nico heard Daniele say, 'There's a big age difference.' He had a point. Jimmy was in his early thirties.

'I'll see what I can do. Ciao. Have fun in Castellina. I have work to do.' He clicked off after Perillo's ciao. It was time to pick up Enrico's bread.

As he walked down to Enrico's, he saw OneWag sitting in front of the shop, ready for whatever Enrico chose to give him. Nico looked at his watch: 11.05. He shook his head in wonder. That wonderful, stubborn mutt had a built-in clock in his head.

CHAPTER FIVE

Pietro Rinaldi's home in Castellina was on a street directly behind La Rocca, a fort that had been built in the fifteenth century to defend the town during the ongoing wars between Siena and Florence.

'He's not here,' Daniele said, after keeping his finger pressed on the buzzer for at least a minute. He felt frustrated, impatient. He'd recently gained some weight, which made his uniform uncomfortable. This trip was turning out to be a waste of time. Coming to Castellina had not been easy. It was not a relaxed drive to begin with, but Perillo's constant comments about his driving skills had made it much worse. The maresciallo had always required patience, something Daniele thought he was handling well, but today he seemed to have lost the ability to accept the maresciallo's ways as part of his job. On the walk through the main street, while Daniele was asking locals for directions to Pietro's house and also leaving messages on Pietro's phone, his boss had gulped down two espressos in two different bars and then stopped at a salumeria to buy half a kilo of caciotta di Piacenza. 'The very best,' the maresciallo had assured him as he handed Daniele the package with the excuse that a maresciallo must not look undignified. His boss obviously didn't care what his brigadiere looked like with a package dangling from his hand.

'Press another buzzer,' Perillo said. 'Someone is bound to stick their head out the window.'

Daniele looked at the four names listed. He pressed Righetti, who lived on the third floor. The other two were foreign names. After half a minute a female voice called down, 'Here I am.' Daniele let go of the buzzer and felt something hit his head. His hat dropped from his hand as he jumped sideways. Daniele looked down on the pavement, saw nothing. A grinning Perillo pointed his index finger upwards.

An empty basket was hanging from a long rope. At the end of the rope was a woman with white hair, round cheeks and a startled expression. 'Holy heaven, I hit a carabiniere!' She shook her head. 'My niece will have a good laugh. I thought you were her with the groceries. I am so sorry. I didn't hurt you, did I?'

Daniele blushed and smiled back. The woman looking down on him from her window had a happy face. 'No, Signora, but I'm glad the basket was empty.'

'How can I help you?'

Perillo took a step back, Daniele assumed to see the woman better. 'Buongiorno, Signora. Forgive the disturbance. We are looking for Pietro Rinaldi.'

'Ah, yes, the poor man. He lost his uncle in that horrible way.' She closed her eyes, and after a quick shudder, leant further out the window. Daniele looked at the flowerpot filled with red cyclamens next to her elbow, put his hat back on and flattened himself against the entrance door.

'He's not in any way involved, is he?' the woman asked.

Perillo shook his head. 'We just need information about his uncle. Do you know where he works?'

'I'm glad to hear that. Pietro's manners are not the best, but he's willing to help an old woman when he has the time. He's painting the interior of an apartment an English lady has just bought at the south end of Via delle Volte. I don't know the number, but it's just past the shop that sells all those white clothes. Her name is on the door. Pennington.'

Perillo lifted his hat. 'Thank you for your help. Buongiorno, Signora.'

'Don't tell him I helped you find him. He has a bad temper.'

'It will be our secret,' Perillo said as he walked away. He'd spotted the store displaying only white clothes after buying the caciotta on the main street. 'Follow me, Dani. I think I know where it is.'

Daniele lifted his hat to the woman in the window. She waved back.

A few doors past the clothes store, a workman wearing a paper hat made of newspaper came out of an open door holding what looked like a lunch box. His clothes were streaked with white paint.

Perillo eagerly stepped forward, Daniele following.

The workman, in his sixties, with a tanned, rugged face, looked Perillo and Daniele over as they approached, clearly unhappy to see them. 'The owner has already cleared everything. The work permits are all in order. If you want to see them again, you'll have to come back. We're on break now.' He shut the door to the small stone house.

'I'm not interested in work permits. I'm looking for Pietro Rinaldi.'

'I'm not the foreman. I don't know last names. We've got two Pietros here.'

'The Pietro who just lost his uncle.'

'First lost, then murdered. That one likes to eat under the vault.' The workman pointed to the stone arch behind him. 'He's a good worker. Steady, dependable.'

Daniele wondered if the workman hoped his words would clear Pietro of any possible guilt in his uncle's death. Perillo strode towards the arch. Daniele thanked the workman and followed Perillo, clutching the cheese package as though it were indispensable evidence.

The vaulted street, laid down next to a rough fifteenth-century stone wall, was dark until they reached the first large window cut into the stone. Daniele, always uplifted by beautiful views, stopped to look down at the spread of trees broken here and there by olive groves and vineyards. '*You'll get tired of looking,*' Perillo had told him once after waiting for Daniele to stop feasting his eyes on yet another soothing view. Daniele had shaken his head. He would never get tired of beauty. And now there was Stella in Florence showing him the beauty of art. The view and the thought of Stella cheered him up.

'There he is,' Perillo said.

Daniele turned and saw Pietro just past a lineup of empty restaurant tables. Cesare's nephew was leaning against one side of another window, eating a sandwich. Daniele tucked the cheese package under his arm and quickly followed Perillo.

'Oh, it's you,' Pietro said with a frown and a full mouth as Perillo and Daniele approached. 'Are you here to tell me you found the Ducati?'

'Buon appetito, Signor Rinaldi.' Perillo made a point of keeping his tone friendly, although he would have preferred giving this man a swift kick in the shins. 'I am here because you were supposed to come to the station at nine o'clock.'

Pietro swallowed. 'The foreman wouldn't give me time off. If he misses the completion deadline, it'll cost him. I guess you haven't found the motorbike yet.'

Perillo didn't appreciate the reminder. Finding the damn Ducati was important. It would tell them where Cesare met his murderer, maybe even his death. He was convinced the murderer didn't haul it into their car along with Cesare's body. Dino and the carabinieri stationed in the towns nearby had been searching an expanding area between Panzano and Villa Costanza since this morning. 'A phone call would have been appreciated, Signor Rinaldi, but let it be. There's a carabinieri station just outside the old town here. We can talk there and also get your fingerprints and DNA.'

'Come on, Maresciallo. Enjoy yourself for a change.' Pietro flung his arm out. 'Carabinieri stations are stuffy. Here I get fresh air and a view. Be generous and ask me questions here while I eat my lunch. The other stuff can come later.'

It wasn't a bad idea, Perillo thought. Why not mollify his number-one suspect, maybe get his guard down? He turned to Daniele. 'Brigadiere?'

Daniele already had his pen and pocket-sized notebook out. He rested the package on the window ledge and quickly slipped his hand in and out of his pocket. Last time he'd had to take notes standing up was next to an old castle parapet. This time he was going to take some notes, but also record the interview on his phone. He needed to convince the maresciallo that a recording was far more accurate than his notetaking. 'I'm ready, Maresciallo.'

Perillo nodded and turned to face Pietro. 'What was your relationship with your uncle?'

'I didn't like him, but that doesn't mean I killed him.' Pietro took another bite of his sandwich of marinated aubergine between two slices of thick country bread.

Perillo watched him chew and felt his stomach twinge with envy. 'Why didn't you like him?'

Pietro swallowed. 'He cheated my father out of everything. My grandparents had two sons. Babbo was the oldest, the one who was devoted to Nonno, took care of him when he got old, but then the prodigal comes back after ten years in Germany. During his time there he never bothered to keep in contact with Nonno – not a word, not a phone call, nothing.' Pietro tightened his grip on the half-eaten sandwich as his voice tensed with anger. 'Zio Cesare appears one day and moves in with Nonno. A year later Nonno's heart gives out.' He squeezed harder and slices of aubergine slid to the floor. 'Who gets everything? My fucking uncle.'

'Your father didn't get anything?'

A bee flew in through the window and buzzed around what was left of the sandwich in Pietro's hand. 'He got what money there was, not much, but it's the land he cared about. It was my great-grandmother's dowry sometime in the middle of the nineteenth century. I told Babbo to fight it in court, but he refused. He claimed Nonno left it to Cesare for a good reason. What reason could there be?' Pietro looked down at the bee that was now examining his hand. With a swift slap of his other hand, he smacked it and flicked it off.

'Didn't it bite you?' Daniele blurted, remembering the excruciating pain on his foot after stepping on one.

Pietro didn't hear him. 'What reason? I kept asking. Babbo wouldn't tell me, because he was making it up. Two years later he died too.'

'We found a will in your uncle's home,' Perillo said.

A smug expression spread over Pietro's face. 'I get the property.'

'Had he told you that?'

'We had a fight about a month ago. I went over to the hotel to tell him he had to sell the land to the neighbour. I was convinced he was going to leave it to greedy Laura.'

Perillo was surprised. Laura Benati had struck him as a gentle, generous woman. 'Why do you think she's greedy?'

'Because she is. All that attention to her bartender? I saw them together enough times to watch how she was all over him, trying to show how much he meant to her, how he was her best friend. It was all fake, an act, you can believe me.'

Daniele blurted out, 'Are you married?' The maresciallo didn't like him to intervene while questioning a possible suspect, but he couldn't help himself. There was nothing fake about Signorina Benati.

'Divorced a year ago.' Pietro took the last bite of his

sandwich and with a full mouth asked, 'What does that have to do with Laura?'

'It's for the record,' Perillo said, having understood what Daniele was suggesting. Pietro might be angry at women in general. Daniele was pretending to write the information down. Perillo was sure Daniele was suppressing a smile.

Pietro angrily slapped his lunch box shut. 'I know she comes across as la signorina perfetta, but it was obvious she was after something, and just as obvious that he loved her, that she was like a daughter to him. I didn't want him to live on my father's land anymore and I certainly didn't want her to have it. He almost hit me he was so angry. He shouted that I didn't know anything, that he would never sell even under torture. I walked away. A week or so later, I got a letter from him telling me that at his death the land was mine.'

'Did you write him back or acknowledge the letter?' Perillo asked.

'Why should I? That land and that house should have been mine the moment the doctor declared my father dead.' Pietro straightened himself up. 'I've got nothing more to say.'

'Do you have the letter?'

'Somewhere.'

'I'd like to see it.'

'Didn't my uncle leave a will?'

'Yes, he did.'

'And I get the land, house and vineyard, what there is of it?'

'Correct.'

'Then you don't have to see the letter. It's private.'

'As you wish, although it would prove you knew you were getting the land before your uncle died, which gives you one less reason to kill him.'

Anger flashed across Pietro's face. 'What other reason do I have?'

'Greed. Why wait until Cesare dies to cash in on Gennari's offer? I'm sure the divorce left you with lightened pockets. One last question for the moment. Did you kill your uncle, Cesare Rinaldi?'

'No, and you can ask the foreman where I've been last week from eight in the morning to seven at night, every day except Sunday. Cesare was dead by then.'

Perillo stiffened. The day and time of death hadn't been released yet. 'What makes you think that?'

'I hear he smelt when you found him Monday morning.' Pietro started to walk back down the vaulted street. 'Let's get those fingerprints over with. I have to get back to work.'

Perillo was tempted to hold Pietro back. He didn't enjoy his prime suspect walking away from him without being dismissed. *Let it be*. At the moment he had no more questions. Besides, he was hungry.

Perillo hurried until he was abreast of Pietro. 'I will probably need to question you further.'

Pietro let out a grunt.

While Pietro was having his fingerprints taken, Perillo walked back to the Pennington house to ask the foreman to corroborate Pietro's alibi. He found only three workers sitting on a drop cloth having lunch.

'Do you know what time Pietro Rinaldi got to work on Friday?'

'On time,' one of them said through the bread in his

mouth. Another one chewed and nodded in agreement. The third man swallowed, clicked shut the metal box that had held his lunch and said, 'Punctual Pietro, the foreman calls him.'

'Thank you,' Perillo said and walked back to the carabinieri station.

Enzo was cleaning glasses behind the small restaurant bar when Nico walked in, his arms holding a large bag filled with Enrico's freshly baked loaves. 'Thanks.' Enzo tossed the dishtowel over his shoulder and held out his arms. Before handing the loaves over, Nico dipped his nose down and took a last sniff. The smell of the loaves reminded him of sitting in the kitchen in the Bronx apartment reading the paper in his pyjamas while Rita's bread baked in the oven. 'On Sundays, Rita always made a big round loaf of bread.' Pane casareccio, the Italians called it. Home-style bread. Nico handed over the bag. 'Hers had salt in it!'

Enzo took the bag from Nico and walked to a table at the other end of the room where he would slice the bread, judging the amount needed as diners came in. 'She must have told you the reason for our unsalted bread.'

'She did. Sometime in the Middle Ages, Pisa hated Florence, for who knows what reason—'

'The obvious reason.' Enzo stacked the loaves to one side of the table. 'Power.'

'Okay, power, and since Pisa had control of the salt trade, she wouldn't let Florence get any.'

'No, Florence could have it if she paid the high tax. Most Florentines couldn't afford it and those who could were too proud to pay.'

'You're both wrong,' claimed Elvira from her armchair in the next room. Enzo shook his head. He was used to being wrong.

'Buongiorno, Elvira.' Nico stepped into the other room. Enzo's mother lifted her face to have her cheeks pecked. She was wearing her green Tuesday dress. Nico kissed her withered cheeks and stepped back.

Elvira patted the stack of folded napkins on her lap as if they held the story. 'The food of Tuscany is rich and is best accompanied by unsalted bread. That's the real reason.' She lifted an admonishing index finger at him. 'You been here long enough to stop sprinkling salt on your bread. I've caught you doing that several times.'

'Old habits like to linger.'

'I'm sure Rita is tired of lingering.'

Nico clenched his jaw.

Elvira reached out and took his hand. 'I'm an interfering old woman who has never been able to hold her tongue. I cared for Rita, and I care for you. She's gone and you are here. Being alive is a blessing. Take advantage of it.'

'I'm trying, Elvira.'

'I'm sure you'll succeed.' She squeezed his hand and let go. As Nico turned to go, Elvira added, 'Your potato tart was excellent, but a little heavy on the salt.'

'I'll tell Tilde. It's in her hands now.'

'Forgive her, Nico,' Tilde said as he walked into the kitchen. 'She's impossible, but she means well.'

'Do you think that when she's nasty to you?'

'It's different with me. I took her son away. She wants to see you happy, and to her, a widow, happy means not being alone. It seems you don't mind being alone.' Tilde had made it perfectly clear she wanted him to start seeing Nelli again. As had Gogol and now Elvira. Their pressures didn't help; they only confused him.

Being alone wasn't the point, Tilde thought, *if that's what Nico wanted*. But she had seen Nico and Nelli together. Seen and felt the lovely feeling they had for each other. Why throw that away? 'You're a grown man. It's up to you to know what makes you happy.' Tilde wiped her hands on her long apron. She'd been washing escarole she planned to sauté with beets. 'Any new recipes coming? The potato dish sold well. And yours was perfectly salted. The one Elvira found too salty was mine. I overdid it a bit.'

'No new ideas for now.' Nelli and the murder had taken over his head.

'We don't really need new ideas, I guess. The tourists are dwindling to a trickle. The hotels are closing at the end of the month. The locals will come but they like their traditional Tuscan foods.'

'Beans, beans and more beans.'

Tilde laughed. Nico didn't favour beans. 'I don't need you now. Probably not even for dinner. We only have a few reservations. Alba can handle them.' She had come to realise that although the restaurant had at first been a lifesaver for Nico, it had now become a place to hide in. Maybe with winter coming and Sotto Il Fico open only for dinner, Nico would need to fill his life with someone else besides his dead wife's family. 'Of course, you can have lunch with us, if you want.'

'I'll skip this time. I'm going to have lunch at the Hotel

Bella Vista.' He wanted to see Laura Benati again but would first stop in Panzano to talk to the vegetable vendor Cesare had gone to before disappearing.

'Ah, you're detecting today.' Solving murders was another crutch. 'Any leads? I know, you'll never tell me, but I will always ask. Have fun. I hear the hotel restaurant is good. It's rated four out of five on Tripadvisor.'

'That's your rating.'

'It is, and we work hard to keep it with your help.' Tilde gave Nico a quick hug. 'Ciao, and be wise.'

'As wise as Solomon.'

'That I have yet to see,' Tilde said as she pushed him out of the kitchen.

Nico said his arrivedercis as he left the restaurant. When he walked out, OneWag ran down the stairs of the church and greeted his boss by sitting down at his feet with a certain look on his face that Nico knew meant, *Time for some fun*.

He couldn't take him to the hotel restaurant, and he wasn't going to let OneWag wander the streets of Panzano, a town the dog didn't know and wasn't known. Leaving him in the car was out of the question. He'd chewed the steering wheel to the point of having to replace it. 'Sorry, buddy, I'm taking you home.'

OneWag lay down flat, snout between his paws, his usual *woe-is-me* stance. It always made Nico laugh.

Enzo laughed too. He had witnessed the exchange between the two from the doorway. 'You can take him if you eat outside.'

OneWag, head still down, cocked his ears.

'The Bella Vista has a back patio. Not as great as ours, but nice.'

OneWag looked up at his boss. Nico held his gaze, then slowly nodded. With a joyous yelp, the dog jumped up and scampered down the hill to where the car was parked.

In Panzano, Nico found an empty spot in the lot below Mac Dario, the more casual open-air restaurant of legendary Dario Cecchini's threesome. Nico was convinced that Panzano had been put on the tourist map because of Cecchini's marketing savvy. Every day his butcher shop, Antica Macelleria, offered slices of country bread with a salame or lard and glasses of Chianti. The tourists came running. Sergio, Gravigna's butcher, had copied the idea, providing Gogol with his favourite breakfast.

Nico reached for the leash in the back seat. OneWag turned over on his back. Having lived on the street, he hated being put on a leash.

'You don't know this town. It's the leash or home. You decide.'

The dog turned around, sat up and studied Nico's face for any trace of give.

Nico met his gaze and silently counted to ten.

No give. OneWag slowly lowered his head.

Nico attached the leash. 'Good boy.'

They walked down the stairs. As they passed a coffee bar, a young woman walked out holding a straw bag brimming with escarole leaves over one shoulder.

'Buongiorno, Signora,' Nico said. 'Where can I find the vegetable vendor?'

She turned towards the piazza and pointed to a road just behind it. 'Nardo's is just a few doors up the road. It's a good shop. You'll like him. He's got good produce and fair prices.'

'Thank you.'

The woman acknowledged the thank-you with a quick smile, said, 'Buongiorno,' and walked past him and the dog.

Nardo's shop was small and crowded with produce laid out carefully in small wooden crates. Nico tied OneWag to an iron ring on the wall. The dog turned his back on Nico.

'Buongiorno,' Nico said, entering, eyeing a crate filled with thin string beans.

'Buongiorno,' Nardo said as he gave the only other person in the shop her change. He was a small man with receding grey hair and the cheerful face of someone who loved his job. 'Be sure to give the pears another day or two, but not in the refrigerator.'

The elderly woman laughed. 'Signor Nardo, I was eating pears when you were still in your mother's belly. I know when a pear is ready to eat, but I appreciate the concern. Buongiorno.' She gave Nico a quick look and walked out of the store.

The vendor turned his attention to Nico. 'Feel free to look around, but please don't touch.'

'Looking is enough for me. I'd like half a kilo of those string beans, please. Also, a head of broccoli, one of cauliflower and two large onions. Oh, and add three or four potatoes to that.'

Nico's purpose in ordering so much was to make the vendor amenable to answering questions. As Nardo gathered his order, Nico said, 'I heard you were the last man to see Cesare Rinaldi before he disappeared.'

'I was. A sad business, but it's not something I want written on my tombstone.'

'I agree. I'm the man who found him, unfortunately.'

'I'm sorry. I didn't mean any disrespect,' Nardo said as he started to put each order in a separate paper bag.

'None taken.'

Nardo assumed Nico was making soup as he added what the Italians called gli odori – the odours – which consisted of parsley, a bay leaf, a carrot and a celery stalk. 'You knew him?'

'No. I'm a friend of the man who owns the car he was found in.'

Nardo shook his head. 'I hope it's already in the junkyard.'

'Did Cesare come here often?'

'Bought all his vegetables here. He said the crowds at the Sunday market gave him a headache. He was quiet, never said much, so I guess he liked things to be calm.'

'Did you notice anything different about him that morning?'

'Not with me. He picked up his apples, paid for them and walked out.'

Before Nico could answer, he heard the ping of a text coming through. He reached into his pocket. The text came from Perillo:

Don't forget Jimmy. I count on you.

Nardo weighed the potatoes. 'That noise on your phone, what is that?'

'Someone sent me a message.'

'I heard that noise when Cesare was here that morning. I forgot about it. Cesare was just walking out, and he did what you just did with your finger, and then he rushed out. A minute later I saw him zoom by on his motorbike. The carabinieri should know what message he got. I hear they have his phone.'

'First you need to find the passcode. That's not always easy.'

'My wife uses her birthday but backward. I stay away from gadgets.' Nardo put the various packages in a large plastic bag, finished adding up the vegetables with a short pencil and handed the bill to Nico.

Nico paid. 'Thank you.'

'Arrivederci. Enjoy your soup.'

'I'm sure I will.' Nico lifted the heavy bag and walked out of the shop. He got no welcome wag from OneWag.

When Nico reached the car park just beyond the tall iron gates of the hotel, a grey Mercedes was coming out, the passenger waving at someone behind her. As Nico drove past the car, he saw Laura Benati standing to one side, waving back, looking lovely in a spring green dress, her blond hair waving down to her shoulders. The loose hair made her look much younger. Nico rolled down his window. 'Buongiorno, Laura.'

Recognising him, she smiled. 'Buongiorno. How nice to see you. Do you need to talk to me?'

'I would like that very much, but I'm actually here for lunch, if it's not too early.' Lunches weren't usually served before twelve-thirty. It was now barely noon. 'I've heard good things about your restaurant. Is your patio open? I've got my dog with me. He gets destructive if I leave him in the car.'

'Yes, it's open.' She wondered if Maresciallo Perillo had sent him to ask more questions, to catch her off guard. Perillo had called her to tell her she was inheriting Cesare's money. A surprisingly big amount. Now she was probably a suspect. This man had a friendly face, the kind that says *trust me*. With Cesare murdered, she wasn't going to trust anyone.

'Choose your parking space. There are only four guests left in the hotel. We close at the end of the month. I'll accompany you to the patio.'

Nico parked under a vine-covered trellis. As soon as the door opened, OneWag leaped over Nico's knees and jumped out. A quick trot and a careful examination of Laura's shoes followed. She bent over and let him smell her hand before giving his back a good scratch.

'Smelling someone's shoes is OneWag's way of determining friend or foe,' Nico said. 'Most people don't bother to acknowledge him.'

'He's cute. OneWag is an odd name,' Laura said, still scratching the dog's back and earning points with him.

'You know English.' She had pronounced the name perfectly.

She straightened herself up. 'Knowing languages is necessary in the hotel business.'

'Of course. OneWag only wags his tail once. The vet says there's nothing wrong with his tail.'

'He's lived on the streets, I would guess.'

'Yes. I've only had him just over a year.'

'Then he has a perfect right to be diffident and proud. Let me take you to the patio.'

The wide semi-circular patio hugged the length of the hotel. The grey flagstone floor held white folded umbrellas next to each round metal table with pillowed chairs. The front edge of the patio overlooked a young vineyard and at the far end stood a stand of oak trees.

'When were those vines put in?' Nico asked as he picked a table next to a tall terracotta jar showing off bright red dahlias. There were flowering jars all along the perimeter.

'Only two years ago. It was a lawn before that, which was costing the hotel far too much money in upkeep. Next year we'll have grapes.' Laura closed her eyes for a moment. 'It was Cesare's idea, his project.'

'Who will take care of it now?'

'I'll hire someone. Sit down. I'll let the waiter know you are here.'

'Won't you stay and have an aperitivo with me?'

An aperitivo would come with questions she would have to answer. 'I have work to do right now. Perhaps a coffee later.'

'Yes, please.' Nico sat down and looked up. He could see that she was now on her guard. 'I look forward to it.'

'The waiter will bring the menu. Buon appetito.'

'Thank you.'

A cautious OneWag waited to take off and explore the new grounds until after this woman with the sweet-smelling shoes went through the wide hotel door.

Two minutes later, a waiter rushed out buttoning the last button of his white coat. He was a thin young man with black curls on his head, a long nose, and ears that stuck out of his head. 'Buongiorno, Signore.' He offered the handwritten menu. Nico opened it, but before he could start reading, the waiter said, 'Besides what is written in the menu, today the chef is offering pappardelle with spinach bathed in a lemon sauce. It's fantastic.'

'You had some?'

The waiter spread his mouth into a wide grin and answered Nico with an exuberant nod.

'Thank you. I'll have that then.'

'Excellent choice, and to drink?'

Nico hesitated. To be loyal to his landlord, he should order a glass of Ferriello, but he was on an adventure. New restaurant. New people. Time for a change. 'A glass of Castello dei Rampolla Chianti and flat water, please.'

The wine, water and a small basket filled with slices of schiacciata came right away. Just as Nico was savouring his wine, a man entered the patio from the same path Nico had taken. He was a short, very large man with tousled grey hair, a weather-beaten face, wearing workmen's boots, stained jeans and a wrinkled sweater. He raised his hand in salute when he saw Nico. 'This is a great day, isn't it?' he said in a loud voice.

'A good day, certainly,' Nico answered, wondering if the man had been drinking.

The man chose the table closest to Nico and dropped down into a chair facing him. 'You're American, right?'

Nico nodded. He hated that his accent continued to give him away, but knew he'd never get rid of it.

'I've never eaten here before,' the man said. 'Prices are too high, but I just got some good news. I should be happy, but it's scary. Money coming my way, that is new to me. Who knows what will happen? What did you order?'

Nico told him and prayed the waiter would come out

quickly with his food. Eating didn't require answers.

'It's bistecca alla fiorentina for me. When the sale is done, I'll get the very best at Dario Cecchini's Officina della Bistecca. He's known all over the world for his beef. You ever go there?'

The waiter's appearance saved Nico from answering. After lowering the hot pappardelle dish in front of Nico, the waiter walked over to the man's table and said something in a low voice. Nico, concentrating on the delicious smell of browned butter and Parmigiano, heard only 'Signorina Benati.'

The man got up and followed the waiter inside. Alone again, Nico happily dug into his pasta and savoured the taste and the silence.

Twenty minutes later, the wine glass was empty, the water glass half empty, and the pappardelle dish wiped clean with a piece of oil-tinged schiacciata. Nico happily sat back and tried to memorise the menu for Tilde's sake.

The waiter appeared and picked up the empty plate. 'Signorina Benati offers her apologies for the disturbance. Would you like to see the dessert menu? It will be on the house.'

'That's very nice, but there's no need. I'll just have an americano. You got rid of that man quickly enough. What did you tell him?'

'I said he knew he was not welcome here.'

'Why isn't he?'

'Because he was Cesare's neighbour,' Laura replied, walking across the patio with OneWag in her arms, 'and made Cesare's last few months miserable with his implorations and threats. Now he wants to celebrate because he's sure Pietro will sell him Cesare's land. If he ever steps on hotel property again, I will call the carabinieri. Your dog was trying to uncover secrets in my office.' OneWag looked perfectly content to stay where he was. 'The right dog for a detective.' Laura lowered OneWag to the floor and sat down next to Nico. The dog settled by Laura's feet.

'I see you know that Cesare left his property to Pietro,' Nico said.

'Yes, and that he left me his money. It was a complete surprise. I hope you believe that. I don't care about the money. I'd rather have Cesare back.'

'Why shouldn't I believe you?'

'Whoever inherits is immediately a suspect in a murder case, isn't that so? It's quite a lot of money.' She stopped speaking as the waiter crossed the patio with their coffees.

Nico waited until the waiter was gone to speak. 'The fact that a man who was a bartender for thirty-eight years has "a lot of money" to give away must have also come as a surprise.'

Laura unwrapped the small square of chocolate that came with her espresso. 'The only money he spent was on his motorbike. The brigadiere told me they haven't found it yet.'

'You spoke with Brigadiere Donato?'

'Yes. A few minutes before you came, I received a call from Maresciallo Perillo. He told me about the will and what money was in Cesare's bank account. He asked me if I had any idea what Cesare's phone passcode was.'

She didn't want them to find the passcode. What was in that phone belonged to Cesare. Only to him. She had sent him a lot of messages after he disappeared. Pleading ones.

Angry ones. Her words were for Cesare's ears, no one else. 'I have no idea what his passcode may be.'

'It's important to see what texts or emails Cesare received. The murderer might have communicated with him.'

'I think it's a waste of precious time. Cesare's killer would have taken the phone or destroyed it if there was anything that could incriminate them.'

'You have a point, Laura, but people often don't know what could incriminate them.'

'I guess I should trust the experts.' Laura finished her coffee and stood up. 'I hope you enjoyed your meal.'

'The meal was excellent and so was the company.'

'Thank you.' Laura thought he sounded sincere. 'We're open every day until the end of the month. We'll reopen in April.'

'Where will you go during those months?'

'I haven't decided yet. Peru maybe. Now that I have money, I may take Nelli with me.'

Nico's stomach clutched briefly. 'I'm sure she'd love that.'

'We'll see. Arrivederci.'

Pleased by her choice of goodbye, Nico said, 'I do hope we will see each other again.'

'Without a doubt,' she answered. At least until Cesare's murderer was found.

Nico and OneWag watched her walk away, her back held as straight as a sword. The meal turned out to be on the house.

Laura found a guest standing outside of her office and put on her hotel smile. 'Mrs Barron, do you need help with your luggage?' she asked in English. The middle-aged woman was leaving today after having spent three months in the hotel. She had arrived with six large suitcases. She was leaving with eight, the new ones filled with clothes from the luxury outlet in Leccio.

Mrs Barron fluttered her small, gloved hand. 'No, no, your porter is taking care of my suitcases. I wanted to be certain you had my reservation for next year. I had such a delightful stay.' She spoke in her fluty voice. 'I cannot wait to enjoy another Chianti summer.'

'Don't worry, Mrs Barron. Your reservation is written down in ink in my ledger.' She had spent her stay charming the staff by never making a fuss.

Mrs Barron's eyes welled up as she put her hand on Laura's arm. Laura clenched her teeth, knowing what was coming.

'I am so sorry, dear. Cesare was such a good man.' Laura nodded.

'Dottor Vittori was horrible to him, snapping his fingers, then getting so angry when Cesare dropped the tray. A very rude man. I'm glad he is not coming back.'

Laura thought that was wishful thinking on Mrs Barron's part. Dottor Vittori had been coming to the hotel since before Laura started working here. 'Of course, you were there that night.' Mrs Barron spent her evenings in the bar, nursing a Pimm's Cup. She had been Cesare's favourite customer, Laura remembered. Mrs Barron sat in silence with her one drink and was always generous with her tip.

'Yes, I was in the bar, studying the other guests, making up stories about them. It's an enjoyable pastime when one is alone in a foreign country. One day I might write them down. For now, I simply remember them.'

'One of the guests who was there that night told me Dottor Vittori accused Cesare of dropping the tray on purpose,' Laura said. 'Is that true?'

'No. He lost his temper and called him an incompetent "babuino." I think that means baboon. It was a horrid thing to say. It was Dottor Vittori's guest who startled our dear bartender.'

'Did his guest say something?'

'Not a word, but as Cesare bent down to serve the drinks, he looked at Dottor Vittori's guest and Cesare's expression completely changed. He was either surprised or startled, and the tray came crashing down. It was as if he'd seen a ghost. I grew up in a haunted house in Sussex. I didn't mind the sweet servant girl who liked to appear in my bedroom. I was an only child and she kept me company. I really should write down the stories she told me. Well, I had better stop chattering. I hired a driver to take me to the Florence airport. Goodbye, my dear.' Mrs Barron gave Laura an unexpected quick kiss on the cheek. 'I hope your memories of Cesare will keep you company.'

'Thank you.' Laura accompanied Mrs Barron to the entrance. 'Have a safe trip. I look forward to seeing you next summer.' She waved as the car drove off. A woman with a strong imagination, Laura thought, but she was intrigued enough to want to find out more about Dottor Vittori's guest.

After the lunch at the hotel, Nico and OneWag drove to the Ferriello winery. As soon as Nico parked and opened the door, the dog jumped out and followed his nose to the Welcome Centre at the far end of the car park.

Arben, the winery's Albanian manager, was standing at one end of a thick, ten-foot-long table. Cinzia was at the other end, ready to lift the heavy weight together.

OneWag looked up at Arben and barked. 'No ball-throwing today, Rocco. I'm busy.'

Walking into the large, wood-beamed room, Nico said, 'Here, let me.' He took over for Cinzia. 'Where are we going with this?'

Cinzia shook her hands, stretched her fingers. 'Lined up behind the other ones.' She had already moved two long tables to the front of the room. 'Thank you for having such excellent timing. These tables are getting heavier by the month.'

'One more wine dinner?' Nico asked as he and Arben moved the table.

'Our last for the season.'

'May Mohammed be praised,' Arben said as he lowered the table with Nico.

Cinzia arched an eyebrow. 'You didn't praise Mohammed for all the tips you got from our tipsy visitors.'

'I praised in silence.'

'How many?' Nico asked. He remembered helping serve dinner to a group of eighty hungry tourists bused in from Florence while Aldo entertained them with lessons in wine production. It was a back-breaking job.

'Twenty-four Germans are coming up from Siena.' Cinzia started moving chairs.

Arben shook hands with Nico. 'Where have you been? You cannot use the murder for an excuse. It has been more than two weeks since you have shown your face here.'

'Longer than that.' Cinzia reached up to give Nico the

double-cheek kiss. She was a small woman, with short dark hair and a slim, well-endowed body, which today was covered by jeans and a burgundy Ferriello sweatshirt.

'It's nice to see your pretty face.' Nico kissed her back. It had taken Cinzia the entire summer to recuperate from the scare she suffered in the spring. Her cheeks were full again. Her eyes sparkled.

Cinzia picked up a chair. Arben took it from her. Cinzia turned to Nico. 'So?'

'I was serving lunches and dinners at Sotto Il Fico, and you were gathering grapes from kilometres of vines.'

'Work is not an excuse. I will accept sadness. Did Aldo tell you?'

'That you're worried about me?'

As if Arben could sense the conversation was heading towards personal talk, he decided to bow out. 'I'll get the wine,' he said and left. OneWag scampered after him. A ball might turn up after all.

'Aldo did tell me,' Nico said. 'I'm not sad, I'm ruminating. I'll happily come to dinner after I check with Tilde.'

Cinzia's face broke into a wide smile. 'I'm glad to hear we can feed you again. I've missed you. Do you need something now? I've got one bottle of last year's extra virgin left if you can't wait for the new.'

'No, I'll wait.' He'd learnt that olive oil was best the year it was produced and kept in the dark. 'Aldo told me you knew Cesare.'

'Poor man. I didn't really know him, but I wanted to. He fascinated me.'

'Why?'

'I felt he was living behind a locked door. Cesare

reminded me of the story of the three locked doors with the tiger behind one of them.'

'Cesare was the tiger?'

'No, I'd say grief. Maybe anger too. And he didn't want to let them out.'

'What gave you that impression?'

Cinzia walked behind the small counter to pick up a dishcloth. 'It's a feeling he gave me every time I was in that bar. The sense that something had gone wrong in his life, something he was hiding behind that locked door. Aldo thinks the drinks went to my head.' Cinzia walked out again and began wiping down the tables.

Maybe Aldo was right, Nico thought. Cinzia was a woman full of energy, a gobbler of what life had to offer her. A couple of drinks served by a man who wouldn't satisfy her curiosity could have triggered her imagination.

'It's a feeling I had. A strong one.' Cinzia started wiping another table. 'Aldo is attached to facts, like most men.'

When he worked in homicide, Nico had learnt to listen to feelings that told him something was off. Sometimes they led him the wrong way. Often, that feeling took him to the real facts.

Outside in the courtyard, OneWag barked, followed by the brief sound of something hitting stone.

Cinzia frowned. 'I hope you don't think I'm a little crazy?'

'Not in the least crazy. Need any help?' Nico asked.

OneWag barked again. And again, something hit stone.

'Yes, I do. Take your dog home so Arben can get back to work.'

'We'll go then. I'll call about dinner.'

'Please.' Cinzia stopped wiping and looked up. 'When

you and Salvatore solve this one, let me know if I'm right.'

'We may find the murderer, but not the key to the door.'

Cinzia went back to wiping. 'Poor, sad Cesare.'

Nico gave her a kiss on the side of her head and walked outside, whistling for his dog. OneWag trotted towards him with his head held high and a tennis ball in his mouth. Arben was nowhere in sight.

An hour later, OneWag was taking a nap in the boss's armchair. Nico was out on the balcony, his feet on the railing, phone against his ear. 'Where are you?'

'Eating a pear in Ivana's kitchen,' Perillo answered. 'I was going to call you when I got back downstairs. Forensics didn't find anything of interest in Jimmy's car and the Villa Costanza videos haven't come in yet.'

'Too bad.'

'I just sent Daniele to Laura's grandfather. Duccio Gualtieri knew Cesare when they were young. Maybe he can tell us something helpful. Cesare's life is fairly inscrutable so far.'

'Good idea. How did the meeting with Pietro go?'

'He persisted in being insolent. Cesare wrote him a letter telling him he would inherit the land after they had a fight. Pietro had been insisting Cesare sell the land to the neighbour.'

'He didn't think Cesare would leave him the land?'

'He was afraid it would go to Laura, and he couldn't forgive Cesare for living on the land that should have "rightfully" belonged to Pietro's father, and after his death, to him. Whether Pietro knew he was inheriting the land from the letter or from finding the will when he and Laura went to Cesare's house doesn't matter. He knew he was getting the land and maybe decided to speed up getting what should have been his in the first place.'

'I wonder why Cesare's father didn't leave the land to his older son, or at least split it up.'

'You never split up agricultural land. It becomes useless. Growing a vegetable garden doesn't qualify. We'll talk later. Ivana has just walked in. As you know—'

'Yes, I know.' Talk of murder was forbidden in Ivana's home. 'Let's get together here tonight. Tilde doesn't need me. I have some news too. Call me. Ciao.' He clicked off before Perillo could answer.

CHAPTER SIX

Laura's parents lived at the end of an uphill, badly rutted road. Daniele, happy at being sent off to question Laura's grandfather on his own, nonetheless regretted the heavy lunch he'd eaten with the maresciallo and Ivana. He was on his motorcycle, trying to avoid the deep ruts and often failing. There were just too many of them.

After twenty minutes of bouncing, Daniele reached the two-storey stone house. *'Look for blue shutters,'* Laura had said on the phone when he got lost. She hadn't sounded pleased about his visit. Daniele turned off the gas and looked up at the shutters painted the bright blue of a summer sky. *A happy house*, he thought. He got off his bike. On one side was a rectangular shed, the sides covered in thick plastic. Behind the plastic Daniele could make out green shapes. An old grey Fiat Palio was parked next to the shed. On the other side of the house, he could see a long vegetable garden with several rows of cabbages and kale, the rest freshly tilled, ready for spring plantings, he guessed. He walked his bike up the stone path that led to the house, rested it against the garden fence and brushed the dust off the blue short-sleeved shirt, which was part of his summer uniform. It was cold. He should have worn the jacket.

His phone buzzed. Stella had sent a text.

Did he catch you recording?

Daniele texted back.

Ciao. He thinks I wrote everything down. I told him I was going to type Pietro's interview tonight. How are you?

Daniele wanted to hear her voice with its gentle Tuscan cadence. She wasn't allowed to use a phone during work hours at the museum. Somehow, she'd found a way to text. He ached to tell her what she meant to him, but he kept quiet. He had no idea if she would consider him more than a friend.

I'm bored. No one's booked a tour this afternoon. When are you going to tell him?

Soon. When are you coming home?

As soon as I can. When are you coming to Florence? We didn't finish the tour of the Accademia.

As soon as we find the murderer.

Well, hurry. I miss you. Ciao. The director's heavy footsteps are coming my way.

Daniele re-read *I miss you* and blushed. When he looked up from his phone, he saw a woman coming out of the greenhouse. He put his phone away, walked the smooth road and introduced himself.

'Carla Benati,' Laura's mother said. She was grey-haired, tall and stout, wearing a home-knit green sweater over a plain grey dress. A large gold crucifix hung from her neck. Daniele would have recognised her immediately. Her handsome face was an aged version of her daughter's.

Signora Benati walked down a short unadorned corridor with Daniele following. 'We know nothing about Cesare Rinaldi. My father is waiting in here. He is not well. Be patient with him.' She turned into a room that held a small sofa and two armchairs of the same sky blue as the shutters.

As Daniele entered, Duccio Gualtieri looked up from the newspaper he was reading. 'Brigadiere, sit down,' he ordered before Daniele could introduce himself.

Signora Benati stayed by the door. 'I'll bring coffee.'

'Two sugars,' Gualtieri said, having gone back to reading the newspaper.

Laura's mother gave her father an exasperated look. 'You have a guest. I'll bring the bowl.'

'Don't break it.' Gualtieri lowered his newspaper and peered at Daniele as if for the first time. Daniele straightened his spine and met his gaze. Sitting on an upright wooden chair by the window, Gualtieri responded with a withering look. He was a big-boned man with strong features and long legs. Thick grey eyebrows sat over deep-set eyes. He had a tremor in one hand, which made the newspaper shiver. He wore a thick grey sweater, jeans and workmen's boots.

A man to be obeyed, Daniele thought. He introduced himself and said he was recording the interview.

'Do as you please,' Gualtieri grumbled, 'but you'll be wasting tape and my time.'

'I'm sorry, Signor Gualtieri, but you have known Cesare Rinaldi for a long time. We need all the information we can get about him. You went to school together, played football together. Is there anything you can tell me about him that would shed light on his murder?'

'He was a good football player, but he had no substance as a man. He was a good friend of my wife's since lower school. Celestina said he made her giggle, not that it took much to make her giggle. She was a brainless woman. I was taken in by her beauty. Beauty can make men brainless too. Go for the brains in a woman, young man, not her looks. Gabriella had both.' Gualtieri pointed at an old bookshelf against a wall. It held rows of framed photos in lieu of books. 'Go on, take a look. You'll spot Gabriella in the blink of an eye. Gabi lights up this room with her beauty, her intelligence. Always has. Always will.'

Daniele stood and walked over to the bookshelf. He spotted Laura as a pretty teenager holding hands with a taller, older girl who was indeed beautiful. There were many pictures of the older girl, always with a smile on her face. Only a few with Laura. None of Laura alone. One photo of Gabriella had been neatly cut, a thin crescent of bloused shoulder showing there had been another woman in the photo.

'What are you doing?' Signora Benati's sharp voice startled Daniele.

'Signor Gualtieri was telling me about—'

The look Signora Benati gave her father was equally sharp. She lowered the coffee tray she was carrying onto a side table. 'Those photographs are personal to the family. Cesare Rinaldi does not appear in them or has nothing to do with them. Please sit down and have your coffee.'

Daniele stole another quick look at the cut-off photo and did as he was asked. He watched Laura's mother drop two tablespoons of sugar in one of the cups and bring it to her father without a saucer.

'No more, Babbo,' she said in a low voice.

No more what? Daniele wondered. *Coffee? Or talk of beautiful Gabriella?*

Laura's mother went back to the table and looked at Daniele. 'Brigadiere, sugar?'

'One, thank you.'

'I hope it's not too strong,' she said, bringing him the coffee.

'I'm sure it's perfect.' As she handed it to him, Daniele noticed that the gold cross on her chest was engraved with a date: 11th January 2011. The day and the month were the same as his mother's birthdate. *A strange coincidence*, Daniele thought, despite his mother insisting coincidences didn't exist. 'Thank you, Signora.' He took the dainty cup of coffee with its tiny saucer and balanced it on his thigh. 'Is there nothing you can tell me about Signor Rinaldi?' he asked the old man. 'We know he went to Germany to work for many years. Do you know where he went? Where he worked?'

Duccio Gualtieri grunted, drank down his coffee and held out the empty cup. 'It could have been anywhere. Torino, Milan, Switzerland. All I cared about was that he was gone.'

'But he came back, visited your home. He took an interest in Laura. Can you tell me anything about him after he came back?'

Signora Benati, taking the cup from her father, asked, 'What does it matter? Cesare came back years ago. He was murdered now, not then.'

Eager to explain, Daniele leant forward. 'Signora—' The coffee cup on his knee wobbled. He quickly grasped it, cursing his clumsiness and the embarrassing heat rising in his cheeks. 'Something could have happened years ago that could help us discover his murderer.'

'I'll tell you what happened,' Gualtieri said. 'He cheated his brother out of his rightful inheritance. I thought Rinaldi's father had more sense than that, but Cesare came back from wherever he'd been, moved right into his father's house and wiled his way into his father's heart. If anyone should have killed him it's his nephew.' The old man raised a trembling hand. 'Cesare deprived people of what was rightfully theirs. Laura can cry her heart to shreds for all I care. The man deserved what he got.' Gualtieri's tremble turned into a shaking of his whole body, causing the newspaper to fall to the floor.

His daughter leant down and stroked his shoulder. 'Shh. Shh, Babbo.'

Gualtieri closed his eyes. His body slowly calmed down.

Signora Benati looked at Daniele. 'My father is tired. No more questions. He's told you all he knows. Come.' She walked out of the room. Daniele reluctantly put the still full cup of coffee on the floor and followed.

At the front door, Daniele apologised. 'I'm sorry I upset him.'

'Brigadiere, you are too young to know the black holes the past can hold for someone. Babbo has had to crawl out of a few in his lifetime. They leave a scar. Old age does the rest.'

From the sadness in her voice, Daniele thought she'd encountered a few black holes herself.

'Laura isn't in any way involved with the murder, is she?'

The sudden and offhand way the question was asked surprised Daniele. He looked at her. Signora Benati's face showed no emotion. Was she afraid for her daughter? 'She's been very helpful with the investigation,' Daniele reassured her. As she opened the front door, he said, 'You also knew Cesare. What can you tell me about him?'

Laura's mother leant against the open door with a resigned smile. 'Enough isn't enough for you.'

Daniele blushed. 'I have to do my job.'

'We all do. I'll tell you this about Cesare. When he came back I heard rumours that he was gay, but my mother said people were just envious of his good looks. He was always nice. Later he was wonderful with Laura. I never had to worry about her when she was with him. I think he was a good man. His older brother was also a good person, but he was always telling his father what to do. Cesare, when he came back, let the old man be. I think that's why Cesare got the property. I'm sorry someone hated him enough to kill him. Arrivederci, Brigadiere.' She moved back and started to close the door.

Daniele put his foot on the doorsill. 'Please wait.' She stopped. Daniele asked, 'Who is Gabriella?'

Signora Benati's hand reached up to finger her cross and she said, 'Someone we love,' then closed the door in his face.

Daniele took out his phone. 'Sixteen thirty-two. End of interview.' He stopped the recording and walked to his motorbike, thinking how a death could bring satisfaction to Gualtieri and regret to his daughter and granddaughter.

Sandro heard clicking on the tile floor and looked up from reading the newspaper behind the counter. OneWag gave him a tail swish of recognition. 'Too late for treats, Rocco.'

Nico followed his dog in and waved a salute. The café was empty. He'd hoped to find Sandro too busy to pay much attention.

'Nice to see you, Nico. We don't often get afternoon visits from you.'

'Tilde has less use for me now that the town is emptying out.' Needing to talk to Jimmy without Sandro made him feel awkward. He liked and respected both these men. 'Is Jimmy here?' He started to walk to the back door. 'I need to ask him something.'

Sandro folded the newspaper and pushed it aside. His friendly expression turned serious. 'He's working in the back. He'll be out in a few minutes. Can I offer you something while you wait?' Sandro's long strides reached the door before Nico could. 'Salvatore sent you, didn't he?'

'Yes, he did. He needs an answer to something and thought it would be easier for Jimmy if I asked him.'

'I'm Jimmy's husband. I know everything there is to know about him. Ask me. Jimmy's been traumatised. He doesn't need to have you or anyone else asking him questions about Cesare. What is the question?'

'I'm sorry, Sandro. It's something only Jimmy can

answer. I'll see you in the morning.' Nico turned around and started walking away.

'Wait. You want to know if there was a relationship between Jimmy and Cesare?'

Nico kept walking. OneWag, seeing his boss aim for the door, scooted out of the café ahead of him.

'Sit down, Nico,' Sandro pleaded. 'Please. I'll tell you.'

Nico chose the nearest table to him and sat. Sandro joined him, with his face alive with feeling. 'The other day I said that Jimmy hated Cesare. That's not true. I am the one who hated him. I say that without fear because I swear on my mother's head, I did not kill him. I love Jimmy so much it makes me horribly possessive. I hated Cesare for being in love with Jimmy.'

'How did you know?'

'When Cesare walked in, his eyes would aim straight at Jimmy and stay there. His face would soften, and he'd smile. Jimmy would just nod and look away. The attention embarrassed him.'

'When was this?'

'It started around a year after we bought the café. A week from this coming Saturday we will celebrate our tenth anniversary as owners. I hope Cesare's death will have been resolved by then. We plan to have a big party for the whole town. They've been good to us from the beginning. As soon as we opened, even the people from nearby towns came to find out about the two queers who had taken over. Cesare came with them, but he kept returning. Italian law didn't allow us to get married then, and I'm ashamed to say I watched over Jimmy like a tiger with her pups. No straying.'

Nico was surprised by Sandro's intensity. He had always seemed like an easy-going man. Nico didn't remember ever being possessive or jealous. His love for Rita had been even-keeled. Maybe Sandro's intensity of feeling for Jimmy came from having to fight for the right to love him. 'Didn't the fact that Cesare was much older than Jimmy ease your mind?'

'I realise I was being ridiculous. The age difference between them was enormous. When Cesare made his first appearance here, Jimmy was twenty-two. Cesare must have been around seventy. I fumed anyway. I was suspicious because Cesare's presence embarrassed Jimmy. Whenever the man walked in, he would stiffen and sometimes retreat to the back room and leave me to handle the clients. Jimmy wouldn't tell me why, which to me meant that there'd been or there was something between them. After two months of these visits, I told Cesare he wasn't welcome here.'

'How did he react?'

'He just said, "Jimmy's a good man. Treat him well." I told him it was none of his business how I treated Jimmy. He left and never came back.'

'Did you tell Jimmy?'

'Jimmy only knows I asked him to leave. He didn't ask why.'

Sandro stood as Luciana walked in for her afternoon snack. 'Salve, Luciana, your fig and prosciutto sandwich is waiting for you. I'll be right with you.' He leant over Nico and softly asked, 'Did that answer your relationship question?'

Your version of it, Nico answered silently. 'Ciao, Luciana. I was going to come by for the flowers.'

'I saved the four chrysanthemums I told you about yesterday just for you. Help yourself. The door's open. Rocco is keeping guard. I told him not to let anyone in. You'll pay me next time.'

'Thanks.' Nico picked up a discarded café bill from underneath the table, wrote on the back his phone number, email address and the word *Please*. He got up and walked to the back door. Sandro's back was turned getting Luciana's sandwich.

Nico opened the door and stuck his head inside. Jimmy was taking his afternoon nap on a chaise longue. Nico flung the piece of paper at Jimmy. It landed a few feet short. Nico wasn't worried. Jimmy kept the small room where he made and baked his cornetti impeccably clean. He would notice the note on the floor as soon as he opened his eyes.

When Nico closed the door, Sandro was looking at him with a stern expression.

'Don't worry,' Nico said. 'I didn't wake him. Please ask him to save two wholewheat cornetti for me in the morning. I might be late.' He hated the subterfuge, but a man's life had been taken and answers were needed if they were ever going to find out who did it. What Jimmy had to say might match up with Sandro's story. Then again, it might not.

OneWag wiggled with happiness on seeing Nico approach, but he did not move from the door. He had a job to do.

Nico tried to enter the shop. OneWag barked a warning.

Nico looked down at his dog. 'You've got to be kidding me.'

OneWag perked up his ears and didn't budge.

'Buddy, you're too much.' Nico picked up his dog, set him down a few feet from the door and stepped inside the shop. Neatly wrapped pink chrysanthemums sat in a glass bowl on Luciana's desk. Before taking them, Nico called Perillo.

'Any news?' Perillo asked.

'I tried to talk to Jimmy. Sandro blocked me. I'd like the three of us to get together tonight and share whatever information we have. I can cook dinner if you can tear yourself away from Ivana's cooking.'

'You'll make her happy. She's got bingo tonight at—' A loud growling sound drowned out Perillo's words.

'What's that?'

'A plough. Cesare's neighbour is having some of his own property dug up. Daniele is on his way back from talking to Laura's grandfather, and I was hoping to bring Gennari back to the station for a talk. According to the workman, Gennari is in Rome.'

'I saw him at lunchtime at Laura's hotel.'

'Well, he could be on his way to Rome by now. I screwed up again, but at least I only smoked two cigarettes today. It's a record.'

'You'll get a gold medal when you're down to zero. Come at eight with Daniele.' Nico clicked off, already thinking of what to cook using some or most of the vegetables he'd bought from the Panzano vegetable store. Nico picked up the flowers and walked out. OneWag took up his position at the door again.

Nico felt a rush of pride. OneWag was taking his guard dog role seriously. Of course, the biscuit Luciana was sure to give him was a great motivator, but still, the mutt had shown the courage to stop even his caretaker from intruding. Nico stopped himself from saying, 'Good boy.' Instead, he said, 'You know where to find me, buddy.'

At the cemetery, Nico got rid of last week's asters and filled the vase with fresh water from the wall fountain. He untied the chrysanthemums and tried to arrange them nicely in the alabaster vase. He'd never been very good at it, but this afternoon his fingers seemed to have only thumbs. Sandro had unsettled him with his strong feelings. He looked at Rita's picture and asked her silently, 'Did I love you enough?' At first, she had overwhelmed him with her strong feelings for love, for life. He responded with caution, afraid of the strong feelings he had witnessed in his abusive father. With time, he and Rita found a good balance, but now he wondered if he had tempered her emotions, made her hold her feelings back. A few days before she died, she had reached for his hand and said, 'You've been a good husband.' He wondered now if she had spoken the truth.

Nico kissed his fingers and pressed them against Rita's photo. 'Buonanotte, bella.' As he turned to leave, he almost stepped on OneWag. The dog was looking up at him with what seemed a look of apology. Nico picked him up and together they walked out of the gate to the land of the living.

Daniele, the first to arrive at Nico's place, dangled a package in front of OneWag, hoping the dog would jump up to get it. The dog looked back at him with patient eyes.

'It's for you,' Daniele said. He had dressed up for the dinner with grey flannel slacks, a blue shirt that matched the colour of his eyes and a navy-blue V-necked sweater that looked hand-knit. 'Don't you want it, Rocco?'

The dog didn't blink, didn't move.

Nico, standing by the narrow counter next to the kitchen sink, caught Daniele's disappointed face. 'OneWag's far too proud to acknowledge a gift,' Nico said. 'When I first found him, he was a scrawny mutt but wouldn't take food from me. I had to leave it and walk away.'

'Last time I tossed the whole package like you told me, but afterwards this room looked like the aftermath of Carnevale in Venice. It must have taken you all night to clean it up.'

'OneWag had fun. After his life on the streets, I'll never begrudge him that. Thank you for bringing him a present.'

'I wanted to bring lemon mousse, but I didn't have time.' Daniele continued to stand in the centre of the room, the package still dangling from his hand. OneWag had lowered himself to the floor, head resting on his paws.

Nico gestured around the room with his kitchen knife. 'Hide your package somewhere in the room and sit down wherever you want. He'll find it soon enough.'

Daniele turned to see what sitting choices he had. His favourite place was the balcony. He liked knowing two swallows or their children came back there every spring to nest on the ceiling beams. The swallows were gone by now and a wind had whipped up, making it too cold to eat outside. He could sit at the kitchen table already set up for dinner or on the small sofa. The hollowed-out seat clearly made the only armchair Nico's place. Daniele scooted his present underneath the sofa and sat down.

OneWag, eyes closed, did not look up. His nose would find it.

Daniele sniffed loudly. He smelt smoke. 'Nico, is something burning?'

'I'm grilling dinner out on the balcony.' Nico unwrapped the sausages he'd bought at Falorni's in Greve, renowned, according to the cognoscenti, for having the best pork and boar products in all of Tuscany. 'Can I get you a glass of wine?'

'Thank you, I don't need anything.'

Nico looked at Daniele. He seemed nervous. 'How are you?'

'I'm frustrated. I can't seem to crack Cesare's passcode. I've tried his birthday, Laura's, his brother's and his father's, plus the date of his death, date of the funeral, countless other combinations. Nothing. If I don't have an answer by morning, the maresciallo is going to send the phone up to the IT people in Florence.'

'Don't give up, Dani. You're as good as they are.' Nico suspected he was exaggerating Daniele's abilities, but the brigadiere was so eager to shine in Perillo's eyes. 'Any news of Cesare's motorcycle?'

'Not so far. I'm assuming the murderer met Cesare in his own car. He kills Cesare, dumps the body in Jimmy's boot and leaves the Ducati at Villa Costanza where anyone could have gone off with it. Keeping it would have been dangerous. There aren't many 1972 Ducati 750GTs still around. He would have needed an SUV to drive off with it.'

'It is worth a lot of money. The same year and model sold at auction in the States for almost thirty thousand dollars.'

Daniele's eyes popped open. 'Really? Do you think the Ducati was the reason Cesare got killed?'

'No. It would have been simpler to steal it.'

'The videos will tell us if Cesare was killed at Villa Costanza.'

'What's taking so long to get them?'

'So long? We only asked for them last night. If Cesare was killed somewhere else, the murderer could have left the Ducati near the body. Someone found it and took off with it. I'm checking the online sales places to see if anyone is trying to sell an old Ducati. Nothing yet.'

Nico smiled as he pierced many holes in the sausages with a fork, enjoying Daniele's new assertiveness.

Daniele eyed the four sausages and felt his stomach groan quietly. Nico must have picked up the look on Daniele's face. 'I have to feed your carnivore boss. You're getting roasted vegetables and grilled scamorza.'

Daniele's blush of relief was interrupted by, 'Buonasera, amici miei.'

Perillo's loud voice reached them before he appeared in the doorway, holding up a loaf of country bread and a closed glass jar. He was wearing his favourite cold-weather uniform: jeans, a burnt orange V-necked sweater over a blue shirt and his for-all-seasons suede jacket. 'I apologise for being unreasonably late, but Ivana made an antipasto that will make you, caro Nico, fall in love with unsalted bread.'

Daniele had stood up as soon as he heard his boss's voice. OneWag waited until Perillo was well inside the room before getting up to sniff the maresciallo's suede boots. They always gave off a different food smell. This time it was something fishy.

'Is your oven on?' Perillo asked Nico, dropping the loaf on one of the plates on the table. 'This loaf needs to be sliced and then toasted. Ivana made a paste of butter, anchovies and capers to put on the toast. One bite and you will both lick your whiskers.'

'Thanks. The grill outside is almost ready.' Nico appreciated the gift, but it was going to throw off his timing. He handed the bread knife and cutting board to Perillo. 'I have to look after our dinner.'

Daniele quickly took the knife and cutting board from his boss before the maresciallo had a chance to hand them over to him.

Perillo nodded his approval. 'Don't cut the slices too thin.'

'Wine is on the table,' Nico said. 'Help yourself.' He bent down to check on the roasting vegetables. They were browning nicely. Nico closed the oven door and reached for the Ferriello Wines apron Cinzia had given him and tossed it to Perillo. He'd never used it, preferring the one he was wearing now, a gift from Rita, which declared I LOVE TUSCANY.

Perillo caught the apron with a surprised look on his face.

'Maresciallo, you're in charge of toasting your bread.' As Perillo looked down at the apron, Nico gave Daniele a quick wink. 'I need your brigadiere to keep an eye on the vegetables while I parboil the sausages to get some of the fat out before roasting them.'

Perillo hooked the apron over his head and threw up his arms. 'As the cook wills.' He was in a good mood this evening, despite not having got far with the murder case. He loved the camaraderie of these evenings, the all-male get-together of friends with a common goal. Perillo tied the apron around an expanding belly – a problem that required a solution he would have to find on his own. 'You have news to tell us, Nico.' He poured himself a full glass of wine from a Ferriello bottle. 'Tell us.'

Nico stepped out onto the balcony and checked the coals. 'Toaster is ready.'

Perillo came out, using the cutting board to hold the slices Daniele had cut to a perfect thickness. 'What did Jimmy say about Cesare?'

'We'll talk after Ivana's antipasto.'

Ivana's concoction did make them lick their whiskers. The three of them sat around the table slathering the anchovy-caper-butter on one slice of toast after another. The sound of crunching covered the noise of Daniele's package quietly being torn into small pieces under the sofa.

When Nico bit into his last toast, he held the butter, anchovy and caper mixture on his tongue for a long time, trying to memorise the taste in order to repeat it.

Perillo noticed. 'You can swallow. Ivana wrote out the recipe for you.'

'It won't help if it's like all the other Italian recipes I've run across. A fist of this, a pinch of that. A touch of the other. I need cups, tablespoons, teaspoons to make sense of anything. Rita claimed cooking was a matter of intuition.'

Perillo pumped up his chest. 'Caro Nico. Do not preoccupy yourself.'

Looking at his boss, Daniele was reminded of one of those strutting pigeons in Piazza San Marco that no one was allowed to feed anymore.

'My Ivana has written down the weights of the three ingredients. In grams, of course. I confess I did not tell her how well we have eaten here. She might get jealous and stop going to her bingo games.' He reached into his jeans pocket and extracted a folded piece of paper, which he gave to Nico. 'Make it for Tilde. Her diners will keep requesting more wine to quench their thirst.' Perillo raised his glass and drank down what was left of his.

'Thank her for me,' Nico said and followed suit. Daniele stuck to water. OneWag came out from under the sofa to show off his new bright red rubber ball.

Perillo ignored the dog and asked, 'You have something to tell us?'

Nico refilled the two wine glasses. 'I'll reveal in order. I bought the vegetables we're eating tonight from Nardo, the Panzano vegetable vendor. He remembered something. Cesare received a text message just as he was leaving the store. Nardo said his expression changed after he read the message and he rushed off on his Ducati.' He walked out on the balcony to turn the sausages and place the split scamorza on the cooler side of the coals.

Perillo looked at Daniele. 'We need to get into that phone.'

Daniele stood up. 'I'll go back to the station and work on it now.'

Perillo shook his head. 'Eat your dinner first. Good food energises the brain cells. You've got all night for the passcode. Nico has more to tell us.'

Daniele sat back down happily. Grilled scamorza and roasted vegetables was his idea of a perfect meal. OneWag dropped his new toy at Daniele's feet and waited.

Nico came back in. 'Five more minutes.' He turned off the oven, let the vegetables sit on the rack and sat back down. 'I then had lunch at Laura's hotel.'

Daniele quietly kicked the ball towards the balcony. OneWag ran to catch it.

Nico drank some of his wine. 'Cesare's neighbour came in saying that he'd soon have money and could afford to eat there. He didn't get a chance because the waiter asked him to leave under Laura's orders. According to her, Gennari had made Cesare's life miserable trying to get him to sell the land. His insistence makes me wonder if there's more to the sale than building a bigger house.'

'Someone else could be involved,' Perillo said, his nostrils catching the enticing smell of grilling sausages. 'Someone who wants to buy both Gennari's land and Cesare's.' Perillo tapped his nose. 'I think the sausages are done.'

Nico stood. 'My nose tells me the same. Dani, would you—'

Daniele was already on his feet. 'Of course, I'll get the vegetables.'

'Thanks.'

Perillo sat back in his chair and took a satisfying gulp of his wine. He would help with the eating.

Nico waited until he served a bowl of apples and pears with a plate of Gorgonzola dolce before telling his friends about his failed attempt to talk to Jimmy privately, then proceeded to tell Perillo and Daniele about his conversation with Sandro.

Perillo touched all the pears in the bowl before picking one. 'Do you believe what Sandro told you?' He spread a generous amount of cheese on his plate.

'I'd like to hear Jimmy's side of the story.'

'In the photo we found,' Daniele said as he peeled an apple with knife and fork, 'Jimmy is wearing football clothes and shoes and looks no older than fifteen. How did Cesare get hold of that photo?' He turned the apple slowly to keep the peel going round and round without breaking. It was something he had learnt as a child, and it still gave him a childish sense of accomplishment. 'Who gave it to him, or did he snap it himself at a game Jimmy was playing?'

Nico quartered a juicy Bartlett pear and cored it. 'I didn't mention the photo to Sandro.' He spread some Gorgonzola on a piece. He noticed Daniele's apple peel bracelet drop on the plate. Nelli liked to peel her apples that way too. He missed her. 'Did your visit to Laura's grandfather give you any interesting information?'

'Yes, it did.' Daniele put the apple down. 'Nonno Gualtieri had no love for Cesare or for his own wife. He called her brainless and said Cesare was good at wiling his way into people's hearts. I think there was more than friendship between Laura's grandmother and Cesare.'

'An affair?' Nico asked.

Daniele felt his cheeks get hot. 'Maybe just a one-sided love.' Like his own feeling for Stella.

'I thought we were going under the assumption that Cesare was gay.' Perillo popped a slice of Gorgonzola-stacked pear into his mouth.

'He may not have started out knowing or accepting his sexual preferences,' Nico said.

Daniele noticed that Perillo looked unconvinced. To change the subject, Daniele said, 'I think Laura had an older sister, Gabriella.'

'She died?' Perillo asked.

'Maybe. Gualtieri once used the past tense in referring to her. She could have just left. It was clear the grandfather loved her very much. He didn't even mention Laura. Signora Benati was upset when she saw me looking at the family pictures. Upset that her father had mentioned Gabriella to me.'

OneWag dropped the ball at Daniele's feet. Absorbed in his telling, Daniele didn't notice. 'When I left, I asked her who Gabriella was. She answered, 'Someone we loved.' That's what made me think Gabriella walked away from the family. If she'd died, why not say it?'

Perillo sat up in his chair. 'I assume you used your trusted phone to record the entire conversation?' His voice was stern.

Daniele's eyebrows shot up, eyes widened. His cheeks turned ashen. 'Maresciallo, I—'

Perillo cut him off. 'Of course, you did. How could you ask, listen and write at the same time? You did as you should. My mistrust of modern gadgets has made your work far more difficult than it need be, and there may come a law court that challenges the veracity of your note-taking.' He had spotted Daniele's thumb clicking something in his trouser pocket a minute before he questioned Pietro Rinaldi. Daniele's lazy pen scratchings confirmed what he suspected. Daniele had turned on an infernal recording machine. Perillo was proud of having controlled the outburst he had felt in his chest.

After several cigarettes Perillo was not going to mention to Nico, he had realised how incredibly selfish he had been to force Daniele to write every word at the speed of lightning. If a midlife crisis was helping Perillo recognise his errors – at least this one for the moment – it was welcome.

Nico had noticed Daniele's surprised and embarrassed

reaction, watched Perillo's pensive expression turn into a smile of satisfaction. 'Anyone for a glass of whiskey?'

From ashen, Daniele now turned red with relief. 'No, thank you. I'm the driver.' Besides, he needed a crystal-clear head to break the passcode. Maybe Jimmy fit in there somewhere. He'd look up his birthdate.

Nico poured for Perillo and himself. 'Tomorrow I'll try getting hold of Jimmy again.'

'Dani and I will talk to the elusive Gennari. The workman said he'd be back by afternoon.'

'One thing I'm curious about,' Perillo added after the whiskey warmed his throat, 'is Cesare's time in Germany. Was he in Germany? When did he come back?'

'The E.U. was formed in 1993,' Daniele said. 'Cesare was back in Italy by then. To leave the country before 1993, he would have had to apply for a passport. We didn't find one at his house.'

'Maybe he never left Italy,' Nico said. 'Do we know when he came back to Panzano?'

'Forty years ago, a year before his father died, according to Pietro,' Daniele said. 'Is it important?'

Nico shrugged. 'Maybe. Maybe not. But the more we know, the clearer the picture should become.' He was thinking of the feeling Cesare had given Cinzia. A man with a locked door.

'Or cloudier.' Perillo put his empty tumbler down.

'Still.' Nico turned to Daniele and said, 'When you get a chance, find out if Cesare had a passport.'

Perillo stood up. 'Thanks, Nico. Another good evening. We'd help clean, but Dani has a passcode waiting to reveal itself and he's the driver.'

Nico laughed. 'Go home, the two of you. May the night bring you wisdom, Dani. OneWag and I will manage by ourselves.'

OneWag, who was lying on the couch with the red ball between his paws, lifted his head. As Daniele passed him, the dog used his snout to push the red ball off the couch. There was no point having a ball no one was willing to throw.

CHAPTER SEVEN

Wednesday morning Perillo walked into the office twenty minutes before his usual time, carrying a tray with a cappuccino and a brioche for his brigadiere, an espresso for himself. The poor young man had surely stayed up all night trying to break the damn passcode. He stopped in the middle of the room. 'Daniele?'

The room was empty.

'Vince!' Perillo bellowed. The tray shook a little. 'Dino!'

Seconds later, Vince's large head appeared behind the door. He quickly swallowed his last bite of ciambella. 'You're here, Maresciallo?'

'No, I'm still in bed. Where's Daniele?'

'Bed is a good bet. You're early.'

'And you're insubordinate. He was supposed to stay up all night.'

Dino's small, thin frame slid by Vince and stepped into the office. 'Buongiorno, Maresciallo. Daniele left me a note to wake him up five minutes ago, which I did. Let me take that tray from you.'

Perillo moved the tray closer to his chest, spilling a few drops of cappuccino foam. 'I want Brigadiere Donato here now! Even in his pyjamas.'

Just then Daniele pushed past Vince and Dino, finishing tucking in his blue shirt. 'Maresciallo, buongiorno! I'm sorry. I didn't expect you so early.'

Perillo put the tray down on his desk, cursing silently. He had stepped out of bed this morning with a burst of optimism. Daniele would have found the passcode. The Greve Carabinieri would then not suffer the humiliation of asking help of the higher-ups in Florence. Now he saw that Daniele's sad face held a different outcome.

Vince and Dino slipped out of the room, surely unwilling to witness a show of the maresciallo's temper.

Perillo sat down behind his desk and picked up his espresso cup. 'Come on, sit down.' He indicated to the chair across from him. 'You look like you need more than a cappuccino and a brioche.'

'Thank you, Maresciallo.' Daniele sat down and reached for the cappuccino. 'I'll catch up on sleep tonight.' He drank it down in three gulps, used the spoon to gather the foam inside the cup. He'd eat the brioche slowly to keep his mouth full as long as possible. He didn't want to talk.

'I can see you're upset, Dani. I appreciate your enormous effort in trying to find the passcode. I should have sent the phone to Florence right away.'

Daniele swallowed. 'I appreciate your trust in me.' The maresciallo was blaming himself. It wasn't fair to hold back. 'The phone can stay here.'

Perillo leant across the desk, a stunned look on his face. 'Are you telling me you found the passcode?'

'I am.'

Perillo slapped his cheek in surprise. 'Gesù, Maria and whoever else you pray to, you are brilliant! How did you do it?'

'Sometime in the middle of the night Santa Monica, the patron saint of patience, revealed a grouping of four numbers I hadn't tried before. I punched them in, and the phone revealed its secrets.'

Perillo sat back in his chair and crossed his arms over his chest, overcome by the need for a celebratory cigarette. 'Brigadiere Donato, I am very proud of you.' He picked up his phone and punched some numbers. 'Our boy did it, Ivana. I told you he would. Prepare the best vegetarian lunch you can think of. Ciao.' He clicked off and looked at Daniele's beet-red cheeks. 'Congratulations. Now tell me who sent the text Cesare received at the vegetable shop?'

The blood in Daniele's face drained away quickly. He stood up, walked to his desk at the back of the room, unlocked a drawer and took out Cesare's old iPhone. He tapped in the passcode as he walked back to Perillo, found the last incoming text and handed the phone to his boss.

Perillo read the message, then took a moment to let the name of the sender sink in. 'I did not expect this.'

'I know, Maresciallo.'

Perillo put Cesare's phone down. 'Well, we know what

we have to do now.' As he stood up and reached for his jacket, someone knocked on the door.

'Yes?' Perillo barked.

The door opened a little and Vince popped his head in. 'A Signor Mattia Gennari wants to talk to you. He says you were looking for him yesterday and this is the only free time he has.' Perillo sat back down with a surprising sense of relief for the distraction. 'Send him in.' He turned to Daniele. 'We have to tell him we're recording his words?'

'Yes, Maresciallo.'

'You didn't tell Pietro.'

'I did while I was fingerprinting him in the Castellina station, and I recorded him acknowledging I told him. You had left the room.'

Perillo found himself between being angry at not knowing and admiring Daniele's defiance. He suspected Stella had something to do with Dani's newfound courage. In a soft voice, he said, 'Never do anything again behind my back, Daniele.'

Daniele nodded, blood rising again to his face. 'Never.'

'Ask Dino to give you the office tape recorder. He records his favourite radio programmes.'

Daniele stared at Perillo. For the past two years he'd typed his fingers to the bone and all the time a tape recorder was sitting somewhere in the station?

Perillo met Daniele's stare with lifted shoulders and an apologetic look on his face. 'I don't recognise my voice on that thing. It makes me sound like a castrato.' He quickly added, 'Yes, I'm vain,' in response to Daniele's barely hidden look of disbelief. His burst of honesty instantly made him feel good. Ivana would be proud. He was improving. 'It wasn't just my voice. The cursed thing kept jamming. You'll have to watch it carefully.'

The office door opened. Before Dino had a chance to announce the visitor, he was pushed aside. 'Here I am, Maresciallo, just back from Rome,' Gennari said, striding on long legs into the office as if it were his own. Neatly dressed in wool slacks, a grey turtleneck sweater and an old tweed jacket, and with his tousled grey hair, neatly combed back, Cesare's large neighbour looked very different from the last time Perillo had seen him.

Perillo stood up. 'Signor Gennari, I am happy you came. I have a few questions to ask you.' He nodded at Daniele, who walked out quickly.

Gennari shrugged. 'I don't know what else I can tell you regarding Cesare Rinaldi. I will not speak ill of the dead.' He drew back the chair in front of Perillo's desk and dropped his weight down.

Perillo took a moment before sitting back down himself. Gennari's cockiness was interesting. The last time he had spoken to him, the man had been angry and frustrated. Now he beamed satisfaction.

'Did your trip to Rome have a good outcome?'

'Very good, Maresciallo. About time too. What more do you want to ask me? I've got workmen waiting for me.'

Daniele came back in with a heavy tape recorder that looked like something Mussolini's people might have used to record his endless speeches. He lowered it onto his desk. The machine worked perfectly; Dino had assured him. Always had.

'Are you ready, Brigadiere Donato?' Perillo asked in his serious maresciallo voice.

Daniele pushed the record button and announced the day, the time, and who was in the room.

'Where were you Friday morning from eight-thirty to twelve?'

'Home, hand-picking my grapes.'

'Can someone corroborate that?'

'I live alone. I guess Cesare could have, if he'd been home.'

'You say you were picking your grapes, yet three days later you were digging up your property.' Perillo kept his voice as deep as possible. 'Why?'

'The few vines I had produced bad wine. I am happy to inform you my land will be transformed into a large successful vineyard.'

'You only have two hectares of land. Does the transformation mean you have been successful in buying the adjacent hectares Pietro Rinaldi just inherited from his uncle?'

'Yes, we signed an agreement. He will sell as soon as the land is officially his. Two or three weeks, maybe a month for the bureaucracy to go through.'

'How much is he selling it for?'

'I don't know,' Gennari said. 'I'm not the one paying. I can tell you that my piece of land is getting a very good price.'

'I see, there's a third party. Who is it?'

'I'm afraid I can't tell you. The buyer wants to remain unknown until Pietro's inheritance has cleared and the double sale is done.'

Perillo turned back to look at Daniele. 'It's not jamming, is it?' He needed time to control his anger.

'No, Maresciallo. The tape is recording every word.' He'd kept an eye on it as he doodled to keep his fingers busy. He wasn't used to being idle and wasn't liking it. It made him feel useless.

Perillo turned back to give Mattia Gennari the benefit of his stern expression. 'Signor Gennari, I am investigating a murder of a man you knew for years. You may not have liked him. If I had known him, I might not have liked him either, *but*' – the word came from the lowest depths of his diaphragm – 'I will find the man who murdered him. Possibly you are that man.'

'No, Maresciallo. I did not kill him. I can't even kill the stupid fox who eats my grapes.'

'To get to the truth I need to know and interrogate everyone who had anything to do with Cesare now and in the past.'

Gennari squirmed in his chair. 'You don't understand. I risk losing the sale. Cesare didn't know about the buyer. Cesare thought I wanted his land so I could build a bigger house. The man already owns—' Gennari stopped.

'What does he own? Land next to yours? There are only woods behind your property. That's protected land.'

'No. He owns a vineyard somewhere. He didn't tell me where.'

Perillo knew Gennari was clearly lying. 'His name.'

'Please, Maresciallo, you don't know how long I've waited to have enough money to leave here, to see the rest of my country. I only got to Rome because it was paid for.'

'Is that where you signed the sale papers?'

'Yes. I swore I would keep my mouth shut.'

'If the buyer needs to keep it secret, it could mean he is doing something illegal.'

'No. It has to do with his in-laws. Something about them not wanting competition.'

'A winemaking family, then.'

'I guess.'

'I need his name.'

Gennari took a deep breath, let the air out slowly. Perillo watched as Gennari's face deflated along with his chest. 'There is no reason to fear the sale of your property won't go through.' He paused. 'Unless you or Pietro or your buyer, or all three of you, killed Cesare Rinaldi.'

Gennari's body seemed to deflate. 'Dottor Eugenio Vittori.' His voice was barely audible.

'Ah, yes, I know that name,' Perillo said. 'I believe he's a frequent guest at the Hotel Bella Vista.' An entitled, difficult guest, Laura had said. Perillo opened the notebook that sat on his desk and pushed it to the edge. He handed Gennari his pen. 'Write down his telephone number and address.'

'I don't have the sale document with me. I only know his mobile.'

'Write it down.'

Jimmy shoved the tray of rolled cornetti into the oven with a bang.

'You've ruined them,' Sandro said.

'No, I have not, and I'm going to talk to Nico.'

'You're not going to tell him.'

'Yes, I am. I understand you're trying to protect me, and I love you for it, but Nico is a friend.'

'He's an ex-policeman who now works with Salvatore. They are going to pin this murder on you.'

'Not if I didn't do it.'

'You are so naïve, Jimmy.'

'Isn't that why you love me?' Jimmy leant over and gave Sandro a kiss. 'I love *you* because you worry. Now let me do my work. Tell Nico I'll talk to him as soon as this last batch of cornetti is done.'

Sandro threw his arms in the air and walked back into the main room of the café. He said nothing to Nico, who was sitting with Gogol at their usual table by the French doors. They'd finished their breakfasts, Sandro noted. Nico's plate held only a few crumbs, and Gogol was dropping the crust of his crostino under the table for OneWag to pick up.

'Is Jimmy still baking?' Nico asked Sandro. *Or was Jimmy not coming out until he left the café*?

'He says he's busy,' Sandro said as he made espressos for a threesome of cyclists, 'but I'd say he just likes me to do all the work out here.'

'Not true! Wait, Gogol.' Jimmy came out of the back room and hurried across the floor with three freshly baked wholewheat cornetti for them. 'I hope you still have room for one of these.'

Gogol stood up, took a cornetto and stuffed it in the already full pocket of his overcoat. Jimmy, convinced that Gogol had ESP, was hoping the old man would help him see what was ahead.

Gogol placed his hand on Jimmy's shoulder. '"Be steadfast in your hope." "Let no lie defraud the truth."'

Good for you, Nico thought. The truth was what he was after.

Jimmy turned to Sandro, who'd been leaning over the counter ostensibly to wipe it down. 'Did you hear that, Sandro?'

'Do as you wish.' *Why do I even bother*? Sandro asked himself.

Jimmy shook Gogol's hand. 'Thank you.'

Gogol nodded, and Nico, Jimmy and OneWag watched him shuffle his way into the piazza.

'That man has a crystal ball in his head,' Jimmy said. 'He just knows.'

Nico wasn't a believer in ESP, but he had to admit that Gogol was good at picking up cues, perceiving what was around him. It was probably a talent Gogol had learnt in his childhood as a way to protect himself.

'Jimmy, do you have time for a chat?' Nico asked.

'Walk me to the car. I need to pick up a new shipment of wholewheat flour at Enrico's bakery. It's parked next to the Coop.'

OneWag heard the name Enrico and scooted off across the piazza.

Nico whistled to stop him. The dog braked and glanced back.

'Coop,' Nico shouted.

OneWag sat. Coop was a word he recognised, but the supermarket came with no treats.

'Salvatore sent you to find out how come Cesare had an old photograph of me,' Jimmy said as they entered the small park that flanked the old town. 'Is that right?'

'Yes. He thought it would be easier for you to explain to me.'

'He's right about that. Let's sit down here on the grass

a minute.' Jimmy sat down and crossed his legs. Nico sat next to him. OneWag came over and sat between them.

'Cesare was a nice, caring man.' Jimmy kept his eyes aimed at the roof of the Coop down below. 'Sandro thought he came to the café because he wanted me. I guess it looked like that. It's my fault I didn't tell Sandro the truth. Cesare was just making sure I was okay. I guess he did care, but not the way Sandro thought. The time Cesare showed up I wanted to give him a hug and sit with him, catch up. Instead, I hid in the back room like the coward I am.'

'Why did you do that?'

'I was embarrassed at first. Then I was afraid of Sandro's jealousy.'

'Wouldn't it have been easier to tell him the truth?'

'Sandro is very possessive and sometimes I need to keep some things to myself. My talk with Cesare was personal and happened before I met Sandro. It's mine.'

'What is the truth?'

'I first met Cesare when I was in high school.' Jimmy's hand found OneWag's ear and started kneading it. 'He sometimes came to watch us play football in the yard behind the school. He liked to give pointers. We listened because we knew he'd been a good player. Some of the boys would snicker after he left and say he was just there to look at us and get a hard-on. Word had spread that he was gay, I think because he was always watching us play and he never had a woman with him. God, this is embarrassing.'

Nico said nothing. In the silence that followed, OneWag climbed into the space between Jimmy's crossed legs. More kneading might be coming.

'I wish I could make it easier for you,' Nico said finally.

Jimmy dug his hands into OneWag's soft fur. 'I'm just remembering how it felt trying to figure out who I was. I suspected I was gay, but I didn't know for sure, and it scared me. I didn't want to be gay. My father would have kicked me out of the house, never spoken to me again. I decided to ask Cesare when he knew, how he knew. Was being gay really the sin everyone made it out to be? I didn't have the courage to ask him directly. After a lot of back and forth, I wrote him a letter and sent him my picture so he would know who I was. I guess I was hoping he'd look for me and talk to me.' Jimmy leant over and buried his nose in OneWag's fur.

'That took a lot of courage.'

'I think it was desperation. I was so confused. Cesare wrote back right away and asked me to meet him at Laura's grandmother's house. He returned the letter and the photo and then listened to all my fears. He told me that whether I loved men or women didn't matter. What mattered was believing in myself and being proud of who I was. And then he said something that made me start crying. If I ever needed him, he would be there for me. No one had said that to me before. Not even my mother. He waited for me to dry up and took me to meet Laura's grandmother. I remember her name – Celestina. She gave me an orange drink and a piece of cake.'

Jimmy let go of OneWag and sat up. He turned to look at Nico. 'While I ate, the two of them held hands. I remember looking at them, registering how happy they were. I wanted to be like them. Happy. Thanks to Sandro I am. Now I wonder if maybe Cesare wasn't gay. Maybe he and Celestina were in love.'

'Could be,' Nico said, meeting Jimmy's gaze. It didn't matter really. Gay or straight, Cesare had understood and helped Jimmy. Nico now wished he'd had a chance to meet the man. What Jimmy had just told him made him want to solve his murder even more. Cesare deserved justice. 'You said he returned your photo. Is the one Perillo found another one?'

Jimmy shook his head. 'As I was leaving, I slipped it in the satchel he'd left at the door. I wanted him to remember me because I was always going to remember him. I feel awful about not acknowledging him the times he came to the café. I did send him a note at the hotel when he stopped showing up. I explained about Sandro being so jealous, but I also told him I was happy, which was true until Cesare showed up dead in my car. I can't make sense of that. Can you?'

'Not yet.' Nico gave Jimmy an awkward pat on the back, thinking of the irony of Cesare dead, perhaps even dying in Jimmy's car. 'Thanks for telling me.'

'I thank you for listening.' Jimmy stood up. 'Blurting it out to you has given me the courage to tell Sandro now.'

Good idea, Nico thought, as he got up. With OneWag between them, they walked to the end of the park.

'Do you think Cesare ending up in the boot of my car has a special meaning?' Jimmy asked, looking at Nico with the gently puzzled look of a sixteen-year-old.

Nico knew coincidences did happen, but he said, 'Why don't you ask Gogol?'

Jimmy's face brightened. 'I will. Thanks. See you in the morning.'

'As always.'

* * *

The Montagliari Chapel was the last remaining building of what had once been a fortification belonging to the powerful Gherardini family of *Mona Lisa* fame. Daniele had looked up the information on his phone and was now eager to share what he had learnt about the complicated history of the family. It kept him from thinking about the text message he'd uncovered. 'There's a drawing of the chapel by da Vinci in the Uffizi,' he said, his foot hard on the gas pedal as the car climbed up the hill. He was going to ask Stella to show it to him.

Vince and Dino, sitting in the back of the Alfa, stopped the flow of Daniele's history lesson with earbuds. Perillo listened only to the rhythm of Daniele's words. He found it comforting. He missed Nico's presence in this important moment of the investigation. He depended on his good sense. Perhaps too much. He'd called Nico once Gennari left the office. Nico didn't answer. He hadn't left a message.

After a long curve, Perillo spotted the small baroque church three hundred or so metres ahead. 'Park here,' he ordered. He wanted them to approach on foot.

The paved road cut across a field thick with trees. A cold wind whipped through the oak and chestnut trees, rattling the leaves, stripping them from the branches.

Daniele shuddered. He was in his shirtsleeves. 'Maresciallo, do you want us to search through the field?'

'The chapel first.' As Perillo got closer, he saw curtains hanging from the upper windows. The entrance was closed by a white gate. He turned to ask Daniele, 'Someone lives here?'

'It's private property. There's a cloister and a house in the back,' Daniele said.

'Not a good place to stab a man in the middle of the morning.' Perillo lengthened his stride and reached the locked gate. 'Is anyone home?' he called out. 'I'm Maresciallo Perillo, and these are my men. Anyone here?' He rattled the gate. No one answered. Perillo backed off. 'Let's try the house.'

A shout from Dino stopped him.

'Here, Maresciallo!' Dino was standing next to a cluster of cypresses fifty metres beyond the church, zipping up his pants. 'I think there's blood on the grass.'

Perillo put on his shoe covers and ran to him followed by Daniele and Vince. He looked down at the spot Dino pointed to. An almost straight trail of something dark ran down a short stretch of ground. Along the trail he could see torn grass, a few clumps uprooted. He remembered that Cesare's body had been dragged. He looked at Dino. 'Were you standing here?'

'No, behind the tree. It's clean.'

'Well done,' Perillo said with a strong pat on Dino's shoulder. Dino's chest surged with pride. An important discovery was a first for Dino.

'Do I call Florence?' Daniele already had his phone in his hand.

'Yes. We need forensics down here.'

Daniele stepped away to make his phone call while Perillo ordered Dino and Vince to cover their shoes and look for Cesare's Ducati. 'I'm going to the house to see if anyone saw or heard anything.'

To his surprise, Perillo was met at the gate by Ida Crivelli, a short, compact barrel of a woman with a short mop of straw-coloured hair. She was dressed in a flowered housedress with a differently flowered apron that reached her ankles.

'Buongiorno, Ida. I didn't expect to see you here.'

'Why not, Maresciallo? I lost one housekeeping job. I had to find another one.' Ida had been the housekeeper of another murder victim. 'I saw your car and your men, so I came out to see why you're here.' She looked up at Perillo with narrowed eyes. 'What is it this time?' She barely reached his chin.

'Are you going to open the gate?'

'What for? The owners aren't coming back until tomorrow. They don't like people to come in. There are enough tourists who bother them about the chapel. We can talk here. When I see you, I know there's trouble. This time I know nothing about your latest murder, if that's why you're here?'

'Have faith, Ida. Were you here Friday morning?' Perillo braced himself for a long answer. Ida liked to tell things her way and did not accept interruptions.

'Of course, I was. Wednesdays and Fridays are my days to clean the house. I do not play hooky just because the owners aren't here. Both days I get a ride with Gemma, who works at the Querciabella vineyard, and I walk the rest of the way. Keeps me healthy. I get here around ten-thirty, sometimes eleven, but I do my five hours, not a minute less. Most often many minutes more. Why did you ask?'

'Friday morning, did you see anything out of the ordinary?'

'I saw a car, parked near the chapel, but that's nothing new. People drive up here all the time. The chapel used to belong to the Gherardini family. You're Neapolitan, but you know who they are, don't you? They are in all the history books.' Ida tilted her head up at him, her expression a doubtful one.

Perillo shifted his weight from one foot to the other. Ida required patience he didn't have. 'I do. What make of car was it?'

'Oh, I was too far to see the make, not that I can tell a Panda from a Ford. I never had a car myself. Never learnt to drive. All I know about cars is from ads I see on television. So this is about the murder. I should have known. Why else is a maresciallo of the carabinieri here? Not to ask how I'm doing. You think he was killed here?'

'Yes. The car. Big? Large? What colour?'

'Oh, Santa Rita, pray for us.' Ida made the sign of the cross. 'Big. Black . . . or maybe blue. The driver . . .' Ida raised her hand when she saw Perillo open his mouth. 'Don't ask. Whoever it was, wore trousers, dark clothes, that's all I can tell you. Could have been a transgender for all I could see. The driver, well, first I noticed the car. I kept walking. Then I saw the driver in the field near the cypress trees like he was looking for something. Then I got a call from Signora Giordani, my Monday employer. She wanted to know if I could—'

Perillo grabbed the gate and shook it as hard as he could. 'Ida, please! I don't have all day.'

She slapped one of his fists. 'Stop that, Maresciallo. You'll break it.'

He released his grip.

She glared at him, her face red with anger. 'I don't have all day either. I was trying to tell you that I didn't see what the driver did after I got Signora Giordani's call. She was giving me a long list of things she wanted me to get for her. I was trying to write them down. I did hear the car drive past me. I have nothing more to add.'

'Thank you, Ida. I apologise for losing my temper.'

Ida nodded her acceptance. 'Will this area be turned upside down? I have to warn the owners.'

'A forensic team from Florence will be descending. They will work as quickly as they can. I'll let them know not to disturb you, unless absolutely necessary.'

'Tell your handsome brigadiere to come visit me again. Daniele is such a nice young man, so polite. I'll make him another raspberry crostata. He really enjoyed the last one.'

On the way back to the car, Perillo called Nico. This time Nico answered.

Laura sat at the desk in her office, dressed in pale grey wool slacks and a long-sleeved wool sweater, paging through the log she kept for frequent guests. She meticulously noted their name, address, phone numbers, favourite room, drinks, foods, and special needs. She liked to add quirky habits she or the staff might notice. Mrs Brennan, for one, insisted on using the pillowcases that had belonged to her mother. Thin delicate ones edged in English lace that had to be washed by hand. Today it wasn't quirks she was interested in. She needed a phone number.

Her phone rang. Laura looked at the number and decided she would call back. She wanted to get her own call over with first. She found the number she was looking for and used the hotel phone to call. She did not want this man to know her mobile number.

'You wish to speak to Dottor Vittori concerning what?'

his secretary asked in her usual superior voice.

Laura moved uncomfortably in her chair. She'd always been caught whenever she lied. 'We found a belt in the room Dottor Vittori's guest stayed in Thursday night. I'd like his address so I can return it to him.'

'Didn't you register him?'

'We didn't know he was staying over.' *At least this part was true,* Laura thought. 'Dottor Vittori did apologise in the morning and paid for the room. I'm afraid I don't even know his name.'

'Dottor Vittori is extremely busy. I will find out for you and call you back with name, address and telephone number. Buongiorno.'

Laura listened to the dial tone and let herself relax. Whoever this man was, he must have known Cesare, if Mrs Barron wasn't inventing one of her stories. A surprise encounter with an old friend would explain what made Cesare drop a tray of drinks far better than anything Dottor Vittori could have said. Cesare was used to Vittori's rudeness.

Her phone rang again. This time Laura picked up. 'Yes, of course . . . No, I have time now. All the guests have left . . . Of course, I want to be of help. I'll be there in thirty minutes.'

Laura sat, waiting. She would leave after twenty minutes. The maresciallo seemed to be a man who expected punctuality. Twenty-two minutes later she heard the phone ring from the end of the hall. She ran back to the office.

'Yes, I'm here.'

'One moment, please,' Vittori's secretary said.

Damn, Laura mouthed. Vittori might see through her

ruse. After a moment that lasted too long, she was greeted with, 'Buongiorno, Laura, I hope you are as beautiful and energetic as ever, despite having lost your bartender. I suggest you replace him with a handsome and personable young man. The bar tab of your lady guests would rise precipitously.'

Laura felt a shudder go through her. 'Dottor Vittori, how nice to hear your voice. I was hoping to get your guest's name and address without disturbing you.'

'No disturbance at all. I've had a frantic morning and I have always found your voice extremely soothing.' His voice made her want to wash her ears. 'Why don't you send the belt to my office and my secretary will make sure he gets it.'

Was Vittori shielding the man? Laura wondered. 'That's too kind of you, but I was hoping to reach him directly in the hopes of interesting him in spending some of his vacation time here at the hotel. Friday morning, while he was waiting to say goodbye to you, he told me how much he regretted his too brief stay here.' In truth, he had only complained about having to wait for Vittori.

'That's an excellent idea. Sirio Reni and I will be partners in an interesting new venture together. Having him nearby next summer could be very helpful. He's staying in Florence at the Lungarno for a few days. My secretary will give you his home address in Genoa and mobile number. He remarked on how very attractive you are, so it should be an easy sales pitch. Arrivederla, Laura.'

He clicked off before she could thank him. Seconds later, his secretary gave her the information.

* * *

'Buongiorno, Maresciallo. I came as fast as I could. I have the name of a man you might want to talk to. He was with Dottor Vittori when Cesare dropped the tray of drinks.'

Perillo did not respond or stand up. 'Please sit down, Signorina Benati.' He indicated the chair in front of his desk.

Momentarily flustered by his brusque order, Laura smiled at the young brigadiere in the back of the room. 'You have news?' She sat down, feeling a flutter of hope in her chest.

Perillo looked back at Daniele.

Daniele nervously turned on the tape recorder. He'd only got two hours of sleep and didn't want to mess up the announcement. 'This conversation between Maresciallo Perillo and Signorina Laura Benati is being recorded at ten-fifteen, 17th October, 2018 – Brigadiere Daniele Donato is also in the room.'

Good, Laura thought, the maresciallo was being efficient. She leant forward, the flutter of hope expanding. 'You do have news then.'

'Yes, we do. Brigadiere Donato was able to unearth the passcode to Cesare Rinaldi's phone.'

Laura's hands turned into fists. They must have read everything she'd texted him when he didn't answer. Pleas mixed with increasingly angry words. *Where are you? You can't do this to me. I'm reliving a nightmare, you know that. Cesare, please. Call me. Come home.*

Laura felt ashamed of what these two men had discovered. They now knew of the neediness she had always taken great pains to keep hidden from everyone except Cesare. She remembered Nonna Celestina's adage and straightened her back against the chair. Straight back, armoured heart. 'Did you learn anything helpful?'

Perillo slipped Cesare's phone into Laura's open hand. 'Please read the text Cesare received at nine-twelve on Friday morning.' Daniele had prudently taken a photo of the text message.

Laura looked down and read:

I need your help. Can you come to the Montagliari Chapel? I'll be waiting for you outside. Please hurry.

She felt a pain inside her chest as sharp as a whiplash. Almost her exact words from that day, almost nine years ago. *I need your help. Please, Gabi, come get me.*

Laura looked up at the maresciallo to remind herself of where she was. He looked back at her with a neutral expression. This was now, she told herself. Now was a message on Cesare's phone, not Gabi's. Laura blinked the memory away and re-read the message. She glanced at the name above the text.

Laura.

Laura sought Perillo's face. 'I don't understand.' His face was a petrified mask. She looked at the brigadiere. He met her eyes with kindness. And trust, she hoped.

'Whatever you say is being recorded,' he reminded her.

Why? 'I didn't write this.'

'The text comes from your phone,' Perillo said.

'No, it doesn't.' She reached into her jacket pocket and took out her phone. 'You look. You'll see I never sent that text.'

Perillo took the phone from her hand and scrolled through the delivered notices. He held the face of the phone across the desk so Laura could see. 'Here it is, Signorina Benati. Laura. Delivered. Nine-twelve.'

Laura dug her fingernails into her palms. Her heart started to bang against her ribs like a caged animal. 'I did not write this. Cesare was my best friend!' She tried to keep her voice from rising. 'He was my *only* friend. I depended on him.' He had removed the guilt, made her feel whole again. 'Never, never would I harm him.'

Perillo wanted to believe her. 'In that case, someone else must have used your phone. Do you always keep it with you?'

Laura unclenched her hands. 'I try to, but sometimes I leave it on my desk or in the pocket of my jacket.'

'Where were you and what were you doing at nine-twelve Friday morning?'

Laura tried to think, but her heart was still hammering, and her mouth was bone dry. Where was she Friday morning? Where was her phone? She remembered waiting for something. Someone. Being annoyed. Why annoyed? Why couldn't she remember? She closed her eyes for a moment.

Daniele had been watching Laura since she'd walked in, now unable to accept her as a suspect. Her initial smile and confidence were shattered. She looked lost, not frightened.

'Were you at the hotel?' he asked, willing to risk the maresciallo's annoyance. Laura needed a prod.

Laura gave her head a quick shake. 'Of course, the hotel. During the season I often sleep there.' Living at home with her mother had stopped being an option once her grandfather moved in. He had never forgiven her. In the winter months, she moved in with Nadia. She paused to let her brain take control of her emotions. 'I was up very early.' The morning came back to her now as clear as the sky had been. 'Dottor Vittori was being picked up at nine to be driven back to Rome and he wanted breakfast in his room at seven. After Vittori's complaints about Cesare the night before, I wanted to make sure everything would go smoothly. At nine I took over at the reception desk so that Nadia, my assistant, could have breakfast. Shortly after that, Vittori's guest from the night before came in. He wanted to say goodbye to his host.' Laura's face lit up. 'Sirio Reni, that's his name. He could be important. Mrs Barron – she's a regular at the hotel – was in the bar Thursday night. She's convinced Reni's the reason Cesare dropped the tray. I have his phone number and address. I think you should speak to him.'

Was this a diversionary tactic? Perillo wondered. 'If it's necessary I will, but we still have a text message that needs an explanation.'

She stared at Perillo, eyes wide. 'It wasn't me. I didn't write it.' Perillo's face turned into her grandfather's angry face. *'It wasn't me, Nonno,'* she'd pleaded. *'I didn't kill her.'* All she had done was send another one of her drunken texts to her sister.

Perillo noticed the great emotion behind her denial. If she was lying, she was good at it. 'Was your phone with you at the reception desk?'

'What?'

'Would you like a coffee or a glass of water?' Daniele asked. Perillo turned to give him a blistering look. Daniele and his soft heart could be irritating at times. Mostly when he hadn't thought of being thoughtful himself.

'Nothing, thank you,' Laura said. *Stay in the present*, Cesare would tell her. Whenever the memory of that night came back and overwhelmed her, he would remind her, *You are here. You are now*. 'I'm sorry. This has been something of a shock.' She looked back at Perillo. 'You asked me something?'

'I asked if your phone was with you at the reception desk.'

'I don't remember making or receiving any calls, but I think so.'

'You say you did not write that text, but whoever used your phone needed to know your passcode.'

'I never put one in.' Laura took her phone out of her pant pocket and held out the phone. 'See for yourself.'

Perillo took the phone and clicked. Her main screen appeared. 'Did anyone approach you while you were at the reception desk?'

'Dottor Vittori finally showed up to settle the bill. His guest had left by then, but he'd left a note, which I handed to Dottor Vittori.'

'Anyone else come by?'

'Nadia came back. It was ten o'clock by then.'

'Do you recall the first time you used the phone that day?'

'I called my mother at lunchtime from my office.' She called her every day. 'I don't remember if I reached in my jacket or whether the phone was on my desk. It's an automatic gesture. I'm sorry. I've been hacked. People get hacked all the time nowadays.'

Daniele cleared his throat. 'Your phone has a very strong anti-virus program, but please add a passcode, Signorina Benati. Add fingerprint identification.'

'What does it matter now?'

'Brigadiere Donato is right,' Perillo said, making a mental note to add fingerprint identification to his phone. 'You are free to go now, Signorina Benati, but please understand that the text sent to Cesare Rinaldi from your phone makes you a suspect in his murder. The fact that he left you a large amount of money in his will gives you a very good motive.'

Laura's heart started banging again, this time out of anger. She sprang up from the chair. 'I didn't know he was going to do that. I didn't even know he had any money!' She didn't care how loud her voice was now. She'd had enough of taking the blame. 'You are out of your mind if you think I killed my best friend. Crazy is what you are.'

Interesting reaction, Perillo thought, and said, 'This interview is over,' forgetting to deepen his voice. He looked at his watch. 'At eleven-o-four.'

Daniele switched off the tape recorder and walked over to Laura. Her outburst had shaken him. Insulting a maresciallo of the carabinieri could get her into deeper trouble. 'Signorina Benati, please, stay calm.'

Perillo joined in, 'Yes, Signorina. Please. You may think I'm crazy, but it is my job to let you know how matters stand at the moment. I will add that you are not the only suspect. Someone may have used your phone to incriminate you, or simply to get Cesare to go to the Montagliari Chapel. Brigadiere Donato will see you out. We will talk again.'

Laura wrapped her arms around her waist and acknowledged Perillo's words with a nod. He had good reasons to suspect her. How stupid of her to lose her temper. Perillo was not her grandfather. Cesare was not Gabi.

CHAPTER EIGHT

Perillo walked into Da Angela's, a popular restaurant in Lucarelli, with Nico and OneWag. Daniele had stayed outside to answer his phone. A pleasant-looking woman in her forties looked up from the reservation book as they came in.

'Ciao, bella,' Perillo said. 'I hope you have room for three hungry men and a dog.'

Angela's grey eyes widened in surprise. 'Well, who do I have here? It's been so long I can't remember.'

'Buonasera, Angela,' Nico said. It was here, just over a year ago, while eating a peppery beef dish and drinking a gifted Brunello di Montalcino that his collaboration with Perillo began. While trying to solve Gravigna's first murder they became friends.

Angela gave him a smile. 'Benvenuto, Nico. *You* are welcome.'

Perillo tried to look abashed. 'You're right, Angela. It's been a long time. Blame it on too much work.'

'No, I blame it on Ivana. I wish she'd come cook for me instead of feeding her ungrateful husband.' She bent down and stroked OneWag. 'I remember you. You have manners.'

'I should have made a reservation.' Perillo tried to look embarrassed. 'But you know how it is.'

'If I didn't know how it is, I'd go out of business.'

'We'd like a secluded corner, as we've got some work to go over.'

'That's right, you have another murder on your hands. You'll have to pay for your own wine this time.'

Angela picked up three menus. 'Where's the third hungry man?'

As if on cue, Daniele stepped inside, his face flushed from Stella's voice. Or the wind. 'Here I am.'

'Good. The wind is whipping tonight, making it too cold for outside. I'm giving you an upstairs room.' Angela gave Perillo a meaningful glance. 'You can share all the dirty secrets you want in there.'

Nico picked up OneWag and they followed Angela upstairs. The small room was welcoming. A milk-chocolate-brown tile floor, a slanting brick ceiling crisscrossed with thick wooden beams. Old black-and-white photographs of vineyards on the walls. A small fireplace edged in green maiolica tile sat in one corner piled with logs ready to be lit.

Perillo sat down at one end of the table and ordered a litre of house red and two bottles of flat water. Nico and Daniele sat across from him. While Angela went to get the drink order, Perillo pointed out the highlights of the menu while OneWag swept his nose over the full extent of this unknown floor.

It didn't take long for Angela to come back with the wine and the two waters. 'I brought an extra bottle of our house red, just in case. Don't worry, I charge by consumption. Ready to order?'

All three ordered pici all'aglione and the aubergine involtini.

'Mine filled with ricotta, please,' Daniele remembered to add, his head still swirling from Stella's *'I miss you.'*

Perillo noticed Daniele's happy face. 'What is it, Dani? Is it Angela's imminent food, or is Stella coming home this weekend?'

The colour of Daniele's cheeks deepened. 'She wants to go to the last Verdi Orchestra concert on Saturday.'

'Good. Perhaps Stella would like an escort. There's nothing like sweet company to enrich music. Unfortunately, we will be at the concert, but on duty to make sure all goes well.'

Daniele's eyes fluttered.

'Let's start sharing the information we both have,' Nico said. 'No sharing before we've had a glass of good wine to stimulate the brain,' Perillo said since Angela was still in the room, lighting the fire. He unzipped his suede jacket and leant his weight on the back of his chair. The old wood creaked in response. 'To go back to the concert. Music, like wine, stimulates the brain, as does a diversion. I think it will be perfectly acceptable to give my very competent brigadiere a few hours off after the concert.'

Daniele gulped. 'Thank you, Maresciallo.'

'It's Salvatore, Dani.' Perillo lifted the glass and took a

sip. 'When we're among friends, I'm Salvatore. That's what Angela calls me.'

'The few times you show up,' Angela said, walking to the stairs. 'Food will be here when it's ready. If you need anything, ring the cowbell that's on top of the mantel. Buon appetito.'

Perillo blew her a kiss and raised his glass to her. 'You're the best.'

'I know I am,' she tossed out as she walked out of the room.

As her footsteps faded down the stairs, Perillo clinked glasses with Nico and Daniele. 'Justice to Cesare.'

Nico took a quick sip. 'I think it's time.'

Perillo instead drank with gusto. 'I'm in agreement. First, the autopsy report. It came in when we got back to the station. Four stab wounds with a sixteen-centimetre smooth-blade knife, the kind used to go boar hunting. One to the heart, two down his chest, the fourth in his stomach. Each one a neat, deep thrust. Gianconi wrote that the killer was a very strong person or an extremely angry person. The back of his clothes was dirty, and grass-stained, indicating that the body had been dragged, which was confirmed by the flattened and bloodied grass. The poor man must have been taken by surprise. Not a defensive mark on him.'

This time Nico took a long drink. He'd heard autopsy reports countless times back in New York. They always tightened his stomach. He put the glass back down. 'Do you know yet if anything of interest was found at the murder site?'

Perillo shook his head, a glum expression on his face.

'I wish. No sign of tire tracks or shoe imprints. The men picked up the usual garbage you find on the sides of roads. They'll go through it carefully, but it will take a few days. What did Jimmy tell you?'

Nico relayed his conversation with Jimmy. 'Do you believe him?' Perillo asked.

'Yes,' Nico said. 'I think you can cross him off your suspect list.'

'What about Sandro being so jealous of an old man?' Daniele asked, then added, 'If he thought Jimmy and Cesare were lovers, he might have killed Cesare and put him in Jimmy's boot for revenge.'

Perillo stared at the flames taking hold of the logs and didn't answer. He held his glass up against the light of the fire. The red of the wine glowed. He didn't want to deal with another suspect. He wanted this case to be over. Maybe he was having a midlife crisis. Or maybe he had simply stopped wanting to deal with cruelty, jealousy, greed, hate, whatever led a human being to kill another.

'Sandro would know where Jimmy parked his car when he visited his mother in Florence,' Daniele added.

'That's true,' Nico said, 'but why kill Cesare now? Cesare hadn't shown up at the café since Sandro kicked him out. That was years ago.'

'Maybe Jimmy and Cesare kept seeing each other,' Daniele offered.

Perillo emptied his glass. Maybe his problem was Della Langhe. The substitute prosecutor hadn't been on his back on this case. He missed the anger that arrogant man provoked – an anger that stimulated him to be his best, to prove the asshole wrong. The thought cheered him. Yes, that's what was wrong. It had nothing to do with aging or a midlife crisis.

'Even if Sandro would have wanted to kill Cesare,' Nico said, 'I don't know how he could have done it. Last Friday Sandro was manning the café all by himself.'

'What time were you there that morning?' Perillo asked.

'Seven-thirty to eight-thirty, something like that.'

The text wasn't sent until nine-twelve, Perillo thought. Enough time to go to the hotel and use Laura's phone. If. If. If. Perillo sighed loudly. *If* Laura was innocent. 'Sandro's guilt is improbable, but I'll talk to him anyway.'

Nico lifted his half-empty glass at Perillo. 'Your turn now. I repeat my question. What led you to the murder site?'

Perillo told him.

The news stunned Nico. 'Laura? That's hard to believe.' He had seen her as a gentle, reserved woman.

Daniele jumped in. 'She was as shocked as you are. Someone else must have got hold of her phone.'

'That's possible,' Nico said.

Daniele bobbed his head in agreement. 'How did you crack Cesare's passcode?'

Daniele's shoulders sagged. 'I wish I hadn't.'

Nico felt for Daniele. 'What was it?'

'One, one, one, one.'

Perillo raised his eyebrows. 'How did you come up with that?'

'Signora Benati wears a cross with January 11th 2011.'

'What does that date have to do with Cesare?'

'Nothing that I know of, Maresciallo. I was half asleep and that date wandered into my head. After I knocked off the 201 from the year, it worked. As I told you, Laura Benati has, or had, an older sister, Gabriella. Her grandfather kept telling me how beautiful and intelligent she was. There were a lot of pictures of her on the bookshelf, very few of Laura. In fact, he never mentioned her. I think in his eyes, only Gabriella existed.'

Perillo took out an unopened cigarette pack and gave it a loving look. 'Laura made no mention of her sister in our talks.'

'I think Gabriella's dead,' Daniele said.

'Let's get back to what's important,' Perillo said. 'It now looks like Laura is our murderer.'

Nico saw Daniele's look of dismay and turned his head to watch OneWag. The dog was standing at the top of the staircase. 'I think Rocco is telling us our pici are coming. Let's discuss who might have killed Cesare later.'

'Yes, please,' Daniele said eagerly.

Perillo tucked his napkin in the collar of his shirt. 'I agree. Food loses its taste with talk.'

OneWag moved aside as a woman old enough to be Angela's mother arrived at the top of the stairs holding a large tray with three mounded plates of pici all'aglione. Daniele quickly stood up and offered to take the tray from her.

Her hands clutched the tray as she turned away from him.

'I'm sorry,' Daniele mumbled, his cheeks picking up the colour of the pici.

'Here you are, Maresciallo,' the woman said. 'I made the pici myself this morning. The sauce is Angela's. These are no supermarket pici.'

Perillo lowered his head in a salute. 'Grazie, Betta. Your arms produce magic.'

Betta lowered the tray at the far end of the table and distributed the plates. In front of Perillo she placed a small bowl with a metal grater and a hunk of pecorino cheese. 'If you need more.'

Nico looked at the pile of thick, glistening strands of pasta that was a Tuscan specialty. During his first year in Gravigna he had stayed away from pici all'aglione, thinking aglione – big garlic – meant the tomato sauce was full of garlic. Nelli had convinced him to try it. Aglione was a different, less pungent garlic, grown in the Val di Chiana just above Siena. Served with a light tomato sauce and lots of grated pecorino, the dish had won him over.

'Buon appetito, Signori,' Betta said with a wave of her hand.

'Grazie,' the three of them responded.

Perillo plunged his fork into the pici and started twirling.

'Eat, Dani,' Nico encouraged in a low voice after taking a few succulent forkfuls of the pasta. 'It's very good.'

Dani lifted a few long strands of the pici and chewed slowly. As the combination of flavours filled his mouth, his eyes widened with joy. Maybe he could bring Stella here after the concert. 'Is the food expensive?' he asked, although he knew Stella would insist on eating alla romana, each paying their own.

Perillo dragged his napkin across his mouth and drank some of his wine. 'If you are thinking of offering Stella the joy of this food, do so. Splurge for once. You deserve to treat yourself.'

Daniele looked back at his boss with a tomato-laced smile.

With all three plates empty, Nico refilled Perillo's glass and his own. Daniele's glass was still full.

'She doesn't look strong enough to heave a body into a car boot,' Daniele said, eager to get back to the reason they were all sitting there.

'According to the autopsy report, Cesare was one metre, ninety,' Perillo said, 'but weighed only sixty-eight kilos.'

Just over six feet and around a hundred and fifty pounds, Nico calculated in his head. 'He was skinny. What does Laura say?'

'We confronted her this morning about the text message. She denies it, of course.'

'I believe her,' Daniele said, lowering his not-quite empty plate to the floor. 'Someone else used her phone.'

Perillo smiled at Daniele. 'Always the Galahad, my trusting brigadiere. You have taught me a great deal about empathy, but we do have to look at the evidence with cold eyes.'

'I believe her,' Daniele repeated. 'I watched her as she read the text. There was surprise. Then pain gripped her face. If she had sent that text, wouldn't she have been afraid?' Her pain had turned to great anger. The maresciallo took it as a guilty reaction. He, instead, thought she was only fighting her pain. 'She has no motive.'

'Cesare had forty thousand euros in the bank,' Perillo explained to Nico. 'It all goes to her. That's a motive. I checked with the owner of the hotel about Laura's salary. She earns two thousand euros a month but has half her salary sent directly to her mother.'

Daniele noisily dropped his elbows on the table. 'That shows she is a good person. If she killed Cesare, why didn't she erase her text?'

'She was overcome by emotion,' Perillo suggested. 'Regret.

Fear. She'd just killed someone who loved her.'

'Who else had access to her phone?' Nico asked.

'It would have to be someone at the hotel. Nadia, her assistant, confirmed on the phone that Laura was at the reception desk Friday morning from nine to ten a.m. She couldn't see me this afternoon because she had to take over for Laura, who claimed she wasn't feeling well. Then there's Dottor Eugenio Vittori, a frequent guest at the hotel. He paid his bill while Laura was still at the reception desk.'

'That's interesting,' Nico said. 'He's another one with motive. With Cesare dead, he got the land he wanted.'

'Daniele looked him up. He's not a medical doctor or a doctor of philosophy. The title is just there to impress the clients whose money he invests. It seems a university degree is not necessary to know how to handle money.'

'How successful is he?'

'The degree of success is hard to find out, as it is a private company,' Daniele said, 'but he has succeeded in keeping Vittori Investments operating for over twenty years.'

Perillo rolled the unlit cigarette between his fingers, fighting the temptation to light it. 'He lives in Rome and didn't have time to talk to me this afternoon. His secretary has set up a telephone appointment for me tomorrow at eleven-fifteen. He's a busy man, it seems.'

'There's also Vittori's guest, Sirio Reni,' Daniele said, happy to add another possible suspect. 'He was near the reception desk Friday morning, waiting to say goodbye to his host. Signorina Benati thinks he might have known Cesare and gave us a phone number to call. I left a message.'

Perillo closed his eyes for a moment to reflect. 'I think the lovely Laura might be trying to add more ingredients to the soup to keep us stirring. That Reni may have known Cesare comes from an English guest who likes to sit at the bar in the evening and, according to Laura's assistant, likes to make up stories.'

'It's worth pursuing,' Nico said, 'but not everyone is eager to get involved with a murder investigation.'

'Of course. Of course.' Perillo was thinking something sweet was needed to aid digestion.

'We'll get Reni's address,' Daniele said, 'and show up at his home.'

Perillo chuckled. 'I venture you're hoping he lives in Florence so you can steal a visit to Stella.'

Daniele picked up his untouched wine glass and tried to hide his face behind it. The maresciallo was a good man, but he didn't know when enough was enough.

'Stop it, Perillo,' Nico said.

Perillo bowed his head. 'You're right, Nico.' He looked up at Daniele's abashed face trying to hide behind the wine glass. 'I guess I'm envious of your youth, of you being in love, the exhilaration, the anxiety, feeling every cell in your body pulsing with life.'

Daniele blushed with embarrassment. 'You're not that old, Maresciallo.'

Perillo beamed a smile. 'I am, but thank you. Soon fifty. I shall tease you no more. Forgive me, Dani.'

Daniele put his glass down and looked at both men sitting in front of him. 'There's nothing to forgive.'

'I think something sweet is in order,' Perillo said, rising from his chair. 'I'll go down to order and save Betta the stairs. You two, what are your stomachs crying for? Angela makes a panna cotta over a bed of melted dark chocolate that can make you sing out Alleluia. That's what I'm having.'

Daniele shot out of his chair, hoping to call Stella back. 'I'll go.'

'No.' Perillo's hand landed on Daniele's shoulder and gently pushed him back down. 'Nico?'

'Nothing for me,' Nico said. 'My stomach wants to rest until tomorrow morning.'

'Dani, what can I get you for dessert?'

Daniele swallowed his disappointment with a shrug. 'The poached pear with strawberry jam, please.'

Perillo grunted a laugh. 'Your healthy food fixation is one thing that does not make me jealous. Come on, Rocco, let's go see if I can get you a cantuccino to gnaw on.'

OneWag jumped up, sending the now-licked-clean pici plate under the table. He ran to catch up with Perillo.

'Thank you, Nico,' Daniele said as soon as Perillo's creaking footsteps down the stairs stopped.

'You're welcome. I hope he keeps his word.'

'It doesn't matter. For someone as proud as he is to ask forgiveness is enough for me.'

'For a young man, you're very wise.'

'I'm not. I find being in love is confusing.'

'It is. I'm not one to give you advice,' Nico said. 'I've got the same problem.'

'You do?' Daniele asked, his voice full of surprise.

Nico nodded.

They both turned to look at the fireplace.

Downstairs, after ordering dessert from Angela, Perillo made a reservation for two people on Saturday night. 'Give him a hefty discount and I'll make up for it.'

Angela wrote it down in her reservation book. 'You are full of surprises. I never thought a soft heart would be one of them.'

'Cara Angela, when was the last time you were in love?'

Angela laughed. 'Who remembers?'

Nico reached over the table and gave Daniele's arm a squeeze. He cared for this young man, felt close to him. 'Your feelings, don't be afraid of them.'

'Afraid of what?' Perillo asked as he and OneWag reached the top of the stairs.

Daniele quickly stood up and walked across the room. 'It's my turn now,' he said as he took the tray with their desserts from his boss.

'Thanks, Dani. I got a plate of cantuccini for Rocco and you, Nico. Also, three glasses of vin santo on the house.' Perillo sat down as Daniele slid the tray on the table and distributed the plates. 'So, afraid of what?'

Daniele threw a pleading look at Nico.

'Afraid we won't solve the case,' Nico said.

Perillo looked up at his brigadiere. 'Have faith, Dani. It might take a long time, but we will.'

'That reminds me,' Nico said, 'have you talked to Beppe?'

'If he has something to tell me, he should come to the station. I'm not going to look for him. He's probably only trying to give himself importance.'

'Maybe, but he still should be heard,' Nico said. 'He won't tell me. Beppe only wants to speak to the top man.'

'To waste my time. I heard you, Nico. We'll put Beppe on the list of people to talk to.'

'I think you also need to talk further with the owner of

the hotel,' Nico added. 'She hired Cesare and Laura and might know something about them that we don't.'

Perillo widened his eyes at Nico. 'Me? You are part of my investigative team.'

'Why don't I talk to her?' Daniele offered. The owner lived in Florence.

'No, Dani, I'm sorry. From the harsh look on her portrait hanging in the lobby of the hotel, Signora Lucchetti strikes me as a difficult woman.' She had sounded perfectly nice on the phone, but he wanted Nico to go. 'Nico has years of experience behind him in getting people to reveal the contents of their closets or anyone else's.' Perillo lifted a spoon and dug it into the panna cotta. 'Let us put murder aside and enjoy our desserts. They will give us sweet dreams.'

Nico looked at the small glass of vin santo. *Sweet dreams and acid reflux.*

Three hours later it wasn't acid reflux that was making Nico toss and turn. Each time he was about to fall asleep, his confused feelings for Nelli would interrupt and start churning in his head. When he had come home too late to call, he started a text.

I miss you, Nelli, every day, but

He stopped typing. But what? *I can't give you enough. You deserve more. If I let myself love you, have I stopped loving Rita? If I love you, will I lose you too?*

What he finally texted was an invitation to come to dinner Friday night . . . It didn't help with his sleep.

* * *

Perillo found Ivana in bed watching *Montalbano*, a favourite programme she had learnt to record thanks to Daniele. He bent over to kiss the top of her head so as not to obstruct her view. 'Ciao, cara.'

'Mmm,' was her response. On the screen, Luca Zingaretti's Montalbano was walking out of the water, showing off his tanned body, luminous drops of water sliding down his chest, his usual satisfied-with-himself grin on his face.

Perillo couldn't bear the man. 'He's got chunky, don't you think?' he said, unbuttoning his shirt.

Ivana turned to give her husband's T-shirted chest a quick appraising look. 'So have you.' On the screen the end credits rolled. She picked up the remote and turned the television off. 'What did Angela feed you?'

'An impepata of mussels,' he said, sucking in his stomach, 'followed by a timballo of maccheroni with peas and sausage. We ended with Babá.'

She laughed. He'd just listed the favourite Neapolitan dishes she cooked for him. Angela wouldn't know where to start. She watched him as he made his way to the bathroom. When he had asked her why she watched a crime show when he wasn't home, she'd answered, 'Montalbano is sexy.' That wasn't the real reason. What watching the show gave her was the illusion of being close to Salvatore when he wasn't home. 'Salva, don't take forever.'

With toothbrush in hand, Perillo looked at Ivana in the bathroom mirror. She'd lifted the bed cover and sheet from his side of the bed. He stuck the toothbrush in his mouth and brushed vigorously.

* * *

Daniele had postponed sleep. After saying good night to his boss, he had slipped back into the office. He sat at his desk in the dark. He wasn't afraid of his feelings. He simply didn't know what to do with them. Keep them inside? Tell Stella he cared? Try to kiss her? He'd thought of kissing her a thousand times, but they were either having a drink in a café or walking the streets of Florence or Gravigna. They were never alone. Over the phone she'd said she missed him. But how? As a friend? Or how he missed her? With an ache that had curled itself in his chest, making it sometimes hard to breathe.

'Oh, shit,' Daniele said out loud and turned on the computer. While he waited for it to come to life, he texted Stella:

I know I already answered that I missed you too, but I just wanted to tell you again. I can't wait to see you on Saturday.

It was late, almost midnight. She'd be asleep, but he waited a few minutes to see if she answered. When no answer came, Daniele turned to the computer screen. He intended to find out if Florence police headquarters had issued a passport to Cesare Rinaldi, but his mind was still with Stella. He looked her up on Facebook again. Her smiling face was gone, replaced by the emaciated face of Donatello's Mary Magdalene. Was Stella sad? Had something happened? He texted her again.

Why did you switch your picture with Mary Magdalene? Is something wrong?

He missed seeing her face, the smile that was like a rush of warm water. Thinking of her smile made him remember the photo he had seen at Signora Benati's house. He clicked search and typed in Gabriella Benati's name. She was still on Facebook, staring back at him with large blue eyes and a wide smile. It was a close-up of the photo he had seen on the shelf. No one had bothered or wanted to delete her. Daniele studied her face to try to get a sense of who she'd been. Her features, her good looks were more incisive than Laura's. With thick, wavy blond hair falling down on her shoulders, she looked vibrant. Laura was a pale copy of her sister.

Below the picture was a string of posts. The first one came from Laura: *Bella Gabi, I will miss you forever.*

Daniele clicked off Facebook and went to the weekly newspaper *Chianti Sette*. He typed Gabriella's name and 11th January, 2011. He found her written up in the following week's edition. The headline read:

TRAGEDY ON THE 222 ON THE OUTSKIRTS OF CASTELLINA.

Twenty-two-year-old Gabriella Benati, a Greve resident and a recent graduate of l'Università di Firenze, met her death on the S.S. 2 when she lost control of the car and crashed into an elm tree. The San Casciano Carabinieri received a call at two o'clock in the morning from a man reporting that a car had smashed against a tree on a curve just before reaching the Castellina town border. He stopped to help, but the woman was already dead. He refused to give his name, saying he had done his duty.

The writer went on to protest the lack of signage warning drivers of dangerous curves.

Daniele stopped reading. He wasn't sure why he had wanted to discover what had happened to Gabriella. Maybe to stop thinking about Stella. Or maybe he was just trying to know more about Laura, now Perillo's prime suspect in Cesare's murder.

Daniele clicked out of the article and went to his station's URL, the first thing he should have done. He sent an email to all the Italian police headquarters asking if Cesare Giovanni Rinaldi had ever been issued a passport. He included Cesare's birthdate, birthplace and residence. With drooping eyelids, he pushed send.

CHAPTER NINE

The next morning, a cold Thursday, while Perillo was spooning a zabaglione into his mouth to restore his energy, he received a text from Laura. Dottor Vittori had made a surprise visit to the hotel late last night.

In his room Daniele was reading Stella's text.

Nothing is wrong. I got tired of seeing my face and I think she's beautiful.

With a grin, Daniele answered with, *I guess beauty is a matter of opinion. Glad all is well. Miss you.*

Forty-five minutes later, Perillo and Daniele appeared at the Hotel Bella Vista dressed in their dark blue jackets and red-striped trousers. Laura met them in the hotel car park.

'Buongiorno, Maresciallo.' Laura added a nod in Daniele's direction. She was dressed in a grey knitted top and darker grey slacks, with a beige wool sweater wrapped around her shoulders. Her hair was tied tightly at the nape of her neck.

'I hope you are feeling better, Signorina Benati,' Perillo said, noticing her drained appearance.

Knowing about Gabriella, Daniele saw sadness.

'Why should I feel better, Maresciallo?' Laura's blue eyes seemed to turn the colour of steel. 'Am I no longer a suspect?'

'I understand how difficult this must be for you,' Perillo said, 'but I assure you there are other suspects.'

'I'm glad to hear that. When are you releasing Cesare? He deserves a proper funeral.'

'I can ask the medical examiner.'

Daniele took a step forward. 'Wouldn't you prefer to wait until we find his motorcycle? He did want it to be buried with him.'

'It may never be found.'

'That is true,' Daniele said, 'but the opposite is also true. Please, give us a few more days.'

Daniele had missed his calling, Perillo decided, for once not annoyed Daniele had taken over the conversation. He should have gone into the priesthood. 'Dottor Vittori's arrival here was sudden, wasn't it? Were you expecting him?'

'No. He called me from the car while I was eating dinner, saying he had business to take care of here and could I have his usual room prepared.'

'Were you surprised?'

'I was. He has always struck me as a very deliberate, methodical man. Someone who always plans ahead. Whatever brought him here must be extremely important to him. He's working by the pool. I'll take you there.'

Perillo followed her gaze and saw a row of closed pool umbrellas. 'Thank you. We'll find the way.'

Perillo noticed the concerned look on his brigadiere's face as he stared at Laura leaving. Perillo felt for the young man. As they descended to the pool area, he said, 'I know you want her to be innocent, Dani, but don't mistake beauty for goodness.'

'It's hard not to,' Daniele answered. He'd actually been wondering what scar beautiful Gabriella's death had left on her younger sister. 'Am I recording the interview?'

'Yes, I will tell him.'

Dottor Vittori was sitting at a white metal table, tapping away on a laptop keyboard. As Perillo and Daniele approached, he held up his hand. 'I'll be with you in a moment.' He was a small man, in his late sixties, with a full head of greying black hair, a sharp nose, and a tightly closed mouth. His eyes were hidden behind aviator sunglasses. Perillo noticed the lushness of Vittori's clothes. A soft forest-green sweater that could only be cashmere, sharply creased grey flannel slacks, black Gucci loafers that cost over six hundred euros. A man who liked to show his success, a man who probably expected reverence.

Daniele admired the speed with which the man typed, but then looked behind the pool area, at the hotel vegetable and flower garden. He let his eyes flow over the rolling sweep of trees to the hotel and farmhouse complex of Vigna Maggio in the distance. Being born and raised in Venice, the vastness of the Tuscan terra firma always enraptured him.

Perillo nudged him to bring him back to the matter at

hand. Daniele gave a quick smile of apology and removed his phone from the pocket of his jacket.

Vittori stopped typing and shut his laptop. Without looking up, he gestured to the nearby chairs. 'Please, Signori, make yourselves comfortable. I am all yours.'

Perillo straightened his back. 'Maresciallo Salvatore Perillo, Dottore. With me is Brigadiere Daniele Donato. We need to ask you some questions regarding—'

'Of course,' Vittori interrupted, reclining in his chair. 'I'm fully aware of who you are and what you want, thanks to Laura. I should thank you for coming to me, although you must admit it is far more pleasant here than in a dreary carabinieri office. Please sit.'

Perillo chose the chair on the other side of the table, directly in front of Vittori. 'You are familiar with the offices of the carabinieri?'

'Certainly not, but they can't possibly have any charm. Laura is a very capable woman and very pleasing to the eye, which is a bonus. I have tried to woo her to work for me, but Laura claims she can never leave this area. I suppose a boyfriend is involved. I'm telling you this in case you suspect her of being involved in her bartender's death.'

As if his opinion mattered, Perillo thought. Why would Vittori think Laura was under suspicion? It was unlikely that she had said anything to a hotel guest she didn't like. 'I hope you don't mind if Brigadiere Donato records our conversation.'

With a wave of his hand, Vittori said, 'Not in the least. As I give many interviews, I am quite used to being recorded. Besides I have nothing to hide. Ask your questions.'

Daniele pressed record on his phone and nodded to his

boss. Perillo stated the time, who was present, and asked, 'You are buying Signor Gennari's property and Cesare Rinaldi's property, is that right?'

Vittori narrowed his eyes. 'So, you know. I suppose Gennari told you.'

'It's my job to know,' Perillo answered. 'Were you keeping the acquisition a secret?'

'Maresciallo, I make a great deal of money for my clients. I try to keep whatever else I do from being a matter of speculation. I don't want anyone to think my attention isn't fully concentrated on increasing their portfolios.' Vittori crossed his legs.

An unbearable man, Perillo was thinking. He sat up straight. 'The carabinieri are not in the habit of divulging information regarding our investigations.'

'Good. I am indeed acquiring Mattia Gennari's and Pietro Rinaldi's properties. Gennari and I signed the agreement in Rome, where I live and work too. I will have to wait for Rinaldi to come into possession of the land, as he has just inherited. Bureaucracy in this country is always slow.'

'Did you have any direct contact with Cesare about wanting to buy his property?'

Vittori gave Perillo a smug smile. 'That would have been foolish. After coming here for many years, I knew Cesare was not the fool Gennari is. He knew who I was and would have raised the price tenfold. I dealt only with Gennari. I offered to buy his property at a fair price only if he was able to buy Cesare's land, which I would pay for. Unfortunately, Cesare refused, even after I told Gennari to triple the price.'

'You were very set on getting that particular property, then.

May I ask why?'

'I have been spending a summer month in this hotel for quite a few years. I like it here. I am used to it. I am comfortable here. Why seek land elsewhere? I am a spoilt man. I am used to getting what I want, and I get it.'

'Cesare conveniently died.'

Vittori knitted his thin eyebrows together. 'I hope you are not implying that I had anything to do with it.'

'His death was very convenient for three people. Yourself, Gennari and Pietro Rinaldi.'

'I am ruthless in business and have sometimes thought how convenient a person's death would be for me, but buying this land and turning it into a small successful vineyard will just satisfy a whim. I needed something to take me away from the money business. I will call it ViniVittori. I already have an idea for the logo.' Vittori slipped a napkin from under his glass of water and with his pen drew two *V*s, one into the other with the *I*s of both words inside the *V*s. He showed the napkin first to Perillo then Daniele. 'What do you think?'

Perillo acknowledged the drawing with a nod, repulsed by the man's self-regard.

'Very clever,' Daniele said.

A wide smile crossed Vittori's face. 'I think so too. I expect to have a great deal of fun with my ViniVittori.'

'I'm sure you will.' Perillo tried hard not to grit his teeth. 'The night before Cesare disappeared you were in the bar with a friend.'

'That's correct. For some reason Cesare dropped the tray

and our drinks spilled all over me. I lost my temper and later complained to Laura.'

'Cesare wasn't reacting to anything your friend, Sirio Reni, had done?'

'What could he possibly have done to justify spilling drinks on me? Reni laughed it off. He is a good sport. Reni will be here tomorrow if you want to ask him yourself.'

'I will. Maybe Cesare had found out you were the one who wanted to buy his land.'

'Yes, I thought of that possibility, but it doesn't matter now.' He tucked the napkin in his pocket and glanced at his gold watch. 'Signori, I must go.' He stood up.

Daniele got to his feet but did not turn off the recording. The maresciallo was still sitting.

'A few more questions, Dottor Vittori,' Perillo said. 'Friday morning, as you were checking out, did you happen to see Signorina Benati's phone on the reception desk?'

'I did. Looking for my credit card I put my phone down on the desk next to her phone. After retrieving my credit card from her, I picked up her phone instead of mine.'

'Did she say it was hers?'

Vittori slid his laptop into a leather case. 'She didn't have to. Her case is hot pink.'

'Did you use it?'

'Of course not. I knew instantly I'd picked up the wrong phone. Hers is smaller. I put it back down. Addio, Signori. I don't think we will be seeing each other again.'

'I prefer arrivederci,' Perillo said. 'You never know.'

Vittori gave Perillo a glowering look before striding off.

'Do you think he's a suspect?' Daniele asked with hope in his voice.

Perillo's eyes followed Vittori. 'I'd love to put him at the top of the list. He has the means. He was near Laura on Friday morning and could have easily sent that text, but is wanting Cesare's property to create a small vineyard enough of a motive?'

Laura had no motive, Daniele thought, *and yet, she was on top of the list*. 'He seems like a man who doesn't let anything get in the way of what he wants.'

'That is true, Dani, but he also has enough money to buy other properties in Chianti.'

'He's been coming to the hotel for years. Maybe he feels at home here.'

'Maybes have to become fact, Daniele. We'll see what we can discover.'

As they left the pool area, a voice called out, 'There you are, Maresciallo!' Beppe appeared from behind a shed. 'I was cycling past the hotel and saw the carabinieri Alfa.' He was wearing a black cycling outfit, short tight pants, and a chest-hugging shirt with BEPPEINFO embroidered in red. 'I was expecting your phone call.'

Perillo stopped and studied his watch to convey he had no time to waste.

'Didn't Nico tell you I had information for you?'

'He did, and I was expecting you to come to the station.'

Beppe pointed a finger behind him. 'Is Dottor Vittori a suspect?' He laughed. 'That would make a great headline for BeppeInfo. *Multimillionaire kills bartender for ruining his Prada slacks*!'

Perillo's eyes opened wider.

'Sure, I know about Cesare dropping the tray. Nadia was talking about it on Friday.'

'How do you know Vittori?' Perillo asked.

'I've known him since I've been delivering the papers to the hotel during the tourist season. I can tell you that he never tips. So, is he a suspect?'

'He is not.' Perillo studied his watch again. 'What is your information?'

'I'll tell you if I'm the first one to know you've made an arrest.'

Perillo started walking. Daniele followed.

'Come on, Maresciallo, soften your heart. I have a blog to fill. Daniele, convince him to give me something. What I saw is important.'

Daniele caught up with Perillo and whispered, 'The motorcycle.'

'Ah, yes,' Perillo said with a smile at his clever brigadiere. He turned around. 'There is something you can help me with, Beppe. Cesare's motorcycle, a 1972 Ducati, has not been found. Perhaps you can ask your readers to help us find it.'

Beppe clapped. 'A treasure hunt! They'll love it. Is there a prize?'

'Certainly, an official thank-you from the Greve Carabinieri. And if the information you want to give me now will help us find Cesare's killer, I will make sure to include that in any report we send to the media.'

Beppe pumped the air with his fist. 'Mamma! Fantastic. I'll get thousands of followers.'

'Your information?' Perillo asked.

Beppe took a moment to catch his breath. Excitement always squeezed his lungs. He looked at the maresciallo and the brigadiere. Their eyes were on him. With his breath back, he straightened himself to his full height. He would take his time.

'I delivered the papers Friday morning as I do every morning. *The New York Times* international edition, *La Nazione*, and since it was Friday, *Chianti Sette*. Only a few copies since most of the guests had left. I left the papers on the big table in the front hall as I always do and went downstairs to grab a cup of coffee in the kitchen. That's where I heard Nadia tell the chef about Cesare's accident with the tray. I hung out for a few minutes knowing I'd soon have to pee. Coffee does that to me instantly. When I left the bathroom, I saw Pietro behind a column. I said, "Ciao, what are you doing here? Are you looking for Cesare?" Not a squeak out of him. He skittered off like a mouse who'd seen a cat.'

'Did you see anyone else?' Perillo asked.

'No. I left right after that. What I saw is important, isn't it? What did Pietro want from Cesare? They didn't get along. Everyone knows that. I don't get along with my uncle either. He thinks I'm wasting my time with the blog. If we find the Ducati, he'll have to flush his words down the toilet. How important is my information?'

Perillo started walking briskly towards the hotel gate. Beppe kept pace. 'You have given us information we didn't have. Thank you. As to its importance, we will have to see. Don't forget to spread the word about the Ducati. Whoever finds it must not move it or touch it and must give the information to the nearest carabinieri station. You know our number. Add it to your blog. I'm giving you a serious task. Be firm with your readers. That motorcycle is evidence in a murder investigation.'

'I will tell them, Maresciallo. Thank you for the trust.'

'Arrivederci, Beppe. Don't be too hard on your uncle. I'm sure he means well.'

Beppe mounted his bike and pedalled off.

Daniele watched him go. 'Do you think Beppe is telling the truth? He seems so hungry for attention.'

'I do. He might exaggerate things on BeppeInfo to give himself importance. He is a good, simple kid from what I hear. Implicating someone in a murder case? No. In any case, tomorrow we'll talk to Pietro and find out more. I now worry about the Ducati. Maybe giving Beppe that assignment wasn't the brightest idea.'

On the other hand, Daniele was proud of having thought of it. 'If it's still out there to be found, we've now got thirty more people looking for it. Once his followers spread the news, there will be many more.'

'That motorcycle is worth a lot of money. Whoever finds it will keep it.'

'I think whoever finds it will try to sell it. That's when I'll catch him.'

'Holy Mary, is everything done online?'

'Just about.'

As Perillo and Daniele were getting into the Alfa, a woman at the hotel entrance called out, 'Maresciallo, wait!'

Perillo turned. The woman walked swiftly towards him. 'Buongiorno, I'm Nadia, Laura's assistant. You wanted to talk to me. I have time now.'

'Ah, yes, I did.' The assistant was attractive and much older than Laura, which surprised him. Somewhere in her forties, he guessed. It couldn't be easy taking orders from someone much younger and of the same sex.

'The morning Cesare Rinaldi went missing, you went on a break between nine and ten. Laura took over at the reception desk. Is that correct?'

'Yes. I went downstairs to the kitchen to have breakfast.'

'Do you know where Laura went after you took over again at ten o'clock?'

'She said she needed some air and was going to take a walk. She looked upset.'

'When did you see her again?'

'When she relieved me for lunch at one-thirty.'

'That's a long walk.'

'Oh, no, she'd come back much earlier. She was in her office when I called her around noon about a bill.'

'You saw her come in?'

'No. There's a back entrance near the patio.'

'You called her mobile?'

'No, the hotel phone.'

'Do you like your boss?'

'She's a very good manager. I've been working here for two years. She's moody sometimes, sometimes unnecessarily sharp, but I know it has nothing to do with me. Yes, I enjoy working with her. The best part is I don't have to worry about her touching my ass every time I walk by.'

'Thank you,' Perillo said. 'No more questions for now.'

'As I work the morning shift, I didn't get a chance to get to know Cesare well. He was a nice man, and I hope you find justice for him.'

'We do too,' Perillo said and got in the car.

Daniele was already in the driver's seat, engine running, not liking what he'd heard. The fact that Laura had taken a walk was bad news. 'Maresciallo, maybe Nadia saw Pietro?'

'Ah, yes!' Perillo leant his head out of the window. Nadia was walking back to the hotel. 'Sorry, Signorina Nadia, one more question.'

Nadia swung back and stopped a couple of feet from the car, her face registering the patient look of someone used to accommodating people's whims. 'Yes, Maresciallo.'

'Do you know Cesare's nephew?'

'Yes, I know Pietro. He was often hovering around the hotel, I guess to talk to Cesare.'

'Was he hovering last Friday morning?'

'I saw him on the patio when I went to breakfast. I asked him if he needed something. He shook his head and walked away. He was here yesterday too. Is there anything else?'

'No, thank you.' Perillo sat back and buckled his seat belt. 'Good thinking, Dani,' he said, despite being annoyed he hadn't thought of asking about Pietro himself. He'd been salivating over Laura taking a walk. It made him think he had his murderer.

Daniele manoeuvred the Alfa out of the hotel car park. 'Taking a walk doesn't mean she killed him,' he said.

'Two hours gives her plenty of time to drive to the Montagliari Chapel, kill Cesare and drive back.'

He saw Daniele's jaw set in *I don't agree* mode and realised they had no time to lose.

'Stop, Daniele! We need to send Laura's car up to forensics. There's a good chance she's going to ask Nadia what she told us.'

Daniele shifted and drove the car back to the spot they had just left. 'Maresciallo, let me be the one to tell her, please.'

Perillo saw the concern in Daniele's face. 'If you wish to.' Daniele's empathy would soften the blow.

'Thank you, Maresciallo.'

Perillo remembered how Laura had lashed out in anger and felt a relief he wasn't proud of.

A red-eyed Nadia ushered Daniele into the manager's office. Laura looked up from writing in the accounts ledger Signora Lucchetti insisted on. 'Thank you, Nadia. Don't worry. I can handle this.' She waited until her assistant was gone to say, 'What else can I help you with now, Brigadiere? A confession?'

Daniele straightened his back and tried to keep a neutral expression.

The brigadiere was nervous, Laura saw. He clearly didn't want to be here. She also didn't want him here. 'It was a joke.' She smiled at him. 'I'm afraid I'm not very good at them.'

'I see, Signorina,' Daniele said.

There was no point in being sarcastic, Laura told herself. It deterred nothing. Certainly not a murder charge. She put her pen down, sat back in her chair and tucked herself into the managerial role that had always served her well. 'How can I help you?'

'The forensic team in Florence needs to take a look at your car.'

'Because I took a walk?'

'Yes, Signorina. Maybe you came back before noon? Did someone see you come back earlier? That would help you. It's a matter of timing.'

'Is it?'

'I'm sorry, Signorina Laura. We'll return the car as fast as we can. I'm truly sorry.'

Laura's fingers rummaged through a pile of keys gathered inside a pewter bowl. 'You are sweet, but don't be sorry. You are only doing your job.' She lifted her car keys.

Daniele hesitated. Her calm confused him. He'd expected anger again.

'They are yours, Brigadiere. I'll walk you to the car.' Daniele took the keys and followed her out of the back entrance of the hotel.

In the car park, Laura stopped beside a Renault, a grey one to Daniele's great relief. The car seen at the Montagliari Chapel was black.

'Tell them to treat her gently,' Laura said. 'She's twelve years old.' Walking away, she added, 'She used to belong to someone I loved.'

'Your sister?'

Laura spun around. 'How do you know I had a sister?'

'I saw her photographs at your mother's house. You looked very much alike.'

'No, she was the beauty in the family, as I'm sure my grandfather told you more than once. The beauty and the brain. You said "looked." You know she's dead.'

'I thought she could be. I'm sorry. It must have been very painful.'

'Do you have brothers or sisters?'

'I'm an only child.'

'Consider yourself lucky.' She noticed Daniele staring at her car, a question mark clearly on his face. 'The night she died, she was driving our mother's car.' Laura turned around and walked back towards the hotel.

* * *

Nico walked from the Santa Maria Novella station to Piazza della Repubblica, enjoying the cool, sunny morning. He had an appointment with Signora Lucchetti, the owner of the Hotel Bella Vista, who had surprisingly invited him for lunch. He had left Gravigna early, excusing himself at breakfast with Gogol, who had mumbled something about necessity, not pleasure. The visit was a necessity, but being with Stella for the half-hour break her work as guide at the Duomo Museum allowed her was going to be pure pleasure.

He spotted Gilli, the coffee bar Stella had chosen, and sat at an outside table facing Piazza della Repubblica. It was his first time back in the city since he'd moved to Tuscany. He'd been here with Rita a few times while visiting Tilde and Enzo in Gravigna. He'd found the medieval city with its famous piazzas and its narrow, dark streets jammed with tourists. He'd had to elbow his way through crowds in the unbearable heat. Rita had bubbled over with joy, proud to show him the beauty of Italian art in the museums and churches. He remembered welcoming the church visit. Finally, a cool, quiet place to sit, he'd said. She'd sighed and called him an ignoramus. Which he had been when they'd met. Thanks to her, a little less of one in the end.

A pair of arms wrapped themselves around his neck. 'Ciao, Zio Nico. You finally made it here.' Stella kissed both his cheeks and swung around to sit next to him. 'Where's OneWag?' She spoke English well enough to pronounce his name.

'I left him with Nelli.'

Stella took off her sunglasses and narrowed her eyes at Nico for a moment. 'OneWag loves Nelli.'

Nico ignored the implication and squeezed her hand, happy to be with her, even happier to see how radiant she looked. Except for her green eyes, she was a young replica of Tilde, with the same pale oval face, and thick chestnut hair that she'd let grow and now wore neatly tied back. The sadness she had carried with her this past year was fading. 'You look splendid.' She was wearing a boat-necked light green sweater that picked up the colour of her eyes with a silk dark blue and green scarf tied around her neck. Cuffed tan slacks completed the outfit. 'And elegant.'

'You need glasses, and you should be ashamed that the only reason you're here is a murder.'

'My eyesight is still fine, and murder is my business.'

Stella wrinkled her nose. 'That's a terrible line from some TV show.'

'That's probably where I got it. I enjoy helping Perillo with his investigations. It gives me a sense of doing some good. May I remind you that you didn't want me to visit you here. I stopped asking.'

'That was true then. Now you can come every day and buy me lunch.'

As Stella was talking, a grey-haired waiter blocked the sun. 'What will you have?' he asked Stella.

'An apricot fruit juice, two tramezzini with tuna and artichokes and later a caffè macchiato.'

'I'll have an americano,' Nico said.

The waiter nodded and left, giving them back the sun.

'I hope you don't mind my ordering so much,' Stella said. 'I won't have time for lunch. Bar Gilli is expensive, but it's peaceful. The Duomo area is a zoo. When are you coming to visit my museum? You can see the original restored Baptistry doors.'

'One day. You look happy, Stella.'

'I'm getting there. The job has helped tremendously. I love opening people's eyes to art. Dani is my favourite pupil. He only knew what he saw in Venice – Veronese, Titian, Bellini, Tintoretto, wonderful painters, but now he's wide-eyed over Raphael, Michelangelo, Leonardo. I'll stop here. Cousin Rita took you around, showed you all our treasures, didn't she?'

'Oh, yes, she did. I had to buy a new pair of sneakers.'

The sun disappeared again as the waiter put their order on the round metal table. The bill was neatly tucked under Nico's coffee cup.

'Thank you,' Stella said and bit into her tramezzino, a crustless white bread triangular sandwich that Nico had discovered was much tastier than it looked.

'Daniele is a good young man,' Nico said. 'I'm very fond of him.'

Stella pushed back a stray lock of hair from her forehead. 'Sometimes a very young man.'

'Yes,' Nico admitted, after drinking some coffee.

'That's what's so beautiful about him. He's so clean inside. He's shy, hesitant, but at the same time so open and sensitive.'

Lovely to hear that, Nico thought.

Stella finished her tramezzino and turned to look at Nico. 'Don't you agree?'

'I do. I think you give him courage. He's recording Perillo's interviews now.'

Stella laughed, covering her mouth with her hand. 'I

know.' With one tramezzino gone, Stella picked up her apricot juice and took a sip. 'It's Dani's fault I drink around three of these a day. I think about him a lot. I miss seeing him. It's wonderful to have a man listen to you, appreciate you, without trying to change you into some ideal of his own.'

'That's how a good friend should be,' Nico said. Without knowing it, Stella had just described Nelli.

'Sometimes I wonder if he's more than that to me.' Stella bit into her second tramezzino. 'I don't know. I have no idea how he feels about me. He's never tried to kiss me or even hold my hand.'

'He's been burnt too.'

'Yes, the gorgeous Rosalba. He told me all about her. Nasty bitch. Sometimes I think she's the one holding me back. She crushed him. He's so vulnerable.'

'He's been over her a long time now.'

'He says he is. Maybe I'm just scared to make another mistake and hurt both of us.' Stella wiped her hands on a small paper napkin. 'What about you, Zio Nico? Are you happy?' She crossed her arms and leant them on her knees. 'Mamma told me you and Nelli aren't seeing each other anymore.'

Nico felt Stella's large green eyes pierce through him. 'Nelli deserves a man who can love her fully. I can't.'

'Why not?'

The waiter appeared with Stella's caffè macchiato, giving Nico a moment to think about his answer.

Stella drank the coffee down, her eyes still on Nico.

Nico sighed. 'I feel disloyal to Rita, too old for romance, and I don't know what else I feel. I've got used to being single. Life is less complicated that way.'

Stella leant her head closer and kissed Nico's cheek. He could smell the coffee. 'Dear Zio, you are, as you Americans say, full of bullshit.' Her eyes met his. 'You'll forgive me for saying that?'

Nico smiled. 'Of course. How am I full of BS?'

'You know perfectly well that complications are what make life worth living. You're just scared. So am I. Maybe we should just get over it and complicate life.'

'Here's another American saying, Stella bella. Easier said than done.'

Stella tilted her head back and laughed.

A happy sound he hadn't heard from a woman in a long time. He missed it.

Laughter over, Stella stood up and rearranged her scarf around her neck. 'I'm sorry, Zio Nico.'

He got to his feet, wanting to hold her back to talk some more about the complications of life, love included.

'I have to go back to work.' They hugged, kissed cheeks. 'Thanks for my lunch. Next time, the Duomo Museum.' She slipped on her sunglasses and started walking. She called back, 'Donatello's *Penitent Magdalene* will take your breath away. Ciao.'

He waved back. Maybe next time. With Nelli.

Signora Lucchetti lived on a large piazza next to the church of Santo Spirito. Nico was early for his one o'clock appointment and wandered through the piazza, looking at what was being offered – stands selling handmade leather bags, ceramics, old jewellery, small antiques, used furniture, colourful vintage clothing. Maybe he could bring back something for Tilde. Some of the vendors were already packing up. When he turned the corner at one end to walk back up to where he'd started, a table displaying a few ceramics caught his attention. The vendor, a young Black woman, smiled at him when he stopped to look. 'They just came out of the kiln yesterday. I did well this morning. I only have a few left. I'll have more next week.'

He smiled back. 'I don't live here.' His eyes fell on a big, tall, grey mug with thin, blue-coloured stripes running down the body. 'It will hold a lot of beer,' the woman said.

Nico pictured a different use and bought it. At the flower stand he bought a small pot of asters to thank his hostess for lunch.

'How very kind of you,' Signora Lucchetti said from her brocaded armchair in the middle of a large room lined with shelves filled with books and a vast collection of old maiolica pottery. Nico had seen broken shards of maiolica for sale at the market below. A small, elegant woman with perfectly coiffed hair, she had a surprisingly strong voice for her eighty-some years. 'I did not expect a pot of flowers for answering questions about poor Cesare.'

'I did not expect lunch for asking,' Nico said in a loud voice, suspecting she was hard of hearing.

Signora Lucchetti smiled with her water-blue eyes, her hand reaching for the double strand of pearls that hung over a pearl-grey sweater the same colour as her hair. She was wearing a darker grey skirt, matching grey support stockings and black oxfords.

A woman from another era, Nico thought, standing awkwardly in the middle of the room, not knowing whether he should hand her the pot of asters or place them on one of the many small tables scattered around the room. He had left the wrapped mug in the foyer.

'It's a pleasure to share a meal with a man,' Signora Lucchetti said. 'With any good person to be truthful. Occasionally I convince one of my women friends to sit at my table, but they, as I, prefer the comforts of their own home. It's what age does to us.' She turned sharply to the woman in a maid's uniform, who had ushered Nico in, and stood by the big double doors of the foyer. 'Adele! Take the flowers into the kitchen. I'm sure they need watering.'

Nico met Adele halfway and handed her the pot.

Signora Lucchetti waved to him. 'Do come and sit down close to me. I detest the hum of my hearing aid, so you will have to speak up. The sofa is close and will give you a nice view of the church.'

Nico walked across the wide Persian rug and sat at the end of a pale blue silk-covered sofa.

Signora Lucchetti nodded her approval, looking at the fractured view two long windows gave her. 'I find the plainness of the facade comforting. As a young girl, I regretted immensely the fact that I was not pretty. My mother tried with great conviction to convince me that what counted was who I was inside. She would use the church as an example. Plain outside, but inside it holds the beauty of God.' She clasped her hands together on her lap. 'I think we should get the sad business of Cesare's death over with before lunch. Now, as an American, I expect you would like a drink? I do have whiskey. I take a sip before going to bed. I find it helps with my sleep.'

'No, thank you, Signora.'

'Maresciallo Perillo has assured me that you, with your

past expertise, have been of invaluable help to him. I am to speak to you as if I were speaking directly to him. I shall do so, although I don't think what I have to say will be of any help.' She sat back and raised her chin to Nico.

Nico leant towards her. 'How did you come to hire Cesare as your bartender?'

'The bartender who had worked for my father, may God bless his soul, quit when I took over, saying he wasn't going to be ordered around by a woman, especially not a pretty one in her forties. At least he waited to leave until the end of the season. I suppose Cesare heard about it and walked in one day and offered himself. He claimed he'd bartended in Germany. Maybe he had. I didn't care. I had bought a good bartending book in case I needed to fill in. I handed him the book and hired him.

'You see, Cesare was very handsome then. I always hired good-looking staff. It brightens the tone of the hotel as much as beautiful flowers do.'

'Did you learn anything about his private life?'

'He was very attached to the property his father had left him and looked after the vineyard his father had started. He'd take care of it every day before work. It was a small one, giving him only enough wine for personal use. I'd get a few bottles each year. I'm afraid the wine wasn't very good, but he was proud of it. "Vino locale," he called it, without bothering to label it. It was odd that his father had left him the land, as he was the younger son. I must have remarked about it to him. I don't remember what I said, but I do remember his answer, "*My father had a son who had not found his way yet.*" There were rumours he was gay and maybe his father believed them and didn't approve, then again Cesare had been away many years. Inheriting the land would keep him home.'

'Did he have friends?'

'I don't know of any. He wasn't outgoing, but the guests loved him. He had a knack for understanding people. Guests would spend many nights glued to a stool unburdening themselves to Cesare. He loved to tell them he'd been behind that bar since he was eighteen, which was nonsense. I think he wanted it to be true. His years in Germany must not have been easy. I asked him if he was gay once. "*Does it matter?*" he asked me back.' Signora Lucchetti looked up at the frescoed ceiling.

Nico waited a moment before asking, 'Did he give you an answer?'

She lowered her head, her eyes on Nico. 'I answered, "*It matters because I'm in love with you.*" I was. He thanked me and said he was flattered, but he was still in love with someone else. I don't know if that someone was a woman or a man, or if he just said it to end any hope I might have had.'

Nico didn't know what to say.

A gurgling laugh from Signora Lucchetti broke the silence. 'Here I am, in the presence of a stranger, revealing all my secrets like a young girl. I should be ashamed of myself, but I am not. Not caring what people think is one of the few advantages of my age. I'm rather hungry and you must be starving. Do you have any more questions, or can I tell Adele to throw the tortellini in the broth?'

'You hired Laura Benati and two years later you left her in charge. You obviously think very highly of her. What can you tell me of her relationship with Cesare?'

Signora Lucchetti reached for the silver bell sitting on the side table and rang it. 'I'll answer that while we have our soup. I'm hungry.'

Adele appeared from another door. 'Yes, Signora?'

'Throw!' Signora Lucchetti commanded.

Adele disappeared and Signora Lucchetti held out a hand for Nico. After he helped her up, she laced her hand in the crook of his arm. 'Through there,' she said, pointing her chin towards yet another door across the room.

She didn't wait for the soup to answer Nico's question. As they slowly made their way to the dining room, she said, 'Cesare had known Laura since she was a child. He suggested I hire her. I think he wanted to help her. He told me she was having a hard time accepting the loss of her sister a few months earlier. She wanted to immerse herself in work. I wasn't sure she was emotionally strong enough to handle the hard work and all the petty complaints guests make, but Cesare insisted she was the right person for the job. He was right. I always thought they were close because they recognised each other's wounds.'

When they reached the oval dining table, she unhooked her arm from Nico's. 'Thank you. I can walk perfectly well by myself, but a walk arm-in-arm with a man is more enjoyable.'

Nico pushed back the chair at the head of the table. After seeing she was seated, he sat down to her right. He felt as though he had walked into the set of a historical movie. The walls of this room were covered in gold-coloured silk with paintings of landscapes in heavy gilded frames. On the table a white embroidered tablecloth – a specialty of Florentine artisans – a white bowl holding a white orchid plant, flowered plates, gleaming silver flatware and etched wine and water glasses, another Tuscan art. The water glasses had been filled. A graceful glass decanter held red wine. He hoped his manners were passing muster with Signora Lucchetti.

Not long after, Adele came in cradling a hot soup tureen. With her free hand, she served two ladlesful of broth and tortellini to Signora Lucchetti, then to Nico.

Signora Lucchetti pointed to the small silver bowl in front of her. 'Please help yourself to the Parmigiano. I prefer without. And please have some wine. I only have a glass for dinner.'

'Thank you.' Nico helped himself and asked, 'You have had no regrets hiring Laura?'

'None. I can enjoy my beautiful home and not worry about the hotel. Of course, I taught her the hotel business, but Cesare deserves a great deal of credit. They trusted each other. Trust is key in any relationship, don't you agree?' She stopped to have a spoonful of the soup.

'Yes.' Nico followed her example.

After she had patted her mouth with a lace napkin, she asked, 'Has the Ducati been found?'

'Not yet. We're still looking.'

'That is a shame.' She spoke between spoonsful. 'It was a beloved possession of my husband's. After he died, it sat in the building's basement for years. I'm not quite sure why I didn't give it away. I wasn't that fond of Iacopo. A few of my husband's friends even asked to buy it from me.' She looked up at Nico and her cheeks puckered into a smile. 'I'm so glad I did keep it. I gave it to Cesare shortly before I met Laura. He was working under a black cloud for several weeks. He was without a car. Something had happened to it. I forget what exactly. Giving Cesare the Ducati and hiring Laura were the two best decisions of my life. Please find it. He would be devastated knowing it was lost.'

Nico had wondered how Cesare had been able to afford such an expensive motorcycle. 'We are trying.'

'He loved that motorcycle so much, he wanted it to be buried with him. Has the funeral been planned?'

'No. His body hasn't been released yet.' Nico was about to ask another question when he heard a buzz from under the table.

Adele appeared quickly and removed their empty soup plates and spoons.

Nico waited until Adele had left the room to ask, 'Did he ever talk about the years he was away? Mention where he'd been?'

'Bartending in Germany was all he said, and that was when I was interviewing him for the job. I did ask a few times, but he made it clear he didn't want to talk about those years. I assumed he was ashamed he'd abandoned his family for so long.' She sat back in her armchair and took a long, slow breath. 'I haven't talked so much for a very long time. I hope you have exhausted your questions.'

'I have. Thank you for answering them.'

'You are most welcome.' She sat back up. 'Let us now concentrate on the good food Adele feeds us: veal scallopine in a lemon and caper sauce and buttered string beans. That is what I asked for. Dessert will be a surprise for both of us.'

Nico got back to Gravigna by four-thirty, parked the car, waved hello to Sandro and Jimmy as he passed by. As he walked across the piazza, the Bench Boys waved to him. He waved back, eager to get to Nelli's studio, ostensibly to pick up OneWag.

'Any news?' Gustavo asked. He was wearing a battered fedora and a coat against the sudden cold.

'Not yet.' He kept walking.

'She's not there,' another voice said.

Nico stopped in his tracks and turned to the four men. Ettore, bundled in two sweaters and a knitted cap, returned his look with a satisfied grin. He enjoyed knowing things.

'Who isn't there? Tilde?'

Ettore raised a finger towards the cemetery. 'She took the dog.'

Nelli then. What was she doing there? Her parents were buried in Panzano.

As soon as Nico reached the gate, OneWag ran to meet him with a series of yelping barks. Nico picked him up. The dog smelt of turpentine. Nelli was standing by Rita's grave, dressed in her usual painting clothes, a large red shawl covering her shoulders. Seeing Nico, she walked slowly down on the gravel path that cut through the graves. If he asked her what she was doing there, she would tell him, even though he would think her foolish. 'Ciao, Nico, how was your visit with Stella?'

'Fun.' He ran his hand down OneWag's soft fur. 'How was your day?'

Now she stood before him, looking up at his face, her long grey braid flopping over one shoulder, her face serious and at the same time luminous. Nico felt the urge to wrap her in his arms. OneWag got the hug instead.

'My day was productive. I was able to finish the portrait

of your wonderful dog. I'm proud of it. I think I caught his street-dog spirit.'

OneWag was squirming. Nico put him down. He settled in the space between their feet, looking up to check for any progress. 'I'll buy it sight unseen,' Nico said.

'I won't let you. He goes in my next show and he's not for sale.'

Was she that angry with him? 'Did you get my text about dinner tomorrow night?'

'I did. Thank you. I would prefer to eat out.'

Damn! He'd been counting on privacy, on the chance they could finally clear the thick fog between them, talk out their different expectations. She obviously didn't want the fog to clear. She'd been the one to stop seeing him, saying their relationship was too confusing for her. When he'd asked for details, she'd said she was tired of thinking about the two of them.

'Sotto Il Fico would be wonderful,' Nelli said. 'I love the food there and Tilde told me she no longer needs you to help, so we can sit and enjoy the night lights. If it is cold, we'll put on layers.'

'Is this Tilde's idea?'

'All mine. I think we need to have dinner together in neutral territory.' His home would bring back too many memories of their naked bodies exploring each other. It would only weaken her resolve to resist him. Lovemaking clarified nothing.

Nico reached out and stroked her cheek. 'If that's what you want, okay, although I'm not sure Tilde's restaurant is neutral territory. She's been tough on me.'

She stepped away from his touch. 'It's a place where we both feel welcome.'

'Eight o'clock then?'

'Perfect.'

Nico used the empty hand to slip the small bag from his arm and hold it out. 'I thought you might like this. I found it at the market in Piazza del Carmine.'

Nelli quickly unwrapped it and turned the large mug in her hands. 'It's lovely. Thank you.'

'I thought you could use it for your paintbrushes.'

Nelli leant forward and kissed his cheek. 'Sotto Il Fico, eight o'clock tomorrow. Ciao.' She bent down, gave OneWag a quick scratch on his head and walked out of the cemetery.

Nico walked over to Rita's grave. A small pot of pink dahlias sat next to his vase filled with the badly arranged chrysanthemums. 'Nelli is a good woman,' he silently told Rita. 'I care for her.'

OneWag swished his tail in approval.

CHAPTER TEN

Gogol aimed questioning eyes at Nico, who was drinking his americano. They were sitting at their usual table by the half-open French doors of the café. Outside the sky was grey, and a chilly breeze swirled leaves along the piazza.

Nico put his cup down and returned Gogol's gaze. 'Go on, I'm listening.' Sandro and Jimmy were both behind the counter taking care of their early morning customers.

'"Your condition raises not scorn, but sorrow in me." "How long lasts the fire in a woman's love if not rekindled often by eye or touch?"'

This time Nico understood the whole quote. He let out an exasperated grunt. 'You keep blaming me.' He leant over the table and spoke in a low voice, not to be overheard. 'I'm not the only one who isn't rekindling. What quote from the illustrious poet does Nelli get?'

Gogol chuckled. '"Open your eyes to what I answer."'

He bit into his lard crostino and chewed slowly, making Nico wait.

'While you think of something wonderfully complimentary for her, I'll exonerate myself. I saw your friend last night. I gave her a present I bought in Florence. We're having dinner tonight. That should satisfy you for now.'

Gogol dropped the remaining corner of his crostino onto the floor where OneWag was waiting. 'To the luminous lady, I said, "Here one must leave all distrust behind."'

'Thank you. Well said.'

Gogol gave Nico a pointed look.

Nico laughed, suddenly feeling better. 'I know. It applies to me too.'

'Ehi!' a man called out from the counter. 'Ciao, Salvatore.'

Nico turned to look at the entrance. Perillo walked in, wearing jeans and his zipped-up suede jacket. He raised a hand in salute to the man who had called out to him, showed two fingers to Jimmy and walked over to Nico and Gogol's table. 'Buongiorno, Signor Gogol. I hope the morning finds you well.'

'For now.'

Under the table, OneWag sniffed Perillo's shoes. Tobacco. No food.

'Ciao, Perillo,' Nico said. 'What brings you here?'

Perillo pushed back a chair and sat down. 'A missing report on Signora Lucchetti.'

'I thought it could wait until this morning.' Last night his mind had been elsewhere.

'Was the lunch good?'

'Very, ending with a dessert I'd never even heard of.'

Sandro was walking over with Perillo's double espresso. 'What dessert can that be?'

'A mound of chestnut puree with whipped cream.'

Sandro put the coffee down in front of Perillo. 'That's a Mont Blanc. Monte Bianco is the highest mountain in the Alps.'

'It was surprisingly light. I enjoyed it.'

'I don't like chestnuts,' Gogol declared, hugging his old coat around him. 'They announce the coming of darker days and bitter cold.'

'That's true,' Perillo said, 'but they are good roasted.' He looked up at Sandro. 'We need to talk. Come down to the station today or tomorrow.'

'No.' Sandro sat down opposite Perillo. 'I have nothing to say to you, Salvatore.' He folded his hands on the table. 'Last Friday, Jimmy was still in Florence, and I was manning the café from six o'clock in the morning until we closed at nine in the evening.' His eyes stayed fixed on Perillo's face. 'If you don't believe me, you can ask all my regulars, Nico being one of them. I may be a possessive, jealous bastard, but I'm not a killer. That said, can I offer you some grappa for that double espresso that's getting cold?'

'Are you trying to bribe an officer of the law?' Perillo asked, pretending he was offended. In reality he admired Sandro's nerve.

'I'm offering a free grappa to a man who has been a good customer for many years.'

'Thank you, Sandro,' Perillo said after emptying his espresso cup in three sips. 'I'll accept your offer another time.'

'Whenever you wish.' Sandro stood up and walked with a straight back to stand behind the counter.

Perillo shifted his gaze to Nico. 'I'll cross Sandro off for now. Did Signora Lucchetti offer anything interesting besides a good lunch?'

'Let's talk later.' The café was filling up.

'Good idea. I have news too.'

Gogol slowly turned to face Perillo. '"Do not fix your mind on one place only."'

Feeling chastised, Perillo frowned at the old man. 'How do you know where my mind fixes?'

A hint of a smile appeared on Gogol's lips, not enough of one to show how much he enjoyed surprising people. 'It is good advice for everyone.'

'Well, that it is.' *Especially for an officer of the law*, Perillo thought, although wanting the investigation over with made it harder. He got to his feet. 'Another drive to Castellina is waiting for me. Arrivederci, until the next time.'

Nico understood that Castellina meant Pietro. 'Have a fruitful trip.'

At the door Perillo lifted his hand to his ear.

Nico nodded.

Gogol reached his arm across the table and patted Nico's hand. '"It is time now to leave this wood."'

Nico returned the pat. 'I agree.' He stood up and reached for his wallet. Perillo had left without paying. 'See you tomorrow.'

Gogol raised himself slowly and gave his standard response. 'Tomorrow, if I live.'

'You will.'

* * *

Nico sat in the discomfort of his Fiat 500 parked behind the café and picked up his phone. OneWag settled down on the forbidden passenger seat.

'Ciao, put me on speaker so Daniele can hear what a euro pincher his boss is.'

'Done,' Perillo said, 'but I've ordered Brigadiere Donato not to listen on pain of having to forego any future tape recordings.'

'It's now eight double espressos you owe me.'

'I'll pay when it's ten.'

'Ha! Now, for my Signora Lucchetti report. It was Cesare who insisted she hire Laura, despite her having doubts Laura was up to it. She thought they were close because they recognised each other's wounds.'

'Laura lost a sister,' Perillo said. 'What were Cesare's wounds, did she say?'

'A lost love, I think. She was upset we hadn't found the Ducati yet. It used to belong to her husband. She gave it to Cesare when something happened to his car.'

Perillo whistled. 'That is a very generous gift.'

'She was in love with him. She urged us to find the Ducati so he can be buried with it. When are they going to release the body?'

'No word yet. Anything else?'

'That's the extent of it,' Nico said. 'What new information have you got on Pietro?'

Perillo let Daniele answer.

'So, Pietro was at the hotel that morning.' Nico turned sideways and stretched his legs out of the car. 'That is interesting news. I'm glad Beppe found you.' He tried to keep reproach out of his voice. Perillo was getting sloppy or lazy. Nico was beginning to miss having the authority that came with carrying a police badge.

Perillo heard something off in Nico's voice. 'I know. I should have listened to you and called Beppe right away. If nothing else, it would have saved us another trip to Castellina.'

'Lesson learnt, as I heard almost every day on my first job,' Nico replied.

'What job was that?' Daniele asked.

'When I was fifteen, I worked as a stock boy in a supermarket for the summer. I used to stock things in the wrong place. My boss would catch me, show me the right place and say, "Lesson learnt."'

'That's a phrase I can use,' Daniele said.

'Very interesting, Nico, but I have something even more interesting to tell you. When Laura's assistant returned to the reception desk after her break, Laura left the hotel, two hours went by before she answered Nadia's call on the hotel phone.'

'That gives her enough time to meet Cesare, kill him, but not dispose of the body in Jimmy's boot.'

'Someone from forensics is coming to pick up her car. It's grey, not black, but it is best to check it out. One of my men has her car keys and is making sure no one comes near it.'

'Good,' Nico said. 'Let me know what Pietro says.' He clicked off, tucked his legs inside the car and turned on the motor. Instead of jumping up and wiggling with happiness that they were finally going somewhere, OneWag pretended to sleep.

Nico noticed. 'Come on, buddy, we're off.' He had

stopped thinking that talking to the dog was crazy. He needed to go to the Coop to shop for tonight's dinner with Nelli at Sotto Il Fico. As long as he kept his mind on food, he knew he wouldn't worry about what to say to her.

OneWag, for once, got to stay on the passenger seat.

Once they'd arrived in Castellina, Perillo skipped the espresso stops and the renowned cheese shop to head straight to Via delle Volte. The front door of the Pennington house was closed.

'You go and bring him out here,' Perillo said. 'I don't want an audience.' What he really didn't want was walking across a floor covered in wood dust, discarded nails and pieces of wood just waiting to trip him up. 'Be careful.'

'I will,' Daniele answered, wondering how he would respond if Pietro assaulted him. He'd never been good at fighting back. He knocked and got no answer.

'To hell with manners, Dani. Just walk in.'

Daniele did as he was told and was overwhelmed by the smell of paint. The small room was empty, the tile floor pristine, the three walls a soft white. He was about to shout, 'Is anyone here?' when he heard banging from above. He crossed the room, turned a corner and was met by a concrete staircase. 'Hello?'

'Get out!' a male voice shouted. 'This is a worksite. Private property.'

'Brigadiere Donato of the Greve Carabinieri,' Daniele shouted back as he climbed the stairs. Halfway up he stopped. A huge man was standing at the top of the stairs.

'Stop where you are,' the man said in a kinder voice.

'We're laying down floor tile. I'm the supervisor here. How can I help you?'

'I'm looking for Pietro Rinaldi.'

Someone laughed. The supervisor shook his head. 'If you find him let me know. He hasn't shown up in two days.'

Daniele let out a loud breath. This he didn't need. In the last case, a suspect he'd gone to pick up had also disappeared. The maresciallo was going to erupt, maybe even think he brought bad luck. He'd heard that a lot of southerners were superstitious.

He walked up four more steps. The supervisor stared down at him and didn't budge, but Daniele was now high enough to see the floor through the iron rails of the banister. Three men were on their knees – one spreading mortar with a trowel, two laying terracotta tiles in a fish pattern. 'Does anyone know where Rinaldi went?' He was mustering hope.

Two men shook their heads. The mortar man sat up with a grin. 'He was going to make a fortune. That's what he said the other night.'

The fortune had to be the sale of his land, Daniele thought. 'Did he say where he was going?'

'Maybe he would have, but I razzed him. Ever since his wife divorced him, all he can think of is money. We've all had enough of his feeling sorry for himself.'

The supervisor twisted his head back. 'Stop spouting, Mario. The mortar doesn't stay wet all day.' His head rotated back to look down at Daniele. 'Brigadiere, if you have any more questions, you'll have to ask them after work. We quit at four.'

Daniele fumbled in his back pocket for his trusted notebook and Bic. 'I need everyone's full name, address and telephone number, please.'

After a muttered curse, the supervisor obliged.

Daniele carefully wrote everything down. 'Thank you,' he said and walked back down, steeling himself for what was to come.

As he stepped back into the sunlight, Daniele shook his head at Perillo and willed his ears shut to the flow of curses pouring out of the maresciallo's mouth.

Tilde walked into the restaurant kitchen where Nico was pouring hot polenta onto a ridged cookie sheet. 'What are you doing?'

'Fried polenta with sauteed porcini mushrooms, garlic and parsley. My new item on the menu tonight. Enzo said you wouldn't mind.' He took a spatula hanging from the wall and smoothed out the polenta to cover the sheet.

'Nelli might like something else on the menu.'

Nico looked up, spatula in hand. 'Oh. You know.'

'She called me to tell me she was looking forward to eating outside, even in the cold.' Tilde leant back against the sink and smiled at Nico. 'I guess you'll have to keep her warm.'

Nico frowned.

'I've made the courgette lasagne; I know she likes that.'

'Well, Nelli can have whatever she wants, but I know she loves porcini mushrooms and fried polenta. I just combined the two. I'll get here early and cut the cold polenta.'

'And leave me to fry it.'

Nico pecked Tilde's cheek. 'It's for Nelli. I've made plenty of sauce for other guests.'

'Well, we'll see which dish she prefers. Yours or mine.' She raised her index finger. 'No telling her the polenta dish is yours.'

'I promise.' Nico's phone rang. He looked at the screen. 'Daniele,' he said, surprised, and walked out of the kitchen. Perillo liked to do the talking. On the terrace, he asked, 'Ciao. Is the boss now passing the reporting job onto you?'

'No. I thought you'd want to know.' Daniele hesitated. Taking the initiative didn't always go down well with the maresciallo.

'I do want to know, Dani. What did Pietro say?'

'Nothing. He hasn't shown up for work the past two days, and he's not answering his phone.'

'Oh, shit. Where's Perillo?'

'Probably smoking and downing espressos corrected with grappa. I mean no disrespect by that.'

'I'm sure you're a hundred percent right. Did you check if Pietro was at home, feeling lazy or sick in bed?'

'I went on my own, praying I'd find him. He didn't answer. I talked to the signora who had told us where to find him last time. Wednesday evening, she was watering her plants on the windowsill and heard the front door of her building shut with a bang. When she looked down, she saw Pietro with a backpack walking away. I knocked at other doors in case someone knew something, but no one answered. Everyone goes to work in the building except her. She also said I'd be wasting my time coming back to question them. Pietro was a new tenant and wasn't liked. He was always complaining. She gave me his ex-wife's telephone number. She now lives in San Casciano. Should I call her?'

'There's no harm in it, but I would wait for Perillo to calm down first. Go find him and get him to treat you to that apricot drink you love so much. You've got Stella hooked on it too.'

'Really?'

'That's what she said.' Nico heard a short laughing sound. 'Make sure Perillo gets a search warrant for Pietro's apartment. It might give us a clue as to where he went. Pietro leaving doesn't necessarily mean he's our murderer. Instead of running away, he might be running towards something. He could be at Cesare's house, now that it's finally his.'

'No, it's still sealed.'

'Of course. Thanks, Dani, for letting me know. Go find your boss before he kills himself with cigarettes.' Nico clicked off and walked back into the kitchen.

Tilde was licking a spoon. 'I was checking your porcini sauce for salt.'

'Oh, really. Does it need three more grains or five?'

Tilde laughed and dropped the spoon in the sink. 'Bravo. It's perfect.'

'For salt or taste?'

'Both.'

'Thank you. Perfect is what I aimed for.'

'But Nelli might still prefer my courgette lasagne.'

'I bet you twenty euros.'

'Done. Now go home and ask Rocco to turn you into a handsome prince for tonight.'

'He doesn't have a wand.'

'Buy him one and let me get some work done. People are coming in.'

'I'll stay if you need me.'

'You've made enough of a mess already. Ciao, Nico. Be wise tonight, okay?'

'I'll try.'

Out on the street, Nico whistled for OneWag. He knew wisdom didn't come easily, but maybe he was finally ready to run towards something good . . . instead of running away.

When Perillo came back down to his office after lunch, Daniele was hanging up the landline. 'Maresciallo, the—'

Perillo held up his hand. 'If it is bad news, it can wait ten minutes. My stomach needs to process Ivana's superb lunch, of which I will give you the only detail that would interest you – roasted potatoes with garlic and rosemary. Yes, I have calmed down. The restorative power of good food and good company is far superior to caffeine and grappa. I can see from your face you are relieved. You checked Cesare's house?'

'I did. He wasn't there, Maresciallo.'

'Salvatore, Dani. Salvatore. We are a team, and we will find Signor Pietro wherever he is hiding. We have set the search for him in motion. We have a search warrant for his apartment thanks to you asking for one right away. The locksmith has been successful in opening Pietro's front door. Was that Dino on the phone? Has he found a photo of Pietro?'

'It was the company that runs the surveillance videos for Villa Costanza. The videos will be delivered sometime this afternoon.'

'Finally.' Perillo lifted his suede jacket from the back of his chair. 'Come on, Dani, off to the café next door. My treat.' On the way out Perillo stuck his head in the back office. Vince shot up from his chair, quickly swallowing the last of his lunch. 'Maresciallo.'

'Let me know if Dino calls.' Perillo shrugged on his jacket. 'If you're done with eating, I'll bring back an espresso.'

Vince grinned. 'Much obliged. Three sugars please.'

'I know. I know.'

Outside it was a typical autumn day, with the sun shining and a light wind cooling the air. Perillo took out a cigarette. As he lit it, he sensed Daniele stiffen with disapproval. 'I'm trying, Dani, but it is hard.'

'It must be. The only thing I have ever tried to give up was my addiction to chocolate for Lent. I was miserable.'

'Miserable only for forty days. Did they say how many videos are coming?'

'Thirty-six.'

'Shit! They sent twenty-four hours of videos.'

Daniele followed Perillo into the café. 'No, Maresciallo—'

'Maresciallo, the usual?' the barista asked.

'Yes, and you, Dani? Apricot juice?'

'A hot cocoa. It's chilly.' He was in shirtsleeves.

'We'll take it outside.' To Perillo's great regret, smoking was no longer allowed inside. He walked back out.

Daniele joined him. 'The company is sending—'

'Stop them. I only want the videos from six o'clock in the evening until six o'clock the next morning.'

'That is exactly what they are sending.' Daniele stepped away from the smoke Perillo was exhaling. 'There are six cameras overlooking the car park and each video runs for two hours. It adds up to thirty-six videos we have to look at.'

'Jesus! It will take us hours.'

'Maybe the murderer put the body in Jimmy's boot early on.'

Perillo looked at his half-smoked cigarette and squashed it down in an ashtray resting on a café table. 'You always look on the bright side, Dani. I wish that I could say that made two of us.'

'You could try, Ma—'

A look from Perillo stopped him for a moment. 'You could try, Salvatore. I bet it's much easier than giving up smoking.'

'For some. Let's drink up.' The bar boy had just placed the espresso and cocoa on a table behind him. 'Vittori's guest, Sirio Reni, is expecting us. For this visit we'll need to put on our uniforms.'

Sirio Reni was waiting for them in a small sitting room just off the large entrance hall of the hotel. He stood up as Perillo and Daniele walked in. Reni looked like a younger replica of Vittori. Same expensive clothes, hair gelled back, face tanned. Reni held out his hand.

Perillo shook it and introduced himself and Daniele. On the way over, Daniele had given him what information he had found on Reni and his company, EOLO. 'Thank you for taking the time to answer a few questions.'

'Yes, of course,' Reni said with an accommodating smile. He sat back down on the leather armchair. Perillo faced him from the opposite armchair. 'Brigadiere Donato will be recording our conversation. I hope you don't mind.'

'Not in the least. I record myself all the time. EOLO,

S.r.l., is young and still small. I go around Europe giving speeches to potential investors.'

'You are in the wind business.'

'Yes, of course. The name tells it all. Eolo, the god of wind. I sell wind turbines built in China. There is a lot of competition, but mine are less expensive and just as good. Italy, for instance, needs to install many more turbines in order to solve all the electrical problems of this country.'

'I agree,' Perillo said. 'My wife can't turn on the dishwasher and the washing machine at the same time. Even using a hairdryer can blow a fuse.'

'Exactly my point,' Reni said, recrossing his legs. The smile came back. 'I don't suppose you are interested in investing. I accept smaller amounts.'

Perillo laughed. 'That would be difficult on my salary. You were Dottor Vittori's guest in this hotel last Thursday evening, correct?'

'I was.'

'You are friends?'

'Business acquaintances.'

'You were trying to get him to invest in your company?'

'Is this germane to your inquiry into that poor man's death?'

'I like to have a complete picture of the people involved. You don't have to answer, as Dottor Vittori mentioned you might be doing business together.'

'Then why ask?'

'The answer always tells me something.'

Reni recrossed his legs. 'Then you will learn that I am impatient. Can you get to the point of this visit?'

Perillo sat up, hands on his thighs. Reni seemed nervous.

'Of course. After dinner you and your guest sat for some time at the hotel bar. The bartender, the late Cesare Rinaldi, was serving you your drinks when he suddenly dropped the tray, spilling the drinks on, I believe, both of you.'

'Mostly on Dottor Vittori, who took it very badly. I was frankly surprised at how he berated the poor bartender. It was only vodka after all. Clear liquid.'

'Was the spill caused by something Dottor Vittori said to the bartender?'

'No, the spill was my fault. I had stretched out my leg and Cesare tripped on it. Vittori reacted very quickly, and so I refrained from mentioning the incident was my fault. It would only have made him look bad, which wouldn't have been good for me.'

And the hell with Cesare, Perillo thought. 'I understand.'

'Can you? I doubt it. As a carabiniere, you have the power of the army behind you. You have a ladder you can climb, from brigadiere to maresciallo to captain and so on. You may have climbed as far as you wish, but you are part of an ordered society.'

In a quiet voice, Daniele interrupted, 'Murder isn't order.'

Reni looked at Daniele as if he had forgotten he was there. 'But you find the culprit and restore order. You are not fending for yourself, trying to make a living, constantly having to kick the hyenas away to create something you can be proud of.'

'You seem to have succeeded,' Perillo said, puzzled by Reni's unexpected outburst.

'Yes, I think so, but it's taken years and an enormous amount of work.'

'I congratulate you then,' Perillo said. 'I'm glad to hear

there's no cutoff age for success. To go back to last Thursday night, the hotel did not have you down as spending the night. Why did you?'

'Dottor Vittori and I talked well into the night, in his sitting room. I started not to feel well. Too much vodka, probably. He didn't want me to drive back to Florence. No one was at the reception desk, so he picked up a key he'd seen hanging there for days and gave it to me. The next morning, I apologised to the manager and paid for the room. I waited to say goodbye to Vittori, but he didn't come down and I had appointments to keep in Florence. Is there anything else?'

'Just a curiosity on my part, which you might be able to satisfy. During the time you spent next to the reception desk, did you notice an iPhone lying there for anyone to pick up?'

'Not for anyone to pick up. At least not at first. When I reached the reception desk, the manager asked her assistant to wait as she'd misplaced her phone. She went off somewhere and came back with it a few minutes later. The assistant went off. I paid my bill and waited for Dottor Vittori to come down for about fifteen minutes. When I left, I noticed she'd put her phone down on the desk. Did someone steal it?'

Instead of answering, Perillo asked, 'How long will you be staying here?'

'As long as Dottor Vittori needs me.'

Perillo stood up. 'Thank you for your time. You have been most helpful. I hope your wind turbines will let my wife blow-dry her hair without fear.'

Reni met Perillo's hope with a wide smile. 'They will. If

either of you win the lottery, remember EOLO, S.r.l. It's an excellent investment.'

'Ah, there you are.' Dottor Vittori was standing under the arched entrance to the room. 'Buonasera, Maresciallo.'

'Buonasera.'

'May I take Signor Reni away from you? You have had him long enough.'

'Just the right amount, but I do have a quick question for you.'

'Ask. I have nothing to hide from Signor Reni.'

'On Friday morning, did you see Pietro Rinaldi at the hotel?'

'Alas, yes. He stopped me as I was leaving the breakfast room. He wanted an advance. I refused. Come, Sirio, we'll talk in the bar room. It's empty.'

'Thank you both for your time,' Perillo said, watching Reni get up and follow Vittori. 'Arrivederci.' He got no response.

'Laura didn't tell us she'd misplaced her phone,' Perillo said as they walked to the car park.

'That's what gave Pietro the chance to text Cesare on her phone,' Daniele responded.

It also gave Laura time to send that text, Perillo thought. 'Maybe, but now we have two witnesses asserting Laura's phone was available on the desk. They both had a chance, while she was dealing with other guests, to send that text. Laura obviously isn't careful with her phone.'

Daniele happily nodded in agreement and unlocked the Alfa. 'Don't you think Reni's outburst was odd?'

'I was puzzled at first.' Perillo opened the door to the passenger side and sat down. He waited for Daniele to get in. 'But it must be very demeaning to be in your sixties and asking people to buy your idea.'

'I understand that Reni's angry because he thinks he deserved better,' Daniele said. 'He didn't want to have to wait so long and work so hard to get somewhere, but why tell us? What triggered it?'

'The difficulty of the job. The possibility that he might fail. He still has to convince Vittori, a man far more successful than he will ever be. He has to keep impressing, maybe fake his success rate, show how trustworthy he is, dress in clothes he probably can't afford, use those fancy words to show he's as educated as men like Vittori. No wonder he thinks a carabiniere's job is easy.'

Daniele drove out to the main road. 'You know a great deal about selling.' He turned left, heading back to Greve. 'Was your father a salesman?'

'No, but I've known a few.' His father was just sperm his mother had allowed inside her. He'd grown up on the streets of Pozzuoli and as Reni talked, Perillo had recognised the need to make an impression, to be someone. Reni could mouth all the fancy words he wanted, but Perillo knew the man wasn't born with a silver spoon in his mouth. 'And your father?'

'Papà was a mask maker. He died of a heart attack when I was twelve.' Daniele turned left.

'What the hell happened to Dino?' Perillo suddenly barked, angry that Daniele had had a father only to lose him so young. It wasn't fucking fair to Dani. *I couldn't miss what wasn't there to begin with*. 'Why hasn't he called?'

'He texted while Reni was talking. I didn't think it was right to interrupt.'

'Why the hell didn't you tell me the minute we walked out?'

'I should have. I'm sorry.'

Perillo swatted the air with his arm. 'Oh, stop being sorry. That man has put me in a bad mood.' He hadn't thought of his childhood in a long time. 'I need a damn cigarette.' He took one out of the pack and put it in his mouth. 'Has Dino got the photo?'

'Dino didn't find any photos.'

'Shit! How are we going to find him without a photo?'

'I gave Dino Pietro's ex-wife's address in San Casciano just in case. She had one she'd forgotten to tear up. Vince has already sent it out. A copy is waiting for you on your desk.'

'Good thinking, Daniele. Thanks.' He put the cigarette back in the pack. 'Take us home.'

CHAPTER ELEVEN

A nervous Nico walked into Sotto Il Fico at ten minutes to eight. The front room was empty. He stopped behind the wide hutch stacked with plates and cups where Elvira sat in her armchair. Nico bent down and kissed her cheeks. 'Buonasera.'

She looked up from her new phone, a birthday present from her son. 'Beh, look at you. A corduroy jacket, flannel trousers. I didn't know you owned proper clothes. You look like a gentleman for once. Handsome too. If I were twenty years younger, I would try to hook you.'

'And you'd succeed.'

'I have no doubts.'

'My outfit is going to keep me warm. We're eating outside.'

'I see.' Elvira's tone indicated she didn't see at all. 'I had a taste of your porcini sauce. If your looks don't do it tonight, the sauce will. My husband didn't know how to boil an egg.'

'And your son isn't much better,' Enzo said, giving Nico a pat on his back as he walked by. 'Nice jacket. If you need something to bolster your courage, the bar is open.'

Nico spread out his arms in annoyance. 'I feel like I'm back in high school with you two. I'm having dinner with a friend, that's it. Okay?'

Elvira's response was a loud *harrumph*.

Enzo laughed. 'Very okay.'

Nico walked into the kitchen, where he found Tilde cutting her courgette lasagne into large rectangles. 'Ciao, Tilde.'

She turned around, knife in hand, and widened her eyes.

'Don't.'

'I won't.' She whistled instead. 'Where's Nelli?'

'She's meeting me here. In case you have the urge to plunge that knife into my hard heart, meeting here was her choice.'

'I know.' Tilde lowered the knife and chuckled. 'Good for her. She'll probably insist on paying her share.'

'I won't let her, and I thought you were rooting for me.'

'Always.' She blew him a kiss and went back to cutting the lasagne.

'Do you have a lot of diners on the terrace tonight?' He didn't like the idea of anyone listening in.

'A few tourists ate early. Now I've got four tables reserved, including yours. You'll be in the company of hardy locals. Don't worry, you'll be sitting at a distance from them.'

'Thanks. The polenta?'

'Is fried and in the oven, keeping warm.'

'Good. I'll go and meet Nelli outside.'

'Bring her here so I can give her a hug.'

Nico heard barking as he left the restaurant. He looked down and saw Nelli coming up the hill with OneWag making a pest of himself by jumping around her feet.

Nelli stopped and looked down. OneWag sat and looked up at her. 'Stop it, Rocco. I can't pick you up. Your paws are filthy.'

'Hey.' Nico waved and went to meet her.

Nelli smiled at him. 'Ciao, Nico.'

'Buonasera.' He kissed her cheeks. 'You look lovely.' She was wearing a long white boat-necked sweater over black leggings and ankle boots. She had draped a black and white wool shawl around her shoulders and done something to her blue eyes that made them stand out.

They kept walking. 'You look lovely too.'

'Lovely?'

'Not masculine enough for you? Would you have preferred handsome?'

Nico lifted his hands in surrender. 'Whoa, Nelli! Give me a chance.'

'I'm sorry. Walking here, I promised myself not to be snappy. I'm a little nervous. I feel as if I need to pass a test tonight.'

'That's exactly how I feel.'

'Good then. We'll study together.'

OneWag followed them into the restaurant. He had always preferred checking the town's street activities while his boss worked. Tonight, his nose told him to stay close. He might be needed.

On the way to the terrace, Nelli cheek-kissed Enzo, then Elvira, who gave her the night's menu, admired her shawl, and said, *'Don't wear out your shoes.'*

Nelli laughed. 'I don't intend to.'

'What does she mean?' Nico asked.

'It's a Tuscan saying. Ciao, Alba.'

Stepping out of the kitchen, with her arms holding her usual load of plates, Alba winked at Nelli.

Nelli didn't mind the teasing. The Sotto Il Fico family was rooting for her. So was Rocco, always ready to be hugged when she needed his furry warmth. Having support made telling Nico how she felt easier. She did feel a little sorry for him. He would have been far happier discussing their situation in neutral territory. She smiled. 'Let me say hello to Tilde and then it will be just us.'

Before he could answer, Tilde came out of the kitchen, her arms outspread.

Nico stood awkwardly in the doorway with OneWag, watching the joy in their faces as they hugged and kissed as if they hadn't seen each other in a long time. During the summer, when he and Nelli were still together, Nelli had often come here late in the evening when most diners were gone. She would sit with a glass of wine while he and Alba cleared the tables. He would steal glances at her face illuminated by a glass-enclosed candle, his blood rushing through his veins, knowing they would spend the night together.

'What should I order?' Nelli asked Tilde.

'A bottle of wine first of all.' Tilde gave Nico a teasing look. 'As for food, the choice is yours. Nico, table twelve. You know the way.'

The sky hadn't turned black yet, but the stars were out. The moon had not reached this part of the sky. Beyond the terrace, dots of home lights covered the low hills. The air was chilly. The only sound came from the soft laughter and mutterings of the diners. As Nelli sat down at the table, Nico's phone rang. Annoyed, Nico quickly grabbed the phone from his pocket. 'It's Perillo. I'm not going to answer.'

'No, do answer. Get it over with or else you'll be mulling the call all evening long.'

She was right. Nico sat down and answered. OneWag lay down under the table.

'We've got thirty-six videos from Villa Costanza to look at,' Perillo said. 'We need your help.'

'I'll be there first thing in the morning.'

'We need you now.'

'I'm sorry. I can't tonight.'

'Are you all right?'

'Yes. I'll see you tomorrow.' Nico clicked off.

Nelli looked up from reading the menu. 'I appreciate you not running off.'

'It wasn't important.'

'I see.' She hid her face behind the menu.

Shit. What was the matter with him? 'I'm sorry, Nelli. That's not what I meant.'

Nelli lowered the menu so he could see her eyes. 'What did you mean?'

'I meant that you are more important.'

Nelli put the menu down. 'Sometimes you can be very sweet and sometimes—'

'A jerk.'

'An oaf. That Tuscan expression you asked about says,

"Between saying and doing, a lot of shoes get worn down." My shoes are already worn and I'm not going to wait for a glass of wine to help me get this over with.' She leant across the table and lowered her voice. 'I fell in love with you, and you didn't fall in love with me. When we were together, there was only a part of you in the room. We made wonderful love together, yes, but five minutes later you weren't there. I'm not talking about the proverbial cigarette-after-coming syndrome. You weren't there then or the rest of our time together. It made me feel as if I was only a body to you.'

'No, Nelli, never.'

'But what? Usually when men find themselves alone again, they are only too happy to find a new companion. Why don't you? Does Rita still have such a grip on your heart that there's no room for anyone else? Do you feel disloyal? Or am I simply not the right woman for you, except in bed?'

Words raced in Nico's head, but they were all a jumble. Nelli's forthrightness came too quickly. He felt bombarded. He needed a moment of silence, an empty space where he could line up his words into sentences that explained how he felt. 'I need some wine,' Nico said and waved to Alba.

'I could use a whole bottle,' Nelli said. She sat back in her chair and hid her chin in the warmth of the shawl. She should have waited to speak until the wine had mellowed both of them. 'What should we order? You must know the menu.'

'The courgette lasagne is always great.' Nico wanted to be fair to Tilde.

'I love it, but I'm intrigued by the new dish – the fried polenta with porcini sauce.'

Nico felt a smidgen of pride. He was acting like a kid, but he wanted her approval, as if liking his dish said she forgave him for being an oaf. 'Let's order both and share,' he suggested, just in case.

'Good idea.'

Alba walked over. 'It's been a while, hasn't it?' She gave Nico a look he ignored. 'To celebrate, the wine is on the house.'

'No,' Nico said. 'I will pay.'

'Not possible. What are you having?'

Nico told her.

'Good choices,' Alba said. 'You're finally taking advantage of the good things in life.' She nodded at Nelli and swung her hips to the other end of the terrace.

'I like her spirit,' Nelli said.

'Sometimes, like now, it's too much.'

Nelli laughed. 'You would think that.'

Nico reached out and took Nelli's hand. 'I've never been very good at expressing my feelings. I always felt it was safest to keep them inside.'

'But you knew what they were?'

'Most of the time.'

'You must have acted out your feelings sometimes.'

'Yes, when I felt safe, when I was sure of them and how they would be received.'

Alba brought over the bottle of 2016 Panzanello. 'Enzo thought you'd enjoy this wine more than the 2018 Antinori you ordered.' Nico knew it was useless to object. He was surrounded. Alba uncorked the bottle, gave the cork to Nelli to sniff. She worked part-time for the GrappoloBello vineyard and knew a lot more about wine than Nico did.

'Nice,' Nelli said after sniffing. She held up her wine glass. Alba filled both of their glasses. They clinked them together, and without saying anything, drank some wine.

Nico put his glass down. 'I left the room, as you put it, because I was scared. I kept thinking that we're no longer kids. What we do to each other has a different weight. Wounds don't heal quickly anymore. At one point I sat down and listed the reasons that scared me. I used to do that when I was trying to figure out a case back in New York. It helped clear my head.' He drank some more wine. 'I listed loyalty to Rita on top when it should have been at the bottom. A few days before she died, she said, "Don't be alone too long. Pick well and enjoy her."' He drank more wine.

'Number two on the list was "I don't know what she wants." Three: "What if I want to back out? What if she backs out? Why not go on the way we are?"'

'That's what you settled on.'

He finished his wine. 'It seemed easier.'

'I'll tell you what I want and don't want. I don't want to marry you or live with you. What I want is to be loved back with open arms. Think about it and let me know. Okay?' Nelli leant into the light of the candle and smiled.

Looking at her radiant face, Nico felt the barrier he'd put up soften, melt away. He smiled back at her, opened his mouth to say—

Nelli placed her fingers on his mouth. 'Don't tell me now, while we're sitting under the stars with a full glass of Panzanello in you. Sleep on it for a few nights.'

'You're wise,' Nico said, feeling grateful. He did need to think about it.

OneWag rested his head on his paws and allowed himself to fall asleep.

With excellent timing Alba brought their two dishes and extra plates. 'Buon appetito.'

'Thank you,' Nelli said and picked up her fork. Having said what she wanted to say, she was now anxious to enjoy the evening. 'This looks delicious.'

Nico watched as Nelli cut into the fried polenta covered with the porcini and tomato sauce.

With Dino and Vince's help, Perillo had brought down his television and his DVD player, since the station didn't have one of its own. Vince set up the equipment. Ivana, relieved the viewing wouldn't happen in her home but concerned the men were missing their dinner, had brought down a huge bowl of penne along with plates, cutlery and cloth napkins.

While Perillo, Dino and Vince helped themselves to the penne, Daniele watched the first few minutes of the 8.10 p.m. videos to find which of the six had filmed the area where Jimmy's car was parked.

'You know what I think?' Dino said, twirling his fork in the air. The men didn't answer. 'My wife needs to take some lessons from Signora Perillo. These penne with fried courgette are heaven-sent.'

'My wife too,' Vince said, swallowing. Perillo ate in silence.

'Victory,' Daniele said. 'Found it in the fifth video. The car is visible at the very bottom edge of the video. The hood is cut off.'

'We only need the boot,' Perillo said and handed Daniele a plate of penne.

* * *

At Sotto Il Fico Nelli and Nico were the only diners left. The moon, four days away from being full, had swung over to their part of the sky, adding a little light. Alba cleared the plates. 'Any dessert?'

'Your cantuccini with a glass of vin santo, please,' Nelli said, breaking the awkward silence that had fallen between them. Alba lifted an eyebrow at Nico. He shook his head. His mind had been fumbling on how to ask Nelli to come home with him without coming off as a bastard who just wanted her body. He wanted to make love, yes, but also to watch her sleep curled up next to him, to be greeted by her heartwarming smile when she opened her eyes and saw him looking at her. Could he say this to her? No, she wanted him to wait and think over what she had said.

'Laura told me she knows you,' Nico said, to give his churning mind a rest. 'She might ask you to go off to Peru with her.'

'That might be fun. I like her. That job has done wonders for her. Gave her back her confidence.'

'I know her sister died.'

'Yes, nine years ago. Gabi worked with me at GrappoloBello and we'd become good friends despite the age difference. She introduced me to Laura. I tried to stay close to her after Gabi died. Laura was overcome with grief and guilt.'

'Why guilt?'

Nelli waited until Alba arrived with a plate and two glasses of vin santo. 'Here they are – Cantuccini d'Alba. Tilde has a hand in it, but it's my recipe. We're going into production November fifteenth.'

Nelli clapped her hands. 'Brava. I'll be your best client.'

'I'm counting on it. You and all the tourists in Italy and, why not, even America.' Alba dropped the bill in front of Nico and sauntered away.

Nico noticed Nelli eyeing the folded bill. 'Should we leave? It's late.'

This is the moment, Nico thought. *Ask her. Would you like to come home with me?* Instead, he said, 'Tilde will let us stay as long as we like. I have the keys.'

'Oh, good.'

She seems relieved, Nico thought. 'Tell me more about Laura.'

'She was a little wild growing up and Gabi worried about her a lot. Laura would find herself too drunk to drive and call Gabi to come get her. It happened almost every weekend. Gabi always went, no matter what time it was. She understood that Laura was just trying to get her family to pay attention. Laura was and is very attractive and as intelligent as Gabi, but she had no faith in herself then. Gabi got all the love, not just from her family. Anyone who met her. She was beautiful, intelligent, generous. She was the top seller at the vineyard and yet no one resented her.'

'Not even Laura?'

Nelli shook her head. 'There must have been some resentment.'

Nico was now genuinely curious. Nelli was describing a Laura different from the strong woman he had met. 'Maybe that's why she used her sister to always get her out of trouble.'

'Possibly. The night Gabi lost control of her car, she was on her way to San Casciano to pick Laura up from a bar.'

'That is tough to deal with.'

'I tried to make Laura understand that it wasn't her fault. I'm convinced someone drove Gabi off that road.'

'What makes you think that?'

'The long gash along the driver's side. I saw that car the day before and there was no gash. I pointed it out to the carabinieri in San Casciano. They admitted someone could have sideswiped Gabi, which made her swerve and lose control, but they wouldn't definitely say it did happen. What tire marks may have been there from the other car had disappeared under many more tire marks. It's a very trafficked road.'

'Who reported the accident?'

'A man called it in, saying she was already dead. He wouldn't leave his name. I think that's suspicious.'

'Did Laura believe Gabi had been sideswiped?'

'No. I think she wanted it to be her fault. It justified how little her family thought of her. I told her mother. I'm not sure she bothered to tell the grandfather. I almost think they wanted Gabi's death to be Laura's fault. It was their payback for all the trouble she'd given them.'

'The usual trouble?' Nico asked.

'Yes, if by usual you mean drugs, alcohol and sex.'

'Negative attention is better than no attention.'

'I did tell Laura's mother that some love for Laura might have helped. She answered that the Benati family was none of my business and asked me to leave.'

'Ehi, Nelli,' Tilde called out as she walked towards them, holding a plastic bag. OneWag saw the bag and slipped out from under the table. She'd taken her apron and headscarf off and let her hair fall to her shoulders. She handed the bag to Nico. 'For Rocco.' OneWag waved his tail in appreciation.

Tilde asked Nelli, 'Did you have a good meal?'

'A perfect one,' Nelli said.

'Which dish did you prefer?'

'I think I will always need to order both, which means I will always have to come here with company.'

'A clever answer. Nico, you can pay tomorrow. I'm going home, and when I come back in the morning, I don't want to find a single cantuccino on that plate or the three of you still here. Buonanotte.'

'Buonanotte,' Nico and Nelli said together, both biting into a cantuccino. OneWag got one too.

Nelli asked Nico, 'Do you have a clean handkerchief?'

'Always.' He pulled it out of his back pocket and handed it over. 'First lesson in fourth grade: a young man must carry a handkerchief in his pocket, a lady in her purse.'

'The nuns?' She opened the handkerchief in her lap and emptied the cantuccini plate.

'Who else?' He watched her tie the handkerchief together. 'To clean that plate we'd have to stay here all night. I guess you're saying it's time to go home.'

Nelli looked up. 'Your home, I hope, but not tonight.'

To hide his disappointment, he picked up his disloyal dog. 'We'll walk you home.'

'No, I'll go alone.' She kissed his cheeks and handed him the handkerchief bundle. 'But thank you for a lovely evening. Will I see you at the concert?'

'We'll be there.' As Nelli walked down the hill, OneWag wasn't the only one yearning to follow her.

* * *

The four carabinieri clustered together as the video fast-forwarded. People and cars came and went, with Vince proudly identifying the cars. No one approached Jimmy's open boot. In the 10 p.m.–12 a.m. video, only five cars were still parked, including Jimmy's. No new cars came in since the tram stopped running at 00.30. The 12–2 a.m. video sped by without revealing anything.

As Perillo and Daniele started watching the 2–4 a.m. video, Dino was snoring lightly. Vince was cleaning the pasta bowl with a fat chunk of bread.

A black car appeared on the far side of where Jimmy's car was parked. Daniele stopped the video, rewound it and pressed the play button. The car reappeared, slowing down as it passed the parked cars.

'That's a Toyota Highlander,' Vince offered. 'Very popular.' As he said that, the car drove out of frame for three minutes, reappearing on the left side of the frame. As it drove by Jimmy's car, it jerked to a stop.

'This is it.' Perillo's voice was triumphant.

'I can't read the license plate,' Daniele said. 'The angle of the camera is wrong.'

'What?' Dino asked, startled awake. Vince stopped eating and pushed his chair closer to the screen.

'We'll catch it later,' Perillo whispered, the tension of the moment tightening his throat.

The four watched in silence as the car swung around, backing up until its rear met Jimmy's open boot. A trousered person got out of the car and walked to Jimmy's boot. The gender was impossible to tell. The person wore a large coat, revealing nothing of the body, wore what appeared like rubber boots, and stayed hunched over. The wide hat kept the face hidden. The person opened the Toyota's boot, lifted it only partially, then lowered Jimmy's boot.

'Whoever it is, he's clever,' Vince said, popping a chewing gum in his mouth. Perillo's eyes were glued to the screen. He chewed silently. 'He knows he's being filmed.'

With the two boots lowered, they could barely see Cesare's body being moved from one boot to the other. Whoever it was acted quickly and sped off.

Daniele rewound the video and replayed the first appearance of the car, stopping it when the angle of the camera allowed him to see the license plate number. The plate was dirty and only the last letter was legible: *V*.

Daniele stopped the video and turned to his boss. Rather than declaring what should be done now, which the maresciallo would not welcome, Daniele asked, 'Do you want me to find who in the area owns a black Toyota Highlander?'

'Also, check the rental agencies and ask if one has been stolen.' Perillo stood up and stretched his back. He'd been sitting for over three hours that felt like twelve. He was tired. 'We'll go over what we saw in the morning. Sleep well. We'll need sharp brains tomorrow.'

At the door of his office, he stopped and turned to look at his men. 'Thank you. And, Vince, if you don't want me to know you're chewing gum in my presence, which as everyone in this station knows annoys me intensely, chew with your mouth shut. Buonanotte.'

'Buonanotte, Maresciallo,' the three chimed in.

CHAPTER TWELVE

Saturday morning Nico cut short his breakfast with Gogol and drove to the carabinieri station in Greve. Perillo's office door was wide open. The room had been cleared of last night's dirty dishes by Ivana before anyone was awake. Dino and Vince had stored the pile of videos Daniele had slogged through in their own joint office. The television set and DVD player, much to Ivana's disappointment, were still on Perillo's desk facing two chairs left over from last night. She was going to miss the morning news on RAI 3.

'Ah, here you are, Detective Doyle.' Perillo spread out his arms. 'You grace us with your presence.'

'As promised. Ciao, Daniele.'

Daniele raised a hand in salute. 'Where's Rocco?'

'Following a smell coming from Vince's room.'

'Vince doesn't share.' Perillo gave Nico a welcome pat on the back. 'Thanks for coming. I forget you're not on the payroll. We're looking forward to your opinion.' He pulled up a chair in front of the television for Nico.

Daniele sat down in his chair. 'You should have come just for Ivana's food.'

Nico sat to one side of Daniele. 'I had a good meal too.'

Perillo took the chair on the other side of Daniele. 'With la bella Nelli, I venture.'

Nico ignored Perillo's remark and said, 'Go ahead,' to Daniele.

After the first go-through, Nico asked to watch it again. Perillo took the opportunity to step outside the station to smoke a cigarette, his first since yesterday.

'What do you think?' he asked, walking back in with a mint in his mouth. 'Woman or man?'

'Someone who doesn't want to show his or her height.'

'Of course,' Daniele said with relief in his voice. 'That's why they're slouching. It's a tall person. Laura isn't tall, so it can't be her.'

Or she wants to appear tall, Nico thought.

'It's Pietro,' Perillo said with conviction. 'He's a big man. He had motive and opportunity. A hunting knife, if you don't already own one, is easy to get. And he's taken off to seek his fortune, which translates to staying out of jail.'

'I saw a roll of the thick plastic Cesare was wrapped in,' Daniele added, 'at the house where Pietro worked.'

Nico put his hands on the back of his head with elbows out and sat back on his chair to think.

'No one involved so far owns a black Toyota Highlander and no one rented one in Chianti. We've contacted other rental agencies and carabinieri stations throughout Tuscany to check stolen car reports.' Perillo sat back down, the mint having melted, the smoke smell gone. 'Nothing yet. The man in the video is Pietro, I'm sure of it.'

Nico opened his eyes. 'But, if it is Pietro, why the hell was he driving into Villa Costanza with a corpse he'd killed ten hours before? Okay, Ida, the housekeeper saw the car in the distance right after Cesare was killed. That explains why the murderer didn't leave the body there. Why didn't he find another place? We have woods, ravines, summer homes now empty.'

'Maybe Pietro panicked when Ida saw him,' Daniele suggested. 'He got scared of being seen again and waited until it got dark.'

'But why pick Villa Costanza? A car park under camera surveillance is not an ideal spot to get rid of a body.'

'He could have known Jimmy's car with the faulty boot lock was parked there,' Perillo said. 'I'm certain he would have enjoyed putting the blame on someone else.'

Nico closed his eyes again. 'According to Jimmy, the only one who knew that is Sandro.' He'd had a lousy night and all the question marks this case was presenting were giving him a headache. 'Gogol and I were with Sandro until nine Friday morning, which leaves him two minutes to drive down to Greve, get hold of Laura's phone and send the text to Cesare.'

'Understood,' Perillo said, noticing Nico's sharp tone. 'It seemed reasonable for a second.'

'Maybe the murder wasn't planned,' Daniele said.

'Of course, it was,' Perillo said. 'He had the plastic sheet ready.'

'We don't know if it was ready before or he got the sheet afterwards,' Nico said. 'Any news of Laura's car?' One of his thoughts during the night had been on Nelli's conviction that Gabi's car had been sideswiped, which had led him to remember something Signora Lucchetti had told him.

'Not yet, I'm afraid,' Daniele said. 'She is being very understanding.'

Perillo scowled. 'It's only been two days, Dani.'

'I know, but she has not called once to ask. She knows it's clean, but she must need her car.'

Nico sat up. 'This is what I think, based on no concrete evidence whatsoever. Call it a hunch. I think our killer,' Nico said, standing up, 'didn't have the time to get rid of the body after Ida spotted them because he or she had to take care of something first.'

'Pietro had to get back to work,' Perillo said. 'His fellow workers said he'd been punctual that morning, but I confess I never did check with the foreman.'

'Laura had to get back to work,' Nico said. 'What about Mattia Gennari?'

'He claims he was home,' Daniele said. 'There's no one to corroborate that, but I thought we'd decided it was Pietro who killed Cesare?'

Perillo threw down his arms. 'Of course, it's him, Nico. He ran away.'

'Hundreds run away every day,' Nico said. 'It doesn't mean they killed someone. Seeking his fortune could mean going off to gamble at the Sanremo Casinò or starting a new life, like I did by coming here.' Nico did not add another possibility. 'Have any sightings of Pietro come in yet?'

'Seven so far came to police and other carabinieri stations. Nothing from this area. They are being followed through, but no results yet. I don't have high expectations from past experience. Some callers are well-meaning, others are delusional, and too many love to have fun with us.'

'It only takes one to lead us to Pietro,' Nico said. 'Pietro Rinaldi does look like he could be our murderer, but let's not close our minds to other possibilities. Daniele, did you ever find out if Cesare had a passport?'

'Passports were only handed out by police headquarters in the past. I sent a request out to all of them. So far only seventeen answered in the negative. It will take time to get all the answers.'

'How many police headquarters are there?'

'One hundred and three.'

Nico scrunched his face. 'I'm sorry, Dani, I had no idea.'

'It took no time at all. I did a mass mailing.'

'I'm glad to hear that. Thank you. Let me know when you hear from the rest.'

'Is Cesare having a passport important?' Perillo asked.

'I'm curious about the years he was gone from home. He may have wanted to get away from his family, but why not answer when Signora Lucchetti or Laura asked? Why the air of mystery?'

'People would find him more interesting,' Daniele suggested. 'It might attract more people to his bar.'

'It did have that effect on Cinzia Ferriello.'

Perillo added his own idea. 'Maybe he'd gone to Holland to live the gay life he couldn't live here. When he finally came home, he didn't want that known.'

'We don't know he was gay,' Daniele said.

Perillo threw up his hands in exasperation. 'Exactly. We can come up with a hundred suppositions as to why Cesare kept his mouth shut. Does it matter?'

'The fuller the picture of who your murder victim was,' Nico said, 'the easier it is to discover why he was killed. The who often leads to the why.'

Perillo nodded, feeling dejected. Nico had much more experience in murders. Nico was always right. Then why had he objected to the passport search? It didn't take up much of Dani's time.

Nico noticed his friend's change of mood. 'I'm sorry. Sometimes I sound like a professor behind a lectern. I used to do that back in homicide when my suggestions were being ignored. Showing conviction is a good defence mechanism. And I apologise for asking Daniele to find out about the passports without asking you first. I guess I too forget I'm not on the payroll.'

Perillo grunted. 'I'm not that insecure, Nico.'

Nico stood up. 'Of course not. You're just suffering from nicotine withdrawal. It makes people crotchety. Rita almost divorced me. Keep it up, though. It does get better.'

'If you say so.' Relief washed over Perillo. His dumb pride wasn't to blame.

'Any news on the Ducati?'

'Nothing so far,' Daniele said. 'I check the selling sites regularly. There are lots of motorcycles for sale, but not the one we're looking for. Beppe has put word out on his blog.'

Nico didn't understand why they'd involved Beppe in the search. 'If one of his followers finds it, there's a good chance he'll keep it or sell it.'

'You're right,' Perillo said, 'but Dani trusts in the good of people.'

Nico gave Daniele a shoulder pat. 'I hope you never have to regret that.'

Daniele smiled. 'Thank you.'

'I'm going home now to work on my vegetable garden and concentrate on more pleasant things. I guess you'll be at the concert in full uniform.'

'Yes,' Perillo said. 'We're on duty.'

'Both? Too bad. I think Stella was counting on having Daniele sit with her.'

A red-faced Daniele straightened his shoulders. 'She understands my work comes first, but we are eating together tonight at Angela's.' He'd asked Vince for a loan after she'd agreed to let him pay for just this once.

Perillo beamed. 'Excellent idea, Dani.' His brigadiere was going to be pleasantly surprised by the bill.

Nico opened the office door. 'Good. I'll see you both there, then. Ciao.' He whistled for OneWag. The dog came out of Vince's room, licking his whiskers.

Nico walked into piazza Matteotti from the main street of Greve with OneWag. He had come early for the Verdi Orchestra end-of-season concert. A crowd had already gathered. Perillo and his men, in full uniform, casually walked around and between the people who were greeting friends they may have seen only a few hours earlier before choosing a seat. Nico waved to Perillo, who walked over briskly. OneWag gave Perillo's boots a quick sniff and then took off to sniff whatever came his way.

Nico eyed his friend's crisp uniform. 'You look important, finally.'

'So do you. You're wearing a jacket for once and what looks like an ironed shirt.'

'It's got cold.'

'It has, but to what do we owe the ironed shirt?' Perillo raised both eyebrows. 'Mm?'

Nico's shoulders slumped. 'Just stop it, will you? You're not funny.'

'I'll be serious then. Take a look at the two men seated at the end of the fourth row from the bottom.'

Nico saw two elegantly dressed men talking to each other. 'What about them?'

'The one on the right is Dottor Eugenio Vittori, a successful money manager. He's the man who bought both Cesare's and Gennari's land.'

'A man with a motive.'

'Exactly. He had access to Laura's phone. So did the other one, Sirio Reni, who is hoping to go into business with Vittori. I was wondering if—'

'If you are asking me to sit near them so I can overhear their conversation, no. I have other plans.'

Perillo gave Nico's shoulder an amicable pat with a look of regret on his face. 'Those plans may have been foiled. Ciao.' He walked away.

Nico turned to look at the row of seats assembled for the concert. The semicircle of orchestra chairs on a stage in front of the statue of Amerigo Vespucci were still empty. Almost half the audience seats were filled with people or saved with wraps and handbags. Children ran up and down the aisles chasing each other, ignored by their parents. Nico thought he had arrived early enough to find two seats for himself and Nelli until he spotted her seated in a centre row. Laura and Tilde sat on either side of her.

Shit, he thought and sat down in the last row. He'd been counting on being near her, enjoying the warm feeling her presence gave him. What was it? A sense of all being right with the world. Why hadn't he asked her to sit with him? Why had he assumed she'd want to sit with him? He could kick himself.

Nico looked up. Enzo was standing at the end of the row. 'My mother insisted we save you a seat. Next to her of course.'

Nico stood up and walked to the end of the row. 'It's very kind of her.' He would have preferred to stay where he was and sulk, or maybe sit behind the two men Perillo had pointed out. He couldn't. Family should never be denied, especially this family who gave him what he'd never had with his own parents.

'I don't see Stella,' Nico said as he followed Enzo.

'She went off to look for her new friend.'

'Daniele?'

Enzo stopped with a concerned look on his face. 'He's a good man?'

'Very good. A piece of bread as you say here.'

'I'm glad to hear that. She's starting to look happy again. I don't want her to get hurt.'

'None of us do.' They resumed walking towards their seats. If anyone got hurt, Nico thought, it would be Dani.

'I warn you,' Enzo said. 'Mamma likes to hum with the music.'

Nico had taken a quick look at the programme. Verdi, Debussy, Puccini, Haydn. 'Elvira knows all the music they're playing? That's impressive.' He was familiar with the opera music thanks to Rita. He was pretty sure he'd never heard the music of the other two.

Enzo chuckled. 'What my mother doesn't know, she

makes up. Sometimes she claims her version is better.'

'It might very well be. Ciao to all,' Nico said loudly as he walked between two rows of seats to join Elvira in a lace-trimmed dark blue suit and the double strand of pearls she wore only on special occasions.

The four women looked up from reading their programmes. He only saw Nelli.

'Ciao,' she mouthed, with a smile that added a light he missed.

He smiled back. Elvira tugged at the shirt he'd taken pains to iron well. 'Sit, Nico, you're blocking my view.' Nico sat and gave her the two expected cheek kisses.

'What view is that?' he asked. 'The orchestra is in front of you.' The musicians were sitting down in their allotted seats: Enrico with his violin; Luciana, the florist, with her oboe; Cesare's neighbour, Mattia Gennari, polishing and repolishing his flute with jittery hands. For Enrico's sake, Nico hoped Mattia's playing would be flawless. He didn't know any of the other musicians, as they weren't Gravignesi.

Elvira leant forward in her seat and started fussing with her handbag. Her head was turned towards Nelli.

'She looks pretty in that blue dress, don't you think?' Nico asked.

'It's about time she dressed like a woman. She smells sweet for a change too. I suspect that's for your sake.'

'I'm a little too far away to enjoy it. My fault for coming late.'

'Your fault for having a cobwebbed heart. It's the hotel manager I'm looking at. Laura Benati. Nelli invited her to sit with us. She doesn't look like a murderer.'

'What does a murderer look like to you?'

Graceless notes began floating in the air now. The musicians were tuning their instruments.

'Cruel. Or crazy. Greedy. Angry. I don't know exactly. At least different from you and me. Laura Benati simply looks sad. Calm. Perfectly nice. It's confusing.'

'What makes you think she is a murderer?'

'People are saying she killed her bartender.'

There it was again, Nico thought. The usual grapevine doing its nasty business. 'Are they saying why?'

'The money he left her. There are voices going around that she killed her sister a few years back. If you kill once, you can kill again.'

'That is pure malicious nonsense. Her sister died in a car accident,' Nico said out of anger, aware he didn't know all the facts of the sister's death. 'I'm surprised you listen to that garbage.'

'I agree. It is mostly garbage, but sometimes you can find a seed that sprouts the truth. What do you and Salvatore think? Did she kill him?'

The first notes of *Aida*'s triumphal march shook the air around them. 'Shh, Elvira. Let's listen to the music.'

Elvira snapped her handbag shut, leant back in her chair and started humming.

Nico sat back too, glad that Verdi had allowed him not to answer Elvira, but she had reminded him of something he needed to discuss with Perillo, something that needed looking into.

During the loud round of applause for Verdi, Stella slipped into the seat on the other side of Elvira. OneWag had followed her in. 'You're late,' Elvira grumbled, looking pleased anyway.

'I'm here now.' Stella kissed her grandmother and leant over her to blow a kiss to Nico. 'Ciao, Zio. Did you see Dani in uniform?' Her jade-green eyes were wide with delight. 'He's movie-star handsome. I took lots of pictures.'

A grunt from Elvira. 'A beautiful vine yields few grapes.'

Stella laughed. 'Dai, Nonna, let me enjoy looking at the vine. I'll taste the grapes later.'

Elvira surprised Nico by chuckling.

The orchestra conductor beat his baton against the lectern. 'Next is Debussy's "Syrinx," played by our excellent flutist, Mattia Gennari. I ask the favour of listening in complete silence. Thank you.'

Stella settled OneWag on her lap. Nico watched Enrico pat Gennari's back. The conductor stepped back and Gennari stood up and walked to the front of the stage. Looking at the man's size, Nico remembered Luciana saying that Gennari should have been playing a tuba. The flute in fact looked like a small toy in his hands.

Stella leant over Elvira again. 'Dani said that the maresciallo wants to see you at the station right after the concert.'

'Did he say—'

'Shhh,' came from Elvira.

Gennari took a big breath, lifted the flute slowly to his mouth and began playing.

Nico sat back and cursed silently. He'd been hoping to catch Nelli after the concert, suggest having a drink together here in Greve, offer to drive her home. Maybe even find the courage to tell her he loved her.

The music lapped over Nico's disappointment, softening it. The notes were slow, sad and haunting. There was total silence in the audience. Elvira, mesmerised, didn't try to hum along. In less than three minutes 'Syrinx' was over. A roar of applause followed. Voices shouted, 'Bravo!' The other players tapped their bows or hands against their lecterns. Mattia Gennari stood transfixed, looking amazed at his success.

Could a man who can play this music so beautifully kill a human being? Nico wondered. He knew little of classical music, but the audience response and Enrico's shining face told him Gennari had excelled. He remembered Rita saying that to excel in music, talent was not enough. It required a heart full of feeling. Generous, good feeling. Not the greed, hate or anger needed to murder. But Gennari had motive. He could only have sold his land if Cesare agreed to sell his. Cesare had not agreed. With Cesare dead, Gennari got what he wanted. He had no alibi for that Friday morning. On the other hand, in his favour was the fact that he hadn't been seen anywhere near Laura's phone.

The overture to Puccini's *Tosca* came next. Elvira started humming. The music was still beautiful, heart-stirring. Nico looked over at Nelli. He could only see her profile, her not perfectly straight nose, the jaw that would tighten with concentration as she painted, the long grey braid that came loose when they made love too long ago. Nico took out his phone and texted.

> *I came early sure that I could snare you to sit with me, but again I was an oaf. I make assumptions based on wishful thinking, like a child. After the concert Perillo wants to see me. I don't know how long that will take. I would love to see you. A drink? A meal? A walk? Ciao.*

He pressed send and let Puccini's romantic music take over.

Nelli's answer came back during the last soaring notes of the overture.

Laura is coming over to my house for dinner. She badly needs support. Ugly rumours are pinning the murder on her. I am always astonished at how cruel and stupid people can be. Let's try for another time.

Nico, disappointed, texted back a raised thumb emoji. As the musicians were rearranging the seating for the Haydn adagio, Nico turned and scanned the piazza for Perillo. He was nowhere to be seen.

'I'm sorry,' Nico said, standing up. OneWag jumped down from Stella's lap.

'What's wrong?' she asked.

Elvira gave a dismissive grunt. 'Men don't know how to hold it.'

'Something's come up. I need to go. See you later.'

'Not me. Dani is taking me out to dinner.'

'Good for him.' Nico brushed knees and almost stepped on a foot as he made his way out. OneWag tunnelled out under the chairs.

Perillo was back in jeans, a sweater and leather jacket when Nico found him sitting on a bench in the park across from the carabinieri station. He had an unlit cigarette hanging from the side of his mouth. He waved Nico over.

Nico climbed the short hill while OneWag relieved himself behind a bush.

'I'm glad you left early.' From where they stood, they

could hear the music faintly. 'We're going somewhere.'

'What happened?' Nico asked. Perillo always liked to keep him guessing.

'Pietro happened.' Perillo put the cigarette back in the pack and walked over to the station. 'Let's go. You drive.'

Nico followed. 'Daniele's not coming?' Perillo never did anything without his trusted brigadiere.

'I don't need him. I've got you and Rocco.' Perillo walked to the Alfa.

Nico got into the driver's seat. OneWag settled down at Perillo's feet. 'Where are we going?'

'To a luxury hotel under construction. Head for Panzano. I'll show you where to turn off before the town.'

The turnoff was a rutted uphill dirt road edged by thick stands of trees, the ground covered in undergrowth. At the top were three half-finished stone walls covered with scaffolding. A cement mixer surrounded by cement bags sat at one end. A small, abandoned vineyard could be seen further down.

Nico found a level spot and parked the car. As soon as they got out, OneWag raised his snout and followed an interesting scent coming from the vineyard.

'Ehi, Rocco, go away,' Vince shouted.

Nico's stomach tightened. Vince had been parading around Piazza Matteotti before the concert. Now dirt clung to the hem of his trousers and his shoe covers. Nico had thought Pietro getting killed was likely from the beginning, but still, he'd held the hope that Pietro had simply taken off for a better somewhere. Living in Italy was making Nico soft. A good thing. Even now.

Vince handed over the wiggling dog.

Nico took OneWag and shut him in the car with the windows half-open. 'Be good.'

Perillo put on shoe covers and followed Vince back into the vineyard. He'd left another pair of shoe covers on the hood of the car. Nico slipped them on and found Perillo standing in front of Pietro's body. The fingers of Pietro's right hand were clasping a vine curled around a low wire.

'He must have tried to get up,' Vince said. Next to Vince was a uniformed carabiniere Nico had never seen before.

'He was stabbed in the stomach.' The blood had already dried. Flies buzzed.

'He could have other wounds in the back,' Vince said. 'I didn't want to move him.'

'He's been dead for some time.' Nico could hear OneWag barking.

Perillo put on gloves, stooped down and went through Pietro's pockets. All he found was an unused Greve to Castellina bus ticket and a tissue.

Perillo straightened up. 'Pietro left home wearing a backpack according to his neighbour.'

'We both walked through the vineyard,' Vince said. 'We didn't find anything. Not even a cigarette butt.'

'We need to find it for his phone. He could have used it to contact his killer.'

All the more reason for his killer to get rid of it, Nico thought. The other carabiniere said, 'Forensics and the medical examiner should be here in about half an hour.'

'Where's the man who found him?' Perillo asked Vince.

'Nanni Gezzi. He's on the other side of the building. I gave him some chewing gum to calm him.'

Perillo raised one eyebrow.

'Chewing does help, Maresciallo. You should try it when you get one of your tempers.'

Perillo kept his temper this time. 'The two of you stay here until the Florence team arrives. Come, Nico, let's hear what Signor Pezzi has to say.' He walked away.

'Gezzi, Maresciallo,' Vince called out. 'Nanni Gezzi.'

'That's what I said, isn't it?' Perillo asked Nico, who was walking behind him. OneWag must have heard their footsteps. His barking was frantic now.

'That's what you said,' Nico said to soothe Perillo. Discovering that his prime suspect had been murdered had to feel like a hard kick on the back of his knees.

Nico opened the car door and picked up OneWag. 'Only if you stay with me, buddy.' His face got tongue-washed. Nico put the dog down and they followed Perillo to the other side of the building.

Signor Gezzi was sitting on a plank placed on two large cement canisters. He was in his eighties, with an almost full head of long curly white hair sprouting over his head in all directions. He wore clean overalls over a knitted shirt. OneWag gingerly sniffed his laced boots.

'It was terrible,' Gezzi announced when he saw the two men approach. 'I almost died.' He wiped his red-veined face with a crumpled handkerchief. 'The instant I saw him, I knew he was long gone. My heart went *pop. Pop, pop, pop*, like corn on the grill. *Pop, pop, pop.*' He took a long breath and let it out slowly. 'Chewing helped.'

With a straight face, Perillo introduced himself and introduced Nico without specifying his role.

'I don't know who that poor man is.' Gezzi stuffed his handkerchief in the pocket of his overalls. 'I never saw him before. I called the carabinieri right away.' He took out a phone from the pocket on his chest. 'A Christmas present from my son, who is convinced I'm going to get lost.'

'Why were you here today?' Perillo asked.

'Ah, that's a long story.' He slipped his phone back inside his pocket. 'Since I found you a dead man, I'll make it short. My father owned this land years ago. I used to play in the vineyard until I was seven years old. Then my father got sick, couldn't work and had to sell. I live in San Martino now. A nice place but my memories of my childhood are here. I put-put up here on my old three-wheeler on the weekends the workers aren't here destroying the place. That poor man has been here at least a couple of days. He's feeding a lot of bugs.'

Perillo jumped in. 'Did you touch him or move him?'

'I kicked his shoe just in case I was wrong. The workers here, you must be wondering why they didn't find him. I'll tell you. I guess none of them had to shit in the past few days. They've turned Babbo's vineyard into a cesspool. That is all I have to say about the dead man and me.' He looked at OneWag, who sat at his feet, staring up at him. 'I'm sorry,' Gezzi said. 'No ball.'

OneWag kept staring.

'Ah, you have a good nose.' Gezzi plunged a hand into a side pocket, took out the crumpled handkerchief, a comb, a box of matches and finally a small package. He unwrapped it and placed the contents at his feet.

OneWag stood up, did his one-tail thank-you wave and bit into a half-dried sausage.

While the dog chewed, Perillo took down Gezzi's personal details on his phone, which Nico was sure Perillo would later e-mail to Daniele. 'Thank you, Signor Gezzi. I will need you to come to the station for fingerprinting and a DNA swab. It will only take a few minutes.'

'I'm happy to oblige. I don't have much to occupy me, and thank you for listening to an old man with memories.'

'I expect you Monday morning,' Perillo said. 'Arrivederci.'

Gezzi nodded.

'My dog thanks you,' Nico said before following Perillo back.

'My pleasure.' OneWag had finished eating and looked up. 'No more.'

OneWag trotted after Nico.

Perillo stood at the edge of the vineyard and called out to Vince and the other man still standing by Pietro's body. 'We're going back to the station. Call me after Gianconi has examined the body.'

'Who's the man with Vince?' Nico asked as they walked to the car.

'He just made brigadiere and is station jumping, getting a feel for the work. He'll be with us for a month. I'm driving.' Perillo yanked open the car door and slipped in behind the wheel.

Nico walked to the passenger side, wishing he could sit behind the steering wheel. Even on a good day, Perillo drove the Alfa Romeo as if competing in the Monte Carlo Rally. 'I value our lives,' Nico said as he got in the car after OneWag.

'I need to get back some control.' Perillo reversed out of the spot and drove down the dirt road at a decent speed. 'We say nothing to Dani, agreed? Pietro's death can wait until tomorrow morning.'

'He won't get upset? He's part of the team.'

'He'll get over it. I want him to have his night with Stella.'

'A whole night?'

'A whole night would be great for him. An evening is good too.' Perillo turned left onto Route 222, tires squealing. 'Pietro was seeking his fortune by blackmail.' He slapped the steering wheel. 'That stupid idiot! How could he think he could get away with blackmailing a murderer?'

Nico glanced at the speedometer. The car was going 170 kilometres an hour on a two-lane road. 'Slow down, please.'

Perillo eased the car down to a tolerable 140. 'Laura just jumped up to the head of the list.'

'Why? You think she's got the strength to lift a body and shove it in the boot of a car?'

'Cesare was skinny and strength comes when you want something badly enough.'

'I've been mulling over something,' Nico said. 'We'll talk about it when we're on firm ground.'

'Americano, we're on asphalt strapped down by seat belts. You'll survive. Tell me now or my right foot is going to get extremely heavy.'

'We should look into Laura's sister's death.'

'Gabriella. Yes, Dani told me about it. She died in a car accident some years ago. He read about it online.'

'I think there might be a connection to Cesare's death.'

'What makes you think that?'

'Something Signora Lucchetti said. Do me a favour. Call your colleagues in San Casciano and tell them you've authorised me to look into the accident.'

'If you wish,' Perillo said, convinced connecting a

nine-year-old accident to Cesare's murder was a stretch. He swung into the parking area of his station and turned off the motor. OneWag jumped from the back seat onto Nico's lap, wiggling to get out. Nico opened the car door. OneWag scooted towards the station. Perillo didn't move. 'Monday I'll send Daniele to talk to the construction crew of the new hotel to see if they saw anyone who didn't belong there. I'll question Laura as soon as Gianconi gives me a time frame for Pietro's death.'

'Mattia Gennari and Vittori need another look,' Nico said. 'They both have a good motive.'

'Mattia has no alibi, but he also wasn't anywhere near Laura's phone. I find it hard to picture Vittori in his fancy clothes plunging a knife into Cesare or Pietro. Besides, with his money, he could buy all the land he wanted.'

'But he wanted that land, didn't he?'

'That's what he said.'

Nico swung his legs out of the car. For the moment the energy to go any further was missing. 'Maybe I'll have dinner at the hotel tonight. I wouldn't mind having a chat with both or one of those two men.'

Perillo swung his legs out of the car too. He felt like kicking something, someone, Pietro if he were still alive. 'What happened with Nelli?'

'Nothing happened, and Tilde won't need me at Sotto Il Fico until the tourist season reopens in April. I have plenty of time to sniff around.'

'Come have dinner with us. Ivana always has enough food to feed the whole station.'

'Thanks, but I think I should go to the hotel. I'm hoping Vittori and Reni are there. Now that Pietro has been killed,

I want to get a sense of who they are and how they fit into the picture.'

'Well, it's a good way to kill time and you'll eat well. Go get Rocco. He's probably found a way to get into Vince's locker.'

'What about you?'

'I think I'll sit here for a little while longer and dream of smoking a cigarette.'

'Sweet dreams then.' Nico got out of the car, whistled for OneWag and made his way around to Perillo's open window. 'Cheer up. We'll find the killer.'

'I don't know. I can't think straight without a cigarette,' Perillo said as OneWag came running out of the station.

Nico saw what OneWag had in his mouth and ordered, 'Drop it.'

Perillo stuck his head out of the window and shouted, 'Bravo, Rocco!'

The dog sat down and looked up at his boss.

'I said drop it.'

OneWag lay down. Nico knew the dog would roll over next. He reluctantly obeyed all commands. Letting go of a found treasure was the toughest.

Perillo was laughing hard.

'You're not helping,' Nico said.

'Wait until I tell Vince.'

'Please don't.' Nico bent over and held out his hand. OneWag sat up slowly, walked over to Nico and dropped a triple pack of chewing gum in his hand.

Perillo got out of the car and went to give OneWag a good scratch behind the ears. 'Thank you, Rocco; you're far better than a cigarette.'

He stood there with Vince's gum pack in his hand and watched owner and dog walk out of the station and towards the centre of town. 'Yes, we'll get whoever it is.'

The sun had set as Stella and Daniele walked into the garden of Da Angela's, but a ribbon of fading pink still floated over to the horizon. Their shoes made noise as they crunched gravel on the way to their corner table next to a laurel bush. A steady flame from a fat candle deep in a glass container dropped a circle of light on the white tablecloth. They were both wearing slacks and sweaters to keep the chill away.

'I'm happy to be with you tonight,' Stella said as she sat down. 'I miss you, Dani.'

Daniele's cheeks did their usual bloom. 'Me too.' This was it, he realised, the moment he could tell her how he felt. He opened his mouth. 'I wanted . . .' The rest of the words got stuck in his mouth.

Stella leant over and kissed him. 'That's what I've wanted to do for a while now. You too, right?'

Stunned, Daniele took a moment to answer. 'A definite yes.' He started to laugh. 'I wasn't sure you'd welcome it.'

'Well, now you know, and we can kiss away after dessert.'

Daniele's laugh turned into a wide smile. 'Why eat?'

Stella picked up the handwritten menu. 'Because we're both hungry.'

Betta, Angela's mother, came over to take their order. She dropped a plate of sliced country bread on the table. 'Order as much as you want and thank the good heart of the maresciallo. So, what's it going to be?'

'What did the maresciallo do?' Daniele asked, worried his boss was up to one of his tricks.

'Me not to say, you to find out,' Betta said. 'Order the chicken cacciatore. It's excellent. I made it.'

'Then I'll have it after the antipasto,' Stella said.

'Me too,' Daniele said, laughing. He was being silly, but he couldn't help it. He was happy.

Stella laughed too as she ordered the house red.

Betta shook her head. 'Panzanello Riserva is what my chicken deserves. That's what you'll get.'

'You know best, Signora,' Daniele said. He hoped he had enough money. The old woman walked away.

An awkward silence followed. Daniele wasn't good at starting conversations.

Stella was wondering if she'd been too pushy, maybe given Dani the idea she was ready to hop into bed. She'd thought a lot about it but wanted to start slowly with Dani. Make sure she would not hurt him or herself.

'I saw Salvatore leave the concert in a hurry,' Stella said, making little balls of bread with her fingers. 'Do you know why?'

'I don't,' Daniele said. 'Maybe his wife needed him. It can't be anything to do with work or he'd have taken me with him.'

'He depends on you.'

'I'll admit to being his buffer.'

His clean way of looking at the world made her feel safe.

Nico walked into the Hotel Bella Vista restaurant. It was empty inside and out. Nelli and Laura had chosen a different restaurant in which to have dinner. So had Vittori and Reni. Nico walked back to his car with OneWag. He knew he was always welcome at Sotto Il Fico, but tonight home was the best place for him. He was feeling down about Nelli, about another senseless murder. A bowl of pasta e fagioli with a couple of glasses of wine would restore his spirits.

Nico opened the car door. 'Come on, OneWag, it's home for us.'

The dog bent his head to one side and gave Nico a long look.

Something was not right.

'Go on,' Nico said. 'Get in.'

OneWag jumped in and waited on the passenger seat for Nico to sit and latch his seat belt.

'Stop staring. I'm fine,' Nico said. 'Down you go.' Nico insisted the dog curl up in the foot space on the passenger side to avoid flying off the seat and getting hurt if he had to brake suddenly. The dog obeyed.

Halfway home, OneWag snuck back up onto the passenger seat, lay down and dropped his head on Nico's thigh.

Dino was on night duty when Daniele walked into the station later that night. 'Ciao, Daniele. What are you doing here? Keeping me company?'

'I want to check up on a few things.' He knew he wouldn't fall asleep, not with his blood galloping through his veins after his date with Stella. 'All is quiet?'

'Now it is. Did you have a good time?'

'I did.' Daniele could still feel her mouth pressed against his as he walked towards the maresciallo's office. He was still holding the door when Dino's comment pierced through his romantic fog. He turned around. 'Did something happen?'

'I'd say so. Pietro Rinaldi got himself killed.' He gave Daniele the details he knew.

'When did you get the news?'

'When we were parading at the concert to make sure no one was going to get shot.'

The excitement of the evening vanished. He should have been with the maresciallo. It was his job. 'Why didn't the maresciallo tell me?'

'He took Nico with him instead. Take two guesses why. No, your head is in the clouds. I'll give you three.'

The clouds cleared and Daniele blushed. 'Oh,' he said, remembering the old woman's words as she took their order. *'Thanks to the good heart of the maresciallo.'* He'd been given a big discount on the restaurant bill and now much more. He felt a jumble of emotions: surprise, embarrassment and pride too. He wasn't just one of the maresciallo's brigadieri. The maresciallo cared.

'The maresciallo's got a mean temper,' Dino said, 'and sometimes he's full of shit, but a shovel will show you he's a good guy.'

'Yes, he is.' Daniele opened the office door. 'I'll see you later.'

'Don't stay in there too long,' Dino said. 'Get some sleep. Tomorrow's going to be a busy day.'

'I won't be long.'

'If I'm asleep, let me be.'

'I will. Sweet dreams.'

'Sexy is what I'm looking for.'

Daniele opened a window to let fresh air in. He clicked on his desk lamp, turned on the computer and sat down. He sucked in a long breath and let it out slowly, hoping it would quiet him down. He couldn't believe his luck. First Stella, then the maresciallo.

The screen lit up. He first went to BeppeInfo's blog as he had done the night before. Beppe now had 506 followers. @ZorroZero had sighted a Ducati in front of a bar, but it turned out to be a more recent model. @Gloriagloris asked why there wasn't a reward for finding the motorcycle. Beppe had answered, 'Money corrupts. Justice glorifies.'

Good for him, Daniele thought with a chuckle. He read quickly through the gossip and the sports comments. There was no other Ducati-related news. *Would the Ducati ever be found?* Daniele wondered. Did it matter? Whatever traces it might have held of Cesare's murder would be long gone by now. Maybe they needed to find it for Laura and Signora Lucchetti so they could grant Cesare's wish.

Daniele switched to the 102 police headquarters that hadn't responded as of this morning. Sixty-three headquarters had not issued a passport for Cesare Rinaldi. The sixty-fourth – police headquarters of Genoa – had a different answer. Daniele wrote down the information. Then he turned off the computer, the desk lamp, closed the window and left the office. Dino was at his post at the front desk, his head cradled in his arms. Daniele wished him a silent good night. He prayed he would be able to sleep as well as Dino. Tomorrow was a church day, but two murders still had to be solved.

CHAPTER THIRTEEN

After his routine morning run, Nico showered quickly and drove to town with OneWag. Normally Nico made his own breakfast on Sundays since Gogol preferred to go to early Mass, but today he was meeting with Perillo and Dani at the station at ten. Before going into the café, he walked over to Nelli's studio with OneWag running ahead of him. The door was locked. The dog looked up at him and whined.

'I'm with you, buddy,' he told OneWag. 'We'll just have to be patient.' OneWag responded with a bark.

'What are you doing here on God's Day?' Sandro said as Nico walked into Bar All'Angolo. Sandro was chewing on a cornetto. The place was empty. Church or sleep kept people away until later.

'Buongiorno. I missed you,' Nico said, paying Sandro

for his coffee and cornetto. At the far end of the counter Jimmy waved and started Nico's americano. OneWag scooted around the very clean floor.

Sandro gave Nico his change. 'You've never missed us on a Sunday before. Why today?'

'Why all these questions?' Nico asked, grateful Pietro's death was not yet a news item.

'You walked in with a very serious look. I thought something new had happened. Rocco, here.' Sandro threw what was left of his cornetto at OneWag, who leaped and caught it.

'I'm curious about something that happened eight or nine years ago. A car accident in which Laura's sister, Gabriella, died. Did you hear about it then?'

'We weren't friendly with Laura yet,' Jimmy said, 'but in this town, if tragedy or comedy happens within a sixty-kilometre radius, it gets talked about, examined carefully, even fought over.'

'What was the general opinion?'

'She fell asleep, she was drunk, she killed herself, someone pushed her off her road. Take your pick.'

'That was around the time Cesare was coming here,' Sandro said.

Nico stayed at the counter to have his breakfast. OneWag aimed all his attention at Sandro. 'Did Cesare say anything about the accident?'

'I remember him walking out when Gustavo and his friends were talking about it. The only reason I remember is because he always stayed much longer. This time five minutes at the most and he was gone.'

Jimmy gave Sandro a long look. 'And you were happy.'

'Relieved,' Sandro answered. 'Why the interest now, Nico?'

'I found out about it a few days ago. It must have been very painful for Laura.'

'Losing a sister is the least of it,' Jimmy said. 'Some people blamed her.'

'Some people have no brains. I'll see you tomorrow. Come on, OneWag, Sandro will give you another chance to leap tomorrow.'

Daniele stood up when Perillo walked into the office at 9.59 sharp. 'Thank you. It was very kind of you to give me the evening off and to get me the discount.'

A discount I'm paying for. 'You deserved it,' Perillo said. 'All you missed was looking at another dead body. Nico is used to that. I'm sure the Florence team took the necessary photographs. We'll have to wait for forensics and Gianconi to tell us more.' He draped his jacket over the back of his chair and sat down.

'When I came back last night,' Daniele said, 'I checked to see if any police headquarters had issued a passport to Cesare. We now have sixty-four who have responded in the negative.'

Perillo shook his head in disbelief. 'Dani, a night off means a night off.'

'I know. I couldn't sleep,' Daniele admitted.

'Ah, I remember those days,' Perillo said with regret. The office door opened. 'Ah, here is our American detective, punctual as ever.'

'Not if I stay in this country much longer,' Nico said.

'Buongiorno. I knew I could count on Daniele to be here.' The young man looked sleepy and radiant at the same time. He guessed love could come up with that combination.

'I am here too,' Perillo grumbled. 'Where's Rocco?'

'He went straight to Vince's room.'

'Dumb question.' Perillo picked up the office phone. 'I'm ordering an espresso. Anyone else?'

Both answered, 'No, thank you.'

'Vince, order a double espresso and an apricot juice.' Perillo put the receiver back in its cradle. 'Don't worry, Dani, you can keep it in Vince's refrigerator for later. He doesn't like the stuff. Our main suspect is dead. Now, let's sit and do some rethinking.'

Nico sat in the chair in front of Perillo's desk. 'Let's talk about Pietro.'

'There's not much to say yet,' Perillo said. 'Pietro must have seen who used Laura's phone and thought he'd found the pot at the end of the rainbow. What I don't understand is why he thought he could get away with it.' He dropped his elbows on his desk and ran his fingers through his thick black hair. 'Dumb, dumb, dumb.'

'Money does that to people,' Nico said.

Daniele had brought over his chair from the back of the room and now sat down. 'I have news,' he announced.

Perillo narrowed his eyes. 'What?'

'Fifty years ago, Cesare Rinaldi assaulted someone who later died. He ended up in jail for nine and a half years. He never went to Germany.'

'Ah, the loner had a good reason to keep to himself.' Perillo stretched his legs under the desk. 'No wonder he didn't communicate with anyone. It also explains why he liked to say he'd worked behind the hotel bar since he was eighteen.'

This was an interesting new development, Nico thought. 'Where was he jailed?'

'In Genoa for most of his sentence. His last year they transferred him to Gorgona for good behaviour.'

'Where's that?'

There was a knock on the door. 'Come in, come in,' Perillo called out.

Renzino, the bar boy, walked in with a small tray.

'Ciao, Renzino,' Perillo said. 'I see you've gone back to your natural hair colour.' He'd been blond in April. A redhead the year before.

Renzino's mouth sagged. 'My girlfriend broke up with me.'

Perillo made room on his desk. 'Sorry to hear that. Put it on my desk. Vince will pay. Make sure he gives you a good tip.'

'Yes, Maresciallo.' Renzino put the espresso and the small bottle of apricot juice on the desk.

As soon as Renzino closed the door behind him, Perillo answered Nico's question. 'It's an island in the Tuscan archipelago.' He drank his espresso in two gulps. 'I'm sure Dani can tell you more. Something is ringing in my head.'

Dani was glad he'd taken the time this morning to look up Gorgona. 'A monastery used to be there in the Middle Ages.'

Perillo sat back and opened his desk drawer. He took out a notebook and started leafing through it.

'It's only one square mile and used to house a hundred inmates,' Daniele said. 'Like your Alcatraz, it is impossible to escape from there. The prisoners grow their own food, cook it. They even make their own wine, learn to—'

'Here it is,' Perillo said, his finger pressed against the sheet of paper. 'Cesare told Laura he was the only Tuscan who mastered winemaking on a small island. When I asked her which island, she said she didn't know.'

'She probably didn't,' Nico said. 'Jail time isn't something you brag about. I'm speculating here, but I think his doing time is the reason his father left him the property. To keep him home and out of trouble.'

'Could be.' Perillo closed the notebook and put it back in the drawer. 'Thank you, Daniele, for being so thorough.'

Daniele nodded and tried to ignore the heat rising to his cheeks.

'So now we know Cesare did time,' Perillo said. 'How does that help us with his murder? Forty years have gone by.'

'Fifty since he was first jailed,' Daniele said.

Perillo raised his hands in surrender. 'All right. If someone was after him back then, he wouldn't wait until now to kill him. He could have got to him at any time. Cesare didn't bother to change his name.'

Nico stood up. 'Giving Sirio Reni another look would be good. Check if anyone by that name was in the Genoa jail or on Gorgona. Vittori too.'

Perillo laughed. 'He would have been no more than ten.'

'You know his exact age?'

'Vittori is sixty-eight,' Daniele said.

'Well, he looks younger,' Perillo said in his defence.

'Thinking it might be important,' Daniele said, 'I did send a request for a list of Cesare's cellmates in the Genoa jail and a list of the Gorgona prisoners while he was there.'

Perillo pointed a finger at his brigadiere. 'You hear that,

Nico? This man I have trained diligently is now after my job.'

Daniele jumped to his feet. 'Never, Maresciallo!'

'Sit down, I'm kidding. Bravo, Daniele. I'm proud of you.' Daniele opened his mouth to speak. Perillo raised his hand.

'Do not thank me.'

Daniele sat back down.

Nico said, 'We also need to find out the name of the man who died from Cesare's assault. This could be a revenge killing.'

Perillo gave Nico a wide-eyed stare. 'We? You hand out work to be done and you are going where, may I ask?'

'To get my dog and drive up to San Casciano to talk to some carabinieri.'

Perillo nodded his approval. 'Maresciallo Sanna is waiting for you. He's an intelligent Sardinian eager to answer all your questions. I told him you are an honorary brigadiere of the carabinieri. Maresciallo would have been an exaggeration.'

Nico accepted the tease with a lavish smile. 'I'm honoured.'

Daniele's chair scraped against the floor as he stood up. 'You are looking into Gabriella's accident.'

'Yes, I am,' Nico answered.

Daniele looked puzzled. 'I read the newspaper account. She lost control on a curve and crashed. It was late at night. She must have fallen asleep. Do you think there might be a connection to the murder?'

'Not necessarily. If I find out anything interesting, I'll let you know. Ciao.'

'Wait.' Perillo pushed himself out of his armchair. 'Ivana

is preparing another fantastic Sunday meal. You're welcome to come. You'll go later to San Casciano.'

'Thanks. Maybe on another Sunday.' Nico was tempted to accept Perillo's invitation, but at the concert he'd caught Nelli looking at his expanded belly. He'd been finding comfort in relentless snacking. With OneWag happily participating. 'As of today, OneWag and I are on a diet. Arrivederci.' Nico walked to the door and closed it behind him.

Perillo shook his head while in the hallway Nico whistled for his dog. 'He doesn't know what exquisite morsels he's missing.'

'No, he doesn't,' Daniele agreed. Ivana's Sunday lunches were Rabelaisian feasts to which he was always invited.

'You also will miss those morsels, but Ivana is willing to relinquish you to Stella.'

Daniele's cheeks bloomed with happiness and embarrassment. 'I thank Ivana and you, Ma— Salvatore.'

'Enough with the thanking. Don't darken my sight until tomorrow morning.'

It was a thirteen-kilometre uphill drive from Greve to San Casciano, with the usual Chianti curves. Nico had been there only twice. The first time, with Rita, he'd learnt that the town went back to Etruscan and Roman times and had flourished for a long time. During the Renaissance it became an important military outpost for the Florentines who built the massive walls that still surrounded the old city. WWII had left the town half destroyed. Now, as Nico walked through the streets, he could see no sign of what the Germans and the Allies had done.

On his second trip to the town, a blistering hot Monday in July, Nico had brought OneWag with him. He needed to shop for pots and pans at the vast market that snaked through many of the streets. Dogs were good at remembering places and today OneWag trotted confidently ahead of Nico, stopping only to sniff passing dogs and interesting corners.

At the carabinieri station, after introducing himself to the brigadiere at the entrance, Nico met Maresciallo Sanna, a nice-looking man of average height, dressed in jeans and a long-sleeved polo shirt. Nico thought he was somewhere in his late forties. After shaking hands, Sanna noticed OneWag checking his sneakers.

'Ah, another dog lover. I have two at home,' Sanna said with a smile. 'I used to bring one or the other with me to the station, but now, because of a mouse situation, we have a cat. Let us go to the café so your dog will not risk losing his eyesight. It is more pleasant there anyway.'

At the café a few doors down from the station, Sanna led Nico to a corner table far from the counter.

'I often do my thinking here,' Sanna said as he sat down after Nico. 'A glass of orange juice to counter fatigue and the brain starts moving like a mill churning water.' They both ordered a glass of orange juice. With the street exploration clearly over, a disappointed OneWag settled underneath Nico's chair.

Sanna didn't wait for Nico to ask a question. 'I have looked over the record of the accident that killed Gabriella Benati very carefully. Luckily the man who prepared the report, now retired, lives nearby, in Calcinaia. After I called him about the accident, he came to the station to explain.

He had seen the fresh dent and long scratch on the driver's side of the car and thought it was more than likely another vehicle had sideswiped Benati in the curve, making her lose control, cross the road and crash against a massive tree. He also found suspicious the telephone call from the man who wouldn't leave his name.'

Nico leant forward. 'Is there a record of that phone call?'

'Not anymore, but let me finish. You will find this interesting and odd. The brigadiere . . .' Sanna stopped to take a long sip of the orange juice the waiter had just brought.

Nico drank his too. 'The brigadiere,' he prompted.

'The one on duty the night of the accident called Benati's mother the next morning to tell her how the accident probably happened. He didn't get to the end of what he wanted to say because the grandfather was on the phone saying he didn't care how his beautiful granddaughter had died. She was dead and if her sister hadn't made that drunken phone call, she would still be alive. Before we could say anything, the grandfather hung up the phone.'

'That was the end of it?'

'Yes. Brocci wrote his suspicions in the report. I have it in my office if you want to read it.'

'Your word is enough. The press made no mention of the possibility of another car being involved?'

'Benati's mother called back and asked us to please not amplify the tragedy with conjecture. Brocci's superior agreed.'

'I see. Thank you for this information.'

Sanna finished his glass and wiped his mouth with a napkin. 'I have more.'

Sanna is behaving like an actor onstage, Nico thought, enjoying the lead role, savouring his lines before pronouncing them. 'I'm listening.'

'Someone else has shown interest in the accident.'

'Yes, I know. Nelli Corsi. She came to your station after the accident to report the dent that wasn't there the morning of the accident.'

'That was almost nine years ago. A month or so ago, I don't have the exact date on my tongue, Gabriella's sister, Laura, asked to see the report. After she read it, she wanted to know if we had a recording of the phone call reporting the accident. She also wanted to know why we hadn't followed through on our suspicions. I told her why and apologised. Had I been in charge, we would have opened an investigation. We should not have allowed the family to influence us.'

'She must have been upset.'

'If she was, she didn't show it. I thought she looked almost relieved.'

Relief was not what Nico had expected. He held out his hand. 'Thank you, Maresciallo.'

Sanna shook his hand. His grip was hard. 'My duty. It's always a pleasure to meet a New York homicide detective.'

'Retired. Now I play at being an honorary carabiniere.'

They left the café together and as soon as Sanna turned his back to return to the station, Nico shook his hand to bring the blood back. On the way to the car, he bought a tuna and artichoke panino, which he shared with OneWag, and called Perillo. Nico let it ring while he finished eating. Perillo didn't pick up. He was probably napping after gorging on Ivana's food. Nico didn't leave a message.

* * *

Stella had taken Daniele to her parents' apartment in the new part of town. Now they were sitting on the narrow balcony eating schiacciata sandwiches made with the only things they had found in the refrigerator: pears and ricotta sprinkled with honey. Tilde and Enzo were busy at the restaurant.

The sun was high in the sky, but a cold wind was diligently blowing away any warmth. Daniele was wearing jeans, sneakers and a cotton sweater.

'It's not too cold for you?' Stella asked, dressed in jeans, ankle boots, a white shirt and the grey wool sweater Tilde had left on the sofa.

'It's nice out here,' Daniele said, avoiding a direct answer. He was cold and the view offered only the row of two-family homes across the street. Between the houses, he could see narrow swaths of greenery from the park. Stella's stunning face with her jade-green eyes was the only view he wanted.

'I hope this is enough to eat for you,' Stella said after taking a sip from her Peroni beer bottle. 'I thought there might be some more food available.'

'It's fine,' Daniele said. Food was the last thing on his mind. 'I'm still full after last night's dinner.' As soon as he had walked into the empty apartment with Stella, he'd felt a tingling in his stomach.

Stella propped her feet on the balcony railing and took a bite of her sandwich, careful not to let the ricotta ooze out. 'We would have had a better meal at Sotto Il Fico, but Nonna Elvira and Mamma would watch our every move.'

Daniele looked at Stella with a wide smile. 'Much better here.'

Stella noticed his eyes bright with what? Excitement? Expectations? Maybe both. She felt a pang of guilt. With legs back on the floor, she met Daniele's look with a serious face. 'I'm sorry, Dani. I brought you here because I thought it was just a good place to talk without anyone looking over us.'

Daniele's body turned hot with embarrassment.

Stella dropped her elbows onto the table to explain herself. 'I like being with you very much. It makes me happy. That's why I kept kissing you last night. I'm not saying I was kissing you just for fun. I wanted more too, but if we make love, it becomes something serious. At least for me.'

'For me too.'

'Then you understand. I'm not ready to be serious about anything except work right now. The catastrophic Gianni breakup was just over a year ago and it was pretty devastating.'

'I know. I'm sorry you had to suffer like that.'

'Thank you. Are we still kissing friends?'

Daniele muttered something quickly.

'Are you telling me to go to hell in Venetian dialect?' Stella asked.

'No, it's just a saying. *Quando l'è finio el vin, va ben anca l'acqua.*' He downed his Peroni with flaming cheeks.

'When the wine is gone, water is also okay?'

Daniele nodded.

Stella squeezed his hand. 'You're too good for me.'

'I'm not walking away from a friend, that's all.'

Stella gave Daniele's hand another squeeze. 'Thank you.' She changed the subject. 'I heard about the second murder. It's horrible. Do you have any idea why?'

'Greed. We think Pietro Rinaldi was blackmailing his uncle's murderer.' He took a large bite of his sandwich.

'You think he witnessed the actual killing?'

'I think he saw who picked up Laura Benati's phone and made the call.'

'What call?'

'I'm sorry, I shouldn't have said anything.'

'Top secret, eh?'

Daniele nodded while taking the last bite of his sandwich.

'I know Laura a little,' Stella said. 'She's a friend of Sandro and Jimmy's. I have a fun picture of her with the two of them and me licking ice cream cones. Nonna took it and put it in her memory book. She used to take pictures of everything, great or horrible, like the ones of her parents in their coffins.' Stella shook her shoulders to shake off the image. 'Laura's the number one suspect in the bartender's murder, isn't she? Mamma said that's what people here are saying.'

'She isn't, and if she was, I couldn't tell you, but she isn't. It's terrible that people think that. I don't know how she finds the will to work and face people. First, she loses her sister and gets blamed for it by her family, and now she loses a good friend, maybe her best friend.'

Stella looked at her wonderful, kind friend, the man she was slowly falling in love with. 'Even if the evidence points directly at Laura, you can't imagine a beautiful woman being so evil as to kill a human being.'

'It's not her looks. It's how she comes across. Kind, gentle and mostly sad.'

In the old part of town, the Sant'Agnese Church bells rang the three o'clock hour.

'My parents are going to come home soon.'

'I know. You need to spend some time with them before you leave.'

'And Nonna.' Stella leant over and kissed Daniele on the lips. 'Forgive me, Dani.'

He kissed her back, harder. 'There's nothing to forgive.' He kissed her nose. 'I mean it.' Her forehead got his last kiss. 'I appreciate your honesty.' She had said being with him made her happy. That was all he needed for now.

Daniele stood up and took hold of his empty beer bottle and plate. 'Let me help you clean up. I'm going to do some work on the case now. You gave me an idea I want to follow up on.'

'What idea?'

'That your Nonna is not the only one who has pictures of memories.'

Once back in Gravigna, Nico called Nelli.

Nelli picked up after two rings. 'How are you, and where are you?' If he was nearby, would she invite him over? No. She'd lead him straight to her bed.

'I'm home and missing you. Am I disturbing you?'

'I was enjoying the book you suggested a while back.' Nelli was stretched out on her sofa, with an 87th Precinct novel by Ed McBain. She had asked to know more about his old job, hoping to understand his emotional guard.

'Should I hang up?'

'The book can wait. I heard about Pietro Rinaldi. That's why you rushed off in the middle of the concert, isn't it?'

'Yes, it is.'

'It's horrible news, and I'm so sorry you are in the middle of it.'

'Nelli, it's my work.'

'Back in New York. You're in Chianti now!'

'The land where you don't have to be something, you can just be.'

'Exactly. Can't you give it up?'

'Perillo asked for my help.'

'You could have said no.' Nelli stopped speaking for a moment. 'I apologise. I have no right to be annoying.'

'You're never annoying, Nelli. Listen, I've done a lot of thinking. I want to see you and talk about us. When can we see each other? Tonight maybe?'

'I just don't know how you stomach violent death.' As soon as the words were out of her mouth, Nelli wanted to take them back.

'I don't stomach it. I hate it.' Nico's voice was full of emotion. 'I do it because murderers have to be stopped, and the people the victims leave behind need answers. Please understand, Nelli.'

'I'm sorry.' Nelli felt the tension leave her body. She loved this man. 'Tonight would be lovely.'

'Great, I'll cook up something. I want to thank you for talking to me about the accident that killed Laura's sister. I just got back from talking to Maresciallo Sanna up in San Casciano.'

Nelli flung her feet to the floor and sat up. 'Why?'

'You made me curious.'

Nelli sucked in her breath. Why had she told him? 'You're going to question Laura about it?'

'I'm going to talk to her. Why don't you come with me?'

'If you want help pinning the murder on Laura, don't count on me.'

'Whoa, that's a jump.'

'For what other reason would you be interested in the accident?'

'I need Laura to open up and tell me what she knows about her sister's death. I found out something today that does not look good for her. It's just a small piece of a bigger jigsaw puzzle. I want to know more, and I'm convinced she can tell me. If she doesn't, I'm afraid Perillo will arrest her.'

'Maybe you believe Laura isn't guilty, but you don't really know. Because she trusts me, she may tell you something that makes things worse for her. I'm sorry, but I can't be part of that. I think you can understand that.'

'I do. I should have reflected before asking you. Dinner tonight then?'

'I think we should wait until you've found your killer. Please be gentle with her. Ciao.' She clicked off before he could say anything more.

OneWag was on the passenger seat, his eyes on his boss. Nico was sitting with his knees hitting the steering wheel, his hand still holding the phone, his eyes staring at the dusty windshield, thinking, *God, what an idiot I am. If I keep making mistakes, I'm going to lose her for good.*

OneWag stretched over the hand brake and gave Nico's chin a lick.

Nico returned the lick with a kiss on the dog's snout. He turned on the motor and shifted out of neutral. He'd face Laura alone.

* * *

Daniele removed the tape in front of Pietro's door and walked into the small one-bedroom apartment. After Pietro had gone missing, he and the maresciallo had searched the place for any clues of the man's whereabouts and found none. They did discover that Pietro had broken into Cesare's sealed house and removed some of his uncle's possessions – three kitchen knives, a pair of scissors, an electric razor, a new bottle of shaving cream, a hiking map and a large envelope filled with photos, belongings that had been in Cesare's house when he and the maresciallo had searched it. Daniele had wondered why Pietro had risked trouble with the maresciallo for so little. Thanks to Stella, now he thought he knew.

Daniele walked into the bedroom, opened the small armoire and lifted the cardboard box holding Cesare's possessions. After dropping the box on the kitchen table, he reached for the envelope. He had already studied these photos during the search of Cesare's house. Five days ago, the only photo of interest had been the one of teenage Jimmy.

Daniele sat down and slowly studied Cesare's memories. An old man holding a large spray can looked at the camera with a smile on his weathered face. A woman with a tired face holding a baby, a little boy holding onto her skirt. A photo of Cesare's father's death announcement plastered on a street wall. A young Cesare with a man who resembled him, both in football uniforms. An older Cesare in jeans and T-shirt next to a row of grapevines with garden clippers in his hands, far in the background what looked like water. A view of a calm sea shot from a height. The last photo was of Cesare with six grinning men of varying ages around a wine bottling machine, each man holding a bottle. Daniele thought of what the maresciallo had read this morning from his interview notes: *'The only Tuscan who mastered winemaking on a small island.'* He squinted, trying to read what was written on the label. He couldn't; the photo had been taken at a distance.

He took a picture of the closest bottle with his phone and magnified it. The label read, La Penitenza. He examined all the faces of the men. He went back to squint at a young one, maybe eighteen or nineteen, with a wide square chin. Did it remind him of . . . ? No. Wishful thinking was making him see things.

Daniele jumped to his feet, gathered the photos, putting the last on top and slipped them back in the envelope. He had found a picture of Cesare on Gorgona, but he wasn't sure it would tell the maresciallo and Nico anything new. That one of those grinning men was Cesare's killer was too much to hope for.

Laura was deadheading the once blue hydrangea bushes that ran along the front wall of the hotel when Nico arrived with OneWag. She was wearing dark green corduroy slacks and a light blue knitted top. The dog went up to her, wagged once in greeting and checked out her shoes.

'Ciao, OneWag.' She did not seem surprised to see them, although Nico had not called beforehand. 'Thank you for finally returning my car, Signor Doyle.'

Nico picked up a dead flower that had fallen on the grass and dropped it in the basket dangling from her arm. 'I'm afraid I had nothing to do with it.'

'But you are part of the investigating team.'

'Yes, I am.' He smiled at her, trying to convey he was not the enemy. 'The maresciallo has made me an honorary carabiniere.'

Laura's expression remained stern.

Nico laughed. 'Not really.'

'Being a New York homicide detective should be enough.'

He had no authority under Italian law. What was he doing trying to trap a perfectly nice woman into admitting she knew who had caused her sister's death?

Laura continued clipping the worn-out flowers. 'If you are looking for Dottor Vittori or Signor Reni, you just missed them.'

No, he was bound by his friendship with Perillo and Daniele. Besides, back in New York, he had encountered many 'perfectly nice' men and women who turned out to be murderers.

Laura kept her face averted from Nico's. 'I've said all I have to say. My car did not have a drop of anyone's blood in it, but if you and the maresciallo still think I'm guilty, have me arrested and get it over with.'

She would have used another car, stolen it, even had an accomplice. 'Can we sit down somewhere private?'

'Here is private. No one is around.'

'I've just come back from talking to the maresciallo at the San Casciano station about your sister's accident.'

Laura snapped the clippers shut with a tight jaw and faced Nico. 'I wanted to know if it was true someone had caused Gabi to lose control.'

'Why after almost nine years?'

'Because I was tired of feeling guilty. I wanted proof it wasn't my fault.' Her voice was low and furious. 'My grandfather hates me for not dying in Gabi's place, and my mother barely accepts my existence. The only one who cared for me after my father was Cesare. Now you and that idiot maresciallo think I killed him because he left me a lot of money. And I'm sure you're wondering how a lowly bartender could have that much. You probably think he stole it.' Her face was red with anger and pain.

'You said he got very good tips.'

'Not that good.' She plunged one hand in the basket and fingered the flowers. 'Signora Lucchetti paid him extravagantly and Cesare never spent a cent except on the Ducati she gave him. You'll never find it, will you?'

'We may not. You must feel better about yourself now that you know someone probably did sideswipe your sister.'

Her hand kept fingering the flowers. 'Discovering that my mother and Nonno stopped the investigation hasn't helped, but I understand why they didn't want Gabi's death being dragged on. I didn't either. It wouldn't have changed anything. I think I wanted to keep wallowing in my own guilt.'

'It was a form of grieving.'

'Maybe.'

'You never wondered then who it might be?'

'No. I blocked out that possibility.' Laura retrieved her hand and dropped the clippers in the basket. 'I'm going to get a glass of water. I'm sure OneWag could use some too.'

The dog had wandered off across the grass, but on hearing Laura's angry voice, he had padded back to sit next to Nico's feet.

'Thank you,' Nico said. 'I would love some water too, if you don't mind.'

Laura gave him a questioning look before saying, 'Follow me.'

They crossed the wide front hall with its dark furniture, the beamed ceiling. OneWag's nails clicked against the dark terracotta tile floor. Nico noted the old tapestries on the wall, and Signora Lucchetti's severe portrait. He had not been inside before. 'It's a very beautiful place.'

'It is, but it needs modernizing. Signora Lucchetti won't permit it.' After walking by a small sitting room, they reached a room that looked more like a library than a bar. Three walls were lined with books of many languages in front of which were two leather sofas, a couple of armchairs and small tables. Laura dropped the basket on the nearest table and walked behind the counter. OneWag followed her. 'Flat or fizzy?' she asked.

'Flat, please. From the faucet is fine with me.'

Laura shook her head and put a ceramic bowl that normally would contain chips on the bar counter. Most Italians considered faucet water unhealthy.

Nico sat on the centre stool. 'You say you blocked the possibility that someone caused your sister's accident. I would have thought you'd welcome it.'

Laura bent down to open the refrigerator below the counter and took out a bottle of flat water. She reached for two glasses from the shelf behind her. 'It wouldn't change anything. I'm still the one who made her get into the car to come get me.'

'If someone did drive your sister off the road and you knew who it was, could you forgive him?'

She opened the bottle and poured water for OneWag. 'I don't see why we are having this ridiculous conversation.'

She bent down and put the bowl on the floor. OneWag swished his tail and eagerly lapped up the water. 'There.' Her voice was soft now. 'I knew you were thirsty.' Laura straightened up.

'I believe someone did sideswipe your sister's car. I think you do too now. Have you thought of who it might have been?'

Laura filled the two water glasses and handed one to Nico. 'I have nothing to go by.'

Nico took a long drink of water, wanting to believe her.

'When I came back from San Casciano,' Laura said, 'I did ask Cesare if he had heard any gossip after Gabi's death. He got angry with me, shouted I needed to stop fixating on the accident and think about the future. That's when I found out Signora Lucchetti had promised to leave him the hotel, but he'd told her he was too old, and she should leave it to me. She has no relatives.' She lifted her glass and drank.

'Would you like that?'

Above the glass, Laura's eyes smiled for a few seconds. 'Yes, very much. I love this place. It's become my home.' She put the glass down, her eyes serious. 'It won't happen now that I'm a suspect in his murder. Signora Lucchetti loved Cesare.'

'What if your name gets cleared?'

'Some people will continue to doubt.'

Nico slipped off the stool. 'Signora Lucchetti seems wiser than that. Thank you for talking to me and quenching our thirst.'

Laura stayed behind the counter. 'I hope you believe me.'

'Why shouldn't I? I do have one favour to ask of you.'

Laura's face tightened. 'What is it?'

He told her.

She thought for a moment. Would complying help her or make things worse? 'Tomorrow morning.' She had so little to lose. 'After ten.'

'Thank you,' Nico said. 'Come on, buddy, it's time we give this lady some peace.'

The word peace made Laura laugh.

As Nico walked to his car, he went over their conversation. Laura had not appeared scared or nervous. She had revealed very personal feelings with what seemed like sincerity. Had she been trying to win him over? Nico didn't know, but he very much wanted to believe her. He hoped it wasn't just for Nelli's sake.

In the car Nico called Perillo. 'Are your Sunday afternoons sacrosanct? I have some news.'

Perillo sighed. 'A long nap has refreshed me considerably, but I do find your zeal and Daniele's, although admirable, annoying.'

'I can wait until Monday.'

'You must not wait. The murder count has grown. I simply wish I had your energy.'

'Blame it on nicotine withdrawal. It's too long a story over the phone. Should I come to your office?'

'I'll come to your house. A nice shot of whiskey will sharpen my ears. Daniele will be with me. He has photos to show us. Not for dinner though. Sunday night with my wife is not negotiable.'

Perillo made himself comfortable in Nico's armchair, looking very relaxed in grey slacks, a red V-necked sweater, white shirt and his suede ankle boots. Daniele sat in a chair next to the kitchen table holding a large grey envelope. He too was dressed nicely in a dark blue V-necked sweater, light blue shirt, dark brown slacks and new sneakers that were intriguing OneWag.

Nico had changed into cargo pants and an old beige crewneck he'd been trying to replace unsuccessfully. Italian men preferred V-necked sweaters.

'Sunday is dress-up day, I see,' Nico said as he poured whiskey into a glass with ice. Daniele had only wanted water.

'I went to church,' Daniele said. He omitted his lunch with Stella.

'As for me, Ivana has made Sunday dinner our night out,' Perillo said. 'She thinks money spent in a restaurant is selfish. I pay her for dinner, and she slips the money in the poor box at church. I get a meal no restaurant could improve, and the poor get the benefit.'

'Back in New York, Sunday was pizza night.' Nico handed Perillo the whiskey glass. He missed those nights. He and Rita would drive down to Greenwich Village and scarf down a large pepperoni pizza at John's of Bleecker Street. Gravigna's pizzeria didn't come anywhere near John's. The first time he'd asked for pepperoni pizza it arrived covered in green peppers. He should have asked for salame piccante. Nico poured himself a glass of his landlord's wine and sat on the sofa next to OneWag. 'Daniele, do you want to go first?' The young man was sitting on the edge, looking eager.

Forever polite, Daniele said, 'No, please, you go first.'

'Yes,' Perillo said, 'tell us first what made you want to look into Laura's sister's accident. I think you said it had something to do with the hotel owner.'

Nico leant over with his elbows on his knees. 'It did, but I want to explain what made me first go off on this tangent. Now that Pietro is dead, Laura becomes our star suspect again. She may not look strong enough to haul a dead body into a car boot but anger can give a person incredible strength. From the start I didn't believe money was a strong enough motive for her to kill Cesare.'

Daniele jumped up as the envelope with the photos slipped to the floor. 'You are right, Nico. She sends half her salary to her mother.'

'You are both wrong,' Perillo argued, waving his glass in the air. 'If she has to send money home, she has all the more reason to want more money.'

'No. If Laura did kill Cesare, it was for a very emotional reason. Not greed.'

Daniele retrieved the envelope from the floor and sat back. He didn't like where Nico was going.

Perillo's hand slapped the desk. 'Laura had an accomplice! That explains how Cesare got into both car boots. Who else but Pietro Rinaldi? He didn't trust Laura but he hated Cesare. Then he made the mistake of blackmailing her and ended up dead.'

'Very possible.' Nico took a sip of his wine and continued. 'While we were having lunch, Signora Lucchetti told me about Cesare being upset and suddenly not having a car anymore around the time of Gabriella's accident. Nelli is convinced someone sideswiped Gabriella's car that night, which could have led her to swerve off the road. She saw a big dent in the driver's side of the car that wasn't there the day before.'

'The carabinieri would have picked up on that.'

'They did and would have pursued it, but Laura's mother and grandfather asked them not to, and I suppose out of respect for their great loss, they obliged. There's something else I find suspicious, besides what Signora Lucchetti said. A man reported the accident to the San Casciano station shortly after it happened, said the victim was already dead, but wouldn't leave his name.'

Perillo took a crisp from the bowl on the side table and bit into it. 'People don't want to get involved.'

'Maybe, but I find it more likely that the caller was the one who caused the accident.'

'What are you leading up to?' Perillo asked.

Nico put his empty glass on the floor. 'Laura was extremely upset by her sister's death. Her family blamed her for it. She probably blamed herself too. She'd made the phone call asking for her sister to pick her up. A few months later, Laura applied for a job at the hotel. Cesare was probably behind it. Signora Lucchetti said he insisted she hire Laura despite her doubts about Laura's emotional strength. Why did he do that?'

'They were friends,' Daniele answered.

'Yes, but how did you find Cesare's phone passcode, Dani?'

Daniele shook his head. 'That was a coincidence.'

'I don't think it was. You found Cesare's phone passcode when you entered the date you'd seen on Signora Benati's cross, the date of her daughter's death.'

Perillo sat up in his chair. 'Are you implying Cesare is the man who sideswiped Gabriella's car? The man who reported the accident after making sure Gabriella was beyond help?'

'That's exactly what I'm implying. Just over a month

ago Laura showed up at the San Casciano station wanting to know more about the accident. She asked to listen to the recording of that call. I was hoping to hear it too, but it was erased years ago.'

Perillo was holding his whiskey glass between his hands, the contents forgotten for now. 'You think she suspected?'

'And maybe asked Cesare. He admitted it and revenge took over.'

'And what?' Daniele asked in an incredulous voice. 'Stabbed him four times?'

Perillo gave Daniele a hard look. 'That's right. An emotional killing. It makes sense, Nico.'

'So far, it only makes sense as a possibility,' Nico said. 'When I came back from San Casciano this afternoon, I went to see Laura at the hotel, and she didn't deny suspecting someone.' He relayed their conversation almost verbatim. 'She was calm throughout. Very natural. Not at all resentful.'

'That's because she's innocent,' Daniele muttered softly.

Nico turned to look at Daniele. 'I want to believe that, Dani, but we have to be thorough.'

'Let's put her aside for now,' Perillo said. 'Dani, show Nico what you have.' Daniele had shown him the pictures back at the station.

Daniele quickly opened the envelope he had kept pressed against his chest. At the sound of crackling paper, OneWag woke up and jumped off the sofa. 'I'm sorry, Rocco, not for you this time.' Daniele took out the two pictures he was sure had been taken on Gorgona and addressed Nico. 'I remember seeing these pictures when we went through Cesare's belongings after he disappeared.

They meant nothing to me or to Salvatore, as we didn't know he had spent jail time on Gorgona. Look, Nico.' He handed over the first photograph.

Nico looked at the one with Cesare alone, turned it around. The back was blank. 'It could be Gorgona. Not a bad place to do jail time.'

'A paradise,' Perillo said, tossing a chip at OneWag, who gave it a quick sniff and jumped back on the sofa. 'Only the reformed prisoners get to go with one or two years left to their sentence.'

'Let me see the other one,' Nico said.

Daniele handed it over. 'The label on the bottle reads, "La Penitenza."'

'Pretty great way to repent,' Nico said. 'Only in Italy.'

'That's right.' Perillo reached for the photograph. 'The good life even for our prisoners. It is not slave labour. They eat and drink what they produce. It gives them a chance to feel human again.' He reached into his leather jacket, extracted a pair of horn-rimmed glasses and slipped them on his aquiline nose.

'That's som—' Nico started to say.

Perillo raised his hand. 'No comments, please. My glasses prove my midlife crisis is over. If I can accept Daniele recording every damn interview, I can accept the fact that my eyes need help.' He turned to his friends. 'Ivana says they look good on me. What do you think?'

'Very professorial,' Nico said, although they made Perillo look more comical than serious.

'Yes, a professor or a lawyer,' Daniele said. The frames were perfect rounds. With them on, the maresciallo looked like an owl. Satisfied by the responses, Perillo examined the faces of the men. 'They look happy, which is nice. I praise your diligence, Dani, but I don't see how these pictures help us with our murders.'

Daniele took a slow, deep breath to stop from blushing, something he'd read on Google. 'I don't either.' The blush didn't come, but the deep breath did nothing to hide his disappointment.

Nico noticed and stepped in. 'One of those men could be our murderer. Dani, you have sharp eyes – did you see anyone who could be Reni or Vittori?'

'Let's be realistic here, please.' Perillo took off his glasses, slipped them carefully in their leather case and raised his thumb. 'First, the chances of one of those men being Reni or Vittori are almost nil.' The index finger came up. 'Second, we need to send their fingerprints to Genoa and Gorgona to see if there's a match.'

'What's third?' Nico asked with a wink at Daniele.

'Third, it's time I get home.' No finger this time. 'I can smell Ivana's cooking from here.'

'That's my loin of pork roasting in milk.'

'Ah.' Perillo stood up and shook his slacks. A crisp fell to the floor, leaving a small oil stain. 'Ivana makes it with veal.'

'It's tastier with pork.' Nico got to his feet and handed the photos back to Daniele, who slipped them back in the envelope.

'Thank you for the whiskey and the chips,' Perillo said. 'Daniele and I will remove the disturbance. Tomorrow I will once again question Laura. By then I'm hoping Gianconi will have Pietro's time of death, approximate as it may be, so I can ask about her whereabouts. I hope you don't mind,

Nico.' His American friend had started to act on his own.

'Perillo, of course not. You're in charge.'

Perillo gave Nico a satisfied smile. 'As the maresciallo, I suppose I am.'

'Always, but please wait for me at the station before you question Laura. I think I might have something that will help you.'

'What?' Perillo asked with a frown.

'You'll find out tomorrow.' Nico accompanied the two men to the door.

'Nico, you're playing games.'

'I learnt from you, Maresciallo.' Nico turned to a discouraged-looking Daniele. 'I'd love to invite you to dinner, Dani, but the only vegetables I can offer are potatoes cooked in milky meat juices.'

'Thank you. I have my dinner. Stella insisted I take home what I hadn't finished at Angela's last night. Now I'm glad I did.'

Nico opened the front door. 'Well then, a buona serata to both and a buonanotte for later. Give Ivana my regards.'

As soon as the door clicked shut, OneWag jumped off the sofa and ran to his food bowl. Overwhelmed by the smell of roasting pork, he used his snout and a paw to noisily overturn the empty bowl.

'I hear you.' Nico laughed and shook his head. 'Sorry, buddy. It's dog food for you.'

CHAPTER FOURTEEN

At ten-thirty Monday morning, Nico walked into Perillo's office with OneWag and the package Laura had given him. Perillo and Daniele had just got back from the coffee bar next door.

From behind his desk, Perillo welcomed Nico with a big grin.

'Buongiorno,' Nico said. 'I'm glad you're happy to see us.'

'I'm happy with myself. Two espressos and not even half a cigarette.' He didn't mention the two he'd had on his after-dinner walk last night.

Nico looked at Daniele for verification.

'He spoke the truth,' Daniele said from his perch in front of the computer, not sharing the maresciallo's happiness. No cigarette meant his boss was going to be in a temper all day.

'Good for you, Perillo,' Nico said. 'Congratulations.' In solidarity with Perillo's efforts, Nico had stopped the one or two cigarettes a day he started smoking after Rita's death.

Perillo's thank-you was a decisive nod. 'What's in the package?'

'Two orange juice glasses from breakfast at the hotel. One with Reni's fingerprints, the other with Vittori's. Now all you have to do is check if they belong to a prisoner in Genoa or Gorgona at the time Cesare was in jail.' Nico gently dropped the package in front of Perillo and sat down in the chair he'd dubbed the 'interrogation chair' because it was always in front of Perillo's desk. OneWag lay down underneath it.

Perillo didn't look happy. 'I was going to ask Laura for those fingerprints.'

'I'm sorry I beat you to it,' Nico said, as a silly phrase popped into his head: *A cigarette a day keeps bad moods away.*

'Don't mind me, Nico. You did well. The only way I can get their fingerprints checked by next year's Christmas is to call in the powers of my esteemed and odious prosecutor, Riccardo Della Langhe. He will want to know why Reni and the distinguished businessman Vittori might be involved in Cesare's murder. I can't tell him we're doing this in the hopes of clearing the most probable murderer, Laura Benati.'

'Maresciallo, that is not the reason,' Daniele spoke softly.

Perillo spun around in his chair. 'Then, for the devil, what is the reason?'

Daniele left his post by the computer and came forward. 'Besides Signorina Benati, there were only three others who could have sent that text from the signorina's phone. With Pietro's murder, now only two. Sirio Reni and Dottor Vittori. Vittori not only wanted Cesare's land, but if Vittori's fancy clients found out he'd been in prison, he would lose his business.'

Perillo interrupted. 'Vittori has been a hotel guest for many years. Cesare would have recognised him.'

'Not necessarily,' Daniele said. 'People's looks change a lot with age. I didn't recognise my grandmother in a picture taken thirty-five years ago. Vittori could have also altered his looks. Maybe something Vittori did recently made Cesare realise who he was. The night before Cesare disappeared, when he dropped the tray and Vittori got so angry, maybe he said something that gave him away.'

Nico sat back and watched. Daniele was speaking with his feet firmly planted on the floor as though the firmness of the ground gave him courage. He was standing up to his boss with intelligence.

Perillo shook his head. 'Conjecture, that's all it is.'

'As for Reni,' Daniele continued as if Perillo had not spoken. 'From what he told you, making a deal with Vittori is extremely important. If he is a jailbird and Vittori found out, ciao ciao to his wind farm deal. The fingerprints will tell us if there is or is not a connection between Cesare and one of those men. I don't see how Prosecutor Della Langhe would object to that reasoning.'

Perillo said nothing.

Daniele waited another moment for his boss's reaction. He looked at Nico, who raised a thumb Perillo couldn't see. 'Maybe Daniele should call Della Langhe and repeat what he just said. You hate talking to the man.'

'I do,' Perillo said, 'but thanks to my brigadiere, I know what to say.' He gave Daniele a begrudging smile.

Expecting anger, Daniele blushed. 'I apologise for speaking out of turn.' In his zeal to shift suspicion from Laura, he now realised he was assuming something. So were the maresciallo and Nico. Maybe they were all wrong.

Perillo dismissed the apology with a wave of his hand. 'You spoke your mind and you spoke well.' He picked up the package Nico had brought. 'Get these glasses dusted for fingerprints.'

Nico watched Daniele hurry out of the room, his arms coddling the package as if it held fresh eggs. OneWag followed him, ready for another visit to Vince's locker.

'Get back here,' Nico ordered. The dog stopped and started a close examination of his hind parts.

Nico shook his head. 'He thinks he's being clever. Any news on the black Toyota?'

'Four stolen in Tuscany, but none with the letter *V* on their license plates.'

'Have you heard from the medical examiner?'

'No. I'll call him now.' Perillo lifted the receiver from the office phone and punched the numbers. 'Buongiorno, Gianconi. Salvatore Perillo speaking. Have you finished with Pietro?' He nodded to Nico. 'Stabbed twice in the stomach. The size of the wounds match Cesare's. Same knife, you think?' Perillo gave another nod. 'When . . . ? Thirty-six to forty-eight hours before we found him? I see . . . Caught by surprise. No defensive wounds. I see. Thank you, Gianconi.'

'When can we have Cesare's body?' Nico asked.

'Ah, wait, Gianconi. Can you release the first body . . . ? Good. Thanks.' Perillo laughed. 'I never want to hear from you again either. Ciao.' He hung up. 'You heard. Pietro was killed thirty-six to forty-eight hours before he was found on Saturday. It won't be easy for our suspects to come up with an airtight alibi for that length of time. I will call Della Langhe and then have another chat with Laura. I need to wait for the results of the fingerprints to interrogate Reni and Vittori.'

'They are at the hotel for now,' Nico said. 'They may leave any moment.'

'I will ask them not to leave the area.'

'You'll need a reason.'

'Nico, you are beginning to weigh heavily on my patience.'

'Trying to help.'

'I know.' Perillo drummed fingers on his desk. After a minute, he exclaimed, 'I have it! The fact that a consummate bartender like Cesare drops a tray of drinks in front of the two of them is suspicious and needs to be investigated further. Now take yourself and Rocco somewhere else while I talk to a surprisingly quiet Della Langhe. Maybe he's sick, not that I wish it for him. Thank you for the fingerprints.'

'Just doing the job you gave me.' Nico stood up. 'I'll leave you now to your prosecutor.'

Perillo waved him off. 'And don't come back!'

'Ciao.'

Perillo picked up the receiver again. His phone rang. It was Dino, whom he had sent to check if the workers at the hotel construction site had seen anything. Perillo dropped the receiver and answered.

'They found Pietro's backpack stuffed down the cement mixer,' Dino said. 'No phone.'

'Shit!' Perillo hung up and opened a drawer of his desk.

He slipped out a cigarette from an opened pack, clamped his lips around it and breathed in the imaginary smoke. Picking up the landline phone again, he exhaled slowly and punched in Della Langhe's number.

Nico drove back to Gravigna and found a lucky spot in the main piazza. Yesterday's cold had retreated. The sky was a cupola of bright blue. The air was still. It was a good day, Nico decided. He stopped by the florist shop.

'Ciao, Luciana, what should I get for Rita?'

Luciana looked up from the bouquet she was arranging. 'You want more flowers?' Usually, Luciana greeted him with big smiles and a tight hug.

'Why not?'

'Take the purple cosmos.' She went back to arranging.

'You're busy.'

'I have lots of orders this week.' She fit a white filler flower in an arrangement of pink roses. 'Cold Januarys equal many October birthdays and I'm not complaining. Not about flowers. About the murders, I am complaining. One was enough. Now we have one more. Is Salvatore waiting for a third one before catching this madman? Keeping us safe is his job, is it not? Yes, it certainly is.'

Nico knew Luciana well enough to know she didn't expect answers. She was sounding out her worry.

'I keep a knife under my pillow now. Enrico's terrified to get in bed with me, but I told him I wasn't going to sleep unless I had the knife. I love my Enrico, but he's a small man. The only time he uses the few muscles he has is with the slicer. I need to protect myself and him. If you're going up to Sotto Il Fico, stop by the shop. Convince Enrico I'm not going to slit his throat in the middle of the night by mistake. Please do that for me.'

'I will next time I see him.' Nico lifted a bunch of cosmoses from a vase on the floor. 'What do I owe you?'

'Nothing. You talk to Enrico. I want him back in bed with me.'

'I will. Thanks.' He wrapped the dripping stems with a plastic bag and walked out while Luciana addressed the roses. 'Who is going to be next I want to know. Not me, not my Enrico.'

'Congratulations on the Fiorentina's win,' Nico called out to the four pensioners sitting on their sunny benches. They were scarved and hatted out of caution, intent on their Monday ritual of discussing Sunday's football games.

Simone, a tiny man well into his eighties, waved his fedora. Gustavo responded with an ecstatic grin. 'I won five euros off of Ettore.'

Ettore elbowed Gustavo. 'Next Sunday, I'll get them back, and some. Stop a minute, Nico. You're always running off somewhere.'

Nico approached the two benches. Knowing where his boss would go next, OneWag ran in the other direction.

'First a bartender gets killed and stuffed in Jimmy's car,' Ettore said. 'That brings it very close to home. Jimmy is one of us. Now another man has been killed not far from here, and I don't see any carabiniere watching over our safety. We could be next.'

Gustavo grunted. 'Who would want to kill you? Your wife maybe.'

'With the wife you've got,' Ettore snapped back, 'you're the one who should worry.'

'Stop it!' exclaimed Pippo. At seventy-nine, he was the youngest of the four. 'They are both fine women, as fine as my Giovanna. The time to berate the fair sex is long gone.'

'Get off the pulpit, will you?' Gustavo grumbled.

Simone looked up at him with a doleful expression, as if to say, *Look what I have to put up with.*

Nico knew they did not mean any disrespect to women or to one another. They were friends who had grown old together, who shared the same frustrations, the same reduced capabilities that came with their age. He would get there soon enough. 'I believe you are perfectly safe.' Simone nodded in approval. 'I'll tell the maresciallo you are worried, and as soon as he has a chance, I'm sure he'll come to reassure you himself.'

'No,' Gustavo said, 'tell him to find the killer first, and you help him. That's a reassurance far better than words.'

'I'm trying. Enjoy this lovely morning.'

Gustavo nodded, as did Simone and Pippo. Ettore did not look convinced.

As Nico walked away from the pensioners, he saw Beppe waving at him from the doorway of Da Gino. Next to him stood lavender-haired Carletta, Gino's daughter. She'd been setting the outside tables for the few tourists that were still around.

Nico acknowledged the wave by raising his hand and walking faster. He was eager to catch Nelli in her studio before she went to work at the GrappoloBello vineyard. First, he needed to let Rita know.

Beppe planted a kiss on Carletta's cheek and ran to catch Nico.

'Ehi, Nico, you're just the man I was looking for. We got

us another murder and my readers are groaning to know some details. What can you tell me?'

'I can't tell you anything, you know that.' Nico kept walking.

'Sure, you can. You're not official. You can tell me everything. Was Pietro stabbed like Cesare? He knew who killed Cesare and tried blackmail, right? It has to be that.'

'It can be anything, Beppe. Any news on the Ducati?'

Beppe grinned. 'Who knows? Maybe any minute now. The wheel of fortune turns in mysterious ways. If you help me, I'll tell you something interesting about Daniele. You'll be surprised.'

Some gossip about Daniele and Stella, Nico guessed. 'Are you going to help me now or not, Nico?'

'I'm sorry, Beppe. I really can't.' Nico looked back at Carletta. She was leaning against the wall of the trattoria, hands in her bright red Da Gino apron, staring at them. 'She's waiting for you.' Nico left the piazza and turned left, headed for the cemetery.

OneWag was waiting for him by Rita's grave. Nico put his phone on vibrate and arranged the cosmoses around the chrysanthemums as best he could. Straightening up, he reached over the flowers to touch Rita's enamelled photo.

'"*Let in someone new,*" you said before you died. I told you never. You got angry with me. You made me promise to try to love again so you could die in peace. Thank you, Rita. I can keep that promise now.'

Nico leant over, kissed Rita's face and left the cemetery. OneWag ran ahead, a dog with a mission.

'Rocco, where are you going?' Nelli called out as she walked out of Bar All'Angolo. The dog did a quick veer to the right and jumped on Nelli. 'Get down, silly. You'll mess me up.' She was wearing a short blue-and-grey-striped dress over dark grey tights and black ankle boots.

'You look lovely,' Nico said as he approached her. 'You're off to work? I thought I could catch you in the studio.' Disappointment in his voice.

'I am. I saw you walk by while I was having an espresso.'

'Why didn't you call out?'

'You had flowers.'

Nico took a step closer to her. He wanted to hold her cheek in his hand, feel her softness, her warmth, but they had an audience. 'I wanted Rita to know.'

She returned his gaze. Her eyes were smiling, welcoming. 'Know what?'

'That I love you. I want you in my life.' There, he'd said it. It felt incredibly good.

Nelli's face changed as though a cloud had released the sun. 'I do too, Nico.'

Nico felt his body lighten. 'Dinner tonight?'

Nelli laughed. 'I hope much more than that.' She leant over and kissed him on the lips. 'Eight o'clock, my place. Ciao.' She was off, striding to her car, her ankle boots hitting the ground with joy.

Nico felt his phone vibrate and slipped it out of his back pocket. 'All is well?' he asked Perillo.

'Della Langhe was in a "joyous mood," his words. His daughter had just got engaged to the "right man." Again, his words. He was only too happy to be of help. He even complimented me on the excellent job I did solving the last murder. I couldn't mention your contribution, of course. I hope you are not offended?'

Nico laughed. 'Perillo, I couldn't care less.'

'You sound happy.'

'I am.' Nico waved at Nelli's retreating car.

'An engagement?'

'An understanding. Did Della Langhe give you a time frame?'

'He knows the Genoa chief of police. We should get an answer quickly. Bad news about Pietro's phone. The construction workers for the new hotel found Pietro's backpack in the cement mixer. His phone wasn't in it.'

'That confirms that Pietro communicated with the killer by phone. Which, by the way, is a plus for Laura's innocence.'

'If she sent that text, why didn't she make Cesare's phone disappear?'

'Precisely.'

'You are assuming that after stabbing a man she had known since childhood her brain was not overwhelmed with emotion,' Perillo added.

'Good point,' Nico said, knowing how eager Perillo was to keep Laura on the suspect list.

'I thought so,' Perillo said in a pleased voice.

'You need to show your face here in Gravigna. People need to be assured they're not going to get killed in the middle of the night.'

'Your town was next. We've already gone around reassuring people in Greve and Panzano. I'll come up tomorrow morning. Save a seat at Bar All'Angolo for me. Enjoy your new mood.'

'Thanks.' Nico clicked off and hoped the fingerprint results took their time coming in. He had a lot of wasted time to catch up on with Nelli. 'Come on, OneWag, let's get a good lunch at our favourite restaurant.'

Halfway up the steep road that led to Sotto Il Fico, a panting OneWag stopped in front of Enrico's shop as he always did.

'Buongiorno, Nico.' Enrico was getting ready to close up for lunch. 'Rocco looks like he needs water.'

'He just came to say hello.' Nico wasn't sure how to bring up Luciana's knife-under-the-pillow comment. 'Mattia Gennari played his flute beautifully at the concert.'

'Mattia was majestic. The relief I felt, you cannot imagine. He brought tears to my eyes.' Enrico opened a bottle of natural Tuscan spring water and poured the water into a bowl.

'You'll spoil him,' Nico protested.

'This is good for Rocco. Don't worry, the bottle comes home with me. Panna water is good for you too. It will cure your kidney stones.'

Nico stepped into the shop and took the bowl. 'Thanks. For the moment I don't have any.' He stepped out again and lowered the bowl to the ground. OneWag dipped his snout in and lapped.

'They will come,' Enrico said. 'You and the maresciallo now have another murder to worry about. The body suffers in face of so much violence.'

'The body also suffers when it's alone. Luciana misses you.'

'You catch that killer and I'll warm her toes again.'

'We will.' Nico handed the empty bowl back. 'Thank you. Arrivederci.'

'For certain.' With the water bottle in hand, Enrico followed Nico out of the shop and locked up.

Nico and OneWag continued up the hill to enjoy a Tilde lunch.

CHAPTER FIFTEEN

Tuesday morning Nelli, Nico and OneWag walked past a small crowd gathered in Gravigna's main piazza. Nelli nodded to a few women as they walked by.

Nico saw Luciana and Enrico in the crowd. 'Are they waiting for Perillo?'

'Yes,' Luciana answered. 'He must have told someone he was coming – that someone must have spread the word.'

'Yesterday I told an enraged Elvira.'

'That's all you need.' Nelli stopped him with her arm. 'I'll join you in a few minutes. I want to drop off this wonderful present at the studio.'

Yesterday afternoon he'd gone to Zecchi's in Florence and bought Nelli some oil paints. 'Don't take too long.'

'I won't.' Nelli wove herself through the crowd.

Nico and OneWag walked into Bar All'Angolo. 'Buongiorno.'

Sandro and Jimmy said their 'ciaos.'

Gogol rose from his chair near the closed French doors. A cold wind had whipped up during the night. 'I greet my friend and remind him, "Here is free from every disturbance."'

'You're right. I'm very late. I'm sorry.' Nico walked over to their table and clasped Gogol's hand. They both sat down. OneWag went to clean the floor of sugar crumbs.

'The usual coming right over,' Jimmy said as he plated two wholewheat cornetti at the far end of the counter.

'Thanks,' Nico said. 'I see you've had a good morning.'

Sandro was picking up dirty cups, saucers, bunched-up napkins strewn along the length of the L-shaped counter. 'We have Salvatore's approaching appearance to thank for that. I'm glad you showed up. We were getting worried.'

Gogol leant over the table and tapped Nico's arm with a long finger. 'I ate both crostini. They were excellent.'

'I deserve that,' Nico said. Sharing the butcher's crostini was a game they played. Gogol always ended up eating both.

'Hail Caesar, we salute you,' Sandro announced.

Nico turned to see the station's Alfa Romeo enter the piazza from the right. On the left Nelli was striding towards him.

Nico turned back to face Gogol. 'The maresciallo is here to reassure everyone about the murders. Do you want to hear him?'

Gogol closed his eyes. 'There is no need. The dying is over.'

Jimmy clapped.

Gogol opened his eyes and looked at Nico. 'The sun shines on your face, although the sky is blanketed. No need to guess the reason. I quote myself. Tell me.'

'Let's have our breakfast first.'

Gogol furrowed his thick grey eyebrows. 'So, what is it? Why, why do you resist?'

'Nico wants to surprise you.' Nelli hugged Gogol from behind. 'Sweet friend, how are you?' She kissed his cheek and sat down next to him.

Gogol's eyes filled with joy. Nelli had been his friend forever. '"And so translucent I beheld her, so full of pleasure."'

Nelli squeezed his hand. 'So full of love.'

The café door opened and Perillo walked in.

Sandro looked up. 'The usual, Salvatore?'

'No, thanks.' Perillo turned to Nico. 'I have news. Come down to the station with me after I'm through here.'

'Can't it wait?' He wanted to enjoy a second breakfast with Nelli before they each went on their separate way for the day.

'That's up to you, Nico.'

'I have to go back to the studio,' Nelli said, surely to make it easier for him. 'And I have news for everyone. I just talked to Laura. Cesare's funeral is tomorrow, ten in the morning at the Santa Maria church in Panzano. The burial will be private.' She looked up at Perillo. 'Can you make an announcement?'

'I'll be happy to. Funerals give closure,' Perillo said. 'We all want that. I'll stop by after I'm through.'

Sandro brought over Nico's breakfast. 'What about you, Nelli?'

'Nothing, thanks. Nico, you'd better go with Salvatore. Whatever it is he wants to share, it's not good. He looked worried.'

'I suspect you're right. But for the next fifteen or twenty minutes, let's just enjoy each other's company.'

'Indeed,' Gogol said, '"For it is not a task to take in jest."'

Forty minutes later, Nico reluctantly followed Perillo down to Greve. He'd left OneWag with Nelli.

'What's the news?' Nico asked as they entered the station. Perillo didn't answer and headed straight to the office. Daniele quickly got on his feet as they walked in. The look on his face was worse than Perillo's.

'There's no match.' Perillo sat behind his desk. 'Reni and Vittori were never in jail. At least not in an Italian jail.'

'That was fast.' Nico sat in the interrogation chair. 'Maybe too fast?'

'No. The Genoa police chief assured Della Langhe he checked carefully. I got accused of wasting his time. Mercifully, Daniele took the call. Now we're back to Laura. I sent Dino to get her.'

'I asked to bring her in.' Daniele aimed his words at Nico. He was still standing in the back of the room, next to his computer.

Perillo turned partway and gave Daniele a long, patient look. 'You are too partial.'

'I did not want her to be scared.'

'My gentle brigadiere,' Perillo said with a smile. 'Pull up a chair and join us.'

Daniele placed his chair next to Perillo's desk. 'May I ask a favour?'

'What is it?'

'I would like to ask her some questions first.' Perillo knit his eyebrows in a frown.

'Why?'

'I don't think she told us the whole truth.'

Perillo lifted his hands in the air in a gesture of disbelief. 'That's what I've been saying all along. What made you change your mind?'

'It's so easy to make assumptions, to see, but not register what you've seen.' After the negative fingerprints report had come in, Daniele had taken advantage of the maresciallo's Gravigna visit to sit on a bench in the park across from the station. 'I went over the case day by day in my mind.' He did not add the two phone calls he made after his thoughts had cleared. One had been to ask a question. The other was a warning.

'Good,' Perillo said. His idealistic brigadiere had come to his senses. 'But why take this unpleasant task on yourself?'

'With gentle handling,' Nico said, 'Laura might even confess.' Had Daniele really changed his mind about Laura's guilt, he wondered, or did Daniele simply want to soften the blow? 'Besides, it would be good practice for him.'

Perillo grunted. 'To steal my job, you mean.' He looked up at his brigadiere standing rigid by his chair. 'I'll give you five minutes.'

Daniele finally let himself sit down. 'Thank you, Maresciallo.'

'I think now I do deserve to be called Salvatore.'

Daniele nodded.

Laura sat rigid in the chair Nico had vacated, facing Perillo and Daniele. She was dressed in a dark blue skirt and a lighter blue sweater.

'May I call you Laura?' Daniele asked with a smile.

'That's my name.'

'The maresciallo is allowing me to ask you some questions first. I am recording this interview.'

'Go ahead. I did not kill Cesare.'

'You must have wanted to.'

'Why?'

'Because he's the man who caused your sister's fatal accident.'

Laura's face blanched. 'No.'

'After you spoke to the carabinieri in San Casciano, didn't you ask Cesare if he knew who had hit your sister's car?' Daniele saw her shoulders relax.

'Yes, yes, I did. He told me to stop obsessing about it.'

'How could you not obsess? You had every right to obsess.'

Laura leant forward, elbows on knees, her eyes wide on Daniele.

Daniele leant into her. Their faces were two feet apart. 'Someone else caused Gabi's death.' His voice was low. The tape recorder was right there on the maresciallo's desk. 'It wasn't your fault. If you would prove it, your mother would love you. Even your grandfather would love you.'

Laura shook her head, unwanted tears gathering in her eyes.

'Didn't you ask him again if he knew who it was?'

She wiped her eyes. 'No.'

Daniele said nothing.

Laura sat back. 'Well, yes, I did. A few days later. I was sure he knew something and didn't want to tell me.'

'I spoke to Signora Lucchetti this morning,' Daniele said. 'She had told you about something happening to Cesare's car, his refusing to drive another one. Did you ask Cesare what happened?'

Laura uncrossed her legs, readjusted her skirt. 'Why are you asking me all this? Cesare's death has nothing to do with Gabi's accident. I did not kill Cesare. That should be enough.'

'It is far from enough, Signorina Benati,' Perillo said. 'Please answer Brigadiere Donato. Against my better judgment, he is trying to help you.'

'Thank you, Maresciallo,' Daniele said. 'I am trying to help you, Laura. Cesare died because he caused Gabi's death and you know it.'

'No!' Laura cried out, her hands clutching the seat of the chair, as if she needed to hold herself down. 'I know nothing.'

'You do know, Laura. He was your friend since childhood. You know what it is like to carry the guilt of a death. You've carried it every day since Gabi died. So did Cesare.'

Laura bowed her head.

Daniele wondered if she was praying. 'I believe Cesare did finally tell you he was the one who caused Gabi's accident. He risked a job he loved, he risked your friendship, but he finally told you anyway, didn't he?'

'No.'

'Why do you think he told you after almost nine years?'

Laura's hands turned into fists. She lifted her head to look at Daniele, her face creased with emotion. 'Please leave me alone.'

Daniele wanted nothing more than to leave her alone. He couldn't. He needed to break her down before the maresciallo took over. 'Cesare didn't leave you alone when you needed help. He took care of you. He loved you. He must have suffered greatly to see you continue to grieve over Gabi, over your family's anger. What made him finally tell you the truth?'

Laura unfurled her fists, laid her hands flat on her thighs. Daniele watched as her whole body relaxed. He let his tension go with hers.

'He'd run out of mint for the bar.' Laura spoke slowly, her head bent. 'The vegetable shop in Panzano didn't have any so I offered to get some from my mother's garden. He drove me over. When I gave him the mint, my grandfather saw us from the window and started shouting for us to leave, that the sight of me or any friend of mine made him sick. I was used to my grandfather's anger and insults, but Cesare was very shaken. When we got back to the hotel, he said he realised I was being blamed for Gabi's death and he confessed it was his fault Gabi died.'

'When did he tell you this?'

Laura looked up. 'Two days before he went missing.' Her face was empty of any expression except exhaustion. It was as if there was no emotion left in her. 'He said I would feel better hating him instead of myself.'

'Do you hate him?'

Laura didn't answer. Perillo was fidgeting in his chair, eager to take over. Nico sat on a stool at the back of the room, the proverbial fly on the wall, admiring Daniele, but also puzzled by him.

After a minute of silence, Perillo's patience ended. 'Laura Benati, I arrest—'

Daniele shot up from his chair. 'Wait, Maresciallo!'

Perillo froze Daniele with a seething look. 'What the hell do you think you are doing?'

Daniele turned off the tape recorder. 'I apologise, Maresciallo. I had no right to interrupt you, but there is more you need to know before arresting her.'

'What is that, Brigadiere Donato?' Perillo's voice had the sharpness of an ice pick.

'I think I know where we can find Cesare's Ducati.'

'And where is that?'

'No,' Laura said with a pleading look at Daniele.

'I'm sorry, Laura,' Daniele said and meant it. 'I have to.'

'No,' Laura repeated in a whisper.

'Where?' Perillo asked again, the sharpness still there.

With an apologetic look at Laura, Daniele told him.

Perillo slapped a hand on his desk with a happy face. He'd been right all along. 'Of course! Where else? Nico, we should have known.'

Nico looked at Laura's frightened face and wished Daniele was wrong.

'Right in her own backyard.' Perillo started to get up when a thought brought him back down with a thump. 'We'll need a search warrant.'

'We won't, Maresciallo. We'll be welcome.'

'Then let's get into uniform,' Perillo said. 'You'll explain that welcome later.'

Daniele drove Perillo and Laura down the rutted road in silence. In the Alfa the ride was far more comfortable than on his motorcycle, but Daniele was too tense to notice, his thoughts on what was to come. Following the Alfa in his little Fiat, Nico felt every rut and wondered what had led Daniele to realise the truth.

The house with blue shutters appeared on the left. Daniele slowed the car and turned onto a paved road just wide enough to hold a car. Nico followed. Beppe was standing by the greenhouse door next to Signora Benati. He had a shovel in his hand. Before the Alfa came to a complete stop, Laura jumped out and ran to her mother. Instead of embracing, they looked at each other, Laura's hand reaching for her mother's and holding it tight.

Beppe walked up to Daniele as he got out of the car. 'Ehi, Daniele, this is exciting. I'm ready to start shovelling. The signora is willing to lend you hers.'

'Buongiorno, Beppe.' Perillo came around from the other side of the car. 'I hope my brigadiere is right about this. I don't want to end up in another police joke about how dumb the carabinieri are.'

'You won't, Maresciallo.' Beppe glanced at Daniele. 'He won't, will he?'

Daniele mentally crossed his fingers. 'Let's get star—' A shout stopped him.

'Get out of my property now, you bastards!' Laura's grandfather was standing at the front door in jeans, a pyjama top and bare feet. He held up a rifle and aimed. 'Out now! And get that drunken bitch out of here too. I'll shoot.'

Perillo put a hand on his gun. Daniele did the same. Beppe snuck behind the Alfa and crouched. Nico had given up guns three years ago. All he could think of doing was slamming his car door as hard as he could to distract the man, shift his aim. The old man kept his eyes on the two uniformed men with guns. Laura was sobbing.

'Get in your cars and leave. You have no right to be here.' Gualtieri's voice broke as he yelled. 'This is private property!'

Signora Benati rushed towards him. 'Stop it, Babbo. Get back in the house. It's too cold. You'll get sick again.'

As Signora Benati tried to push her father back inside the house, Daniele handed his phone to Nico and walked towards them. 'Buongiorno, Signor Gualtieri. I'm sorry we upset you. We should have called beforehand.'

Gualtieri pushed his daughter aside and squinted at Daniele. 'I know you.' The hand on the barrel was shaking.

Daniele kept walking. 'Yes, we had coffee together the other day. I had come to ask you about Cesare Rinaldi.'

Gualtieri spit on the ground. 'That son of a bitch deserved what he got.'

'He was in love with your wife, wasn't he? Did she love him back?'

'She was a stupid cow. Him taking off for years, that was my doing. I told him I'd kill him if he ever got near my wife again.'

Signora Benati tried to lower the barrel. Gualtieri tightened his double-handed grip, one finger still on the trigger. 'Why don't we go inside, Babbo?' Her anguished face turned to Daniele. 'Come, Brigadiere Donato, come inside with us. I'll make coffee.'

'That would be nice.' Daniele was now only an arm's length from Gualtieri. 'Cesare deprived people of what was rightfully theirs. You told me that, remember?'

'Yes, a vulture. A filthy stinking vulture.'

'He took your wife. What else did he take?'

Gualtieri let out an anguished cry and raised the rifle to Daniele's face.

Perillo aimed his revolver, yelling, 'Down, Dani!'

Instead of down, Daniele lurched towards Gualtieri's chest. The rifle went off, the bullet making a hole in the smooth path. Signora Benati screamed. Laura hid her face in her hands. Perillo and Nico ran to help. Gualtieri was on his back, kicking and punching. A boot landed on Daniele's cheek.

Nico slapped the old man hard. Gualtieri grew quiet and looked up at Nico. 'He had to pay for taking the only one I ever loved.'

'Only Gabi got love. Not his wife, not me, not Laura,' Signora Benati said as the three men lifted Gualtieri to his feet. 'The two of us kept hoping, didn't we, Babbo?' She grabbed his shirt and pulled. 'We begged for it. We deserved to be loved.' She looked at Daniele with tear-filled eyes. 'All I got were reprimands. In his eyes I am only his servant.'

Did she know? Nico wondered. Did she wash his bloody clothes hoping to be loved for it?

Laura appeared at her mother's side. 'I love you, Mamma. Let's go inside.'

Perillo slipped handcuffs on a calm Gualtieri.

Signora Benati whispered, 'His head is not right anymore.'

'I understand, Signora. You'll need to come to the station in the morning.'

'We'll be at Cesare's funeral.'

'Right, after then.'

The two women closed the door behind them. Perillo told Gualtieri he was under arrest for a double murder. Daniele read the old man his rights.

'This is unnecessary.' Gualtieri's voice was calm. 'You have to understand. We had coffee together, but I don't remember your name.' He was looking at Daniele.

'Daniele Donato.'

'Please let me explain, Daniele.' He sounded like a parent trying to clarify an unpleasant rule to a child.

Perillo pushed him forward. 'You'll explain later.'

'That was crazy,' Nico told Daniele as they walked behind Perillo and Gualtieri. 'He could have killed you. You too need to do some explaining.'

'I will after we send Gualtieri off to a Florence jail.' He looked down at the phone Nico was holding. 'Is there power left? I think he wants to keep talking.'

'Not much.' Nico took his own phone out and handed it to Daniele. 'Use mine. It's fully charged.'

As the group approached, Beppe left his safe post behind the Alfa. He puffed out air. 'Mamma, my readers are going to eat this up.'

Perillo said, 'Not a word until I say so,' and lowered Gualtieri into the back seat.

Beppe mouthed a swear word and looked at Daniele. 'And what about the Ducati? Isn't anyone going to help me dig for it? I mean, it is here, isn't it?'

'I think so,' Daniele said. 'Try that patch of tilled soil in the vegetable garden.'

'What if he buried it really deep?'

'It will take longer, but you'll get all the credit.'

'That I like. A sore back I don't.' Beppe slung his shovel over one shoulder and made his way to the vegetable garden.

'I'll drive,' Perillo said. 'You get in the back and keep him calm.'

'Happy to, Maresciallo.' Daniele sat down next to Gualtieri. Maybe he would get answers to what had puzzled them about this case.

Nico would have liked to ride with them, but he had his car to drive back.

As soon as Perillo drove onto the rutted road, Daniele asked, 'What did you want to explain, Signor Gualtieri?'

'You have to see I had no choice. He needed to be punished. You do understand that? I acted correctly. He deserved to be killed by me. No one else, but me. He chose me by bedding my wife, by killing my Gabi. It was his destiny.'

'How did you know it was Cesare's car that caused the accident?'

'A lesson for you, young man.' Gualtieri wagged a finger at Daniele. 'If you want your life to be in order, you must stay alert, be prepared to hear even the squeak of a mouse. Laura squeaked to her mother. I was alert.'

'I see,' Daniele said softly. 'If you like order, why didn't you dump Cesare right away?'

Gualtieri let out a raucous laugh. 'Yes, yes, I like order. I planned carefully. My Fiat Palio is too small to fit the Ducati in, so I looked for a big one. Where do you find cars just waiting to be stolen?'

'Villa Costanza?' Daniele asked.

Gualtieri nudged Daniele with his knee. 'A beautiful Toyota Highlander was waiting for me. Left my car in its place.'

'How did you get out without a ticket?'

'Hah! I'd lost it, said I'd been there two days, paid and drove off.'

Daniele shuddered at the look of sick pride on Gualtieri's face. 'Why didn't you leave Cesare where you killed him?'

'That was my first intention. Leave him right there to rot. I heaved the Ducati in the boot. Heavy but worth a lot of money. A woman appeared at some distance. She was coming to me. I had no choice but to gather what strength was left and drag the carrion into the boot. I was very tired despite doing fifty push-ups a day since I was eight. I needed to rest as God rested on the seventh day. I brought the bastard home, parked the Toyota behind the house, took out the Ducati and hid it. I had my lunch, my nap while that shit of a man was slowly rotting on my property. Had my dinner too.' Gualtieri chuckled. 'The thought gave me comfort.'

'Enough talk,' Perillo said. 'We'll get your statement at the station.'

'I am speaking to this young man, not you. I don't know who you are.'

Daniele leant forward. He was sitting directly behind Perillo. 'I'm recording.'

Perillo acknowledged the information with an emphatic nod.

'Why did you take him to Villa Costanza?' Daniele asked Gualtieri.

Gualtieri raised his thick eyebrows in surprise. 'To put the Toyota back with him in it and pick up my car.'

'Weren't you worried about all the cameras?'

'They didn't catch me stealing the Toyota, did they? I waited until dark. And as if ordained by God, that faggot from Gravigna left his car there for me. With the boot open. It was perfect. I had a good laugh. Let the faggot end up in jail where he and his so-called husband belong. You understand, don't you, Daniele?'

'It was Laura who would have gone to jail for Cesare's murder, not Jimmy. You went to the hotel that morning and used her phone.'

'How else to get him to come to the chapel? Oh, I had luck that day. If it did not bless me that day, I would have tried again. I have never let anything or anyone stop me, you understand? A few guests saw me, but I was dressed like a gentleman.' The old man looked very pleased with himself.

'Pietro Rinaldi saw you, didn't he, and tried to blackmail you?'

'A stupid man. He wanted the Ducati. I knew I would find her phone abandoned somewhere. She was always losing things around the house since she was a little snot.'

'Did you want to punish her?'

The question seemed to surprise Gualtieri. 'She sent Gabi to her death.'

Gualtieri slumped back in the seat. 'I'm tired now. I did what had to be done. The judge will understand.' He closed his eyes and didn't speak for the rest of the car ride.

At the station, Perillo handed Gualtieri over to Vince. 'Fingerprint this man, please, then bring him to my office. Nico, you go with Vince.'

Ten minutes later Vince brought Gualtieri to the office. Perillo took off the old man's handcuffs and sat him in the interview chair. Daniele took up his post by the computer with the office tape recorder.

Perillo sat down and made a call to Vince's room. 'Are you settled?' Having a civilian present while he was interviewing the prisoner could lead to trouble.

'I am,' Nico answered. He was munching on a piece of chocolate Vince had offered.

'We'll talk later.' Perillo put the receiver behind the phone. This way Nico would hear what was happening in the room.

'Signor Gualtieri, would you like a coffee?' Perillo was eager to have one himself.

'Food is what I want,' Gualtieri said, 'and a glass of red. Where's my daughter?' He looked around the room. 'Where is she?' He half rose from his chair, a look of panic on his face. 'Where did you put her? I need her. I'm hungry. She takes care of me.'

Perillo stood and gestured for him to calm down. 'She's at home with Laura.'

'No, I need her here. I'm hungry. I need to eat.'

'We'll get you a panino. Is prosciutto and mozzarella all right?'

'No! My daughter feeds me. Take me home.'

'Daniele, start recording, please.' Perillo announced the date and time, so happy with the morning's results he forgot to lower his voice. 'Did you, Duccio Gualtieri, kill Cesare Rinaldi?'

'I had no choice.'

'Did you also kill Pietro Rinaldi?'

'I had no choice.'

'Is there anything you would like to add?'

'I want my daughter to feed me.'

Perillo announced the time and end of the interview. He dropped the receiver back in its cradle. Daniele stopped the recording.

'Thank you for your honesty, Signor Gualtieri. Now, would you like a sandwich while Daniele types up your confession? I will need you to read and sign it before you leave for Florence.'

Gualtieri looked up in surprise. 'Florence? I always loved eating from the street vendors. The lampredotto is the best.'

The idea of eating the fourth and final stomach of a cow was revolting in Perillo's view. The old man clearly had lost his connection to reality.

'I am hungry. I would enjoy a schiacciata with salame and mozzarella.'

Perillo picked up the phone and ordered the flatbread sandwich. Daniele delivered the printed statement to Perillo. Gualtieri signed it and left for Florence with his wrapped schiacciata in hand, accompanied by Vince and the new brigadiere.

Nico walked into the office after they were gone. 'Is Gualtieri crazy or clever?'

'I'm sure his lawyer will get him to plead guilty by way of insanity. I think he is a sane, despicable man.'

'What Laura had to go through is cruel, unnatural,' Daniele said from the back of the room.

Nico sat in the interview chair still warm from its previous occupant. 'I don't think her mother fared much better. Pull up your chair, Dani, and paint us a picture on how you zeroed in on Gualtieri.'

Perillo wagged no with his finger as he picked up the receiver. 'Della Langhe first.'

Barbara, his wonderful secretary, answered. There was no direct line to the substitute prosecutor.

'We got him. That is, Daniele did.'

'Evviva! Give him a kiss for me.'

'I will let someone else do that.' Perillo knew Barbara had a crush on Daniele's voice and manners. She'd never met him. 'What is His Excellency's mood today?'

'Still jubilant. I'll switch you over. Ciao.'

When Della Langhe answered in his usual haughty tone, Perillo relayed the good news.

'Well, I am pleased to hear you have arrested the culprit. And you have a confession. Excellent. I can cross you off the list then,' Della Langhe said. 'You will send me the details. Good work, Maresciallo.'

'Brigadiere Donato is the man who solved the case, not me. I am very proud of him.'

'Ah, the Venetian. I remember him. He is extremely polite, which is unusual in the young. Extend my compliments to him.' Della Langhe clicked off.

'He extends his compliments to you,' Perillo said. 'I do too.'

Daniele's face turned a justified red. 'Thank you.' Gualtieri's boot had left an even redder mark just below one eye.

'No thanks needed. They are very much deserved. Your cheek is turning into a hill. Put some ice on it or a Dario Cecchini steak. Isn't that what Americans do, Nico?'

'Only in old movies. A pack of frozen peas would be better. I'll go to the Coop and get you some.'

'No, no,' Daniele protested. 'Please. I'm fine.' He didn't mind having something to show off for his effort.

Perillo settled back on his desk. 'We should eat before doing anything else. My stomach has been thundering with hunger.' He lifted the receiver, pressed two buttons. 'Dino, three schiacciate filled with salame, prosciutto and caciotta. One with aubergine for Daniele . . . no, make it five. One for you and Vince too. We're celebrating.' He put the receiver down and looked back at Daniele, who had stayed by his desk.

'I am as eager as Nico to learn how you pinpointed Laura's grandfather. I'm sure your eagerness to prove her innocence had much to do with it, but there must be more.'

'Oh, there is more,' Daniele said in a dispirited voice. 'Can it wait? Della Langhe will need the transcription of the confrontation with Gualtieri that my phone recorded as soon as possible. I also need to get back to Beppe and help dig out the Ducati. It would be nice if Cesare could be buried with it tomorrow.'

'It would make Laura and Signora Lucchetti very happy,' Nico said. 'You are sure it's buried in the vegetable garden?'

'I hope so. I know nothing about farming, but the freshly tilled soil in late October made me wonder.'

'Then I'll grab my sandwich and go help Beppe dig,' Nico said. 'We'll manage without you, Dani. You showed a great deal of courage today.'

'And foolishness,' Perillo added with a stern expression. 'You have a crimson mound of a cheek to show for it, but I am proud of you, Dani. I need to make sense of why I did not come to Dani's conclusion. Is it a matter of age, I ask myself?'

'I didn't get there either,' Nico said.

'Of course not. You are years older than I am.'

Nico laughed. 'Indeed I am.'

'Maresciallo, it has nothing to do with age. You couldn't

suspect Gualtieri because you didn't meet him.' Daniele sat down. He was tired, but he might as well explain now before the maresciallo started fixating about getting old again. 'I heard Gualtieri's anger, witnessed his treatment of his daughter. How he hated Cesare and loved beyond measure the granddaughter who died. I saw the plastic covering the makeshift greenhouse, the same plastic he probably used to cover Cesare's body. I saw the freshly tilled earth. I didn't connect all these elements then. It was when Laura was the only suspect left that I looked for another possible suspect.'

'You had no concrete evidence,' Perillo said with awe in his voice. 'You gambled on a hunch.'

Daniele gave Perillo a weak smile. 'I gambled on the conviction that plunging a knife four times into someone you've known since you were a child takes an enormous amount of hate and anger. Gualtieri had both. Laura has only sadness.'

Perillo got up, strode to Daniele and gave his brigadiere a bear hug that lifted him right out of his chair. 'Thank you, Dani. You're the best.'

'And you deserve the best,' Nico added. 'A raise for one. You have a talent for reading people.'

Daniele blushed as expected. Nico and Perillo looked the other way. Renzino knocked, and without waiting for an answer, swept in with a tray of sandwiches and drinks.

Nico grabbed the one with *N* on the wrapping: caciotta and mortadella. 'Thanks. I'll shout if we find it.'

Perillo waved him away. 'We await your shout.'

* * *

Fifteen minutes later Nico was back with OneWag in tow. Nelli had delivered the dog outside the Greve Coop since she had to go to work at the vineyard where dogs were not welcome.

Sandwiches quickly eaten, Daniele was already at his computer, transcribing Gualtieri's threats, his own controlled voice.

Perillo was at the bar, wondering if he could reward himself for Daniele's success with a cigarette.

Nico dropped a bag of frozen peas on Daniele's desk. 'Take care of yourself.'

Daniele thanked him and pressed the bag against his cheek until Nico and OneWag had left the room. The cold felt good, but he had a job to finish.

CHAPTER SIXTEEN

Rain was falling in hard sheets when Nico and Nelli ran into the silence of the Santa Maria Church in Panzano. There had been no warning. They were both drenched.

'I thought it rained only at movie funerals,' Nelli said in a low voice, as she dried her face with a handkerchief. Drops from the hem of her grey dress dripped to the floor. The rain on Nico's dark blue suit, one he'd worn at his wedding and Rita's funeral, had released a faint smell of camphor. Twenty-five years had elapsed between the two previous events. Before the outburst of rain, it still fit him, although he had to keep the jacket unbuttoned.

Nelli tucked her handkerchief in her pocket and looked down the aisle. A smile lit up her face. 'He will now rest in peace.'

'It's what he wanted.'

In front of Cesare's closed coffin stood the much-searched-for Ducati, its gleaming body reflecting the hanging lights of the church. People were staring at it and whispering to each other.

In the last row of pews, Perillo raised his hand to get Nico's attention. Daniele sat next to him. Nico walked over to them and noticed their uniforms were dry.

'You got here early,' Nico said.

'We were the first ones here, as is right.' Perillo raised his chin towards the front of the church. 'A beautiful sight.' Daniele sat up straight, looking proud, despite the purple splotch on his cheek. 'I tried to call you last night, but you didn't answer.'

Nico had been with Nelli, who had stopped to talk to a friend.

'The owner of the Toyota finally retrieved his car.'

'What took so long?' Nico asked.

'He just came back from Australia and he wasn't very happy to find the boot covered in blood . . .'

Nico let out a long breath. 'Well, then I hope he enjoyed his vacation.'

Nelli joined Nico and said a quiet hello to the two carabinieri.

'Sit with us?' Perillo asked. Funerals gave him the jitters.

Nelli shook her head. 'I want to be closer. Laura's a friend.' Laura and her mother were seated in the front row. Don Alfonso was bent down talking to them. 'I want to give her a hug,' she told Nico. 'You pick where to sit. I'll find you.'

Nico watched her hurry down the aisle. 'What is happening with Pietro?' He turned back to Perillo. 'Has his body been released?'

'Yes. His ex-wife in San Casciano is taking care of the burial.'

'I see Jimmy,' Nico said. He was sitting at the end of the pew with Gogol, who never missed a funeral or a christening if he could find a ride to take him there. 'I'm going to say hello.'

Not many people had come to Cesare's funeral, Nico noticed. Nelli would easily find him. Walking down one side of the church, he raised a hand in silent greeting to Nardo, the vegetable store owner whose observation had given a start to the investigation. He nodded at Cinzia and Aldo sitting across the aisle. Gustavo and the other Bench Boys were seated several rows behind them listening to Beppe with camera and notebook on his lap, probably telling them how he'd found the Ducati. In the pew behind them, Tilde smiled at Nico and twirled her finger, a sign that meant *later*. He smiled back and nodded. A few rows further down, on his side of the aisle, he joined his café friends.

They greeted each other in low voices. Gogol's cologne was very faint. Jimmy mumbled, 'He should have come.'

'Sandro had to man the café?'

Jimmy gave Nico a resigned look. 'I wanted to close it down for a couple of hours. Money man refused with the excuse Cesare wasn't from Gravigna. Gogol sat with me to keep me company.' Gogol patted Jimmy's hand with his own bony one and whispered, '"I cannot deny what you ask me."'

'Thank you, Gogol. There is an elegant lady here looking for you, Nico.' Jimmy turned to look around the church. 'Ah, there she is.' He pointed.

In the front row, across from Laura and her mother, sat Signora Lucchetti, dressed in black with a small, veiled hat sitting at an angle on her white head.

'Thanks for telling me.' Nico slipped out of Jimmy's row and walked down to sit next to her. She smiled at him, her eyes filling with tears. 'I can't thank you enough,' she said in a barely audible voice. 'You fulfilled Cesare's wish. My wish too.'

'Brigadiere Donato deserves your thanks, not I.' OneWag had done his part too.

'My poor gentle Cesare.' Above the Ducati, lying on a bier, Cesare's coffin was covered in a blanket of chrysanthemums. 'The woman he loved was Laura's grandmother, wasn't it?' The news of Gualtieri's arrest had been leaked earlier. Nico suspected Beppe had spread the news.

'It seems so.'

Nelli slipped in to sit on Nico's other side. Before he got a chance to introduce her, the organ began playing and Don Alfonso began the Mass. Forty-five minutes later the funeral Mass was over. Cesare's coffin was guided down the aisle by Nardo, the vegetable vendor, and three men Nico didn't know, followed by Laura and her mother with the Ducati.

The mourners filed out. Nico and Nelli accompanied Signora Lucchetti to the front. Outside the church, she held out her black-gloved hand and thanked him again. The rain had subsided to a light shower. Signora Lucchetti, her arthritis giving her forewarning, had come with a flowered umbrella. Nico watched her join Laura and her mother in Laura's car. Once she was settled, the car followed the hearse towards the Panzano cemetery for a private burial.

'I think I need a drink,' Nico said. The funeral had

brought bad memories. What he wanted most was to get away from the whole sad business and be with Nelli.

'So do I,' Perillo said from behind Nico. 'Let's have one together. The Three Musketeers, plus one.'

'No, thanks, Perillo. I've had enough of you two for a while.'

'Nico and Nelli have a date with me,' Tilde said from behind the foursome. 'I have some good news to catch up on from these two. Come on, let's get out of this rain and get that drink.' She dashed down the stairs.

'I'm with you.' Nelli ran after her.

'Don't forget Laura and her mother are coming to the station this afternoon,' Perillo reminded Nico. 'Are you going to listen in?'

'No. You can tell me all about it later. Ciao, you two.'

'Thanks for your help,' Perillo said with regret in his voice.

'Anytime, but not too soon. I'll see you at Bar All'Angolo's anniversary party on Saturday.'

'Maybe,' Perillo answered.

Nico skipped down the steps, praying OneWag, who he'd left in the car because of the downpour, hadn't shredded the seats.

Perillo was ready to go upstairs, change into his civilian clothes and have lunch with Ivana, when Beppe caught him walking out. For the funeral he had put on a tie over his sweater which hung over jeans and worn-out sneakers. 'Maresciallo, how about that scoop you promised for BeppeInfo?'

'You didn't find the motorcycle.'

'I helped.'

'Write your own scoop. You were there.'

After a few blinks, Beppe grinned. 'That's right, I was.' He raised his camera. 'Give me a smile of triumph. "Justice Is Done" is going to be my headline.'

Perillo covered the lens with his hand. 'No, but I'll make sure your help will be mentioned in the press release as promised.' Daniele would make sure he kept that promise.

After changing into civilian clothes, a lunch of spinach ravioli with a pistachio mushroom sauce, breaded chicken cutlets, broccoli salad, an apple and an espresso, followed by a thirty-minute nap, Perillo was almost ready to bring the Cesare Rinaldi case to a close. A cigarette would have eliminated the 'almost,' but he resisted the urge.

Perillo walked into his office. His brigadiere was already there, seated by his computer. 'Ehi, Daniele, did you have a good lunch?'

'Excellent.' Daniele had spent his lunchtime eating crisps and texting Stella about the funeral.

'Let's go for another coffee for me, an orange drink for you. Come on.' Perillo opened the door to find Dino in front of him.

'What, Dino?'

'They are here.'

'Good.' Perillo stepped into the corridor. 'Come in, please,' Perillo said, his arm indicating the open door of his office. The two women were seated on the bench next to the front door, backs straight, hands in their laps, staring back at him, one a younger copy of the other, both still in their dark funeral dresses.

'Thank you for coming on such a sad day.'

Laura stood up. 'We want this to be over.' She strode across the floor. Her mother, clearly frightened, stepped forward gingerly.

Daniele nodded a greeting to them both as they entered and immediately lowered his head. He felt awkward, embarrassed, even guilty. He hadn't wanted to face them again. Yesterday their lives had been upended. Maybe Laura was relieved she would not go to jail, but Gualtieri was her grandfather, la Signora's father. What were they feeling? What did they think of him?

The women sat in the two chairs placed in front of Perillo's desk. He sat down in his armchair.

'This should not take long if you answer truthfully. Daniele, please start the recording. Signora Benati, I will start with you.' Perillo noticed Laura reach out for her mother's hand. 'When your father came home for lunch after killing Cesare, did you not see bloodstains on his clothes?'

'I did. When I asked, he said he had helped our neighbour pull out a calf having trouble birthing.'

'You believed him.'

'Why shouldn't I? That's what neighbours do for each other. He's always had a gentle touch with animals. And I know nothing about that motorcycle. I was sleeping when he came home that night, and I am the one' – she started pressing her finger against her chest – 'who tilled the garden. I will plant kale, and cabbage and brussels sprouts. My father never set foot in my vegetable garden. It was my space.' There was anger in her eyes. Her finger kept pressing against her chest.

'Mamma.' Laura reached up and pushed her mother's hand down to her lap.

'After Cesare's body was discovered, didn't you suspect your father?'

'No. I worried about Laura. For all this time we had blamed her for Gabi's death and now she knew it was Cesare's fault.'

Laura clasped both her mother's hands. 'I forgave him, Mamma. I told you. He didn't hit Gabi's car on purpose. He was tired and closed his eyes. He bore the guilt of it as long as I had. I forgave him.'

Signora Benati retrieved her hands and drew herself up in the chair. 'Then you are a better person than I am.'

'No, I'm not.'

'And you, Laura?' Perillo asked. 'You must have suspected your grandfather.'

'Mrs Barron, an English guest who had been at the bar when Cesare dropped the tray of drinks, said something that made me think Signor Reni had killed Cesare.'

'And when he was cleared?'

Laura looked over at Daniele. He hesitated to return her gaze. She owed him her freedom and smiled to thank him. She wished she could be grateful. 'I thought he could be the one.'

'You should have shared that suspicion,' Perillo said. 'I could charge you with being an accessory after the fact.'

'I had no proof.'

'We would have found the proof.' Perillo studied her face. It was a mask of calm. 'Do you mean to tell me you were willing to go to jail for a grandfather who treated you miserably?'

Laura looked again at Daniele. There was compassion in his face. She turned back to Perillo. He simply looked unbelieving. 'I don't know, Maresciallo. Family is complicated.'

Perillo sat back in his chair and looked down at the many scratches on his desk. In his teens, a kind carabiniere, instead of arresting him, had offered a home and his street life had ended. He'd been lucky. He could charge Laura, but to what purpose? Gualtieri would never kill again. She'd been through enough. Daniele would never forgive him.

'End of interview.'

Daniele's heart skipped a beat as he said the time into the recorder and turned it off.

Perillo got up from his chair. 'Signora, Signorina, you are free to go.'

Hand in hand, the two women walked out of the office. Perillo picked up his leather jacket from the back of his armchair. 'Come on, Dani, that coffee and orange drink are waiting for us. And a cigarette too. I think I deserve one.'

Daniele agreed silently.

CHAPTER SEVENTEEN

When Nico and OneWag walked into Gravigna's main piazza, the anniversary party was already underway. A semicircle of rainbow-coloured balloons and lights hung above the wide-open café door. Lady Gaga's 'Always Remember Us This Way' billowed out onto the piazza from a speaker propped next to the café's entrance.

People were strolling around, greeting each other, chatting, munching hors d'oeuvres, sipping prosecco, going in or coming out of the café. Children played tag or licked their ice-cream cones.

A much-needed joyous feast, Nico thought, to celebrate Sandro and Jimmy's ten-year ownership of Bar All'Angolo. He hadn't felt this good in a very long time. Nelli was part of his life again. The murders had been solved. The day had been warm and sunny. Now, at five o'clock in the afternoon, the sun was dropping westward. The intense blue of the sky was fading, but the old lampposts had taken over, helped by the strings of Christmas lights circling the piazza from one lamppost to the other.

'Ciao, Nico,' Luciana called out, waving her arm. She was jiggling to the music on a bench, her usual black tent dress substituted by one covered in splashes of colour. 'We're celebrating.'

She flung an arm over her husband's shoulder. Enrico raised his red wine glass.

At another bench, Gustavo and his friends also raised their red wine glasses. 'Alla salute,' they said in chorus.

'And to yours!' Nico called out. 'I need to get some of my own.' He walked ahead. OneWag trotted off to greet the various dogs their owners had brought.

A newspaper flashed in front of his face, stopping Nico. 'Did you see, Nico, did you?' Beppe's face flushed with happiness. '*Chianti Sette*, I'm in it. Right here on page five.' He lowered the paper and recited by memory, '"Beppe Fantoni, creator of the local news blog, BeppeInfo, was instrumental in helping Maresciallo Salvatore solve the murders," et cetera, et cetera, "by finding the missing Ducati along with Domenico Doyle, an American resident of Gravigna."'

'I've read it, Beppe. Congratulations.'

'Overnight I got a hundred and twenty-two new subscribers. I'll get a lot more, won't I?'

'I'm sure you will.' Through the open French doors of the café, he spotted a grey braid. 'Excuse me, Beppe, I have to go.' He hurried over.

'There you are,' Nelli said, coming out of the café with an espresso cup filled with olives. She met up with him and reached up to kiss him lightly on the lips. 'Gogol was asking about you. So were Jimmy and Sandro.'

'You weren't?' He watched her lips spread into a smile.

'Not yet.' She popped an olive in his mouth.

He chewed. 'You look nice.' She was wearing a deep turquoise scoop-necked sweater over wide-legged dark green slacks that were far more flattering than the oversized shirts and paint-splattered jeans he had mostly seen her wear. 'And no turpentine smell.'

Nelli gently punched his arm. 'That's my Nelli 5. Get used to it. I had no time to paint today. I oversaw the prosecco supply for this party. I got them a great discount from a vineyard near Asolo. Aldo provided his Ferriello red practically at cost. It was very generous of him. He and Cinzia are inside too. Come on, your friends are waiting for you.'

'Perillo?' They hadn't spoken since Perillo had let Laura and her mother go without charging them.

'Uh-huh. Daniele is with Stella. They look sweet together.'

Seeing Nelli, OneWag ran over and squirmed in greeting. 'Ciao, bello mio.' She bent over and scratched his ear. 'Maybe bringing him isn't such a good idea. He'll get trampled.'

Nico picked up OneWag. 'I'll hold him.'

They had to elbow their way into the café. The crowd stood shoulder to shoulder. During a pause in the music, Nico heard a growl that sounded like 'amico.' He turned towards it. Gogol was sitting at his usual spot by the French doors with his coat wrapped around him. Elvira sat opposite him, doing the crossword puzzle. Theirs was the only table and chair; the others had been cleared to make room. Nico bent down to kiss Elvira's cheeks.

‘Tell your friends to get rid of that music,’ she grumbled. A new song was playing. Nico nodded and turned to Gogol. ‘Ciao, amico. How are you? I haven’t seen you since this morning.’

With a lopsided smile, Gogol raised a half-eaten mini cornetto filled with prosciutto. ‘“Love can quickly take the gentle heart.”’

Nelli bent down and kissed his cheek. ‘Not so. It took him forever.’ She slipped by Nico and wove her way between bodies to where Sandro, from behind the counter, was handing out ice-cream cones. The length of the counter was covered with cups of olives, squares of salame and caciotta, schiacciate, mini cornetti, bruschettas and bowls of grapes.

‘Nico’s here,’ she said.

‘Thanks,’ Sandro answered.

Nico spotted Tilde sitting on top of the counter at the far end in a bright red dress that made her look years younger. She was filling flutes with prosecco. Jimmy was sitting next to her, handing them out along with glasses of red wine Alba was filling.

Nico raised his arm to get Tilde’s attention. Crossing the room would have taken some heavy shoving.

Tilde looked up, saw him and clapped her hands. He clapped back. With Prince’s ‘Purple Rain’ at full blast, shouting over the chatter would have been useless. She mouthed *Enzo* and pointed to a spot. Nico tried to find him and instead saw Aldo, his landlord. Aldo lifted Cinzia up so she could wave at Nico. Nico blew her a kiss. Enzo stayed hidden. Nico shook his head at Tilde. She shrugged and continued to fill the flutes.

A red wine glass appeared in front of Nico. It was a very

welcome sight. He turned to see Perillo and Ivana.

He kissed Ivana's cheeks and leant into Perillo to be heard. 'Thanks. Where's Daniele?'

'He's with Stella stuck in a corner. He wanted to leave but Sandro asked him to wait until you got here. Same thing with me. So now you're here and we can enjoy our drinks outside.'

Nelli leant in from behind them. 'We can't. Sandro is going to give a speech.'

Perillo groaned.

'Stop it, Salva,' Ivana muttered, and with a normal voice, added, 'We have to raise our glasses to them first.'

Mid-song, Prince stopped singing. Sandro clapped his hands for attention. OneWag barked. Everyone quieted down. OneWag stopped. 'Thank you, Rocco. You'll get a day-old cornetto every time you visit.'

'If there are any left,' Jimmy added, which got a few chuckles.

'Always has to have the last word.'

Nico turned to see Sandro behind the counter suddenly dominating the room by standing on a chair.

'My friends, thank you for coming to celebrate the ten years we have owned Bar All'Angolo. Jimmy and I are honoured and happy to have served you for all these years. Jimmy, come join me.'

'I'd love to, but I'm stuck!' If he moved, he risked shattering glasses on one side, knocking the food to the floor on the other.

'Well then, I'll come to you.' Sandro got off the chair, took it with him to the end of the counter and got back on. He looked down at his husband. Jimmy looked up at him.

'Jimmy, I haven't been the best of husbands lately. I want to say in front of these wonderful people that I'm sorry. I love you. You make me very happy.'

Sandro's words were followed by an embarrassed silence. Nico sensed the Gravignesi weren't used to public declarations of love between gays.

Somewhere in the crowd, Daniele squeezed Stella's hand.

Jimmy winked at the room. 'Of course, I make him happy. I swelter by the oven or the espresso machine while he coolly collects the money.'

The room laughed.

'I love him too, and I love all of you, as long as you keep buying my cornetti and telling me how fabulous they are.'

More laughter. Nico clapped loudly, almost dropping OneWag. Nelli took the dog and held him against her chest.

'We'll stop talking about ourselves now,' Sandro said, taking the glass of prosecco Jimmy held up for him. 'I want to thank our excellent Maresciallo Perillo, Brigadiere Donato and our own Gravignese, Nico Doyle, for once again catching the culprit. They never let us down. We can sleep soundly again.'

'For now,' someone said, followed by loud shushes. People clapped, yelled out thanks. Perillo's shoulder got patted. Daniele blushed proudly.

'Before we raise a glass to all of us honest Gravignesi, several men here want to ask Nico the same question. Do you mind, Nico?'

'That depends on the question.'

'Was the Ducati really buried in the vegetable garden?'

'No, it wasn't.'

'I knew it,' Gino shouted, standing above the crowd.

He was a tall man with a bushy moustache and a girth that showed he enjoyed the food he served at his trattoria. 'No way could Gualtieri have enough strength at his age to dig a big enough hole. So where was it?'

'I had your same thought, Gino,' Nico said. 'Or maybe I was being lazy. I decided Beppe and I should look around before digging. The first thing we found was a rabbit that my dog started chasing.'

Someone booed.

'No, Rocco did a good thing.' OneWag's furious barking had led him to a large U-shaped stack of logs standing against the back wall of the house. 'His chase caused the rabbit to find a place to hide.' Leaning down to pull OneWag away, a flash of light in the small opening between logs had caught his eye. After removing only a few rows of logs with Beppe, the side-mirror of the Ducati had flashed sunlight back at them. Beppe had whoopped for joy.

'The Ducati and the rabbit were hiding behind a stack of logs.'

'Did the rabbit get away?' asked a young voice.

'He ran off as fast as lightning. Rocco has not forgiven me.' People clapped. Some yelled out, 'Evviva!' and 'Bravo, Rocco.'

OneWag perked up his ears.

'Thanks, Nico,' Gino said. 'I just won twenty euros. You have a meal at Gino's anytime you want. Bring Nelli and Rocco too.'

A man standing next to Nico, whom he recognised as one of the grammar schoolteachers, held out his hand. 'I hope you plan to stay here.'

Nico shook the man's hand. 'Gravigna is home now.'

'Glad to hear that.'

'Aren't we all,' Nelli said silently, giving OneWag a gentle squeeze.

'And now,' Sandro said loudly enough to stop the chatter that had resumed. 'Please raise a glass to Gravigna and all the Gravignesi.'

OneWag raised his head and howled.

ACKNOWLEDGEMENTS

Once again COVID-19 kept me away from my friends in Chianti, but they were with me nonetheless as I wrote this third story. The internet kept them close. A thousand grazie to Lara Beccatini, Ioletta Como and Andrea Sommaruga for their friendship. I will forever be indebted to now-retired Maresciallo Giovanni Serra, who continues to answer my questions virtually. I miss all the Panzanesi friends I made writing this series. I wish them good health and I hope to see them very soon.

In New York, I thank Barbara Lane for her unerring eye. There is not a typo or misplaced comma that she doesn't catch. I have an excellent new editor, Yezanira Venecia, who smoothed out my sometimes-choppy prose. Publicist Alexa Wejko is always great at spreading the word. Thank you to both.

To my first reader, my fantastic husband, Stuart, I am grateful for your love and patience.

LIST OF CHARACTERS

in order of appearance

Nico Doyle – American ex-homicide detective who has made Gravigna his home

Salvatore Perillo – maresciallo of the carabinieri in Greve-in-Chianti and Nico's friend

OneWag – Nico's adopted dog, also known as Rocco

Vince – a gum-chewing brigadiere at the Greve-in-Chianti carabinieri station

Laura Benati – a guilt-ridden manager of the Hotel Bella Vista

Cesare Rinaldi – the hotel bartender who kept quiet about his past life

Daniele Donato – blushing Venetian brigadiere and Perillo's right-hand man

Stella Morelli – Daniele's art-loving friend and Tilde and Enzo's daughter

Dino – a quiet brigadiere at the Greve-in-Chianti Carabinieri station

Elvira Morelli – a grouchy widow and owner of the Sotto Il Fico restaurant

Tilde Morelli – Rita's cousin and concerned chef at the restaurant

Sandro Ventini – co-owner of Bar All'Angolo

Gogol – Nico's Dante-quoting friend who won't renounce his overcoat or cologne

Jimmy Lando – cornetto baker, co-owner of Bar All'Angolo and Sandro's husband

Luciana – hug-loving owner of the Gravigna florist shop

Nelli Corsi – artist who has lost patience with Nico

Pietro Rinaldi – Cesare's angry nephew

Giovanni Sant'Angelo – café manager at Villa Costanza

Miremba – counter person at the Villa Costanza café who gives a time frame

ALDO FERRI – owner of Ferriello vineyards and Nico's landlord

ORESTE – the town barber

GUSTAVO – an opinionated pensioner, leader of the Bench Boys

ETTORE – a gentler Bench Boy

GINO – owner of Trattoria Da Gino who asks the last question

ENRICO – owner of the town's salumeria and Luciana's worried husband

BEPPE – always eager for news to add to his BeppeInfo blog

TINO – the butcher's son

ENZO MORELLI – Elvira's dutiful son and Tilde's loving husband

NARDO – vegetable vendor in Panzano who hears an important click

MATTIA GENNARI – Cesare's flute-playing neighbour

MRS BARRON – English hotel guest, has her own take on what happened

ARBEN – Albanian manager of the Ferriello vineyards

CINZIA FERRI – Aldo's wife who's intrigued by Cesare

CARLA BENATI – Laura's grieving mother

DUCCIO GUALTIERI – Laura's angry grandfather

RITA DOYLE – Nico's deceased Italian wife, buried in Gravigna

IDA CRIVELLI – talkative housekeeper in Montagliari

DOTTOR EUGENIO VITTORI – frequent guest at the Hotel Bella Vista who wants a change

ANGELA – patient owner of Da Angela's restaurant in Lucarelli

BARBARA – works at the prosecutor's office

BETTA – Angela's pasta-making mother

NADIA – Laura's assistant at the hotel

SIGNORA LUCCHETTI – widowed owner of the Hotel Bella Vista

ALBA – hip-swinging Albanian waitress at Sotto Il Fico

SIRIO RENI – Dottor Vittori's guest, eager for investors

NANNI GEZZI – an old man who finds something unexpected

CARLETTA – Gino's daughter

RENZINO – the bar boy

MARESCIALLO SANNA – of the San Casciano Carabinieri station

DON ALFONSO – the local priest

IVANA PERILLO – the maresciallo's patient wife

Hungry for more?

Nico Doyle returns in

MURDER AT VILLA SALVIATI

Read on for a taste of the next Tuscan mystery . . .

CHAPTER ONE

A Monday in May, 5:05 a.m.

Nico's cold feet searched under the bedcovers for Nelli's warm ones, found them and dropped back into his dream. In the adjacent room a phone started to ring, heard only by OneWag, curled up on the sofa. The dog raised his head seeking the source of the persistent sound. The thing on the table. He allowed himself a low growl of protest. He'd been chasing rabbits. The ringing continued. OneWag jumped down, padded over to the bedroom door and pushed it open with a vigorous thrust of his snout.

The louder ringing finally woke Nelli. She lifted herself up on one elbow and nudged Nico's back. 'Wake up, your phone is ringing.'

Nico hugged his pillow. 'Mmm, no. Yours.'

'Wrong. Mine's right here by the bedside table.' She glanced at the clock radio and started shaking Nico's shoulder. 'Get up, Nico. It's five in the morning. It must be important.'

Nico mumbled, 'It's some joker having fun.'

'You're impossible.' Nelli started to climb over him to get to the phone.

Nico pushed her back. 'I'll go. I'll go.' He gave her a quick kiss on the nose and grunted out of bed. Yesterday's mind-blowing meal was still sitting heavily in his stomach, and he took his time reaching the phone.

Seeing Nico, OneWag wagged his tail in greeting but was ignored. Miffed, he jumped back on the sofa and gave Nico his back. The ringing stopped just as Nico picked the phone off the table. He rubbed his eyes to read. *Missed call.* Great. Back to sleep. As he turned back, the ringing resumed. Perillo's name gave Nico a jolt. He swiped. 'What's wrong?'

'I need your help.'

'Are you okay?'

'Just fine. For the past twenty minutes I've been standing with a dead woman at my feet and an alive English one who doesn't speak Italian.'

'Do you want me to talk to her?'

'Please.'

In strongly accented English, Perillo said, 'Signora Barron, my friend speak English.' Then Nico heard a strong female voice declare, 'Thank God for small mercies,' followed by the sound of soft footsteps and Perillo's phone changing hands.

'Sir, what has happened to my friend is an abomination. I will not say any more until we can speak in person.'

After the phone shifted hands again, Perillo asked, 'What did she say?'

'She wants me to come over. Where are you?'

'A few kilometres south of Vignamaggio. Just past a

very sharp curve you'll see an uphill road flanked by cypress trees. The villa is on top of the hill. Villa Salviati.'

'Give me time to get dressed and I'll be there.' Nico clicked off.

'Who was that?' Nelli called out. She was out of bed, tying her wool bathrobe around her waist.

'Perillo.' Nico walked to the bedroom and started dressing.

'What happened?'

Nico told her while he buttoned up a plaid collared shirt.

Nelli handed him his grey corduroy slacks. 'Who died?'

'I didn't ask.'

'How sad.' Nelli's forehead creased. 'A heart attack?'

Nico didn't think the carabinieri would get called for a suspected heart attack but said nothing. There was no point in alarming Nelli. He reached for the dark blue sweater she had given him for Christmas. 'I don't know.'

Nelli crossed herself as she walked to the stove. OneWag jumped off the sofa and ran to greet her. She picked up the dog and kissed his head. 'I'll put the moka on.'

Nico ran the electric shaver over his cheeks and chin. For some reason, he felt he needed to make a good impression. The English lady had sounded very refined. He combed his still-full head of greying hair and brushed his teeth.

The moka was gurgling when he came into the living room/ kitchen. 'I don't have time.'

'Two more minutes,' Nelli said, not wanting to see him go.

'I can't, Nelli. Perillo needs help. Drink a double for me. Ciao, bella.' He meant to kiss her lips, but she moved her head and he ended up kissing OneWag. Nico took a moment to study her face. Her expression was soft, still full of sleep. 'Are you upset I'm going?'

Nelli smiled. 'The reason upsets me. Don't worry. Rocco will keep me company.'

Nico kissed her lightly on the lips. She kissed him back. 'Let me know.'

'I will.'

After Nico left, Nelli poured herself a double espresso, added some milk and took her cup back to bed. OneWag stretched himself out against her leg while she sent a little prayer to whoever was listening in the sky. *Please let it be nothing more violent than a heart attack*. These past five months with Nico not playing homicide detective for Perillo had been good. He was cheerful and loving, the sadness he seemed to carry almost gone.

Nelli leant back on her pillow. And yet she had noticed a restlessness in him. Nico had told her he had not enjoyed his detective work in New York, but it was obvious he liked working with Perillo and Daniele. Here he was needed in a way that maybe he had not been in New York. He had more experience with murder than Perillo. It was clear he loved being helpful. It was how he had entrenched himself in his Italian life. He helped at Sotto Il Fico, coming up with new recipes for Tilde, but during the winter months, with Gravigna empty of tourists, the restaurant had only opened for weekend dinners. She had enjoyed more of his company, his love, the attention he gave her.

Nelli shrugged and finished her coffee. If it was murder, he would have less time for her. Maybe that would be good for both of them. She had a job she loved at the Querciabella vineyard, and she'd have more time for painting.

CAMILLA TRINCHIERI worked for many years on films in Rome with directors including Federico Fellini and Luchino Visconti. She emigrated to the US in 1980 and received her MFA in Creative Writing from Columbia University. Under the pseudonym Camilla Crespi, she has published seven crime novels.

camillatrinchieri.com
@camillatrinchieri